JEFFERSON PARISH

MICHAEL W. HULL

PAGE PUBLISHING, INC.
Conneaut Lake, PA

First originally published by Page Publishing 2020

ISBN 978-1-64701-621-0 (pbk)
ISBN 978-1-64701-623-4 (hc)
ISBN 978-1-64701-622-7 (digital)

Printed in the United States of America

For
Mom and Dad

And anyone who has ever been categorized
as an "other" in their lifetime.

Chapter 1

JEFFERSON PARISH, 2001

The world is a very big place though no one from Jefferson Parish, Louisiana, would ever call it that. Not unlike most other southern towns in the United States, Jefferson Parish has certainly had its problems throughout its history, but on this day, Matthew Laurent would be facing a predicament he never could have imagined.

Sitting alone in a small windowless drab green interrogation room, like the color often associated with and often used in insane asylums, Matt notices the lack of "things" in the room. A table, two chairs, one on either side of the table, a CCTV camera in the corner of the room pointed in his direction—he can't help but wonder who is watching him… And even more perplexing, what are they thinking?

In the corner of the sturdy steel-framed table, an ashtray sits with two crushed-up cigarette butts in it. *No doubt from the last man who sat in this seat*, Matt thinks to himself. Reaching over to it, he tries to pick it up but discovers it is bolted down to the table. Just then, the lock on the heavy door unlocked and the door opens and in walks Sheriff Darnell Kennedy. Everyone in the Parish knows Sheriff Kennedy, and he liked it that way. From Father John, as he was called by his parishioners down at St. Patrick's Church, to the ladies of the United Daughters of the Confederacy and everyone in between knew Sheriff Kennedy to be a tough, no-nonsense lawman. Standing six feet four, black, and the law on his side, it's fair to say that there were plenty of citizens in Jefferson Parish who didn't much care for the sheriff. That being said, he was a fair man, a reasonable man, and people knew it, even those not particularly fond of people of color.

"Hey, Sherriff?" Matt says in a tone filled with uncertainty.

"How you doin', Matt?"

The sheriff shut the heavy door behind him; it locked from the outside. The sound of a large steel interrogation room door locking is one that is intimidating and unmistakable and often heard in prisons or jailhouses movies. Or at least that's what Matt equated it too.

"Well, to be honest, Sheriff, I'm wondering what the hell's goin' on."

Sheriff Kennedy walked over to the table, putting his curled-up fists down on the table, resting all his 260 lbs. on his knuckles, looking down at Matt and asks, "How long have I known you, Matt?"

"Jesus, Sheriff," Matt says as his eyes turn toward the ceiling as he thought for a few seconds. "Grade school, maybe?" Matt responds but looked to the sheriff for confirmation.

"Ya know, Matt, down here, most black folks have learned to deal with bullshit. It's the way it is…been like that forever. This ain't news to you. You know my uncle Calvin was strung up not two miles from where we sit right now? I was only eleven years old, but I remember it like it was yesterday. That's somethin' you don't easily forget. You understand? But that was forty years ago, and yet here I stand, sheriff of Jefferson Parish, Louisiana. A black man, a nigger some in the Parish still think of me but have the right good sense never to say it to my face. At least not anymore. Now you know I'm a man of faith. I believe in the good book and believe that Jesus has a plan for all of us and gives each and every one of us tools to work with. He certainly did with you. But he gave me some tools as well, and that, I thank him for every day," the sheriff says, looking down at Matt.

"Do you know what those tools are, Matt?"

Matt looks up from the empty table and at the sheriff and says, "No, sir."

"Size and the ability to sniff out bullshit," the sheriff responds, not missing a beat.

Pulling the heavy steel chair out from under the table effortlessly, he sits across from Matt. Looking at the sheriff, Matt says, "Billy's funeral."

"That's right, son," the sheriff responds. "Billy's funeral. Now why don't you do what's right and tell me what the fuck is goin' on?"

Matt, his eyes now raised toward the ceiling, remembering that night from all those years ago, was like going back in time. He wished he could forget, but like the sheriff said, the Lord gives all men certain tools that help sustain him through good times and bad, and while Matt's memory was often a blessing, other times it was a curse. This was not one of the blessed times. Matt always wondered why the Lord hadn't given him the ability to do better in math or science, but it was his memory, almost photographic, that was one of his divine tools. Hell, the athletic ability of his big brother, Billy, would have been a more welcome blessing. But it was times like these that Matt cursed his memory and his ability to go back without ever leaving the present.

Chapter 2

APRIL 7, 1980

Down on Huey P. Long Avenue is Redd's funeral parlor; Davis Funeral Home it's called. The Davis Funeral Home has been around for more time than most folks can remember, but if you ask Redd, he'll make sure to tell you his great-great-granddaddy started the home just after what he and many other Southerners call the Great War—the Civil War.

Inside, just off the hall is the smaller parlor; the larger parlor, being toward the back of the building, was used for people with more social status as well as more friends and family, but in the small parlor at the head of the room lay a casket. A simple closed casket, but by no means shabby, held the body of sixteen-year-old William Laurent Jr.—Billy to family and friends. Karen, Billy's momma, was kneeling in front of the casket, disheveled and crying hysterically like any mother who just lost a child would be, clutching her rosary beads to her chest. Billy was handsome, athletic, and one of the more popular kids his age. He had a barrel load of friends, but most had come and paid their respects and were gone at this point. Only a few mourners remained, of them was Billy's eleven-year-old brother, Matthew, seated in the first row of seats, alone, his head hung low, but no tears were coming.

He wondered then, and many times since, why he didn't cry that night. Heck, everybody else did, but he never could figure it out. Karen's best friend, Doris, of over thirty years and Karen's momma,

Edith, did their best to comfort her. While stroking Karen's hair, Edith asked her grieving daughter, "Why don't you come and sit down, honey? Can I get you a glass of water?"

Edith was not an emotional woman, at least not at this point in her life, and it's not that she didn't love her grandson; it's just Edith was hardened over time, galvanized by pain and time. Surprisingly, Matt, at just eleven years old, was much more like his grandmother, Edith, than either of his parents, but he didn't mind at all.

Doris had gone to the lady's room to get Karen a cup of water when Edith helped Karen to her feet. Weak-kneed and fearing she'd fall over, Edith held on to her daughter's arm so tight Karen would have a bruise the next day as a reminder of her mother's strength.

"Here you go, honey, drink this," Doris said as she handed Karen the cup of water, only half filled. With both hands free, Doris helped Edith guide Karen over to the first row of chairs.

"Where is William?" Karen asked in between taking small sips of water.

"Johnny took him next door to get a drink," Doris said.

Clearly agitated, Karen mutters, "Son of a bitch! His damn son is lying here in a coffin and he's drinkin'! Any goddamn excuse!"

"Karen!" Edith responded to blasphemy.

"Well, Momma, it's no wonder his son's killed in a car wreck drunk. His father's a drunken fool. You know how many times Billy seen his daddy come stumbling in the house three shades to the wind puking all over his self?" she asked rhetorically.

"I know, I know, honey. Believe me, I know," Edith said.

"Come on, let's go to the ladies' room and clean you up a bit," Doris said in a whisper. The three women got up and walked past Matt without saying a word, though only two knew exactly where they were going and the third was totally reliant on the two. Edith glanced back at her youngest and now only grandson sitting alone.

With his head hung low, staring at the dark burgundy-colored carpet, he was thinking about Billy—Billy and fishing. Just a week ago tomorrow, Billy had taken Matt fishing for the first time. Matt was hoping it would be the first of countless fishing trips to come. He was hoping they'd go fishing so much that in time he'd never be able to remember the first time because they'd get all mixed and confused together. This was the first time Billy had given in to Matt's never-ending pestering about taking him along, but frankly, he didn't mind at all. And now, unfortunately, he'll never confuse this fishing trip with any others because there would be no others. He never told his brother, but Billy was Matt's hero, and he just now realized he'd never get to tell him.

"Hey there, Matthew," a voice said to the young boy.

Looking at the hand resting on his shoulder, Matt's eyes slowly made their way up to Father John O'Conner's freckle-filled face. Father John, a relatively young man at only thirty-nine, hair thinning, and slight in stature, was fairly new to the Parish and only recently assigned to Saint Patrick's Catholic Church. Nonetheless, a man who carries a lot of weight with his parishioners. The church just a short walk from Redd's funeral parlor over on Sixth Street, Father John is often at the funeral parlor, much more so than he'd like to be, but it comes with the job, and he knew it. As most priest know, like any other job in the world, even working for God has its difficult days.

"Hey, Father," Matt responded in a somber, faded voice.

Sitting beside Matthew, Father John said, "You know, Matthew, death is never easy to deal with, especially when they are so young," as if he has had to say that same line far too many times as he looked up at the closed casket while putting his hand on Matt's knee.

"As difficult as it seems right now, you must trust in God and his plan. He has a unique plan for each and every one of us. And you can be sure he has big plans for you, young man."

Raising his head and looking at Father John, he asked, "You think so?"

"Absolutely, Matthew. It's understandable at times like these doubt that seeps into our minds and we question God. We ask, 'Why, God? Why did this terrible thing happen?' But that's what faith is, believing in something greater than us. You must not let this divert you from the plan that God has set in place for you, for you, Matthew," Father John said, shaking Matt's knee slightly, eliciting a response from the quiet young boy. Looking up again at Father John, Matthew let an ever so small smile encroach on his face.

"He took me fishing last week," Matt said softly.

"I know. He told me."

Looking at Father John with an inquisitive look on his face, wondering how Father John knew about the fishing trip. "Remember Billy was painting the recreational hall in the basement of the church?" Father John reminded Matt.

"Oh yeah," Matt said as his eyes turn upward. Thinking to himself for a few seconds, he asked, "So who's gonna finish painting it?"

Looking at the young boy, seeing hope slowly seeping back into the youngster, he asked, "Do you think you could handle such a job?"

"Oh, heck yeah, Father, I can do it. I help pop at home all the time with stuff," Matt said, momentarily excited, referring to the two or three times William had asked him to hand him a screwdriver or a wrench from his toolbox. He didn't see no harm in a little exaggeration since he'd be working for God.

"Can you say a prayer with me for Billy, Father?" Matt asked sheepishly.

"Of course." Father John took great pride in helping his parishioners through difficult times. He also knew that children who suffer a loss are often damaged on the inside and it isn't until later in life that the pain rises to the surface. They walked over to the casket, and both got down on the kneeler. In unison, they started to pray, "Our Father, who art in heaven, hallowed be thy name…"

* * *

Drinking Jamison Whiskey as he often did, William, along with Johnny, Doris's husband—well, common-law anyway—dealt with most of the difficult aspects and many of the not-so-difficult aspects of life the same way: via the bottle. Redd's Tavern, not nearly as old as the Davis Funeral Home, was the brainchild of Redd some twenty-five years ago. When the space in the building next door to the funeral parlor opened up after the five-and-dime closed down,

Redd, the consummate businessman and always observant, had, for years, watched his mourners, mostly men but sometimes women, take shots from flasks or even bottles wrapped in brown paper bags hidden in their inner pockets. So when Redd saw the iron was hot, he struck. It didn't hurt that Redd wasn't averse to the drink himself and is often his best customer.

William, not particularly tall at five foot eleven, was a sturdy man, thick with muscles from a life of hard work. At only thirty-five years old but often mistaken by those who didn't know him personally to be in his forties or even fifties, he wasn't a bad man though no one has ever gone out of their way to claim he was a good man either. He was one of those guys that not many people paid much attention to, but that's just the way William liked it. Oh, if you were a friend and needed a couch moved or your truck looked at, you could count on William, but most people knew where to draw the line when asking him for things. Sitting on the same twenty-five-year-old stools Redd bought when he first opened the place can sometimes be precarious. Just two weeks ago, Johnny Miller, quite a big man though a different Johnny altogether, had one of those old barstools collapse right from under him while drinkin' a Rollin Rock. Though that was Johnny Miller's mistake for not checking the rickety old thing and when he complained to Redd and threatened to sue, Redd simply told ole Johnny to go fuck himself. They settled out of court for a beer and a shot.

"Ya never know, ya just never know," Johnny said while looking forward but meant for William to hear.

"Bullshit," William responded, also not bothering to turn to look at Johnny.

Johnny, surprised by William's response, turned toward William. "Leo, another Jamison," William said, still not diverting his eyes from the mirror directly in front of him. Though he wasn't looking at himself or anything in particular in the mirror, it just happened to be in his line of sight. Leo, Redd's son-in-law and former schoolmate of William and Johnny, poured both men a double. He turned to put the bottle back in its rightful place when he realized he'd just be back for it in a minute or two and decided to place it on the bar and gave William a pat on the forearm before going back to his newspaper. He wasn't really reading it; it was just an old trick that Redd had taught him to make customers think you weren't listening to their conversations.

"What do you mean sometimes you know?" Johnny asked William.

"Sometimes ya just know. Ya just know. Death is right around the corner and there ain't shit you can do about it. Leo, a pack of Red Apples," William said, his focus now on the glass in his hand as he raised it to his mouth and gulped down the drink.

Leo turned from his paper to the back side of the bar, grabbed a pack of Red Apples, and slid it down the bar toward William. William took the package of cigarettes and packed them firmly into his hand, compressing the tobacco in each cigarette. Slowly opening the pack, still staring into the mirror and past his own reflection, he raised one of the cigarettes to his mouth. Leo, never known to be the sharpest tool in the toolbox, was at least well trained by Redd and always had his Zippo ready for a smoke. In a smooth double action of first opening the lighter and then igniting it, William didn't have time to even ask. As he took a long drag on the harsh unfiltered cigarette, his eyes diverted down from the mirror to the red-hot end of his cigarette, exhaling a cloud of smoke that billowed up and over his weathered face.

"I saw it in Vietnam. I saw it in Nam all the time. Death ain't the sneaky bitch people think her to be. Sometimes…you just know she's comin'. I was in country during my second tour. It was '67 and I only had three months to go. We were in Ong Thanh on a patrol and we came across a dink bunker."

Leo couldn't pretend to be reading the newspaper any longer and looked up at William. He reached down in the cooler in front of him and grabbed a cold bottle of beer. Redd didn't mind so much if Leo had a few beers per shift, just as long as it wasn't too busy. Johnny poured another shot for William as he picked up his glass and, in a single gulp, emptied his. Sliding his empty glass toward Johnny, he knew William was ready for a refill.

"So what happened? With the bunker I mean?" Johnny asked, never hearing this story before as William wasn't the kind to share such things.

"We did like we were trained to do. We called in air support. They came in, F-4s, two of them, and dropped a shitload of napalm."

"Holy shit," Johnny said.

"Yeah, you ain't never seen anything like it," William said before taking his next shot. "It ain't like them damn movies with John Wayne. It's fucking hell on earth."

Looking over at Johnny and in Leo's direction, he said, "We ended up finding seventeen dead Vietcong, burned beyond all rec-ognition. A lot of them Vietcong were women, but after they were burnt up, you couldn't tell the difference. It's the most horrifying thing you can ever imagine."

"Fuckin' gooks," Leo said as he took a swig of beer. William looked at Leo with a bit of contempt in his eyes for a man who never experienced war and never would. In a weird way, and in a way that he would never talk about, William had more respect for the enemy he fought in Vietnam than he did for most men, especially American men who never served.

"Leo, give me a beer," Johnny said. "Doris is gonna shit if I don't take it easy." Johnny took a twenty-dollar bill out of his pocket and put it on the bar. "Give Billy one too," he said. Leo grabbed two more cold beers from the cooler, popped the tops, and placed them in front of the guys.

"The fucked-up thing about war is, just when you think the worst is passed, just when you think things might be okay, well, that's when shit can really hit the fan." For a quick few seconds, Johnny's mind wandered but was quickly drawn back in to William's war story once he continued.

"After we counted the bodies and collected whatever intel wasn't burnt to shit, we started taking incoming from three sides."

"Jesus Christ," Leo said.

Taking a sip of his cold beer and wiping away the sweat from the bottle with a paper napkin, William continued, "Yeah, well, Jesus didn't have nothing to do with that day."

"What did you do?" Johnny asked with anticipation in his voice.

"We took cover. Hunkered down. We called in for more air support, but a couple hours had already passed and they weren't available. Probably dropping more bombs somewhere else," he said before taking another longer swig of his beer. Johnny reached over and grabbed the pack of Red Apples on the bar and took one out, and before Leo could get his Zippo out, Johnny had it lit.

"So what happened next?" Johnny asked.

"We fought. We had no choice. It was either that or get cut to shreds trying to make a break for it. There were 142 of us when the incoming started."

"How many of them fuckers?" Leo asked.

"Who knows, maybe a thousand."

"Motherfucker!" Johnny said.

"You know, I would have been there with ya if it weren't for my damn knee," Leo said as he reached down to rub his knee. William again shot Leo a condescending look his way. William knew Leo his whole life, and while a pretty okay guy and a decent friend, Leo wasn't the kind of guy to sacrifice anything for anyone. Back when they were all in high school and fights broke out, Leo was that one guy you find in almost every group of guys who happened to disappear when the shit hits the fan. William was never under any illusions as to how Leo would have handled himself in Nam.

"If I hadn't torn up my knee in the Thanksgiving game in '65, I would have been right there with you, Billy," Leo said, holding out his beer in an effort to toast and looking for some recognition, though he was looking in the wrong place if he thought he would get it from William. Seeing William wasn't about to raise his bottle, Leo sheepishly clanked his bottle against William's still resting on the bar.

"Damn, I haven't thought about that game in years. How many touchdowns did you score, three?" Johnny asked Leo.

"Four." Leo made sure to correct Johnny quickly.

Leo, feeling a bit more like a hero than a few minutes ago and never shy about talking about himself or his old glory days, continued, "Four touchdowns, three rushing, and one punt return. And it might have been five if it hadn't been for the big black motherfucker from Lafayette that clipped me."

"Fucking Lafayette," Johnny said to know one in particular before taking a swig of beer.

From the other end of the bar, Margret called for Leo, "Leo, Beefeater and a beer!" Leo, annoyed he had to interrupt his story to go serve Margret, did it as quickly as he could on his bum knee so he could get back to his story. Margret was a regular, at least in her sixties had been a regular at Redd's Tavern since they opened. Not originally from Jefferson Parish, or even Louisiana for that matter, she moved down here with her husband in '56. Tony was his name, and they weren't here more than a month when he was killed at the furniture factory. Crushed by two tons of oak planks. When they finally got the loader in there to lift all those oak planks, there wasn't much left of him; he was squashed pretty good. He was laid out at Redd's funeral parlor, and she was the only one there being that they hadn't made any friends yet and had no family in Jefferson Parish. After the service, she walked into Redd's Tavern for a drink and pretty much never left.

Leo grabbed the bottle of Beefeater and beer on his way down to the end of the bar. William looked at Johnny. "Yeah, he would have been right there with me, huh? If he hadn't hurt his knee, he would have been off to LSU banging cheerleaders and calling me baby killer."

Johnny, finishing up his beer and placing the bottle down, turned to William and asked, "So what happened?"

"What?" William asked, his head not as clear as it was just a short time ago.

"What happened after the attack?"

"Oh yeah. Sixty-four dead, seventy-five wounded."

"Holy shit!" Johnny said. "What happened to you?"

"Nothin'. Not a scratch," William said just before drinking the last swig of beer from his bottle. "I have to get back."

William walked out the door of Redd's Tavern and into the Davis Funeral Home just next door, walking past his wife, Karen, and his son, Matt, and directly to the coffin. He kneeled, performed the sign of the cross, and said a prayer. After what seemed to be only a minute or so, he got up to his feet and crossed himself again as any good Catholic does, and as he walked in the direction of Karen and Matt, never stopping, he said, "I'll be in the car. Say your goodbyes," and continued walking out the door.

Chapter 3

E very child knows school can be a difficult place even in the
best of situations. Children can be cruel at times, often not
knowing the damage they cause, but there are those kids, and
they exist in every school, who know all too well the damage they
cause and they enjoy it.

PGT Beauregard Elementary School was not dissimilar to other
elementary schools around the country built just after the turn of the
century in 1909. By 1980, the old schools' best days were behind it.
It was built in the Baroque style as many schools and other buildings across the United States were back then, but especially down
here in Louisiana with all the French influence. Some seventy years
after its opening, many things have changed though at Beauregard
Elementary, too many things remained the same. For instance, there
ain't no air conditioner like that new school they built over in Lafayette
Parish. So the kids here at Beauregard—Beauregard, that's what folks
down here called it—the kids at Beauregard Elementary agonize in
the sweltering heat in late spring and in early September especially.
On real hot days, it can be ninety degrees outside and one hundred
degrees inside. So a few years back, the school committee bought a
half dozen of those big stand-up fans, but they didn't have enough
money to put one in every class, only half. Mrs. Thompson's class was
one of the lucky ones on the account of her age and seniority.

And while plenty of progress has been made down here in the Deep South, there are still plenty of problems that need addressing. Heck, it was just twenty years or so ago that the school became integrated with the black kids. That didn't go over well down here for many of the white folks, and sometimes they still go out of their way to let the black folks know they ain't too pleased.

It was Monday, April 14, 1980, 8:05 AM and the first bell had just rung; the second bell rang at 8:10 AM, and if you ain't in your seat, Mrs. Thompson's gonna make you stay after school and clean erasers and wash blackboards. But on this day, Matt was in his regular seat, dead center of the class as usual. This was Matt's first day back to school since Billy was killed a week ago this past Saturday. He had been driving back home from a concert in Baton Rouge with his two friends, Clarence Bonnaire and Peter Perrot. There were all drinkin' and Billy lost control of the car and slammed head-on into a tree. Luckily, Clarence and Peter weren't hurt too bad, just a few broken bones, but they'd be home from the hospital in a few weeks. But being this was Matt's first day back, he was just feelin' a bit uneasy.

"Come on, children, take your seats. You back there, Tommy Martel. Perry, take your seats so we can gets started," Mrs. Thompson said loud enough for the whole class to hear.

"Bitch," Tommy said under his breath and out of earshot of Mrs. Thompson. While Tommy's ignorance and defiance gave Tommy's friends, Perry and Albert, a chuckle, most of the kids just rolled their eyes at their idiocy.

The kids always took a bit more time to get settled in their seats on a Monday morning. A weekend of freedom would always carry over a bit, but they eventually quieted down enough where Mrs. Thompson could address the class. Standing in front of her large wooden desk that had to be as old as the school itself and in front of the first row of student desks, Mrs. Thompson said, "Matt... Matt, the whole class would like to tell you just how sorry we are for your loss." Her hands folded and with a look of pure compassion on her face, she looked at Matthew, who was looking down at the cover of his history book and only because that was in his line of sight. "Matt?" Mrs. Thompson said. Matt, at that point, looked up from his book and at his teacher. Mrs. Thompson turned toward the young girl in the first row. "Emily?"

Emily Moulin, the cutest girl in Matthew's class and in PGT Beauregard Elementary School for that matter—well, that's what Matt thought anyway—stood up from her desk. But it wasn't just Emily's beauty that Matt was attracted too, it was her personality, her sweet nature and most of all, she was different from all the other girls.

"Matthew," Emily said. She always called Matt by his full name, Matthew. "Matthew," she said as she looked at him with sadness in her eyes, "the whole class wishes to tell you how sorry we are for your brother dying." Looking down at her shoes at times and occasionally raising her head to make eye contact with Matt, she handed him an envelope with a card in it. He wasn't sure if should open it or not, so he turned to Mrs. Thompson for conformation.

"Go on, open it, Matthew."

It read, "*From the whole class, we wish to extend our sympathies for your loss.*" Each of the children had signed the card; it took up most of the two inside pages of the card. Matt was looking down at the card. He was looking for Emily's signature, when he found it, close to the bottom; he saw she had drawn a small heart after her name.

"Okay, Emily, take your seat, honey," Mrs. Thompson said.

Emily sat back down in her chair, but Mrs. Thompson remained standing in the front of the class.

"Class, before we get started, I would like to introduce a new student, Jamal Jenkins. Jamal, would you please stand up?"

Jamal, a black boy, was sitting just to the left of Matt. He was big for his age, but he also had a timid nature about him that any-one with eyes could see. Jamal looked around the class and gave a half-hearted wave and stat down as quickly as he could. Having just moved to Jefferson Parish, a white parish for the most part, from a predominately black parish, Jamal didn't look none too thrilled. No doubt he left behind a lot of friends in his old school and was feeling a bit out of place.

Mrs. Thompson made eye contact with Matt; she gave him a little wink before walking around her desk and sitting down. "Let's get started, children. Turn your history books to page 192."

After their history lesson was complete, Mrs. Thompson moved on to science. This year, the kids were learning about the Milky Way galaxy. Matt was never a big fan of science; he was a good student overall, but science he could do without. What he really loved was history, and it showed in his grade each year—straight As every year so far. His historical hero was Thomas Jefferson. Lots of people down in Jefferson Parish thought it was named after Jefferson Davis, the Confederate president, but Matt knew better; in fact, it was named after Thomas Jefferson just a year before he died.

Every forty-five minutes, the bell would ring throughout the school and in each class. This would let the teacher and the kids know that it was either time to change subjects or go to lunch or recess. But of course, the most important bell of the day was always the final bell. After the science lesson was the morning recess, so every day at about nine twenty-five, the kids start getting restless in anticipation of the recess bell at nine thirty. Mrs. Thompson, like all the teachers at PGT Beauregard Elementary School, knew this and had her hands full trying to keep the kids focused for that last five or ten minutes as most of the eyes in the class were watching the clock that last five minutes. Precisely at nine thirty, the bell rang, and twenty-five kids jumped to their feet and rush out the door. Not wanting to waste even thirty seconds of that recess time, the kids, boys and girls alike, are out the door faster than coonhound on a scent.

As the kids rushed out the door in and into the schoolyard, Matt certainly wasn't himself yet. Normally he'd be right out the door as fast as the others, but today he took his time. As he walked by Mrs. Thompson's desk, she said, "Matt?"

"Yes, Mrs. Thompson?" Matt responded.

"I just want to again…extend my condolences and let you know if you need anything, you let me know. If you need a little extra time on your homework or just someone to talk to."

"Thank you, Mrs. Thompson, but I'm doing okay," Matt said as his eyes again moved from the floor to Mrs. Thompson and back to the floor again.

MICHAEL W. HULL

"Well, you let me know if you need anything." Mrs. Thompson took Matt into her arms in a warm embrace that shocked Matt a bit, but he quickly reciprocated and was happy for it.

"Now go outside and have some fun," she said.

"Yes, ma'am," Matt replied and headed out the door.

As Matt walked down the dimly lit stairway off the main hall and opened the door to head out into the schoolyard, he was momentarily blinded by the bright sunlight. Standing in the doorway for a few extra seconds to let his eyes adjust to the extreme difference, he could hear a commotion.

"Fucking nigger," Matt heard. His eyes still not adjusted, he couldn't see what was happening just yet but had no doubt whose voice he heard—Tommy Martel.

A second or two more and Matt's eyes came into focus. Scanning around the schoolyard, looking to see what was going on, he saw over toward the old willow tree Tommy, Albert, and Perry had the new kid, Jamal, surrounded. Jamal was cornered between the willow tree and the back of the schoolhouse with nowhere to escape. Matt could see all three of them, teasing and spitting on Jamal, calling him coon and nigger.

"Fucking nigger! Why'd you move here anyways?" Albert said. Lots of kids call Albert Fat Albert after the cartoon even though he wasn't that fat, just kind of chubby though he is one of the biggest boys in the school. Jamal, almost frozen except for his hands, shaking and clearly afraid, had a look of terror on his face.

"My father told me all you niggas only want to steal white women and make half-nigga kids," Perry said as he spit a big loogie in Jamal's face. And what made it even worse was Perry, like Tommy and Albert, chewed tobacco. So it wasn't just spit; it was brown slop. As Matt watched, he could feel his blood boil. Standing there without even knowing it, his hands balled up into fist.

"Nah, he wouldn't know what to do with a girl anyway, white or nigga," Albert said.

"You niggas are ruining everything. My daddy said all niggas need to go back to Africa wheres they came from," Tommy said as he pushed Jamal to the ground.

22

Jamal got up quickly, wiping the dirt off his clothes, and said, "I ain't from Africa, I'm from Orleans Parish."

Not a second after Jamal finished his sentence, Tommy swung with all his might and walloped Jamal right in the eye. He fell to the ground quicker than a drunk woman's top at Mardi Gras. Jamal, humiliated and scared, this time didn't rush to get to his feet. Matt had seen enough and rushed over.

"Hey, why don't you leave this boy alone!" Matt said, trying to get the bullies' attention.

"Hey, Laurent, fuck you!" Perry said. Just then, Tommy noticed that Jamal has pissed his pants. It wasn't something that he could hide as some of the dusty dirt had started to cling to the dampness.

"Ha ha! Hey, look, Matt, the nigga pissed his pants like a big baby," Tommy said loudly, trying to get as many kids to hear as possible. Tommy, even though only twelve, was already an expert at causing pain. He had a good teacher, his father, Tommy Sr., a well-known racist and neo-Nazi around town, though he had been in prison for the last five years after he was found guilty of killing a black man in a bar fight. He got ten years for manslaughter.

"Just leave him alone already," Matt said in a much-firmer voice.

"Or what?" Albert asked Matt. "Or what?" he asked again.

"He didn't do nothin' to you, so just leave him alone!" Matt exclaimed.

"But he's a nigga, and my daddy says us white folks are superior than niggas," Tommy said, obviously trying to repeat what he had heard from his daddy but probably didn't have a clue of what it meant or what the hell he was talking about. No one ever accused Tommy Martel of knowing much about anything but being mean.

"Come on, Jamal. Let's go get you cleaned up," Matt said while doing his best to position himself between Jamal and the boys.

"You're just a fuckin' nigga lover, Laurent," Tommy said as he pushed Jamal one more time to the ground. As Matt extended his hand to Jamal, who was now sitting on his backside, Tommy sucker punched Matt in the side of his face. Matt fell to the ground but got to his feet right quick and jumped on Tommy. Matt started punching Tommy in his face, belly, and anywhere else Tommy couldn't cover up fast enough. Albert and Perry just stood there, a bit shocked because no one ever punched Tommy before. Tommy was usually the one doing the punching, and they just didn't know what to do. Within a minute or so, though it felt much longer to both Tommy and Matt, as most fights do, Mrs. Thompson and Mr. Orlando were approaching.

"You boys stop that this instant!" Mrs. Thompson yelled. "Break it up! Break it up, Mr. Orlando."

Mr. Orlando, the black custodian, now well into his fifties, who had been employed at PGT Beauregard Elementary School since he was sixteen years old, quickly pulled Matt off Tommy, leaving Matt open for another sucker punch from Tommy. Mr. Orlando quickly let go of Matt and grabbed Tommy.

"Get your fucking hands off me, nigger!" Tommy yelled. As Mr. Orlando was doing his best to restrain him, his necklace broke off and fell to the ground—a silver swastika necklace, a gift from his daddy that Tommy had worn every day since his father went to prison. His father said to him, "Take care of this until I get out" as he handed it to him in the courtroom on the day he was convicted. Tommy's daddy would never get to wear the necklace again as he would be killed in prison just six months from his release date. They believe he was shanked by two black men in his cell though no one was ever charged. Tommy would cherish that symbol of hate until the day he died.

"Thomas Martel! You stop this instant!" Mrs. Thompson said over and over again. "Mr. Orlando, you take Mr. Martel to the principal's office and you have him wait for me." Mrs. Thompson noticed Tommy's swastika on the ground and picked it up. She handed it to Mr. Orlando and said, "Take this trash as well."

When Tommy noticed his necklace has come off his neck, he got even more agitated all over again, saying, "That was my daddy's! Give me my fucking necklace!"

Mr. Orlando walked off toward the principal's office with Tommy in one hand and the swastika necklace in the other, just shaking his head in disbelief as they walked away. Jamal had gotten up off the ground, still shaken from the whole ordeal; Mrs. Thompson started brushing the dirt off his back and his backside. "Can someone tell me what's going on here?" she asked to no one in particular.

Perry quickly sounded off, "This nigga started it!"

"Bullshit!" Matt yelled.

"Matthew!" Mrs. Thompson said in rebuke.

"Perry, you get your behind to the office as well and wait there for me," Mrs. Thompson said, having just about enough of all this nonsense.

"What did I do?" Perry asked as he walked toward the building. "You heard me, just keep walking and you wait until I get in there." Albert, who had, all of a sudden, gotten really quiet, kicked some dirt at Jamal at one last effort to get the better of him and that was all it took.

"You go!" Mrs. Thompson said to Albert as she pointed toward the office. "Office now!" Albert walked off, clearly pissed off like the rest of them.

Looking at Jamal, Mrs. Thompson asked, "Are you okay, son?" Looking down at the ground, embarrassed and probably still scared, Jamal just shook his head, "Yes."

"Matthew, why don't you take Jamal down to the boiler room and wait for Mr. Orlando to come back? I'll make sure he'll let you boys use his lavatory to clean up."

"Yes, Mrs. Thompson," Matt said.

Matt, with Jamal following close behind, both brushed dirt from their clothes as they walked around to the rear entrance of the school, the quickest way to the boiler room. As they walked, Matt was a few steps in front of Jamal.

"Thanks," Jamal said.

Matt turned around to look at Jamal and said, "That's okay. Those guys are assholes anyway."

Chapter 4

GRADUATION DAY, 1987

M uch time had passed since that fateful day when Jamal would come into Matthew's life in a fashion that would impact Matt for the rest of his life. As well, Jamal found in Matt a contradiction of his past experiences and lessons that were instilled through valid past experiences. To say the black folks didn't really trust the white folks and vice versa would simply be stating the obvious. Class, social standing, and above all, race, even in the 1980s, were still a big part of the South, and trust that crossed over between the races wasn't easy to find.

Over the course of their friendship, Matt and Jamal complemented each other very well. Just last year, Pope John Paul II was making a trip to New Orleans and was to speak at St. Luis Cathedral, mostly to Catholic clergy and other dignitaries. In addition to the clergy and other political figures from New Orleans and around the state, the presidents of each senior class in New Orleans and the surrounding parishes were also invited to attend the service. Jamal, being the president of the senior class of 1987, was extended the invitation. Though a southern Baptist and knowing right well Matthew's Catholic convictions, Jamal was suddenly struck with a severe case of food poisoning on the day of the visit, and coincidentally, when Principal Dodd called Matthew, the class vice president, to replace Jamal, Matt just happened to be dressed in his Sunday's best, sitting by the phone.

This day would be a bit of a culmination, at least for now for both Matt and Jamal, as well as their families. The senior class of J.V. Brown High School, named after a local civil war hero, the confederate side of course graduation was only moments away. It was a typical mid-June day down in Creole country, hot and humid, the southern ladies, both black and white, dressed impeccably and not one of them without a handheld fan. It was controlled chaos that preceded the ceremonies and anyone who ever attended an event like a graduation knows exactly what I mean. Matt, in his cap and gown, stood with his grandmother and his momma and daddy. Edith was beaming and couldn't be more proud of her only grandson.

"I can't believe you're gonna be gone in a few months," Karen said to Matt with a self-serving tone.

"I know, Momma. But you know I've been wanting this for so long. I busted my ass for this," Matt said.

"Matthew!" Edith scolds.

"Sorry, Grandma."

"I just don't know why you can't go to LSU or Xavier. Xavier was right good enough for Emily," Karen said, looking to strengthen her argument.

"Momma, Emily applied to Columbia and didn't get in."

"You know Columbia isn't a Catholic college?" Karen said as she made a point not to make eye contact with Matt and pretended to be surveying the goings-on around the event.

Matt, knowing his decision to attend a northern school wasn't the most popular, knew to just let it go and move on to another subject he might get a fair shake at. With his hand shielding his eyes, Matt scanned the grounds; the sun was high in the sky and so bright it lacked an orange glow, replaced with a blinding white light.

"There's Emily and her family," Matt said.

"You know it's different up there? The people are different. They ain't like us, Matthew," Karen said, looking at Matt, trying to catch his eye though Matt was still looking off in Emily's direction. A few seconds passed and he turned and looked at his grandmother, seeing the look on her face and the subtle nod of her head indicated to Matt that she agreed with Karen. He gave Edith a kiss on the cheek. That was his way of reassuring her of his love and not to worry.

"I know, Grandma, that's why I wanna go to experience something different. Something new. I mean, the farthest I've ever been was that class trip to the Johnson Space Center in the eighth grade."

William, never known as much of a talker, not even by his friends down at Redd's, was indeed proud of his youngest son and said simply, "You just stay out of trouble up there and hit them books. Don't piss all your money away either. You been working for the last five years to save for this, so don't blow it, boy."

"Pop, I got a scholarship."

"Yeah, well…"

"Can y'all excuse me for a few minutes? I wanna go say hi to Emily and her folks," Matt said. "Momma, look." Matt gestured over toward the parking lot. "Doris and Johnny are here." Karen swung her head around and made eye contact with Doris and waved. "Come on, Momma, let's go say hi." Taking Edith by the arm and with William in toe, they made their way over to meet Doris and Johnny. Matt, taking advantage of the opportunity he created, looked around for Emily and spotted her talking with a friend. He wasted no time walking over to her in the most direct route.

"Hey, Em…Shelly. Hi, Mrs. and Mr. Moulin. How y'all doing?" Matt asked as he extended his hand to Mr. Moulin. Emily's parents always liked Matt. In Jefferson Parish, like most places in America, there were two sides of the tracks even if there weren't any real tracks to speak of. Emily's father was a hometown lawyer who never left the neighborhood, but because of his occupation and income, it placed them clear on the other side of the tracks from Matt and his family. Though, Mr. Moulin was a good man and treated everyone with respect even though he'd be justified in having some animosity against some folks. He and Mrs. Moulin had some tough times. But they liked Matt, both of them—probably because of how well he treated Em. And Mrs. Moulin, well Matt just thought the world of her. There was no doubt that Emily took after her momma when it came to her beauty—her hair, complexion and even her ability to cook all came from her momma. Mrs. Moulin worked as a secretary at Mr. Moulin's law practice and took classes at the community college at night. They could see better than most that Matt was a young man with integrity.

"Hey, Matthew," Emily said with a smile that extended from ear to ear, a reaction that she found to be reflexive whenever she saw Matt. She threw her arms around his shoulders and gave him the same big hug she's been giving him for the last three years of their relationship. She always had to reach up to do so as Emily was only five feet one compared to Matt's six feet one, a clear difference that often made them the butt of some good-natured jokes.

Over the crackling loudspeaker, Principal Dodd said, "Good afternoon, folks. We're about to get started with the ceremonies, so, parents and family members, can you make your way to the guest seating area? Students, make your way over to your assigned seating, and we'll get started in about ten minutes."

"Well, I better get back and show my folks to their seats," Matt said.

"Emily, we're going to find our seats and get out of the sun. We'll see you in a little bit, honey," Mrs. Moulin said as she and Mr. Moulin walked under the tent and out of the bright sun.

"Okay, Momma. I'll see you in a bit." She turned back toward Matt and quickly around again, watching her parents, to make sure they found their way into the shade under the tent. "Wish me luck!" she yelled out in their direction. A faint "Good luck, baby!" came back in return. Turning back toward Matt, one of his hands in each of hers, she looked up at him as was needed.

"You know I love you, Matthew," she said.

"I love you too, Em." Matt gave her a kiss on her forehead, then a peck on the lips, and another quick embrace. "I gotta go find my family. You know them." Emily laughed and said, "Oh yeah." Matt started walking back to where he'd last seen the family venture off to and spotted them. He started walking over toward them to rustle them up and get them in their seats as soon as he could. Matt always regarded any function with his entire family as an attempt to round up cats. Not one of them were known for punctuality or being where they needed to when they need to.

"Atticus! Atticus!" Matt heard someone yelling.

Stopping in his tracks, he looked in the direction from where he was being called, but before he even turned, he knew exactly who it was.

"Jamal!" Matt yelled back.

When the boys were in eighth grade, in Mrs. Hicky's class, they had read *To Kill a Mockingbird*. When Jamal was halfway through finishing the book, he started calling Matt Atticus on occasion. He did it out of reverence for his friend because, even at that young age, Jamal saw that Matt always tried to do the right thing, even in difficult situations. A few years back, Matt had been with a group of boys lighting grass fires, nothing big but something they shouldn't have been doing. Well, one of those little grass fires got out of control, and it ended up catching Mr. Foxworthy's fence on fire. It was only about a ten-foot section, but it was ruined. When the boys saw they couldn't put it out, they ran. But Matt waited for the fire truck to arrive. He told the fire chief and Mr. Foxworthy what had happened and was willing to accept whatever punishment was headed his way. The chief and Mr. Foxworthy both agreed that if Matt helped to rebuild the fence, they could keep this between them. And that was what they did.

Matt quickly glanced at his watch as he slow jogged over to Jamal and his momma. Matt was the first in the Laurent family to truly understand the meaning of punctuality. He had heard the story of his parents' wedding day numerous times throughout his life, most often when Karen was upset with William. Apparently, on the day of their wedding, William decided to go crawfish trapping with Johnny and was close to an hour late for the ceremony. William always blamed the tardiness on a broken-down boat motor, but Karen had always suspected cold feet or too many cold beers to be the culprit.

"What's up, bro?" Matt said. "Shouldn't you be rehearsing your speech or somthin'?" he asked.

"Nah, I got it memorized."

"How you doing, Mrs. Jenkins? You must be proud of our boy here." Matt asked as he gave Mrs. Jenkins a hug.

Jamal's father had been diagnosed with throat cancer a few years back, and even though he had all kind of fine quality treatment, nothing helped. He only lasted seven months.

"Oh, Matthew, praise Jesus! I'm the proudest momma here today, you got that right. Amen!" People down in the South have a habit of saying amen after things. Even the people not so religious like William would say amen every time LSU would score a touchdown or he'd catch a big catfish. There didn't seem to be no rules when or when not to say it; people just said it.

"Momma, can you find your seat, all right? I wanna talk to Matt for a second," Jamal said.

"Sure, baby." Mrs. Jenkins stilled called Jamal baby even though he stood six foot three and weighed in the neighborhood of 220. I guess for a mother a son will always be her baby. "You do me proud and remember to stand up straight when you give your speech. Big fellas like you look terrible when they get all hunched over." Mrs. Jenkins said as she started to walk off.

"Of course, Momma. I'll see you when it's all over. Now go get out of this sun."

Mrs. Jenkins, fanning herself, walked off toward the tent, stopping along the way and asking someone for help finding her seat. As Mrs. Jenkins head off, Matt caught the eye of his daddy and held up his left arm and pointed to his watch. William, not acknowledging Matt but reaching over and saying something to Karen, turned and headed toward the tent. Jamal extended his hand and Matt took it, shaking his best friend's hand. Matt glanced back again at his family to make sure they were heading where they needed to be; he saw Karen and William walking under the tent, but Edith was heading toward him and Jamal.

Seven years had passed since that day in Mrs. Thompson's fifth-grade class when the two boys met. Unfortunately, Mrs. Thompson had passed away two years ago, and as quiet and reserved as Mrs. Thompson always was, she didn't go quietly. She had a massive heart attack right in the middle of the homily during Easter mass. Father John did his best to keep everybody calm, and David Duke—no, not that one—David Duke, the deputy chief of the Jefferson Parish

Fire Department, was there, as he always was with his wife, Sissy, and their two boys started CPR right away. Unfortunately, poor old Mrs. Thompson, now in her seventies, didn't make it. Both Matt and Jamal were honored when Mrs. Thompson's son, Donald, who lived in Florida, asked them to be pallbearers at her funeral. You never heard from either Matt or Jamal or most any of the kids in her classes ever say a bad word about Mrs. T.

Jamal and Matt had been through a lot since that day they met, and while both boys excelled academically as well as playing multiple sports, Jamal was on a path he, at one point, never thought possible. Becoming the valedictorian and having been accepted to Harvard, he was excited about his future. Matt, on the other hand, was not accepted to Harvard or Yale or Princeton, and while Jamal could have taken the opportunity to gloat, he never did. Instead, he talked about Columbia, Matt's destination, and all about their political science program and how cool living in New York City was going to be.

"You better get going before Dodd has a shit fit," Matt said as he gave his best friend a pat on the shoulder.

"Yeah," Jamal said as he glanced toward the front of the stage.

"Look, he's over there talking to Mayor Ferguson. He ain't going anywhere until the mayor is ready." Matt looked over.

"Thanks, brother," Jamal said. "I couldn't have got here without you."

"Bullshit. Of course, you could have. Okay, brother, good luck with your speech," Matt said.

"Thanks, man."

Jamal headed off to the front row where the valediction was assigned to sit, and Matt, seeing his grandmomma heading his way, rushed over to her to close the gap and save time.

"What are you doing, Grandma? You gotta get to your seat," Matt said with urgency in his voice, looking at his watch one more time. "Shit."

"Matthew! Watch your mouth!" she scolded him.

"Sorry, Grandma, but—"

"But nothing. You just give me a minute. We won't have many more like this left."

"Okay, Grandma, okay."

Taking her grandson's hands in hers, she, looking up at him as most of the women in Matt's life were forced to do, said, "You know, Matthew, after your brother died, we were all worried about you. I know your momma and your daddy don't exactly show it much, but they love you very much. And they're proud of you, just like I am. Your daddy just ain't never been the same since he came back from the war. Oh"—clasping her hands together and looking up to the sky—"your daddy was so different, Matthew, so don't be too hard on him."

Matthew bent over a bit to kiss his elderly grandmother on the cheek and said, "I know, Grandma."

"Grandma, you got to get to your seat."

"Just one more thing."

"What's that, Grandma?"

Matthew noticed his mother, Karen, making her way through the crowd and heading toward them, no doubt to collect Grandma. "Here comes Momma for you," Matt said, looking back over her shoulder.

She reached into her purse and pulled out a white envelope. She handed it to Matt and said, "This is your graduation present."

Looking down at the seemingly full envelope, the contents challenging its very structure, he asked, "What's this?"

"It's $3,200," she replied with a satisfactory grin on her face.

"Grandma, where did you get this?"

"Bingo! Being Catholic has benefits besides everlasting salvation," Edith said with a hint of gratification in her voice.

"Seriously?" Matt asked in disbelief as he stared down at the envelope. "Grandma, I can't take this," he said as he tried to hand it back to her.

"You most certainly will take that. You take this money and go to New York and live. Enjoy your life, Matthew. No one deserves it more." Not knowing what to say in response to her generosity, he gave her a hug bigger than any he had since he was probably ten years old. Looking back up at Matt, she said, "Your granddaddy would be so proud of you."

"Grandma, I don't know what to say. Thank you," Matt said humbly, knowing full well Grandma, as well as Momma and Daddy, could use that extra money.

Just then, a voice over the loudspeaker. "Good afternoon, graduates of J.V. Brown High!" A roar went up in the crowd.

"Momma? Momma?" Karen said as she came to collect Edith.

"Thanks, Grandma. I gotta go get my seat." Matt ran off under the tent toward the student section.

"Momma. Come on, Momma, we got to go take our seats," Karen said as she took Edith by the arm.

"Did you bring enough film for the camera?" Edith asked Karen as they walked off and disappeared into the shadow under the tent.

Chapter 5

NEW YORK, 1991

O ver the last four years, a lot has transpired for Matt and everyone around him for that matter. In his fourth year at Columbia, he, not surprising, was an academic standout. Emily, well, Matt and Emily had tried their best to make things work, and they did for some time. After Matt's first year of college was completed, he returned to Jefferson Parish for the summer, spending much of his time with Emily, talking about a future, enjoying the summer nights and beautiful sunsets down on the bayou. But Emily was...well, at her core she was country girl. She had dreams of a family in a nice quiet farmhouse outside town, Matt would have a small law practice once he finished law school, maybe run for parish president, and they'd live happily ever after. But Matt was anything but a country boy. Matt's dreams of leaving the parish had long been cemented. As much as he tried to warm up to the idea of a simple life back in Jefferson Parish, it just never took root.

By Christmas of 1988, Matt had realized he needed to do the right thing and end things with Emily. He had put it off as long as he could in a way hoping he'd change his mind. Hoping that the thought of a simple country life would find a place in his heart though it never did. It wasn't an easy conversation, but one he felt he owed Em. Lots of tears were shed by both Matt and Emily, and he did his best to convince her it was for the best for each of them. Emily and Matt loved each other very much; they shared memories that were no one else's and only their own. In time, their hearts would heal, separately of course, and they would move on. Even falling in love again.

Then one day, he met a girl. Her name was Samantha.

Sitting at the Columbia University Library, Butler Library, a beautiful space with soaring ceilings and grand chandeliers, surrounded by books both open and closed, looking around, Matt suddenly noticed that he was nearly alone. A girl, sitting at one of the library's heavy oak tables at the other end of the reference hall, and two other boys, one he recognized from one of his classes last year but couldn't seem to remember his name. And of course, the librarian sitting at the desk near the entrance though looking not at all like the stereotypical librarian we all grew up knowing. In fact, this librarian was a usually very talkative, though not tonight. Matt looked down at his watch and saw the time. It seemed odd, a bit early. Shaking his wrist and then holding his watch up to his ear, he realized it had stopped. He looked over to the large clock over the window and saw the time, the correct time.

"Shit!" Matt said, much too loudly for a library setting, for which he drew the requisite sneers from the remaining four others and quickly offered up an apology. "Sorry, sorry," he said as he collected all his books, pens, and notebooks that would be useless to any others and threw them into his backpack in a haphazardly fashion and ran toward the exit. That earned him yet another admonishing stare from the librarian as he mistakenly tried to exit through the entrance turnstile, slamming his pelvis into the immovable object. Realizing his error, he quickly stumbled through the exit turnstile while, again, offering the requisite apology, "Sorry, sorry. I'm late."

Running down Amsterdam Avenue with his jampacked backpack, through the crowded Manhattan sidewalks, he did his best to avoid running into people, passing the Church of Notre Dame, the closest Catholic church to Columbia and a fixture in Matt's life since arriving in New York four years ago. He crossed himself as any good Catholic would as best he could while in full stride and being thrown off-balance by his awkwardly heavy backpack. Weaving in and out of people and the hustle and bustle for what New York is known, around such obstacles as mailboxes, fire hydrants, and the random rat scurrying away from a five-foot pile of garbage bags, he completed the eight-block run. Looking at his watch, forgetting it had stopped, he wondered if that run was done in record time. Though he had no clue of how fast he had made the trek, he couldn't help but be impressed with his time, then reality set back in. A bit disheveled, Matt looked first into the window at his reflection of Augie's to fix his hair, then adjusting his sight through the glass to look for Sam.

Augie's was a jazz club that served Cajun and Creole dishes like étouffée and gumbo, among other things. They sometimes even served frogs legs on Saturday nights, and Augie's gave Matt a little piece of home in the city. But in New York, well, they got everything; that's why Matt had come to love New York. They have everything here. Matt, from a young age, was an expert frog catcher. His father had taught Billy when he was about eight or nine, and the summer after Billy was killed, he taught Matt. William had made Billy a frog net made from a hickory branch and an old pair of Edith's pantyhose. William didn't bother to make Matt his own frog net, but rather when Billy passed away, Matt kind of inherited his. But being it was Friday night, frogs were off the menu.

He was making his way through the crowded restaurant, the band in full effect, jammin' as they always did on the weekends. Matt loved this place.

"Hey, Matty," said a waiter as he passed, carrying a full tray of food, Matt going in the opposite direction.

"Hey," Matt replied, not realizing who it was but looked back to identify him. *Clifford*, he thought to himself. Moving past the stage, the bandleader and fixture at Augie's, Frenchy, playing his alto sax, gave a slight nod of recognition to Matt as he passed without ever missing a beat.

"Hey, baby, I'm sorry," Matt said as he put his pack down and under the table before taking a seat at the table for two. With a bit of disappointment in her voice, Samantha responded, "It's okay. I understand."

"No, it's not okay," Matt said in a tone he thought sounded like one of him taking responsibility yet hoping to be forgiven sooner than later. Holding out his wrist and pointing to his watch, he said,

"My damn watch stopped!" He held it up to his ear for effect. The waiter arrived just as Matt took his seat and, upon looking up, Matt realized it was Luis. "Hey, Luis, how's it goin'?"

"Fine, fine, Matty. Busy as always on a Friday night. Hey, Sam," Luis said. Sam responded with a smile. "You guys going to be around for a while? Terry B. is coming in later to do a set."

Looking at Samantha for approval and not getting it, he looked to Luis and said, "No, no, not tonight, Luis."

"Drinks?" Luis asked with his pen and server's pad at the ready.

"Why don't you bring us a bottle of white wine, Luis?" Matt said.

"I'm just drinking water," Samantha said, which surprised Matt.

"No wine?" Matt asked.

"Not tonight."

"Okay, well, then just bring me an Amstel," Matt said, looking up at Luis.

Luis headed to the bar, and Matt took the opportunity to look around the room for familiar faces. He saw Kenny, David, and Scott standing over at the bar, drinking their usuals, shots with beer chasers, and working three coeds who looked three sheets to the wind. They couldn't be more than nineteen, he thought to himself. Freshman probably, sophomores maybe. It was common knowledge that Augie's didn't always adhere to the required New York State laws when it came to legal age of alcohol consumption. That's why it was so popular with freshman and sophomores. Matt moved the small candle that sat in the middle of the table to the side and reached across and took Samantha's hand in his.

"I'm sorry I'm late. It's just this final paper is driving me nuts, and I lost track of time and this…this damn watch," pointing to it yet again.

"Matt!" Samantha interrupted.

"Yeah, babe?"

"It's okay," Sam said with a smile. "Forget it. In two years, this is the first time you've been late. I'll give you a pass," she said just before biting into a piece of bread.

"Oh," Matt said, relieved. "Awesome! Happy anniversary, baby," Matt said enthusiastically.

"Happy anniversary," Sam said as she looked at Matt's face with the candlelight dancing across it in the dimly lit bar.

Luis returned to the table, setting Samantha's glass of water in front of her and then opening Matt's Amstel and placing it in front of him. Taking out his pad once again and flipping it through until he reached an empty page, with pen in hand, he asked, "Food?"

"We don't have any menus," Samantha pointed out.

"Shit! Menus! Right! Be right back," Luis said.

"How was your day, honey?" Matt asked Sam as he lit a cigarette, which earned him a cross look.

Knowing full well of the look, he said "I know, I know, I'm going to quit. So how was your day, babe?"

"It was okay. I got my grade from my sculpture class."

"And?" Matt asked with anticipation.

"A-," Samantha responded with a sense of relief.

Samantha was in her third year of the BFA program at NYU. Matt was never one to take an interest in art, let alone try to understand it. But over the last two years, Sam had made great strides in educating Matt on the history of art through the centuries and eventually getting Matt to understand the cultural significances. While Matt had always been interested in other cultures, he never paid too much attention to the art of these cultures, and it was Samantha who made him realize the importance of art.

Sam enjoyed teaching Matt about art and why people, for thousands of years, needed to express themselves in various forms. First taking him to the Met and the Museum of Natural History and then the Frick and, eventually, the Guggenheim, Matt would start to see this part of humanity through Sam's eyes and learn to appreciate it in all its forms. While at first it wasn't always easy, knowing Matt's love of jazz music, Sam used it to explain the creative process of an artist. Before Sam, Matt didn't necessarily see music, not even jazz; he only heard it. But Samantha would change his whole outlook on art and artist.

"Baby, that's great!" Matt said with enthusiasm. Finishing off his beer, he said to Sam, "I think that calls for a drink. You sure you don't want a drink, a glass of wine, a beer?" Matt asked, knowing Samantha isn't averse to alcohol.

"No," she said, taking a sip of her water. "Water is fine tonight."

Just then, Luis returned with the menus, placed them on the table, and hurried off to another. Matt yelled, "Amstel, Luis!" as Luis moved through the crowd, but raising his hand to let Matt know he had heard him. Matt and Samantha started looking at the menus when Matt reached into his pocket and removed a small black box with a simple white ribbon wrapped around it. He placed it on the table, behind the menu, waiting for Samantha to put hers down.

"Do you know what you want?"

"Can we get oysters Rockefeller?" she asked.

"Of course, what about for your entrée? I'm going to have the jambalaya."

"I think I want beignets," she said with a smile.

"Really?" Matt asked and then laughed. "Desert for your meal? Okay," he said, always appreciating her little quirks and uniqueness that made her so special to him. Matt's levelheadedness and reasonable nature surprisingly fit perfectly with Sam's little peculiarities, which often made him think that he would go utterly mad to spend the rest of his life with someone like himself. Her way was simply something that he couldn't resist, and they fit as well as a hand and glove.

Putting his menu down and waiting for Samantha to notice the box, she began to ask him about his schedule the following day and whether he'd have time to go to the park for a picnic.

"I can pick up some chicken salad and rye bread at the deli and make some sandwiches. Kelly's on Ninety-Sixth has the best pickles I've ever had," she said with delight in her voice. Matt, still waiting for her to notice, started to chuckle, and she asked, "What's so funny?"

"Nothing, nothing at all," he said, laughing even louder.

"Matthew!" she exclaimed, getting frustrated.

"What's in the box?" Luis asked as he put Matt's Amstel down in front of him.

Sam threw her hands to her mouth and covered it as she finally noticed the box.

"Need a minute?" Luis asked.

"Yeah, thanks, Luis," Matt said.

"Happy anniversary, baby," Matt said as he slid the box across the table. Sam picked up the box and slowly started to untie the ribbon, her eyes moving back and forth from the box to Matt's eyes and back again. Removing the cover of the box, she saw a simple silver necklace with a pearl pendant.

"Oh my god, Matt, it's beautiful!" she said. "Can you help me put it on?" she asked. Matt quickly moved around the table to help Sam clasp the necklace around her neck.

"Do you like it, honey?"

Looking down at it, now hanging around her neck, and back up to Matt, she said, "I love it!" as she leaned forward over the small table, looking for a kiss. Matt, excited that she liked it as much as she does, leaned forward and gave her a kiss. After the first kiss, their faces still only inches away from each other, they gave each other another tiny kiss and then another and another. With their faces just inches away from each other, Matt said, "I love you, Sam."

"I love you too, baby," Samantha responded.

Luis returned and Matt gave him their order. Sam commented on how smoky it was in the bar that night, even more so than usual. All the while, Matt wondered and finally asked, "How long are you going to keep me waiting for package you have under your seat?"

"How could you see that from your chair?" Sam asked in disbelief that he noticed the gift that she tried her best to hide before he arrived.

"I saw it when I walked in," he said with a chuckle. "So?"

"Close your eyes," Sam said, to which Matt complied, clinching his eyes tightly.

Reaching under the table, it took two hands for her to lift to the table. Luckily, the food hadn't arrived yet as there would be no room for both the food and Matthew's gift. "Okay, Matthew, open your eyes." Opening his eyes, he couldn't help but notice the wrapping on the gift.

"Wow, did you wrap this?" Matt asked.

"After last Christmas, you're asking me if I wrapped this?"

"What can I say? I have a wrapping deficiency. Thanks again. By the way, Grandma just assumed I wrapped her gift and I didn't want to disappoint her when she mentioned what a good job I did," Matt explained his logic. He started to open his gift.

"Some would consider that lying by omission," Samantha said jokingly.

"What? I confessed the following Sunday," Matt responded as he did his best to collect the little bits of paper falling to the ground.

"Seriously? You confessed that? You are such a Catholic," Samantha said with a laugh.

"Yeah, I know. By the way, I told my family you were Catholic too."

"Matt!" Sam said, surprised at his statement.

"What? I had to. They don't understand," Matt replied.

"Well, does that mean you…?"

"Yes, I confessed that as well," Matt said, cutting Sam off before she could finish the question as he finally got the gift totally unwrapped.

"Matthew Laurent, you are unbelievable."

Looking up from the package at Sam, Matt said, "Sam, my family hasn't wandered far from Louisiana. They think most people are Catholics or, at worse, a Baptist." He continued unwrapping. "And frankly, they'd be disappointed if they knew the truth. Better for them to believe a lie that makes them happy than hurt them with the whole truth."

With the paper finally removed, Matt lifted the top of the plain white box. His smile slowly departed, and a serious look emerged on his face. Looking down into the box, he saw a patent leather attaché case with his name embroidered in fine gold thread on the flap. Not saying anything and still looking down at it, Samantha asked with anticipation, "Do you like it?"

"It's beautiful, honey. I love it," he said with a frog in his throat. Running his fingers over the gold embroidery, Matt said, "I absolutely love it!" Sam, with a big smile on her face, was relieved as this wasn't her first choice for a gift. She almost bought him a first pressing of Chet Baker, *Chet*, down at Rainbow Records in the village. Not willing to ruin the moment and see disappointment in Matt's face, Sam thought better of telling him about the Baker album until the time was right. *Let him enjoy the moment*, she thought to herself.

"Oysters Rockefeller for the happy couple," Luis said as he held the dish, waiting for Matt to remove the case from the table. Matt put the case carefully by his seat, Luis put the platter down on the table, and the couple began to eat.

Chapter 6

Moving to New York City, almost four years ago now, was a culture shock for Matt but one he anticipated and openly accepted. Initially, Matt's plans were to take a Greyhound bus from New Orleans to New York, a cost of $59, which he paid for with the money his grandma had given him. A trip that would have been a thirty-six-hour exhausting bus ride with stops all over the South. Mobile and Montgomery, Atlanta and Richmond, on to Philadelphia and then to New York. Now Matt is as frugal as they come, so when he found a better deal by airplane, only $46, he bought the ticket. Matt had never been in an airplane, but he wasn't scared or nothin'; in fact, if he was describing it, he'd call it anxious excitement. He wanted this next chapter of his life to be filled with experiences he hadn't had the opportunity to have before. So being he had been on a bus before, when the opportunity arose to fly, he took it.

The only problem Matt had now was he was stuck with a useless one-way bus ticket to New York. He tried to get a refund and spent nearly two hours at the bus depot in New Orleans pleading his case to three different employees. First, there was the ticket counter girl, a really pretty girl who couldn't have been more than a year or so older than Matt and seemed as concerned with Matt's problem as she is at getting a date for Saturday night, not very. When she got sick of him, she walked over to one of the desks behind the counter; there was a man by the named Johnson, the assistant manager, who frankly hadn't given Matt the time of day either, seeing he was trying to watch the races at Saratoga on a little nine-inch black-and-white TV with terrible reception. Finally, Matt got to talk to the manager, Mr. Tingle, when he returned from his lunch break though he insisted Matt call him Billy-Jo; he was the nicest of all three of them. In the end, Mr. Tingle, or Billy-Jo, heard Matt out and decided to give him a 50 percent refund on his ticket to be used within a calendar year. Matt saw this as a victory and thanked Mr. Tingle, or Billy-Jo, put the $29.50 voucher in his pocket, and went on his way.

The day Matt left Louisiana to start this new chapter of his life wasn't easy, nor did he expect it to be. Jamal had already left a week earlier to head to Boston, but gathered at the Laurent home was Karen and William, Edith, Father John, and of course, Emily. Since Matt's flight wasn't until 7:15 p.m., Karen and Edith did a lot of cooking that included jambalaya, boudin, pork ribs, corn still on the cob, and all kinds of sweets. Doris and Johnny showed up later in the day; they had some family birthday party they had to make an appearance at first, but they showed up. They were good and reliable like that, and they did love Matt. Matt liked when Johnny was around because it gave his daddy someone to talk to even though Johnny did 85 percent of the talking, and when William did talk, it was usually to correct something Johnny remembered wrong. He always found that interesting; as much as William drank, he always seemed to be able to remember things. Maybe that was the one thing he got from his daddy, Matt thought to himself.

After all his goodbyes were done, Karen's being the longest and had involved the most crying, Emily took Matt to the airport, Moisant Field, which would later be renamed Louis Armstrong New Orleans International Airport. Emily had borrowed her daddy's Buick '79 Park Avenue with a big bench seat in the front. This was the first time either of them had ever been to the airport, let alone taken a plane anywhere. Emily and Matt found the whole thing a bit confusing. First off, Emily took a wrong turn twice, and they had to drive through the arrivals area, where people were coming in from all over the United States, probably from all the world. But after a few tries, they got it right, and after a bit of time, Em was finally able to park the large car between two others in the parking lot, all without hitting anything whatsoever. It was getting a bit late, already 6:10 p.m. Wishing they had had more time to say goodbye and get in a bit more kissing in the car before they left, they had to cut it short. Emily held Matt's face with her two hands, looked him in the eyes, and said, "I am so proud of you."

"Proud? Why you proud of me?" Matt asked.

"Because you set a goal and you're moving toward it. That takes courage. Hell, most people down here talk about moving away or going to New York, but they never do. You've been talking about this since our first date at the summer carnival. You remember that night?"

Matt's eyes moved up as he recalled that day, which led into night and they had their first kiss, the first for either of them. "That was a good day, wasn't it?" Matt asked rhetorically.

"Best one of my life," Emily replied as she pulled Matt's eyes back down to hers.

"You let me touch your boobs on the Ferris wheel," Matt said as his eyes moved back up, remembering as he let out a little chuckle.

"I did not!" Emily exclaimed as she swatted at his shoulder. "Well, okay, maybe I did, but don't you go around telling anybody, Matthew," she admitted meekly, with her eyes facing down in a bit of embarrassment.

Using his finger, moving her chin up to catch her eyes with his, he said, "Never. That day will always be ours, nobody else's." With tears running down her cheeks, she put her arms around Matt and gave him the tightest hug she had probably ever given anyone in her life. While still in the embrace, Matt looked at his watch over Em's shoulder and said softly, "I got to go."

Matt stroked Emily's hair and gave her a kiss on the forehead and exited the car, removing his duffel bag, his daddy's duffel bag which he got when he was in Vietnam, from the back seat and made his way into the terminal. He told himself he wasn't going to look back at Em as he walked away, but he couldn't help himself. He did.

When Matt got into the terminal, he was overwhelmed—people moving in every direction, seemingly lost, scurrying around, and all of them seemed to have their tickets in hand. Looking around the big open space, Matt noticed a booth with a big sign over the attendant, Information. He walked over.

"Good evening, sir. Can I help you?" the woman at the desk asked.

"Evening, ma'am."

"Where you headed?" the woman, probably as old as Edith, asked Matt.

"New York City," Matt responded as he fumbled to take his ticket out of his very full duffel bag.

Handing the woman his ticket, she saw he was on the 7:15 p.m. Eastern Airlines flight 703 with a stopover in Charlotte and a final destination of JFK, New York City. Searching around his duffel bag again, he finally pulled out an envelope, already sealed and pre-addressed with Emily's address. The blue-haired woman, now with Matt's full attention, pointed him in the direction of the Eastern Airlines boarding gates.

"Just walk down that way there and veer left. Your gate is 37," she said, concluding with a big smile.

"Thank you very much," Matt said. "Do you happen to know if there is a mailbox in the airport?"

"Sure is." She pointed over to her right, Matt's left, not thirty feet away.

"Okay, thank you." Matt walked off toward the mailbox which happened to be in the same direction as the Eastern Airlines gates.

"Have a nice flight," the woman said as Matt walked away.

A week or so earlier, he and Em went down to Barny's Used Auto lot. Em had been saving up for a down payment on a Jeep she had her eye on, but when they got down there, Emily realized she didn't have enough money for a down payment. Matt hated seeing how disappointed she was, and he knew just how much she hated driving her daddy's big ole Buick around. As hard as he tried to make her take the money, she would have no part in it. But when he got home, he knew exactly how he would solve that problem. He wrote out an envelope with her name and address, took $500 of his New York money, and put it in that envelope, along with a note. It read,

> *Dear Em,*
>
> *I couldn't go away knowing I had a pocket full of money and you needing some. I enclosed $500. That should cover the rest of the down payment and the cost to get it registered and all that. I figure you'll probably have a few bucks left over, so you can use it to buy a nice dress or maybe use it to help buy books for your classes at Xavier.*
>
> *We been through a lot together over the last few years, and it wasn't always easy. The night we went to see* Dirty Dancing *at the Paramount Theater, you rested your head on my shoulder during the movie; my heart melted right then. But when we came out and that bunch were giving us a hard time, when they called you that word, I wanted to protect you so badly. I wanted to kick their asses so bad! But they ended up whooping my ass pretty good. When you wiped the blood from my nose while I was still on the ground, I knew I'd always love you.*
>
> *I will always love you for that!*
>
> *Love Always,*
> *Matthew*

Matthew dropped that letter into the mailbox and made his way to his gate.

After checking his bag in and getting on the plane, seat 23A, a window seat, Matt's nerves started to act up. Now Matt wasn't one to frighten easily; in fact, every summer when the boys and some girls would go down to the Robert E. Lee Bridge, Matt was always the first to jump. It was only about seventeen or eighteen feet down to the water, but standing up on the rail made it seem a hell of a lot higher. But every time, without exception, Matt always went first.

Even from a young age, Edith always said Matt had a healthy curiosity that would likely get him into trouble one day. From the time when he was in his crib, Karen would notice that instead of playing with his toys or napping like most young toddlers do, Matt would stand up, holding on to the bars and watch what was going on in the room. Whether William had the boys over for a poker game or an LSU game or Karen and Doris were sitting around gossiping, Matt was always observing. As Matt got settled into his seat, he was taking in everything around him. Watching people struggling down the aisle with their carry-on bags, mothers calming their children down, he realized the plane was much smaller than he had thought it would be. He noticed the terrible fabric that covered the seats and was astonished at how loud it was inside the plane.

The flight was uneventful except for the occasional turbulences, which almost made Matt shit his pants the first time. The captain's voice came over the intercom and started rattling off a bunch of information—stuff about speed and altitude and maybe something about the weather in New York—but Matt didn't get it all because the stewardess was asking him if he wanted steak or fish for dinner at the same time. It wasn't long after he finished up his Salisbury steak, mashed potatoes, peas, and peach cobbler before the captain made another announcement to look out the left side of the plane and you'd get a good look at the New York skyline. Matt just about pressed his face up to the small oval window, trying to get the best look he could. He had never seen so many lights in one place before.

After landing and pulling up to the gate, the stewardess said, "Welcome to JFK airport. You may now deplane." That grabbed Matt's attention as many random things did and made him wonder that if they are deplaning now, he therefor must have planed when he got on. Didn't make much senses to him and didn't feel it was worth thinking about anymore, so he didn't.

He made his way off the plane and followed the crowd down to collect his duffel bag. After waiting for what seemed like forever, he assumed that because he had looked at his watch four times in a nine-minute span. First at 12:25 a.m., then 12:30, then 12:33, and finally, at 12:34. Already exhausted from a long day, the bags started to come out of this little stainless steel doorway at 12:36 a.m., Matt's duffel bag was the sixteenth to come out.

With his duffel bag slung over his shoulder and the address of the Columbia freshman dorms in his hand, Matt made his way to the subway. Matt had never, in his life, taken a subway but was certainly looking forward to the experience. Though most folks back home would often talk negatively about New York, the rumors about the New York subway were legendary. Doris told Matt to be careful on the subway because her cousin's husband was in New York a few years back and witnessed three coloreds as she called them mugging some white guy. Matt listened politely, nodded and looked appalled at all the right points in the story but didn't give it much credence. This was only one of many horror stories Matt would hear from different people, none with personal experience mind you, before he left. He gave them the same credibility he would give a spooky campfire story—very little.

When Matt got to the subway platform, he noticed people exchanging cash for tokens and then putting them into a turnstile; not wanting to look like some hick, instead of asking, he simply did the same. Matt had taken $100 dollars of his $4,800 which included the money his grandmother had given him plus his savings and put it into his front pocket before he had left the house. He kept the remaining $4700 buried deep in his duffle bag and except for a dollar he used for a Coke he had bought when he was in the airport in New Orleans, he had all $99 left. Reaching into his pocket and peeling off a five, he slid it under the window and asked the man for tokens. The man slid five prestacked tokens under the window without even lifting his head from his *New York Daily News* paper.

"Can you tell me what subway I take to get to Columbia University?" Matt asked the clearly uninterested man in the booth.

"Take the LIRR to Jamaica Station, then to Penn Station, and then the 1 or 2 to Columbia," the man said without lifting his head from his paper and faster than Matt has ever heard anyone talk before.

"I'm sorry, can you say that again?" Matt requested, feeling more self-conscious about his Louisiana drawl than ever.

Finally looking up at Matt and now clearly annoyed, he said, "Take the LIRR to Jamaica Station, to Penn Station, and then the 1 or 2 to Columbia." A bit dumbfounded, Matt knew he best not ask him a third time. He took his tokens and looked around. Seeing a big subway map on the wall, he made his way over to it. Standing there, trying to make heads or tails of what looked like a wall of multicolor lines going in all different directions that could have been drawn by a third grader, a voice behind him said, "Where you tryin' to get?"

Turning around, Matt saw the man, not more than twenty-five years old, well-dressed in a suit and tie though the tie was loosened quite a bit. "Columbia," Matt replied.

"No shit? I'm headed uptown myself," he said.

"Is Columbia uptown?" Matt asked.

The man laughed and said, "Where you from?"

"Louisiana," Matt said in response.

"Yeah, Columbia is uptown. I'm headed up to 103rd Street. You can tag along with me if you want," the man said. Extending his hand, he said, "I'm Juan."

Matt shook his hand and said, "Matt. Matt Laurent. Thanks a lot. I really appreciate it."

"No problem," Juan said. "Come on, follow me."

Juan put a token in the turnstile and passed through, turning to wait for Matt. Matt, feeling a bit relieved, followed Juan's lead and head through as well. They only waited on the platform for a minute or two, in silence, before a train pulled into the station at a high rate of speed accompanied by a loud roar.

"We can take this one," Juan said as he turned to Matt.

"How long is the subway ride to Columbia?" Matt asked.

"Probably about an hour," Juan replied. "But we have to change trains a few times." Juan rushed into the train car as soon as it stopped to ensure they would get seats. They were lucky the crowd at that time of night wasn't too bad and they both got one. All along the way to Jamaica Station, Juan was telling Matt about life in New York.

"I was born and raised here in the city," he said to Matt.

"Really? What's it like?" Matt asked.

"Just like any where's else, I guess," he replied.

After a twenty-minute ride from the airport to Jamaica Station, the men changed trains to head into Manhattan. This station was much busier, and the men were forced to stand for about ten minutes before two younger kids, teenagers, got up and moved down the train car. Matt and his first New York friend quickly jumped into the seats. Matt was relieved he was getting so close to Columbia as he was getting more and more tired by the minute. He had woken up earlier than usual, 5:30 a.m., and just assumed it was excitement that set off his internal clock. He had hoped to take a nap earlier in the day before people arrived, but that didn't materialize. He could feel his eyes getting heavy.

"Put the strap from your duffel bag around your leg. In case you fall asleep, you can tell if someone's trying to steal it," Juan said.

"That's a good idea," Matt said and took the advice; he put his bag on the floor between his legs with the strap looped around his leg.

"I'm sorry, it's been a long day, what was your name again?" Matt asked.

"Jose," the man replied.

"Jose?" Matt asked again.

"Yep, Jose," he replied.

The men arrived in Penn Station and quickly made their way to the uptown train platforms. Matt, looking at his watch, realized he'd been awake for nearly twenty hours and couldn't wait to lay his head down, somewhere, anywhere at this point. The number 1 uptown train arrived, and again, they got lucky and were able to get seats. As the train moved uptown, Matt crossed his arms as he listened to Jose talk about his job at the freight terminal at the airport. He closed his eyes while listening to Jose; with the occasional interruption of the subway engineer announcing the stops, Matt dozed off.

"Forty-Second Street," a voice over the speaker said.

"Times Square."

"Columbus Circle."

Matt was only half asleep on the train, the kind of sleep where you can still kind of tell what's happening around you but not really aware. Matt heard, "116th Street, Columbia University." And he jumped in his seat. Shaking out the cobwebs and getting his bearings, he realized Jose was gone. *He must have gotten off at 103rd Street like he had said,* he thought to himself. Collecting himself along with his duffel bag, he thought to himself, *I guess I'm detraining,* as he got off and walked up the stairs leading to the street. Looking around, he reached into his pocket for his New York City map that Columbia had included in the orientation package they had sent him. He frantically started checking all his pockets, first the front and then the back, and while he still had his map, his $94 was missing.

"That son of a bitch!" Matt said loudly as he stood on the sidewalk, realizing he just learned his first New York lesson. Reorienting himself, he started walking the short distance, all the while muttering, "Juan my ass. Jose my ass. Just wait if I ever see you again" though he knew in a city of eight million people, that would be unlikely and better just chalk it up to inexperience. He was just glad at this point that his orientation director, a woman by the name of Shelia, had told him he could arrive anytime and to just head to the freshman dorm and they'd have his room assignment.

Sheila was right; they were expecting Matt, and he was led up to his room where he took the bed closest to the window and fell asleep within minutes, fully clothed.

Chapter 7

COLUMBIA, 1991

ollege came pretty easy to Matt, and he was always surprised and thankful that he was able to have some downtime, time he could spend with Samantha or, on Saturday mornings, where he could just be lazy. So often on those Saturday mornings, he would lie in bed and relax, think, read, relax some more, and sometimes fall back asleep. He found life to be much different in New York than down in Jefferson Parish. Back home, William always found something for Matt to do. And then when Billy was killed, well, his chores just about doubled. So when Matt got to Columbia, he realized that college was a whole lot more than just studying, and you needed to take advantage of any downtime that presented itself and get as much sleep as possible.

Life at Columbia had changed dramatically over the last two years in comparison with the first two. While Matt was on a full academic scholarship, during his first year he was required to live in the freshman dorms, as all freshman must during their first year. After that first year was behind him, he tried his best to figure out a way to get his own apartment, but it just wasn't doable. But after he had completed his sophomore year, he got some great but also unexpected news.

To say Matt was frustrated having to live in the dorms would be an understatement. Okay, okay, he thought in regard to freshman year, but sophomore year? See, most of the kids that went to

Columbia came from families that were much more well-off than Matt. Hell, there was this one guy, Mitchell Gillette, Mitch people called him, who was related to the people who make the razor blades. Well, he had his own two-bedroom apartment down on 88th, and his parents only lived on the other side of the park at East 106th. But Matt figured, when it comes to money, sometimes you do what you got to do. And he did. But in the final semester of his second year, in May, he received a letter with a pretty fancy envelope. It was embossed with gold lettering, like the kind on his new attaché case that Samantha had given him, and it had a fancy official coat of arms on it as well. When he opened it, he was beyond shocked to read that he had been awarded the Fulton-Shockley Political Science Scholarship for outstanding merit in the field on international politics.

As Matt was reading through the letter, it stated that his political science adviser had nominated him for the award for an article that Matt wrote and was published in the *American Political Science Journal* back in December. The scholarship awarded him $10,000 for each of the next two years. And since Matt's tuition, books, and food were already covered through his academic scholarship, he knew right away he'd now be able to afford his own place. Well, his own in that he'd have to find a couple of roommates. New York was still New York, and apartments ain't cheap even if you do got a spare $10,000. Within a week of asking around if anyone was looking for a roommate, he found a fella by the name Stephen Miller. Matt and Stephen were in a freshman class together though they never spoke during the class. Matt swears it was freshman English while Stephen contends it was some other though he could never recall which class he thought it was, but he was firm it wasn't freshman English.

And that was Stephen, with a *PH*, a fact he made known after every time he said his name. "Hi, I'm Stephen. That's with a *PH*," he'd say every time he'd introduce himself, which Matt found odd, but not odd enough to not share a place with him. Steve was a microbiology major and was a pretty good student, a bit of an odd duck, but Matt thought he was okay for the most part. He came from Chicago, Oak Park neighborhood, and was almost always quiet though the two exceptions over the last two years were Stephen's birthday. The boy like to celebrate his birthday—a lot.

Matt's other roommate was a young woman by the name of Petra Shah. Petra was from Lebanon and studying law at City University of New York. Matt had posted an ad in the *Village Voice*, the *Columbia Spectator*, and a few other school newspapers, looking for a second roommate. He had already found a three-bedroom apartment on West Eighty-Fourth Street, and the landlord had agreed to give Matt a week to find the third roommate. Petra responded on the second day the ad was placed.

Petra was a few years older than Matt and had a difficult upbringing. Matt and Petra became good friends rather quickly. Petra was brought up in a small village outside Beirut, surrounded by civil war. She was able to escape to England in 1985 with the help of some well-connected family friends. There she attended City, University of London, earning her degree in economics. Matt admired Petra. Her ability to overcome obstacles in her life were nothing less than inspirational.

Now Matt's life down in Jefferson Parish wasn't always easy; in fact, at times when William didn't have enough work because of a bad shrimping season, Karen had to go down to see Father John for some help. Father John ran a small food pantry out of the basement hall of the church, the same hall where they had bingo every Tuesday night and the church pie sales and every other kind of function Father John came up with though some weeks Father didn't have enough food for those in need and often had to hand out a few bucks here and there so kids didn't go hungry. But Petra, that girl had to walk to school through a war zone. Forget about not eating dinner before you go to bed. This girl had to avoid bullets and bombs dropping nearby. Matt recognized strength in Petra that did not go unnoticed.

Another thing Matt liked about Petra was that she spoke French. Matt, being from Cajun country and being French himself, spoke the language, but his French didn't sound much like Petra's. Edith and Karen would speak to both Matt and Billy in French at home from an early age. Being from Louisiana and with so many people down in the bayou still only speaking French, it was a necessity. But with Matt's Louisiana drawl and his lack of practice over the last few years, Petra and Matt would have a blast having conversations and laugh hysterically between their two very different dialects. As a part of his curriculum, Matt was also required to take a foreign language. He was surprised that there were so many different options for languages at Columbia; there was German and Italian, Chinese and Japanese, French and just about every language spoken on earth. But the decision wasn't that difficult for Matt. It was down to Arabic or Farsi. Farsi is a Persian language spoken in Iran and only a few other small pockets in the Middle East, so he settled on Arabic. With his political science studies focused on Middle East policy, the decision wasn't that difficult after all.

When he met Petra at a little coffee shop down in the village to discuss the apartment and found out she spoke Arabic and French, in addition to German and Spanish, he was fascinated. Add on that she was one of the most pleasant people he'd come across in New York in two years, he was convinced she was the right choice. As a matter of fact, Matt had made appointments with three potential roommates all to meet him at the same coffee shop, forty-five minutes apart, Petra being the first. Though Matt waited around for the two other fellas to give them the bad news that the apartment was taken, neither took the news too bad.

On this Saturday morning, Matt was taking his time getting up. He wasn't one to flounder around much, but Saturdays were often the exception. After waking up, being all twisted in the sheets as he often was, he decided to just lie there and look out his window. The view wasn't much to look at, just the building across the street, especially from the angle he was looking still being in his bed. If you stand up and look out the window, often you see people moving about, but not from the comfortable position Matt was currently in. He could hear Petra down the hall making breakfast; she was always an early riser, being that she had to get up to pray.

"Matt!" Petra yelled loud enough to make sure her voice carried through Matt's closed door.

"Yeah?" he responded.

"Do you want coffee?" she asked.

"No, not right now, thanks. I'm just gonna relax for a bit."

A meek knock on the door, it slowly opened. Petra, poking her head around the door asked, "You sure? I'm going to be heading out soon."

"No, thanks. I'm just going to lie here a bit," Matt said. "Where's Steve?"

"I'm not sure. I'm not sure if he even came home last night," Petra said though not so surprised. Steve did have a lot of girlfriends and from schools all over the city. Matt never could figure out how he could keep track. Once, he was seeing these two girls, both named Jessica. They didn't know about each other, but Matt never could understand how Steve could tell them apart when they called. He just figured it was due to all the practice Steve had.

"Okay then. I'll see you later on," Petra said as she closed the door.

Lying in the single bed that was located up against the outer wall of the room, Matt would sometimes look to his right at the empty space between the bed and the door. Back home, that empty space was occupied by Billy's bed as the two brothers shared a room. Even though it had been ten years since Billy's death, not a day went by that Matt didn't think about his older brother. Matt usually wasn't a "what could have been" kind of guy or the kind of guy who spent too much time thinking about the past, except when it came to Billy.

Over the years Matt had often wondered what Billy would have done with his life, what he would have accomplished, and where he'd be. He had crafted a life for Billy in his imagination that he hadn't had the chance to live out. Billy was set on going into the Army just like his dad and wanted to make a career out of it. Sometimes he'd say to Matt in their room late at night while they both lay in their beds, "What better job in the world is there than serving your country?" Matt could never find a reason to disagree, so he never did. So Matt had determined that Billy, by now, would be Staff Sergeant Laurent, often stationed in hot zones around the globe, helping people and serving his country proudly. He was married to a sweet girl, one of Billy's ex-girlfriends from back home, April, with two children, William III and little Clarabelle. Sometimes Matt would change up

Billy's life, depending on what kind of mood he was in. If it was around Christmas, Matt would always imagine Billy was stationed in the states, Fort Bragg or maybe Fort Campbell, with his family. Matt liked the idea of being an uncle. But if it were summertime, Matt would imagine Billy stationed somewhere in Italy or some tropical place, single, surrounded by beautiful woman, all fawning over him in his uniform. Matt never once doubted, had Billy lived, that he would be successful at whatever he did. Boy, Matt sure did miss his big brother.

Matt started reading a book while he lay in bed, a Steinbeck, but it wasn't too long before he had fallen back asleep. When he woke up, for the second time, he looked at his watch and realized it was close to noon, eleven thirty-three exactly. Still not overly motivated, he realized he should make some phone calls. Saturday was the day he made his phone calls. After he got out of the shower and before he was fully dressed, he grabbed the cordless phone that Steve had bought when they first moved in. It was a great convenience because you could move room to room without pulling a long cord around with you though sometimes in the back hall and out on the veranda the signal would break up and get all staticky. But being he was in the kitchen making breakfast, that didn't much matter.

Matt always called home first on Saturdays because they expected him to call. And he did regularly though there was one time he forgot to call after Steve's last birthday party and he didn't hear the end of that for weeks. His momma still brings it up occasionally when he calls later in the day on Saturdays, "I thought you forgot about calling like last time." Karen would say like it was the first time she ever said it. But being it was still before noon, he figured he was safe.

"Hello?" Karen said as she answered the phone.

"Hey, Momma," Matt said.

"Matthew, baby. How are you? How are your classes going? How is Samantha?" she rambled off in quick succession.

"Good, good, good," Matt responded.

"And how about that Muslim girl?"

Matt, sitting at the table in the kitchen, the cordless phone in one hand and a forkful of corn beef hash in the other, rolled his eyes.

"Petra?" he asked, knowing full well she remembered her name. "Petra's fine, Momma," he said, again as he had to do regularly every time Karen asked about Petra, always conveniently forgetting her name. But that wasn't a can of worms Matt wanted to open right now. Karen would usually do most of the talking during their calls; she would update Matt on all the goings-on down in the parish— who got married, who died, who was out of work, who had a child out of wedlock and all the gossip she could muster during the week so she could share with Matt on Saturday. Not that Matt really cared about much of it, but he knew Karen enjoyed telling him, so he obliged.

The one bit of news that took Matt by surprise was about two months ago when she told him that Emily had gotten engaged. It had been about two years since he and Em had called it quits, but Matt still felt a bit weird about hearing she was going to marry another guy, Tim Lukas. Matt didn't know him too well, but from what he could remember, Tim was an okay guy.

After talking for about twenty minutes, enough time for Matt to finish his breakfast and almost finish washing the dishes, Karen put William on the phone, and that conversation only took two minutes. It was pretty much the same conversation every week with his daddy. "How are you, son? You staying out of trouble?" And it would usually end up with some version of "Don't trust anybody up there" though sometimes William would change it up and remind Matt how "those people are different." None of this was new to Matt, and he just went along with the program as to not cause trouble. The way he saw it, he's their only kid left, and why make a fuss about something that he can't change?

He said goodbye and gave his best to Grandma, who happened to be working down at Father John's food pantry. Saturday was the collection day for food. Sometimes when Dave, the manager over at the Piggly Wiggly, would order too much of one product or had food that was going to spoil sooner than later, he'd bring it down to the church. But most of the donations came from other regular folks in the parish. They would collect all the food and then bag it up. Usually there was pasta, rice, canned beans, and corn bread mix, but on good weeks, there might even be some fresh greens in there or even some chicken. After mass on Sunday morning, Edith and a bunch of the other ladies from the church would disperse it to those down on their luck.

After he got off the phone with his folks, he made his bed and straightened up his room as best he could. It wasn't easy with all kinds of books and papers and notebooks and such, but he did the best he could. Keeping a clean space was a habit that was instilled in him by Karen when he and Billy were still young. She just wouldn't tolerate a messy room. He appreciated this virtue instilled in him by his momma so long ago, but sometimes he had a habit of nitpicking with his roommates about the way the might leave things hanging around. Steve was always good at losing the remote for the TV, and Petra would regularly drink all the juice and forget to tell anyone until someone would ask, "Who drank all the juice?" Inevitably she'd say, "Oh, that was me. Sorry."

Matt was just about to call Jamal up in Boston when the phone rang; it was Sam.

"Hello? Hello? Hello?" Matt said into the phone, a short pause between each, each one louder than the next. He could hear Sam talking to her roommate, Benny, in the background but couldn't make out what she was saying. Benny was a cool guy, also an art student at NYU and very gay. Now Matt didn't have a problem with homosexuality whatsoever, but Benny was certainly a character. Believe it or not, Matt and Benny had a lot in common. Benny came from a small southern town on the Florida Panhandle. Benny had a tough time growing up there, always getting picked on because he didn't like playing ball with the guys or fishing like most boys; Benny liked hanging out with the girls. And he paid a price for it. But when he got to New York, he found a whole new world where he felt totally at home. He found a community where he fit in and wouldn't be judged for who he was, and he never planned on going back home—well, what used to be his home anyway.

"Matt?" Samantha said back into the phone.

"Hey, beautiful. What the heck's going on over there?" Matt asked with a chuckle.

"Oh my god. Benny is driving me crazy. He wants to borrow that paisley silk scarf you bought me for Valentine's Day, and I told him no and he's all pissed off," Sam said in an exacerbated manner.

"Just let him wear it. It's just a scarf," Matt said, trying to resolve the situation.

"But it was a gift from you," she said, hoping Matt would agree with her but knowing he probably wouldn't.

"It's only a scarf, baby."

"Okay. Hang on." Sam dropped the phone and Matt could hear her tell Benny, "Here, be careful with it. It was a gift from Matt."

"Hey, Matt!" Benny said, with Matt not being too surprised when he picked up the phone. He usually does when he gets the chance. "Thanks for letting me use the scarf. I'll take good care of it, baby," he said before dropping the phone.

"No problem, Benny," Matt responded, knowing Benny had already dropped the phone.

"Hey, babe. So we going to the park?" Samantha asked.

"Yea, sure. What time do you want to meet?"

"Well, why don't we meet at the Central Park Zoo? I picked up the chicken salad this morning and made some deviled eggs, and I got you a surprise. I'll bring it and we can eat in the park after the zoo. Sounds good?"

"A surprise, huh? What is it?" Matt asked while he sat on the edge of his bed, tying his shoes.

"Ooohhhh, you're just going to have to wait and see, rebel."

"Okay, whatever," he said, trying his best to not show his curiosity. But he was damn curious. "I'll meet you out in front of the zoo at two, okay?" he asked, straining a bit as he balanced the phone between his shoulder and ear as he tied his shoe.

"Okay, babe, see you in a bit," Sam responded.

Now just because Matt always called Jamal on Saturdays doesn't mean he was always successful at getting him on the phone. Calling Jamal was hit or miss with him being home because he was always doing something. Lots of times they played phone tag and would leave messages on each other's machines. Matt's were always short and to the point, "Hey, Jamal, Matt here. Call me when you get a chance." While Jamal, on the other hand, well, his could take up the whole sixty seconds of a recording. Sometimes Matt would wonder why he even needed to call Jamal after listening to one of his messages, but he always called back. So before he headed out, he called Boston.

"Hello?" Jamal said when he answered.

"What's up, brother?" Matt said, always happy to hear Jamal's voice.

"Oh, you know, getting things done."

Jamal was finishing his first year of law school at Harvard; he had completed his bachelor's degree in business in just three years, finishing third in his class. Most folks would be damn proud of such an achievement, but Jamal, as thorough and as competitive as he is, always analyzed everything to figure out where he could have improved. But Matt knew that's what made Jamal so good at whatever he did; he was always trying to figure out what he did wrong and correct it.

"So have you heard back yet?" Matt asked Jamal.

"Well, yeah," Jamal replied but waiting for a response from Matt.

"Well, yeah what?" Matt asked with a sense of urgency in his voice.

"I got picked!" Jamal said

"You son of a bitch! No shit? You really got picked?" Matt asked as he wandered around the apartment, watering the plants. Matt never paid that much attention to plants or trees or things like that in the past, but when he got his first apartment, he bought himself a fern. He liked how it looked so much, so he bought himself a second fern and then a cactus, and well, now he has well over ten.

"You really got it? You ain't pulling my leg?"

"I really got it," Jamal said with a sense of pride in his voice. "I'll be heading down to Washington in a few weeks."

"Damn, a black boy from Jefferson Parish clerking for Justice Anthony Kennedy. Damn!" Matt said.

"Hey, what the hell does black have to do with it?" Jamal asked in a joking manner.

"You're right, you're right. I'm just messing with ya," Matt said meekly. "Listen, black, white, green, or gold, it doesn't matter. What matters is that they picked the best man for the job," Matt said, clearly happy for his friend.

"When you getting down there?" Jamal asked.

"I think it's around June 20, so a few weeks. Do you have a place to stay yet?"

"Nope," Jamal said.

"Well, you can crash in my place. It's only a one-bedroom, but you can sleep on the couch."

"Brother, I'm damn glad you offered because money was going to be an issue. I got a $2,000 stipend, but that wouldn't cover rent for the summer, let alone food or anything else," Jamal explained to Matt. "How's Sam doing?" he asked.

"Man, she is great. I'm meeting her in the park in a bit."

"She seems like a good girl."

"She is, she really is."

"But an artist, Matt?" Jamal asked with a sense of unsureness in his voice.

"She's a great artist."

"Yeah. I'm just saying they don't all become Picasso."

"Yeah, I know, but I really love her. She doesn't have a pretentious bone in her body. Her daddy is the CEO of a Fortune 500 for Chrissake, and it took me two months of me asking about her family before she told me."

"Hey, I think she's great. I haven't spent much time around her, just those couple of visits, but she is a nice girl. I'll give you that. And damn sexy for a white girl," Jamal said to lighten the conversation.

"Hey, white, black, green, or gold, she's damn sexy!" Matt said in response. "Oh shit!" Matt said as he looked at his watch. "It's getting late, bro, and I got to go meet Sam. I'll call you during the week with all the information on the apartment, address, and such," Matt said as he looked into the hall mirror, checking his teeth and using his hands to fix his hair a bit.

"Yeah, okay. That sounds good, Matt. I'll talk to you soon."

Matt put the phone back into its cradle, grabbed an apple from the bowl on the small table near the door, and walked out the door. The building is what they call prewar, which meant it was built before World War II but often usually meant it was a good excuse when the elevator wasn't working, like today. Matt made his way down the winding stairs, all four flights and out into the sunlight of a beautiful spring day in the city.

Chapter 8

Now for those of y'all who haven't been to New York City, well, it's a pretty big damn place. So being that Matt lived up on West Eighty-Fourth Street, two blocks from the park and was heading down to the Central Park Zoo over on Fifth Avenue, he had about a thirty-minute walk, but he didn't mind. It was only one o'clock, so he had all of an hour to meet Samantha.

Being that Matt spends most of his time in classrooms or in the library, he always enjoyed spending time in the park whenever he could. Down in Jefferson Parish, Matt always spent as much time outside as he could, most of the time down by the bayou, fishing or catching frogs, but he also worked two summers at the Mitchell pig farm, Hog Heaven it was called. Matt and Jamal both worked there over their freshman and sophomore years in high school. Matt's daddy, William, knew Josiah Mitchell, the owner of Mitchell's Hog Heaven for years, so when William asked old Josiah to give the boys jobs, he obliged. The boys would feed and water the hogs, clean up the pens, and then round them up at the end of the day, which some-times could be a bitch. There was this one hog, Ms. Tilly, old man Mitchell called her, who was the biggest female hog in the pen and didn't much like humans. When the boys would get her cornered, she'd think nothing of charging one of them to get out of the situ-ation, which would often end up with one of the boys on their ass covered in mud and pig shit.

Mr. Mitchell was an okay guy, being he didn't care much for black folks, and even though he didn't say it, Matt and Jamal could always tell by the way he talked differently to the boys. But he wasn't no worse and certainly no better than most folks down there. But that was the problem. Jamal and Matt would always laugh about the name of the farm, Hog Heaven, and always questioned it since once the hogs were full grown, they were sent off to the slaughterhouse. So it never much sounded like heaven to them.

Matt walked down Eighty-Fourth Street and then turned right on Central Park West. He could turn left and crossed over to the park at Eighty-Sixth Street, but Matt always liked walking down to the Museum of Natural History at Eighty-First and crossing over there. Matt enjoyed seeing the groups of people outside the museum, taking pictures, eating hotdogs and ice cream they'd get from the corner vendors. He really enjoyed seeing the groups of school kids that came from all over the city and, who knows, maybe even the state. He'd watch the kids interacting and having a good time and assumed, as most kids do, just enjoyed being out of the classroom. The kids would fool around and run about and inevitably watch their teachers try to round them up. Matt just got a kick out of that. It also made him think about his own childhood; he missed being a kid sometimes, sometimes an awful lot. Being it was Saturday, there were a lot of people outside the museum, young and old, but Matt didn't have time to people watch today since he was on his way to meet Samantha.

Central Park was really like an oasis in the middle of a steel desert. Once you walked off the sidewalk and in through one of the countless park entrances, you are truly transported to another place. In a span of just a few steps, a person goes from the steel, stone, and paved jungle, cars whipping by and millions of people moving about from this place to that to a green, tranquil, quiet place that New Yorkers flock to whenever possible.

As Matt walked through the park, he passed by Belvedere Castle. Belvedere Castle is this old building that looks like some medieval castle in Europe that was built when they created the park. Matt never knew exactly what it was or used to be, but now it's a tourist information center and gift shop. The one thing Matt appreciated most about the castle was that they got bathrooms in there which can come in handy from time to time. Looking at his watch, Matt saw he was making good time and didn't feel any need to rush. Rushing around anywhere on a Saturday, or even Sunday for that matter, was something Matt always tried to avoid. Even though he had been living in New York for the last four years, and sometimes even felt like a New Yorker, when he would see tourist, all lost and looking at their maps and up at the tall buildings, it reminded him that he was and probably always will be a laid-back Southern boy. Just another tourist on an extended stay.

When Matt first arrived in New York City, he was surprised by most things. The sheer size of the city for one. He never thought a place could be so big. It's one thing to see it on TV or in the movies, but a whole nother to be right in the middle of it. When Matt first got to New York, on some of his first excursions into the park, he was a bit hesitant because he had heard some bad stories of people being attacked or mugged and even raped. There was a case that happened not long ago that people all over the city were talking about. A white woman got raped in the park, and these five black guys were found guilty though lots of people thought they were innocent. Years later, through this new technology, they call it DNA, these boys would have their convictions overturned. The city would pay them forty-one million dollars.

Matt made it through the park, unscathed as usual, and on to Fifth Avenue; he came out on Sixty-Seventh Street. It was one forty-five, and he didn't see Sam, so he sat under a big shady oak tree not far from the entrance to the zoo and took out his well-worn copy of *To Kill a Mockingbird*. Matt was an avid reader and loved the classics; *Mockingbird* was his favorite book and had been since he first read it years ago. He'd read dozens even hundreds of books since the first time he read *Mockingbird*, but he never found one he liked better though he also liked Hemingway and Vonnegut, and on occasion, he'd read Jack Kerouac, but only *On the Road* and, of course, Salinger. He had barely found his place in the book when heard Sam.

"Hey, babe!" she yelled from a good fifty feet away while waving her hand. Matt looked up just as Scout and Jem found the knothole in the tree filled with cement, but being Sam was still walking in his direction, he didn't bother to get up just yet.

As Samantha was walking toward Matt, he didn't want to look away for even a second. Sam was a beautiful girl with long blond hair; she wasn't short but wasn't exactly tall, maybe three or four inches shorter than Matt's six feet one. Well, maybe she was a bit taller than most girls. As she got closer and closer, he couldn't take his eyes off her, and being that it was past noon, close to 2:00 p.m., the sun was shining behind, casting her in silhouette; her hair looked like millions of flowing gold strands, a slight breeze messing them about. Looking at her, he couldn't remember a time he was this happy. Standing over him, still beyond comfortable under the tree, Samantha extended her hand to help Matt up.

"Hey, beautiful," Matt said as he looked up, shading his eyes with one hand. He took Samantha's hand with his other. He pulled her down on his lap for which she gave little resistance and, once in his lap, welcomed the gesture.

"How long you been here?" she asked Matt as she closed the book cover just enough to read the cover. "Again?"

"Ah, not long. Just a few minutes. You take the train?"

"No, I walked. Benny, Carol, and me went shopping for a bit," she said as she stroked Matt's brown hair and then kissed the side of his head.

"Big surprise," Matt said.

"What? What are you trying to insinuate, Mr. Laurent? Are you saying I shop a lot? I spend too much money?" she questioned Matt in a joking manner, squeezing his cheeks together enough that made his lips look like some funny-looking fish.

"Well," he said as best he could with his temporary lip disfigurement.

"Chose your words wisely, Mr. Laurent," she said while interrupting each word with a small kiss to his puckered lips, finally releasing them at the end of her sentence.

"I'll says this, Samantha McCain. You are one lucky girl," he said as his eyes darted to his left for a moment as a woman walked by with a small yellow dog on a leash and then back to Sam's eyes in a conscious manner. A small grin of approval creeped onto her face.

"Are you referring to my privileged upbringing?" Samantha asked as she took Matt's face into her two hands, forcing him to look into her eyes. "Now can I help that my father is successful?" she asked him before kissing him on the lips yet again.

"Babe, you got me there. Not your fault at all! You wanna go look at some animals?"

"Hell yeah! I read they got a new leopard, snow leopard, I think," she said as she stood up off Matt's lap and helped him to his feet. Sam jumped on Matt's back in a surprise move, making him lose his balance momentarily and enjoyed a piggyback ride to the front door.

"Did you remember the sandwiches?" Matt asked.

Nibbling on Matt's ear and still on his back, she said, "Shit yeah! I made some fruit salad as well."

"Made?" Matt asked with a bit of skepticism in his voice. Often when Sam said she made something, it really meant she made the trip to the market or deli. Samantha put a little more tooth in her nibble on the next bite of Matt's ear.

"Ouch!" Matt yelled out. "Damn, baby. I was just kidding."

Pulling back slightly to get a better look, still on Matt's back, she said, "I think I drew a little blood. Sorry, babe." She kissed Matt's ear and hopped down.

Matt rubbed at his ear and said, "Freakin' vampire."

"I'm sorry. Don't be upset with me. I'll let you take it out on me later," Samantha said as she used two big hop steps to get around the front of Matt, walking backward and looking back at him as he continued forward.

"Oh really?" Matt asked, very pleased. "I'll take you up on that, young lady. Hello, two tickets, please," Matt said to the ticket attendant.

"Fifteen dollars," the attendant responded.

"Wait! I got this. Not complaining about my rich daddy now, are you, Matthew?" she said while laughing and reaching into her purse for cash. She looked back up at Matt from her wallet and gave him a simple wink of the eye.

"Love you, babe," Matt said as he gave her a kiss on the side of the head.

After they wandered around the zoo for about an hour, both thoroughly impressed with the new snow leopard, they headed into the park and up to the carousel. As they walked through the park holding hands, Matt made a point of not talking about the future, something they will have to deal with much sooner than later.

"You know, that bear was badass," Matt said.

"He was a big boy. But that leopard was so beautiful! I want one."

"Oh, you want one? And how you think Benny's gonna react coming home to a snow leopard?"

"Ha! Are you kidding? He'd love it. He'd buy him a rhinestone collar and walk him down Park Avenue," Samantha said with absolute assurance.

"Yeah. You know, I believe it. Now bring home the grizzly."

"Oh, that's when he shits himself," Samantha said with a chuckle.

"So you going to tell me what my surprise is?" Matt asked Sam.

"Oh, baby, not yet. Wait until we get to the carousel."

With the carousel in sight, Sam took off running toward it. With a pretty big head start, she yelled back, "Last one there!" Matt didn't even hear what she said next and quickly made up ground. Matt was always one of the fastest kids in school, even going back to middle school. And he was still as fast as ever. It didn't take him long to blow by Sam and laugh out loud while doing so.

"Cheat! You cheated!" Sam was yelling as Matt passed her up.

Matt, a bit out of breath, sat down on the grass, pulled his knees up to his chest, and watched Samantha as she gave up running and reverted to walking, staring Matt down as she approached. "You know, I got this big backpack full of food, and you don't have anything. Therefore, you cheated," Samantha said, doing her best to try to convince Matt of his what she saw as unfair advantage but, in actuality, doing her best to convince herself. Looking up at her and laughing, he loved her always creative excuses; that was one of the things he loved most about her—her creativity. She had a vulnerability in her that Matt found to be adorable and always endearing. Even when Sam would lose at Monopoly or scrabble or anything for that matter, she would always have an inventive excuse, at which point Matt would concede victory to her. Her face would light up, knowing full well Matt embraced defeat for nothing more than her momentary happiness. It was his giving nature that she so loved most about Matt. When she reached Matt, he looked up at her and said, "You know what, babe, you're right. It wasn't fair. You win."

Samantha, always happy to win, jumped in the air and pumped her fist in the sky. "Yay! Yay! The winner!" she yelled loud enough to make everyone within fifty feet look over at them as she collapsed herself to the ground on the side of Matt. "You know what?" she asked.

"What's that, sweetie?"

"I think it was a tie," Samantha said, relinquishing some of her glory for her guy.

"I'll take it. Now where's them sandwiches?"

The couple sat back and watched the kids on the carousel and the guys playing baseball on the diamond closest to them; they ate their chicken salad sandwiches and then the fruit salad for desert and then they lay back on the grass and watched the clouds roll across the sky. They held hands as they often did, occasionally turning their heads toward each other to indulge in a kiss. Samantha felt something hit her legs, so she turned back on her elbow to get a better look at where it came from. It was a tennis ball. And chasing after it was a little girl, about two years old, with her mother in close pursuit, but letting the little girl make good use of her little legs, gaining confidence with every stride.

"Hi, sweetie," Sam said to the young girl. Holding out the ball to her, she only smiled back at Samantha, not yet reaching for the ball. Her mother was only a few steps behind her but didn't interfere with the little girl's new curiosity. Looking up at the woman,

Samantha said, "Oh my god, she is so beautiful." Matt, at this point, leaned up on his elbows himself. "How old is she?" Sam asked.

"Twenty-two months," the young woman responded.

The little girl's big blue eyes, almost too big, but in a good way, were still fixed on Samantha, a smile exposing only a handful of baby teeth soon followed, and Sam couldn't help smiling back at her if she tried to. Sam extended her hand with the ball toward the girl. The little girl reached her tiny hand forward toward the ball, and once it was back in her little grip, her excitement couldn't be contained.

"She is so adorable!" Sam exclaimed. "What's her name?"

"Annabelle," the woman said in a voice that was filled with happiness. Samantha extended her hand toward the woman. "I'm Samantha, this is Matt." She used her head to gesture his way.

"Hi," Matt said.

"I'm Lori," she said, her eyes moving back and forth quickly between Samantha and Annabelle.

"Oh, oh. I have something for Annabelle!" Samantha said with excitement in her voice as she reached into her bag. "But only if it's okay?" she asked the woman. "It's a cookie."

"Yeah, sure, that's fine. She loves cookies."

As she fished around in her bag, she found the small package of cookies she had bought for Matt. She looked over to Matt and said, "Surprise!" Annabelle, a bit occupied with her ball, did not notice the cookie yet until Samantha called her name. "Annabelle, would you want a cookie?" Sam asked as she held out the cookie toward Annabelle. The little girl's eyes somehow grew even bigger than before. She took a step closer to Sam, reaching for the cookie, but toppled over onto Samantha, not yet mastering her little legs and the opposing forces of gravity.

"Oh my goodness, honey, you are so beautiful," Samantha said as she helped Annabelle to her feet and handed her the cookie. Annabelle put good use to the few little teeth in her mouth, taking a bite much too big for her little mouth, paying the price as half of the cookie fell onto the grass. Annabelle reached for the cookie before Lori stopped her. "No, honey, leave that there."

Sam handed Lori another cookie and said, "For later."

MICHAEL W. HULL

"Thank you," Lori said with gratitude in her voice.

"Do you know what time it is?" Lori asked Matt, noticing he has a watch on.

"Yeah, it's, ummm, four ten," Matt said.

"Oh boy, we're running late, Annabelle. Daddy's going to be home soon."

Annabelle, hearing the word *daddy*, turned toward Lori and repeated, "Daddy?"

"You want to go see Daddy, honey?" Lori asked her little girl. Clearly excited to see her daddy, she reached up to her mother. Bending over to shake Matt and Samantha's hands one more time and thank them for the cookies, Annabelle opened her arms to embrace Sam. Almost falling into her again, Sam opened her arms and hugged the little girl.

"You are so precious," she said as she released the little girl.

Lori took Annabelle by the hand and said, "Say bye-bye, Annabelle." Annabelle, holding on to her mother's hand, started waving her other rapidly, clearly showing her mastery of the wave and saying bye-bye, as they turned and walked away.

"I can't believe you," Matt said as he opened the package and removed the last cookie.

"What?" Samantha said, looking at him surprised.

"You gave that little girl all my cookies," Matt said, joking around as he bit into the chocolate chip cookie. "Mmmm, these things are awesome."

"Aww, poor baby, I'll buy you some more tomorrow," Sam said as she reached over to give him a kiss on the cheek.

"You think I'm going to say no, don't you? Well, you're wrong. I'll take them," Matt said, laughing as he jumped to his feet. "Come on, let's go back to my place." Matt reached down and took Samantha by the hand and pulled her to her feet.

"Wasn't she so cute?" Sam asked Matt as they start walking toward Central Park West.

"She was a cutie, for sure."

"Want to watch a movie and I'll make us some dinner later on?"

"Why don't we just order pizza?" Sam suggested.

74

"You do know I have a 4.0 GPA and can tell when you're telling me I don't know how to cook, little lady," Matt said as he started pinching at her ass.

"Matthew! Matthew!" Samantha yelled while trying to escape. She took off down the path in a jog with Matt in hot pursuit.

Back at the apartment, Steve was in the living room watching cartoons, which never surprised Matt or even Samantha at this point. Petra was out back on the veranda reading and taking advantage of the beautiful day and the afternoon sunlight. Her room was the darkest of the three, and even though she's been meaning to buy new stronger lightbulbs for weeks, it's the one thing she keeps forgetting to buy when she goes to the store. Hearing Matt and Samantha come in, Petra yelled from the back, "Hi, guys! I made some falafel and salad if you want any." While Matt made his way toward his room, Samantha head out the back to say hello.

"Hey, Petra, how you are doing?" Samantha asked as she reached down to steal a grape out of a bowl on the table.

"I'm good, Sam. Busy," she said as she lifted the book she was reading off the table, indicating such.

"Where are you guys coming from? The park?" Petra asked Samantha, relieved they had come in as she was looking for an excuse to take a break. Walking out the back door and taking the only other empty chair at the table, Matt said, "Hey, P."

"What a Southern gentleman you are. You don't even offer your girl the seat," Petra said sarcastically.

Slapping his hand on his lap, he looked at Samantha and asked, "Seat, baby?" Turning his head toward Petra, he said smugly, "See? Southern gentleman." Then he started eating grapes. Looking up at Sam and yawning, Matt said, "Hey, babe, how would you feel about a nap? I know, I ain't been up all that long, but I'm exhausted." Looking at his watch, he saw it was five. "Come on, babe, just for a bit, then we can order pizza when we get up."

"You know what, Matty, that doesn't sound like such a bad idea," Samantha said with a wry grin appearing on her face. "We aren't going anywhere tonight, right?"

"Nope, nowhere. What are you doing tonight?" Matt asked Petra.

"I'm going to a party in Brooklyn later. Just a few of us," she said, looking up from her textbook. "My friend just got offered a job at Stern & Camps and she's pretty excited. She starts on Monday."

"What kind of law?" Matt asked just before throwing a grape up in the air and catching it in his open mouth, barely having to adjust his head, just as a seal would catch a mackerel from its trainer.

"Impressive," Samantha said, nodding at Matt.

"Civil rights mostly. They do some work for the ACLU and some nonprofits. Wrongful evictions, denied disability claims, that kind of stuff." Matt nodded in approval before throwing another grape in the air only to have it fall to the ground and roll off the edge of the veranda. No doubt a delightful sweet treat for a city squirrel or possibly even his despised cousin, the lowly rat.

"I'll probably head out at about seven. We're going to grab something to eat before the party. David, you know David? He's staying back at the apartment and getting things set up to surprise her when we get back."

"Do you know what Steve is doing?" Matt asked.

"No clue," Petra responded without looking away from her book.

Starting to feel a bit tired herself, Samantha grabbed Matt by the arm, pulling him to his feet and said, "Come on, big boy, let's nap." Not putting up any resistance, Matt started through the door. Samantha, stopping quick, turned to Petra and said, "Oh my god, we saw the cutest little girl in the park today." While Matt was pulling her through the doorway and into the apartment, Samantha yelled to Petra, "I'll tell you about her another time! Have fun tonight!" The last few words were somewhat muffled by the emptiness of the hallway.

"You too!" Petra yelled back, realizing her excuse for a break from her studies just walked back into the house and reluctantly went back to reading.

* * *

Samantha woke up from their nap before Matt but just lay next to him, still not wanting to wake him up but simply enjoying watching the reds and yellows of the small bit of sky she could see out the window and just above the building across the street. Reaching back to the bookshelf at the head of the bed, she started pulling books out one at a time, reading titles, and returning them to their rightful place. Rubbing her fingers down Matt's arm gently, from his biceps to his forearm, finally reaching his watch, she sat up a bit, conscious of the sleeping man to her side, leaning over just a bit to get a better look at his old watch, trying to read the dial.

"What are you doing?" Matt asked but not yet moving from his comfortable position.

"Just looking at your watch. It's old," Samantha remarked.

"Yeah."

"Where did you get it?" Sam asked, lifting Matt's wrist to get a better look. "You should get a new one."

"I don't want a new one," Matt responded, taking his wrist back from Samantha gently to help himself sit up.

"Yeah, but—"

"Sam, I don't want a new one!" Matt snapped as his voice raised. Surprised by his quick and boisterous response, she jumped up from the bed and walked into the kitchen, not bothering to look back. Opening cupboard after cupboard and slamming them shut, looking for a pot to boil water to make coffee, though she knew exactly in which cupboard the pots were kept, Matt realized he had to explain. Sitting on the edge of the bed and grasping that he was too harsh, he walked into the doorway separating his bedroom with the kitchen and leaned against the dark-stained doorframe. Looking down, somewhat ashamed at how he responded, his right hand holding his old watch on his left wrist, Matt said in a tone just loud enough for Samantha to barely hear from her position at the sink, "It was my grandfather's."

Turning around from the sink where she was running water into the small pot, she looked at Matt but didn't say a word.

"He was wearing it when he was killed in Germany during the war." After a short pause, he said, "My dad wore it throughout his two tours in Vietnam, and Billy was wearing it when he was killed."

Feeling a bit embarrassed for even suggesting he get a new watch, she walked over to Matt and wrapped her arms around him. He responded and did the same.

In a soft voice, she said, "I'm sorry."

"It's okay. You didn't know," he said, moving her away just enough to see her face, lifting her head, still hanging in embarrassment. "Baby, it's okay. Forget it." He kissed her on her forehead, then hugged her firmly once again. "What kind of pizza do you want?" he asked.

"Veggie" she said meekly into his ear.

"Sal's?"

"Sure," she said as she continued to fill the pot, placing it on the rear burner since you needed a match to light either of the front two.

Matt walked into the living room, grabbing the phone from the cradle, and plopped his whole body weight down on the sofa. "Baby? Can you make me a cup?" he asked as he turned the TV on and only then realized Petra and Steve must be gone. Looking at his watch, he saw it was well past seven—seven twenty-three to be exact. Without having to look up the number to Sal's, Matt dialed from memory. Just like his parent's number or Jamal's number, Sal's was imbedded in Matt's mind from constant use.

"Yeah, hi. Can I get a large veggie for delivery?" Listening to the person on the other end of the line parrot the order back to him, Matt responded, "Yep, black and green olives. Can I get a Greek salad also?" Waiting for a response, Matt started flicking through the channels on the TV. "That's it. 910 West Eighty-Fourth, apartment 4B, fourth floor. Okay, thank you."

"About forty-five minutes!" he yelled to Samantha in the next room.

"Okay, babe."

Samantha walked into the living room, each hand with a hot cup of coffee. She placed Matt's down on the table in front of him and sat beside him though in a much more graceful manner, folding her leg under herself as she sat down.

"Thanks, honey," Matt said without looking away from the Yankee Red Sox game on TV. "I got fifty bucks on the Yanks. Jamal thinks the Sox got a chance this year." He was still not looking away from the screen. While Jamal and Matt were both lifelong Atlanta Braves fans, they each adopted the teams of their current cities.

Stroking his hair without Matt seeming to notice, she looked down at his watch and then to his face and back to the watch. She thought that there was so much they don't know about each other. What was his childhood like? What is his family like? What is Jefferson Parish like? All these questions started to rush into her mind, but not sure if she was ready to broch the subject. Was there a reason he hadn't offered up all this information in the last two years? There was no mistaking who they were; she knew early on in their relationship that she was the talker and he was the quiet one; she was the extrovert and him the introvert, but she realized just then that she wanted to know more. Reaching over and taking the remote from Matt's hand, Samantha turned the TV off. Matt swung his head around and looked at Sam as if to say, "What the hell?"

"Let's talk," Samantha said.

Seeing the look on Sam's face, Matt realized then he'd have to watch Sport Center later on to get the final score.

* * *

Sunday morning rolled around, and Matt woke up with Samantha on his side. She was devoid of any covers, not so much as a sheet as Matt was tangled up as usual; she lay there naked. Matt did his best to unwind from the single sheet without waking Samantha up but found it as difficult as one would find unwinding a large spring. Finally untangled, he laid the sheet gently down on Samantha, wiped the sleep from his eyes, and walked to the bathroom. When he came back into the bedroom, he noticed Sam hadn't moved; he stood in the doorway and leaned on the doorframe for a minute or two, looking at and appreciating her beautiful shapes and how the sheet, now draped over her body, flowed over her like the marble sculptures Samantha had shown him at the Met. Her hair was in disarray but not a fraction less beautiful than if she was prepared for a night out, and a slightly exposed section on her bottom made him feel as grateful as he ever had to that point in his life.

Opening his dresser drawer, Matt removed a pair of shorts and a Nike T-shirt, quickly throwing them on and taking a seat in the only chair in the room, not wanting to sit on the edge of the bed as he normally would out of fear of waking Sam up. After finishing tying his sneakers, he reached for a small pad off the table beside him. Flipping through and looking for a clean page, he started writing Sam a note. He took a minute to think before he wrote, tore the page from the pad, and folded it in three. He went into the kitchen and came back into the bedroom a few moments later with a glass of orange juice and set it on the nightstand by the bed. He laid the note at its base, and though he thought about kissing her gently on her head, he thought better of it, not wanting to wake her up.

Matt made his way down the stairs, the Out of Order sign still hanging on the elevator door. Matt and the other tenants are getting far too used to using the stairs. Out on the morning sidewalk, Matt looked at his watch, noting the time, seven twenty-three, and started his run toward the park. Matt ran almost every morning, except those when it was raining too hard or his schedule was too busy. He loved running in the morning best because, at six or seven in the morning, the city is still asleep, especially on a Sunday morning.

He made his way into the park and started his run on his regular route. It was a winding route through the park that brought him by the lake and Strawberry Fields and down to Columbus Circle. Then parallel with Central Park South and around the pond, past the statue of Thomas Moor, behind the zoo, and all the way up to the reservoir and then west back toward his apartment. Matt knew from the four years of living in New York and talking with fellow runners that his run was almost seven miles total. He was usually able to complete the run within an hour and half, but on this day, he took a bit longer.

Throughout his entire run, he could not stop thinking about Samantha, not that he was trying. Matt enjoyed running not just for the exercise, but because it was a good way to clear his mind and helped him to focus. Normally, he'd think about his family back in Louisiana, fishing down in the bayou or very often, Billy. But today, his thoughts were filled with his beautiful girlfriend, currently lying naked in his bed. As he was well into his run, Matt's memory took him all the way back to the night they met.

It was the early fall of 1989 and Matt was at Washington Square Station waiting for the C train, heading uptown. It was about midnight, and he had just finished a date with a girl, a student at Cooper Union. She was a lovely girl, Japanese, with an exotic beauty to her, an engineering student and quite brilliant—well versed on world affairs and though not yet in the United States six months and already more competent than most regarding US politics. Matt boarded the C train heading uptown.

The train was packed with people as it always is on Saturday nights; at that time in the city, trains are full of people heading uptown, some heading downtown, and some crosstown. People heading out to dinner, even at midnight, to bars and clubs, and thousands just hanging around Times Square. Matt always remembered overhearing a conversation between Mrs. Thompson and Ms. Dune one morning before classes started back in Jefferson Parish. Mrs. Thompson had taken a trip to New York with her cousin Alma, and Matt never forgot it. When describing the trip to Ms. Dune, Mrs. Thompson said of New York, "It's alive." And this Saturday night was no different. Matt really understood what Mrs. Thompson meant. New York was alive.

Standing up for a few stops, holding on to one of the straps that hang down from the top of the car, the train packed full, a girl caught Matt's eye; it was Sam, sitting alone, reading a book, a romance novel Matt assumed because of the artwork on the cover. You know the kind? With the overly muscled, square-jawed chiseled man holding on to the fragile, helpless damsel in distress. You know the kind? As the train continued on, Matt started to get nervous that this girl would get off the train before he had a chance to talk to her. First Ninth street and then Fourteenth. Matt didn't want to stare, but he had already thought to himself that if she got off before his stop, he'd just have to get off and say something to her. But at the Twenty-Third Street stop, more people had gotten off than the previous two and the seat on the side of this beautiful girl became vacant. Matt tried to move quickly to grab the seat before someone else did but, at the same time, didn't want to look too obvious. Siting there, beside this beautiful girl, engulfed in her book, he searched his mind for an opening line that wouldn't come off too corny. Nothing was coming to mind, and out of pure fear she'd get off at one of the next stops before he thought of something witty, he blurted out, "Hi."

The conversation continued, stop after stop, until Matt had willingly missed his stop. Sam was heading up to 125th Street; she was staying with a friend because her dormmate was having a boy spend the night. When she found out that Matt had purposely missed his stop, she asked if he'd like to get a cup of coffee. They talked in this little coffee shop on 123rd Street until 3:30 a.m. Matt walked her to her friend's building where they shared a kiss—their first.

They met for lunch the next day, where Matt hesitantly admitted he had just returned from a date the night before. Samantha found that to be extremely funny because she too had just finished a date. She went on to tell Matt how her date was rude and had bad teeth and never stopped talking about himself. When Sam asked about his date, hesitant to tell her the truth that she was a very nice girl, he chose to be as diplomatic as possible. "She was nice, but she's not you," he said.

When Matt got back from his run, Sam was in the kitchen making pancakes. When she got out of bed, she just threw on Matt's shirt from the night before, which, because of their size disparity, was long enough on her to cover everything though neither Petra or Steve were out of bed yet anyway.

"Hey, honey, pancakes?" Matt asked.

"And eggs, scrambled. You want some?" she asked as she turned her head around from the stove to look at Matt.

Matt came up from behind her and gave her a hug, kissed her ear, and said, "Sure, I'm going to jump in the shower real quick."

When Matt got out of the shower, he walked into the kitchen, combing his still-dripping wet hair. "You're dripping all over the place," Samantha said, looking up from the table, just before she put a forkful of eggs into her mouth.

Looking down, Matt said, "The floors ain't been washed in a while. It ain't gonnna hurt none." Sitting across from Sam, he started eating, making sure to compliment her on the food, something his grandma always told him he should do. "Always compliment a meal someone prepares for you even if it ain't too good," Edith would say though, in this case, it was the truth; he always liked Samantha's eggs and pancakes.

"What time is church?" Sam asked Matt in between bites.

"Eleven," Matt said as he took the last bite of pancake into his mouth. "You want to come?" he asked.

"No, not today. I have to get home and work on that project I have from my contemporary art class."

Matt brought his plate over to the sink and started washing dishes. Samantha always complained about doing dishes. She said it pruned her fingers, and the chance of breaking a nail was always a possibility. Being that she grew up with money, she had all the luxuries one could have back in California. Her daddy, Mr. McCain, back when he was a graduate student at Stanford, had created some program for computers that the military used for some of their new surface to air missile systems; he made millions. There wasn't nothing that man didn't know about computers. By the time Samantha was born, well, the McCains were pretty well-set. The difference between Samantha's upbringing and Matt's was as different as a pink alligator and a can of tomato soup.

Being brought up just outside San Francisco, Sam was exposed to all the benefits of an urban environment—nice restaurants, muse-ums, classical concerts—so when she and Matt started seeing each other, she exposed him to a lot of things he had never paid much attention to. Within six months of their relationship, Sam convinced Matt to go to the opera, *Swan Lake*. He loved it. She took him to Broadway shows and symphonies at Carnegie Hall and taught him so much about art, the periods, the artists, the styles, and the meth-ods. Matt sometimes felt embarrassed by how much he didn't know about the art world, but Samantha never made him feel inferior in anyway. In fact, she explained things in such a way that made Matt want to learn more. And over the last year, he read more books on artists and musicians than he ever imagined he would.

As much as he knew he liked Sam from the moment they met, he wasn't sure it was going to work. He didn't think they'd be able to get past the social class differences. But after those first few months, he realized he was wrong. Sam was just as open and interested in his life and his upbringing down in the parish as he was about hers in California. Before she met Matt, she had never had gumbo or jambalaya and forget about a crawfish boil. In New York, they got everything, especially foods from all over the world. There's this fish market in New York called the Fulton Fish Market, and they have everything that could possibly come out of the sea. So on occasion, Matt would go buy a bushel of crawfish and make a boil using his grandma and momma's recipe. Samantha loved it; in fact, she loved all of Matt's cooking, especially his gumbo. She'd ask him to make it at least every other week.

Neither Matt nor Samantha had any doubts how the other felt; they loved each other very much. The question is, where do they go from here? And they knew it. Matt was leaving for Washington in a few weeks to start an internship at the State Department and law school at Georgetown in September. Samantha would be in New York for at least another year and wasn't sure if she wanted to go back to California or stay in New York after her classes were over. The other option was to go down to Washington, DC, to be with Matt though DC isn't known for its art or artist, and that was the problem.

Samantha finished her breakfast and brought her dishes over to the sink. "Want me to help?" she asked him, resting her chest on his back. With a very vocal laugh, he said, "Ha ha! No, I'm okay."

Walking back over to the table, Samantha sat back down and said, "Just thought I'd offer."

"Well, thanks, babe," Matt said. "Thanks for breakfast."

"I've been doing a lot of thinking about what we talked about last night," Sam said.

Catching Matt's attention, he turned around and leaned back on the vanity of the sink, the water still running; he said, "And?" He turned around to shut the water off and walked over and sat across from Sam. He took her hand into his and said for the second time, "And?"

Looking up from the table and into Matt's eyes, she said, "I'm going to DC."

A bit taken aback by her answer, being that in their conversation last night she was leaning toward going back to California and getting an apartment in San Francisco. Leaning forward a bit, he said, "What's that?" wanting to be sure of what he heard.

"I'm going to DC."

Matt's response was subdued. He got up and walked over to the sink, turned the water on, and began doing the dishes again. Samantha, after the pregnant pause that had overtaken the room, walked over to Matt and said, "Listen, I want to go. I love you and I want to be where you are." Matt was touched by the gesture and was hoping that she would eventually join him after she finished her senior year, but he wanted her to decide for herself, so he made a point to not put any pressure on her.

"Are you sure?" Matt asked, trying to keep his emotions in check.

"Well, Jesus, Matt, you don't seem to excited about it!"

"Baby, I am thrilled, more than you know. I just wanted you to do what you thought was best for you."

"Being in DC with you is where I want to be. That's what's best for me, for us."

"Who made pancakes?" Steve said, walking into the kitchen, rubbing his eyes.

"Morning," Matt said.

"Hey, Sam, you moving to DC, huh?" Steve asked as he reached into the fridge for some orange juice.

"You heard that?" Matt asked.

"Thin walls," Steve said as he poured himself a glass of juice and sat at the table. "Any more pancakes?" he asked to whoever wanted to answer his question.

"What else do you hear?" Samantha asked inquisitively.

"Don't worry, I put a pillow over my head when I heard you guys having sex."

"Steve!" Samantha said in embarrassment.

"What, I can't help it! You guys are loud," he said before taking a sip of his juice.

"I am not loud!" Samantha said, still clearly embarrassed.

"Not you, Matt."

Looking over at Steve, Matt said, "Dude, I was just going to offer to make you pancakes too."

"What? No shame in being loud. This isn't church. Hell, I bet I'm loud too."

"You are very loud," Samantha said in a joking manner as she walked into Matt's room.

"Who's loud?" Petra asked as she walked into the kitchen.

"Oh, forget it," Matt said. "Who wants pancakes?" he asked.

"Me," Petra replied excitedly.

"Me," Steve followed.

Samantha hopped in the shower and got ready while Matt made his roommates pancakes before leaving the apartment together. Sometimes they'd shower together when they were alone in the apartment, but this day, that was not an option. Matt walked Samantha to the Eighty-Sixth Street station and then headed up to 114th Street to the Church of Notre Dame for the 11:00 a.m. mass.

Matt's grandma, Edith, was always happy that Matt kept his religion. Now she wasn't oblivious when it came to Matt and Sam, or any of his girlfriends before her, but she thought it's a different time today than when she was a kid, and as long as he went to confession regularly, then Jesus would save his soul. He went to confession every week, right after mass, to clear his conscious, cleanse his soul, and make his grandma happy.

After mass, Matt would sometimes go outside and have a smoke while he waited for Father Jefferies to start doing confessions. He didn't smoke much; he's always talked about quitting, but never got around to it. Sunday mornings were tough though; sometimes there'd be twenty people waiting for confession. Matt figured that most were there feeling a bit guilty for all the sins they committed on Saturday night. Sometimes people would be in the confessional for twenty or thirty minutes, and Matt always wondered what in the world did these people do that they need to confess for that long. But then Matt would always remember that he was no better and always managed to rack up his fair share of sins in a week.

After his turn in the confessional, Matt walked out of the church and into a spring shower. Matt hadn't brought an umbrella and started a slow jog across Morningside Park and over to Fredrick Douglass Station to get the train back home. Even though it wasn't raining to bad, by the time he got to the station, he was as wet as a waterlogged sponge.

Chapter 9

MONDAY, JUNE 10, 1991

onday mornings are no different in New York City than anywhere else in the world, and for some reason, they always rolled around too quick, and like every Monday for the last eleven Mondays, at 8:30 a.m., Matt was sitting in Professor Adkins's class. Sitting in the seventh row, dead center as usual, the class of 105 students filled every last seat. Some days, there'd be students sitting in the aisles because students who couldn't get in the class that semester would often sit in on the class anyway. Professor Adkins, the dean of the Columbia School of Political Science, was a Middle East expert and loved nothing more than an engaged and lively classroom. Yanni, a friend, well, more of a classmate of Matt, sat down in the open seat next him.

"What's up, man?" Yanni said as he sat down.

"What's up, dude?"

"Hey, when do you leave again?" Yanni asked Matt.

"The twenty-fourth. Two weeks from today," Matt responded.

"No shit? You must be excited."

"Good morning, class!" Professor Adkins said as he walked through the doorway.

Setting his briefcase down on the desk and turning to the whiteboard, he began to write. With his back to the class, Professor Adkins said, "Would anyone like to comment on the current instability of the Middle East and how we, as political scientists, can best explain or use our knowledge to inform those who cannot afford a Columbia education?"

Leaning over to Matt, Yanni whispered, "You having a party before you leave?"

"Yeah, it's going to be at Samantha's apartment. I'll give you the info after class," Matt whispered back.

"Come on, people! This is Columbia, not Brown," Professor Adkins said, which drew a collective laugh from the class. Matt raised his hand.

"Mr. Laurent, do you have something to say on the matter?"

"Yes, well, I think this being an advanced class and since most of us in here are seniors and since this is, in fact, Columbia and not Brown"—polite giggles engulfed the class again—"I think we have a very difficult responsibility since we have acquired this knowledge, and it would be irresponsible if we don't share it with those who lack it."

"Keep going."

"Well, the Middle East is such a unique place. But it doesn't exist in a vacuum. Heck, they didn't a thousand years ago, and they certainly don't know."

"Explain," Professor Adkins said as he hopped up onto his desk.

"Well, we have become tribal. Before the Gulf War, most people couldn't find Iraq on a map, most probably still can't." More polite giggles come from the class. "But we, Americans, Westerners, have to understand the complexity for what it is…and why it is."

"And why is that, Mr. Laurent?" Professor Adkins asked.

Thinking for a second and looking up at the ceiling, Matt said, "Well, I'm a Catholic from the Deep South, and while Jesus is my Lord and Savior, as he is to Protestants and Baptist and Orthodox Christians, but hell, to say I'm the same as a Protestant from Memphis just because we pray to the same god and are from the same country is, well, idiotic. Over the two hundred-plus years of the United States, with a more or less secular government, depending what religion you are, we have learned how to coexist with one another, even with our countless views on religion and politics for that matter."

"Okay, keep going."

"We have to stop thinking that we are always right," Matt said.

"What do you mean? Can you expound on that?" Professor Adkins asked.

"Well, like I was saying, we, as Americans or even Westerners, have lots of similarities—the belief in democracy, freedom of speech, freedom of religion."

"Okay, so—" Professor Adkins interrupted.

"But just look around this class," Matt continued, pointing around and looking from side to side. "While most of us in here are Americans or Westerners, we are different in more ways than we are alike. But we are also more alike than not as well. We're all human first and foremost. To assume everyone wants to be like us is ridiculous. We are a melting pot, they are not. Many of their nations and customs are thousands of years old. We are barely a toddler still in diapers. In Saudi Arabia, women can't drive cars. Now I'm not judging their culture because they have a nonsecular government. New York City is different, but down in Jefferson Parish, Louisiana, businesses can't open on Sunday. Well, why is that? Religion. Well, that's all well and good for me because I am a Catholic and believe in the Sabbath, but what about that poor atheist that needs to keep his business open seven days a week to feed his family? We criticize others for their nonsecular views and policies but fail to acknowledge our own."

"So what do we do about it, Mr. Laurent?" Professor Adkins asked.

"Inform, educate, and tolerate. Teach people that it's okay to be different, that all people don't need to be like us to be good people. People who don't look like us, pray like us, eat what we eat does not mean they are wrong. We don't have a great reputation over there for many reasons."

"Give us one."

"Okay, well, after World War I, Great Britain really screwed Prince Faisal over. I'm just saying, that we can't keep expecting them to change their whole way of life, the way the dress, the way the pray and be more like us and, if they don't, condemn them as evil people because when we do, they become less than, others. Our country was founded on that premise, and luckily, we were strong enough to eradicate slavery and pass the Civil Rights Act of 1964. But racism is alive and well here in the good old USA and that *othering* is often projected onto other countries because they are not white European, but black Africans and brown Middle Easterners or Mexicans," Matt said.

"Well, Mr. Laurent, you make a few valid points, and like you, I wish more people took the time to understand the complexity of the world and others would stop trying to dumb it down for the masses. But that probably isn't going to happen this morning. So turn to page 158 of Fleming," Professor Adkins said.

After class was over, Professor Adkins called out to Matt before he could leave. "Mr. Laurent, can you please see me before you leave?" As the students were collecting their books and backpacks, Professor Adkins yelled out to the class, "Remember, final papers are due on June 12, midnight! Got that?" looking around for acknowledgment but not receiving any.

Before Matt made his way down to the front of the class to speak with Professor Adkins, he ripped a page of paper out of his notebook and wrote Samantha's address down, along with the time and date of the party for Yanni. They shook hands, like people do, and Yanni walked off.

"Later, bro!" Yanni yelled back, raising his fist in the air but never looking back as he walked out the door.

"Professor Adkins," Matt said, standing at the front of the class while Professor Adkins was writing something in his journal while sitting behind his desk. Still writing and looking down, the professor asked, "When are you headed down to Washington?"

"The twenty-fourth, sir, twenty-fourth of this month. Just a few weeks," Matt replied.

Standing up from his chair, looking at Matt, he said, "I just wanted to give you some advice about DC. I actually worked down there myself for a while, back in the sixties and seventies. It's a swamp down there."

Shaking his head, Matt said, "Yeah, I heard it can be pretty cutthroat."

Looking up from the papers he was gathering and putting in his briefcase, he said, "No, I mean it's a swamp, literally. The humidity is terrible in the summer."

Reaching his hand out to Matt, Matt took it and shook his hand well—with a firm grip, not holding it too long but not letting go too soon either, just as his father had taught him when he was only five. William wasn't one to show affection; he was what some called a man's man, and a man's man didn't hug other males, not even his own boys, William Jr. and Matthew. So he taught them to shake hands very early. As Professor Adkins walked toward the door, he looked back and said, "Good luck, Matt. Make our country proud, young man." And he exited the door.

Chapter 10

SUNDAY, JUNE 16, 1991

A week had gone by and Matt had finished all his remaining classes. He did well in all of them, including Professor Adkins's class, and was only waiting for his final grade in advanced Arabic. Though he was confident that he did well because since meeting Petra, he would always have her check his work before he turned it in. She would point out the few mistakes he made but was very impressed with his lack of errors. The improvement he made in his last two years were a direct result of his friendship with Petra, and he knew that. Matt, who some would call obsessive, would break down his grades constantly. It was a habit he formed in his freshman year. He knew that to have any chance to get into law school one day or work at the State or Justice Department, he'd have to keep his grades up. So throughout each class, in each semester, in each year, Matt would recalculate his grade with every new assignment, sometimes even before getting his grade back, speculating, first with a higher grade and then with a lower grade, though Matt had a 3.92 GPA without Arabic, so it wasn't going to fluctuate much either way.

Matt had spent the last week packing the things he was taking to D.C., while giving away the things he wouldn't need. He was taking the train down to DC and was only allowed two bags, so not much else besides clothes, books, and photos would be making the journey. Steve was more than happy to take Matt's TV he had in his room since it was better than the one in the living room. That TV always came in handy when Matt and Samantha would lie in bed and watch *Wheel of Fortune*, and it came in handy when they'd turn up the volume to mask the sounds of their lovemaking. Sometimes they simply lie in each other's arms, naked, with just the glow from the TV screen to light up the room. All these thoughts and memories were going through Matt's mind as he was moving things into Steve's room and putting clothes into boxes, taping the tops before bringing them down to Goodwill.

Being it was Sunday, Matt and Sam were going to meet in the park at about noon. They were planning to watch a friend of Samantha play in a softball tournament; Debbie was her name. Sam was in her apartment, making a picnic lunch to take along though this time she was making tuna salad sandwiches, a Greek salad, humus, and chips. She was making more than she normally would because Benny hadn't made up his mind if he was going though it didn't help that it was eleven fifteen and he was still in bed. So Sam thought it better to be safe and make a bit more. She figured if they didn't finish it, there were always plenty of homeless people around they could help out.

As Sam was cutting cucumber for the Greek salad, she paused, and holding the knife in her right hand with her eyes turned up, she looked over to the calendar. Walking over to it, she noticed it was still on May. Lifting May's page, she saw June's page wasn't there, just July. Having a sneaky suspicion, she walked to Benny's room. She knocked quick and walked in.

"Where is June?" she asked.

With the covers still over his head, he said in a muffled voice, "What?"

"June! June! Where is June?" she exclaimed.

Throwing the covers off his head, exposing himself as well as another young man, he said, "What?"

"June, the calendar. Where is June?" she asked in a calmer voice.

"Oh, I used it last week to write down my number for David." With his hand gesturing to the young man lying next to him in bed, he said, "Meet David. David, Sam, Sam, David."

"Hello," David said without lifting his head from the pillow but offering a big wave of hello.

"Hi, David," Sam responded. "Do you have a calendar in here?" she asked.

"Yeah, my planner. It's on the desk over there," Benny said, pointing toward the general direction of his desk. "What's wrong?" he asked, noticing her seemingly excited state.

Walking over to the desk, Samantha picked up Benny's pink day planner with bright flowers on the cover, flipping through the pages of April, May, and June. With her finger, she moved it up and down the page.

"Are you going to tell me what's wrong?" Benny asked, sitting up in his bed now, alert to Sam's concern.

"I just realized Matt's leaving in a week," she said as she put the planner down and walked out of the room.

"What the hell was that about?" David asked, looking up from the pillow only slightly at Benny.

"Her boyfriend is moving to DC next week," Benny replied.

"Ohhh, that's too bad. Is he hot?" David asked in a joking manner.

"Marky Mark hot," Benny said.

Lifting his head off the pillow finally, David said, "Really?" He got a quick slap in the head from Benny and quick admonishment. "Slut!" Benny got out of bed and headed into the kitchen. Samantha was putting on her jacket and walking toward the door. Benny asked, "Where are you going? Don't we have Debbie's game in, like, an hour?"

"Yeah, I'll just be a minute. I need to go get some Feta for the Greek salad. I'll be right back. Do you need anything?"

With his head in the refrigerator, he said, "Skim milk. We're out of skim milk."

"Okay, I'll be right back," Sam said as the door closed behind her.

Benny was anything but a morning person. After his first semester of being late to every morning class, and even incurring some point deductions from his grades, he had decided to never take a morning class again. He has not taken a morning class since freshman year. Reaching into the cupboard, Benny grabbed for his favorite cereal, the one with the leprechaun and the marshmallows. Opening the box, he was clearly disappointed that there wouldn't be enough for a full bowl but grabbed a bowl from the sink strainer and emptied the box into it. Sitting on one of the two stools at the kitchen counter, his face resting in his hands still not fully awake, waiting for Samantha to get back with the milk, he noticed a slab of Feta on the cutting board by the cucumber.

About ten minutes later, Sam came walking through the door. Placing the CVS bag down on the counter and pulling out the milk first knowing Benny was waiting for it, she took out the chunk of Feta and put it on the counter. Benny asked, "What's going on?'

"What do you mean?" Samantha asked dismissively.

"Samantha, now I know I'm not like a whole lot of other people, but I am not stupid like most people either. What did you go out for?" he asked, knowing in his gut something wasn't right.

Sam pulled the home pregnancy test from the crumpled-up CVS bag in her hand she was trying so hard to hide. "Oh my god!" Benny said. "Are you late?"

"Yeah. It's been seven weeks since I got my last period," she said nervously.

"Are you going to take the test?" Benny asked while pouring far too much milk into his bowl. "Shit!" he said as the milk spilled over the top.

"Well, I didn't spend $12.95 not to take it. I'm afraid. What if…"

"What if what? What if nothing? Just go take the test before you get all worried. You wouldn't be the first girl to miss her period without being pregnant, Missy." Benny always called all his girlfriends Missy. He then took a mouthful of cereal, spilling milk all down his chin. Walking toward the bathroom and doing her best to stay calm and not over react just yet, she looked back and said, "What would you know about periods?'

"I know I'm not late, Missy," Benny said without looking her way in a joking manner.

Samantha flipped him the bird as she walked into the bathroom. Knowing Sam's typical response to Benny's sarcasm, he didn't have to see the finger to know it was there, to which he replied, "Love you too, honey."

* * *

It was twelve twenty and Matt had already been waiting in the park for thirty minutes. Matt skipped his run that morning, so after mass, instead of taking the train, he jogged the forty-plus blocks down to the ball fields. He had stuffed a blanket in his backpack before he left the house and now had it spread out near Heckscher Fields with a good view of the ball field. It was the bottom of the second, and Debbie's team was up 2–0. At Debbie's first at bat, she hit a line drive into the gap, which rolled all the way into the next field, seeing there weren't any fences. Debbie drove in a run and made it all the way to third standing up. The girl after Debbie would drive her in on a sacrifice fly to right field.

Matt was sitting with his legs crossed, reading the US State Department book of rules and guidelines. He was always a quick study, but needless to say, he was nervous about interning at the State Department and wanted to be as prepared as possible. This was a big opportunity for Matt, and he was even going to miss his graduation for this chance to fulfill a dream. His emotions were all over the place, pulling him in different direction, and they had been for the last few weeks. It's funny how human emotions can pull us in different directions at the same time. He was excited and nervous about working at the State Department over the summer, anxious about starting law school in in the fall, and sad about leaving Samantha yet overjoyed that she had decided to join him in DC after her senior year. But at the same time, he also felt enormous pressure that Sam had changed her plans to be with him. But he was also excited that he and Jamal would get to spend the summer in DC together. It would be the first time in a long time since they'd spent that much time together. He was on an emotional roller coaster.

Standing up to stretch his legs, Matt looked up at the mostly blue sky, just a few random fluffy white clouds that reminded Matt of marshmallow fluff, one of Billy's favorites. Billy loved peanut butter and fluff sandwiches though Matt never cared for them. It was another beautiful day in the city, something that didn't go unnoticed by Matt. Standing up, he couldn't help but to look around for Lori and Annabelle, the mother and cute little girl he and Sam had met the last time they were in the park though he didn't see them. The park was full of people—runners, cyclist, other picnickers, and plenty of families enjoying the fine-weathered day. While Matt was stretching his arms up to those fluff-like clouds, he peeked at his watch; it was twelve twenty-three, and he noticed Samantha walking his way with her bag, no doubt full of food. Matt was happy for that because he hadn't had anything for breakfast.

"Hey, babe!" Matt yelled out to Sam as she got closer and closer. Sam responded with a smile spread across her face and a big wave.

"Hi, honey," Samantha said as she wrapped her arms around him. "Beautiful day, isn't it?" she said happily. "Are you hungry?"

"Oh, hell yeah! What did you bring?"

"Tuna."

"Nice!"

"Salad, humus, and chips," she added.

"Cool," Matt responded as he sat back down, reaching into the bag. Pulling out container after contained, he opened the pita chips and humus and started eating.

"I guess you're hungry. Who's winning?" Samantha asked, looking over to the field.

"Debbie! Debbie!" Sam yelled, waving toward right field, Debbie's position.

Samantha sat down by Matt, her legs crossed, as she took out the plates and handed Matt a napkin. Opening the containers, she made each of them a plate.

"Crap! Did you bring water?"

Without saying anything, Samantha reached into the bag and pulled out two bottles of cold water she had bought from the guy who sells ice-cold water out of a cooler at the Columbus Circle entrance.

Using one of the napkins, Samantha wiped the condensation from the plastic bottle and handed it to Matt.

"How was your morning, sweetie?" Matt asked while taking a bite of his tuna sandwich.

"It was okay. Benny has a new boyfriend," she responded.

"Nice. What's his name?"

"David."

"What's he like?"

"No idea. I only saw his head on the pillow and just said hi," Samantha responded as she started eating her Greek salad.

"Debbie's up," Matt said, gesturing to home plate.

Looking up from her salad, Samantha reacted. "Come on, Deb!" she yelled out, trying her best to cover her mouth, still full of salad, but not wanting to miss the opportunity to encourage her friend. Debbie and Samantha had been friends since sophomore year, and Debbie was also from the Bay Area though they had only met once in New York.

"Is Benny coming by?" Matt asked.

"No, no. He said he was going to go for lunch with David. He said he'd make it up to Deb."

"Oh, that's too bad. I was hoping to see this David. Benny just doesn't have a type, does he?" Matt asked.

"What do you mean?"

"Well, his past boyfriends have just been so...different from each other."

"He doesn't discriminate. He has eclectic taste," she responded.

"I guess."

"Well, you're pretty eclectic."

"What do you mean?" Matt asked, inquisitively looking away from the game and over at Sam.

"Well, Emily was black. I'm white and Protestant. Like I said, you don't have a type."

"Em was half black, biracial. Actually, I do have a type," he said.

"Oh, plus remember that Japanese girl you cheated on me with?" she said, exhilarated.

"What!" Matt snapped back, somewhat muffled by a mouthful of tuna. "Cheated on you?" he asked, trying to keep the food from falling out of his mouth.

"You know, that Japanese girl you went on a date with the night we met," she said nonchalantly.

"Ohhhh, you mean the girl I went on a date with before I met you?" Matt said while rolling his eyes.

"Technically," she said as she bit into a piece of celery.

Looking over at Matt, blocking the sun from her eyes, she asked, "So what's this *type* you speak of?"

He thought for a second and said, "I'm a sucker for sweet." He leaned his body over to her, and after making him wait a split second for effect, she leaned toward him and they met in the middle of the space between them with a kiss.

"Think that's going to get you laid?" she asked. He gave her a squinted look, partly due to the sun in his eyes and also because that's the sex look he gives her whenever the time is right.

"Yeah, okay, it worked. Later," she said, giving him her sex look, which was a lowered head, eyes up, and a slight bite of her bottom lip. That always drove Matt wild, but since they were in the middle of Central Park, surrounded by people, it would have to wait.

After they had finished lunch, Samantha took off her tank top, underneath wearing a bikini top. Sam had fair skin, almost milky, though she did tan and, throughout the spring, had acquired a nice base. Rubbing lotion on her legs and then upper body, she gestured to Matt to take his shirt off, and he did. He was lying on his stomach and started reading his book where he had left off. Squirting the cold lotion on Matt's back, he recoiled from the chill. As Samantha rubbed the lotion all over Matt's back and shoulders while keeping an eye on the game, she asked with purpose, "So what does our future look like?"

Looking up from his book and over his shoulder, though not able to see her face, Matt said, "Perfect."

Sam used her finger to draw a little heart on Matt's back in the lotion before incorporating it. "No, really?" she asked.

"What do you mean?" he asked, not looking up from his book.

"Like how is this going to work? What do you see for our future?"

"Well, after you finish school, you'll move down to DC."

"And?"

"Once I finish law school, hopefully I get a job at the State Department," he said.

"And?"

"You'll work on your career, establishing yourself as the next great artist of this generation."

"Oh really? I like the sound of that," she said, shaking her head up and down slightly.

"We'll get married, maybe I'll get stationed overseas. All you need is studio space wherever we are in the world and then eventually back here to the States. A few kids, maybe a dog. White picket fence," he said with certainty in his voice.

Samantha was looking around the park, at the game, the endless stream of runners passing by, the cyclists, and families, lots of families. She asked, "What if it doesn't work out that perfectly?"

"What do you mean? Why wouldn't it?" he said, looking back.

"Well, life doesn't always work out the way you want it too. Things happen. What if you meet someone else down in DC?" she said.

Turning over to make eye contact with Sam, he said, "Baby, you're the one for me. I don't want anyone else. I will never want anyone else."

She bent down just enough to give him a kiss, and she sat back up and said, "You better love me that much!" as she swatted his backside. "I'm not going to spend the rest of my life with someone who doesn't love me that much."

"Of course, I love you that much. Don't you love me that much?" Matt asked, laughing out loud, before leaning back down, continuing to read his book.

"I do, I absolutely do. But what about our religious differences?" she asked. Samantha was a Christian as were her family, Protestant though nonpracticing.

"What about it?"

"Well, you're Catholic, I'm not. How would we get married, in a Catholic church if I'm not Catholic?" she asked, knowing how important Matt's religion is to him while her religious convictions are, at best, flexible. Still watching the game, she said, "Debbie's up again."

"She's got a good swing," Matt said as he looked over to the ball field.

"Stop worrying already. That doesn't matter right now. We have a lot of time and ground to cover before we get to marriage and kids."

"Oh really? And you figured this out in your spare time?" Sam asked with a bit of sarcasm in her voice.

"Yes, in my spare time. I like to be prepared, you know, like the Boy Scouts?" He looked back at her. "Even though I was never a Boy Scout."

"And what if I got pregnant before we got married?" Samantha asked hesitantly while running her fingers through Matt's thick brown hair.

"Yeah, well, that's not going to happen."

"Why do you say that?"

"Because we need to get married first."

"And why is that?" she asked.

"Because it says in the Bible. Deuteronomy, I think. It's bad enough, I have to confess to Father Jefferies, that we have sex every week," he said embarrassed.

"Really? You confess that every week?" Sam asked, a bit surprised.

"Hell yeah," he said, closing his book.

"Details?" Sam asked meekly.

"Oh my god, no!" he exclaimed before he started laughing.

"Well, how the hell would I know? I didn't know what you confessed in the first place. Ass," she said, feeling embarrassed.

Looking back at her once again, he said, "Besides, you're on the pill, so that's nothing to worry about. It's already bad enough that we're not supposed to be using birth control as a Catholic, let alone having sex to begin with." With no shame expressed externally though feeling shameful moments after he said it for not feeling it in the first place.

"But I'm not Catholic!" she said sharply.

"Doesn't matter."

"You do know the pill isn't 100 percent effective?" Samantha said.

"It's 98.9? That's pretty damn close," he said quickly in retort, as if he was reading the stat from a report of some kind or he had it memorized.

Sitting up and folding his legs beneath him, he reached in the bag for the container of humus and the bag of pita chips. Using just his index finger to lift her chin and looking into Samantha's eyes, he said, "Babe, you're the only one I want to marry. You are the only one I want to have my children. I just want to do it right. We'll get married in a few years after I finish law school. Maybe I can get stationed overseas at an embassy. Paris, maybe London."

"Tokyo? Istanbul? Cairo?" Samantha said in quick succession, seemingly accepting Matt's view into their future, doing her best to induce a reaction.

"Can you imagine?" Matt asked, with a clear sense of wonder in his voice. "Wouldn't it be nice to expose our kids to other cultures, other ways of life than just this? Though this isn't bad," Matt said as he looked around the park.

Now sitting face-to-face, each with their legs folded beneath them, Sam leaned forward and wrapped her arms around his shoulders; she hugged him, and Matt did the same. Kissing her on her right ear, a habit he had going back to Emily. He loved to kiss ears. He kissed it again and again. Whispering in her ear, he said reassuringly, "We're going to be fine, honey."

Doing her best to hide the single tear rolling down her face, she refused to release Matt from the hug when he tried, reestablishing the embrace until she could wipe it away without his knowledge. Samantha, looking over his shoulder, still in the embrace, yelled, "There's Annabelle!"

Chapter 11

A lot can happen in a week. Jesus was dead and had risen from his tomb in less than a week. The Battle of Gettysburg was fought and over in less than a week. Though it doesn't have to be an extraordinary week for much to occur, it's just the way life is. And this past week, much had transpired. On Tuesday, less than a week before he was headed down to Washington, Matt had gone by the Church of Notre Dame to see Father Jefferies. Matt and Father Jefferies's relationship, now four years in, had become similar to Matt's and Father John's back in Jefferson Parish. The beginning of that relationship took hold within the first few months of his arrival in New York. Feeling very alone and very much a stranger in a strange place, Matt reached out to the one place he always knew he could—the church. On Tuesdays, there's only a 7:00 a.m. mass, so Matt went by Notre Dame at ten o'clock, figuring the father would have finished any confessions he had after mass. Luckily for Matt, Monday night isn't the biggest night for sin and found Father Jefferies reading in the rectory. He invited Father Jefferies out for coffee to which the father was more than willing to accept.

They walked over to Tim's Diner on 112th and Broadway to get two black coffees to go. Tim's was one of Father Jefferies's favorite restaurants; he thought they had the best matzo ball soup in the city. Matt had never tried matzo ball soup until one night, in those first few months of being in New York, the father had taken him over to Tim's after bingo. Back then, Matt would often go for walks and inevitably end up at the church. This was not lost on the father, and he took the opportunity to let what he saw as a scared and lost young man know that he was not alone, neither in the city nor in life. As it turned out, Matt loved the soup. It was the first time he had tried Jewish food, but not the last. Growing up in Louisiana, there wasn't much opportunity to eat Jewish food; in fact, Matt had never met a Jew until moving to New York. Over the last four years, Matt had eaten many meals in Jewish delis around the city though he found the best Jewish restaurants to be in Borough Park in Brooklyn.

After ordering their coffee, Matt reached into his pocket for some money to pay, but Father Jefferies stopped him, telling him, "You got last time, I got it." Thinking to himself and remembering that he did pay last time, Matt said, "Thanks, Father." They walked east down 112th street toward Morningside Park, reaching Amsterdam Avenue, and looking at the massive Cathedral Church of St. John Divine, an Episcopal denomination. Father pointed and said, "My competition," which drew a laugh from Matt. They made their way across the park and found a bench at the monument of Lafayette and Washington.

Father Jefferies was much older than Father John was, in his seventies. Father Jefferies had seen a lot, a lot of good and a lot of bad over the years. Sitting down for a few minutes, both Father and Matt watched the people walking by, going about their day, the pigeons wallowing around, pecking at the ground, no doubt much more unsuccessful than successful with each peck to the ground. Father Jefferies asked, "Are you ready, son?"

Taking a sip of his coffee and pausing for just a few seconds to consider his answer, Matt said, "I hope so."

"Matt? Why the self-doubt?" Father Jefferies asked, a bit surprised at Matt's response since he usually found Matt had projected such self-confidence.

"I don't know, Father. Everything. Change," Matt said as he picked up some pebbles from the ground and fidgeted with them in his hand, shaking them as though they were a pair of dice.

"Ah, change. That explains it."

"Is it that obvious?" Matt asked, looking at the elderly holy man.

"Well, I'd love to lie to you, son, but you know that's against rules."

"Yeah," Matt said, throwing the pebbles off into the grass one at a time.

Leaning back on the bench, crossing his legs, and looking up to the sky, Father turned to Matt and asked, "Did I ever tell you about when I was your age?"

Shaking his head no while still throwing his pebbles and in a low tone, Matt said, "No, no, Father, you haven't."

"Well, it was 1942, and I just graduated seminary at Boston College. We hadn't been in the war that long at that point. Only six months prior, the Japanese attacked us. But my parents, on the day I graduated, they were so proud that day."

"I bet they were," Matt said, looking toward the father, sipping on his coffee in bigger sips as it had cooled off slightly.

"The world was a mess back then," Father said as he rubbed his hand on his chin. "They were proud of me, and as hard as I tried not to be, I was awful proud of myself too. You know I had an older brother too?" Father Jefferies asked, looking toward Matt and putting a hand on his knee.

"Really, Father? I didn't know that," Matt responded, looking back at the old man.

"He was killed two weeks before the Pearl Harbor attack. We weren't even officially in the war yet. He was a pilot," he said with pride.

"I'm sorry, Father," Matt said as he continued to look toward Father Jefferies.

"It was a long time ago, son."

"He had volunteered for the RAF, the Royal Air Force," he said, making sure Matt knew what he meant. "The UK needed pilots and asked for volunteers from the United States military, and he volunteered, along with a lot of other brave young men. Not a big surprised to me though." He looked over at Matt. "Didn't really surprise my mother or father either. Though my mother tried to talk him out of it. Harry wouldn't have it. Harry wasn't as fond of the church as I or my parents, but he loved this country. He was a patriot for sure."

"What happened to him? If you don't mind talking about it, Father?" Matt added, realizing he had asked a question that might have been a sore spot for the father.

"No, no, quite all right, son," the father said, reassuring Matt. "He was stationed in Northern Ireland. They said he was out on patrol…at night, and he didn't return. They sent out a search party in the morning and found some wreckage in the Channel. But they never found Harry. They said it was most likely some sort of catastrophic failure. Explosion of some sort."

"Oh my god, Father."

"That was the toughest thing for my mother, not being able to bury him. So we buried an empty casket, just some old photos and personal items we each put inside."

"We did the same with Billy. We all put some things in his casket too."

Looking over at Matt, he said, "It's not easy losing a brother, is it?"

"No, no it's not."

"Well, after we buried him, things slowly went back to normal at home. Life had to go on, but things quickly got worse for the world. I joined up in June of 1943."

"I didn't know you were in the military, Father," Matt said, looking at a rather small, meek old man beside him, trying his best to imagine him as a strong young man in his prime on a battlefield with little success.

"Sure was. Army, Ninetieth Infantry Division, clergy, of course," Father Jefferies said with pride. "I went ashore in the fourth wave at Omaha." Father Jefferies did his best to keep his composure and not get emotional about something he clearly was. Matt, almost too afraid to ask any details or even make a comment, waited for Father to continue.

"What I saw that day…on that cold, wet beach reaffirmed the decision I had made in life to serve God."

"How's that, Father?"

"War is a terrible thing, Matthew. Boys…just boys," the father said, becoming more emotional than before and before a momentary pause. Matt gave the father the requisite time he needed to continue. "I saw what man is capable of doing to one another. Right or wrong is not the point. What the point is that all men have the ability. Mankind needs God." He looked over to Matt, silent until Matt looked back at him. "We all have a purpose, Matthew. Mine is to serve God and to offer his salvation to those who accept it. Yours is to go to Washington, finish your schooling, and do some good. I don't doubt you will do just that."

A smile slowly developed on Matt's face, the first of the day for him. Father Jefferies sipped his coffee and noticed Matt was wearing a watch. The elderly man felt his own wrist, just then realizing he had forgotten to put his on earlier that morning. His more recent forgetfulness was not lost upon him. "What time is it, Matthew?" he asked.

Looking down at his old watch, Matt said, "Just past eleven."

The priest's eyebrows raised and was accompanied by a slight nod of the head before he said, "Well, I better get back to the rectory. Work to be done." He rested both hands on his weary knees to brace himself and used the leverage to stand up. Picking up his coffee cup, he finished it off and looked around for a trash can.

Matthew said, "Leave it, Father. I'll throw it away."

"Are you heading back my way?" he asked.

Looking around for just a moment, Matthew said, "No, no. Not yet. I think I'll just sit here a bit longer. The father nodded his head once again and started off.

* * *

The days of the month of June had passed faster than any other Matt could remember since being in New York. He had received his grade in Arabic, an A-, which overjoyed Matt and impressed Petra. He hadn't spent as much time as he wanted with Samantha in his last week being she also had finals to finish and, on Wednesday, had come down with a summer bug of some kind. Matt had offered to go by and nurse her back to health, but Sam said, "I'd hate for you to get sick before you head to Washington."

Now Saturday, June 22, just days before Matt was to head down to DC to embark on what he hoped would be a successful career working for the State Department. Matt had just a few more things he need to get done before his going-away party later that night. When he woke up that morning, he lay in bed, looking out his window for a while, thinking of the past four years he'd spent in New York. While there was no doubt Matt was a Southern boy through and through, he had done a good job at becoming and transplanted New Yorker, something that gave him a sense of pride.

Like anyone from the South or anywhere for that matter who moves to New York City, it can be a bit overwhelming at first. Matt couldn't help but remember his first day when Jose or Juan or whoever he was stole his wallet and taught him a valuable lesson. Matt had spent his life giving people the benefit of the doubt, and just because he was wronged, that wasn't going to change. After the initial anger wore off, he always assumed that Jose or Juan just needed the money a bit more than he did. Some might call that naive, Matt just thought of it as kindness.

"Yo, you getting up today? It's eleven o'clock," Steve said to Matt, standing in his doorway.

Looking over to Steve, Matt said, "Yeah, I'm getting up. Just going to call Sam."

"You want breakfast?" Steve asked.

"You're going to cook breakfast?" Matt asked in astonishment, being that in the last two years Steve might have cooked a total of five meals. Steve was always more apt to order in food or wait until Matt was cooking and then get in on that than cook his own food.

"Shit no!" Steve exclaimed. "I'm ordering, Carol's Corner. French toast and bacon okay?"

"Yeah, that sounds great," Matt said with a hint of a grin on his face, realizing how much he was going to miss Steve and all the controlled crazy he brought to Matt's world.

"Cool," Steve said as he walked back into the kitchen.

Matt rolled over on his side and was quickly scanning his now very empty room. He reached back for one of only two books he had left on the shelf behind his headboard, *Slaughterhouse Five*. Flipping through the book he had read countless times, he grabbed the cordless phone he had left on the nightstand the night before. He dialed Samantha's number, but it just kept ringing. Matt rolled out of bed and hopped into the shower while he waited for the food to be delivered.

Walking into the kitchen in her pajamas and surprised to see Steve setting up the table for breakfast, Petra asked Steve, "Where is he?"

Turning toward her for a quick second, he said, "I think he's in the shower. Do you want any breakfast? I ordered from Carol's."

"No, no, thanks. I'm going to meet a friend in a bit. We'll grab something."

As Matt walked into the kitchen and sat down at the table, Petra walked over to him and draped herself over him like a blanket, hugging him harder and longer than she had in the past two years. Matt could hear her start to cry ever so quietly though she did her best not to reveal her emotions. Matt kissed her on the side of her head and hugged her back, and she walked off toward her room.

After breakfast, Matt went back into his room to call Sam. The phone had been in his room the whole night, and he had forgotten to put the phone on the charging cradle in the morning, and it was now dead. So he realized he'd have to go out to use a pay phone. As he was walking out the door, Petra yelled from the living room, "What time is the party?"

"Eight o'clock," Matt said as he looked at his watch.

"Okay, I might not be here later, so I'll see you at the party. I'll make sure Steve gets there too," Petra said, knowing full well Steve was often late for or totally blew off engagements regularly.

Matt laughed, knowing full well Petra's inference to Steve either missing or being late to events. "Okay, see you tonight," he said as he walked out the door. Matt walked out to Central Park West and made his way down to the Museum of Natural History where there was a pay phone outside he had used plenty of times over the last few years.

Putting a quarter into the phone, Matt dialed Samantha's number while still not understanding why it cost a quarter to make a call in New York City while only a dime in Jefferson Parish. The phone rang once and then twice, Matt looking around at the hundreds of people, more children than adults; he noticed the sky was starting to get dark. It looked like rain, he thought to himself, when Benny finally answered the phone after the sixth ring. Out of breath, Benny said, "Hello?"

"Hey, Benny, it's Matt. Is Samantha around?"

"Ummm, no, she's not, Matt. She's at the library. But she said she'll see you tonight at the party."

"Oh, okay," Matt said, disappointed that she wasn't home.

"She's been really busy, Matt. She's been trying to catch up after being sick," Benny said, trying to reassure Matt.

"Yeah, I understand. All right then. I'll see you later tonight, about eight, right?"

"Yep, eight o'clock. See you then, Matty," Benny said before hanging up.

Matt decided he'd go for a walk through the park for the last time in what could be a long while. He walked over to the carousel and bought an ice-cream cone, vanilla. After about thirty minutes of sitting on a bench, watching the children ride the carousel horses go around and round, he decided to hop the train and head down to Battery Park. He wanted to visit Lady Liberty one more time before he left New York.

During his time in New York, Matt had lost count of how many times he had gone out to Liberty Island to visit the old girl. It had started to spit rain just a bit, but New Yorkers, being some of the best opportunist in the world, there were already two men selling umbrellas as he walked up and out of the train station. They were the kind that broke after the first or second use, and between Matt and his roommates, they must have had a collection of twenty nonfunctioning umbrellas at the apartment though they did come in handy when they had guest and someone needed one when it was raining. They were good enough when you hand nothing at all.

It had been sometime since Matt had walked up the steep steps and into her torch, so he figured he'd spend the extra $8.95 it cost and take one last look at the view. Over the years, Matt had realized that few New Yorkers ever visited the Lady and often heard visitors on Liberty Island speaking many different languages. After taking in the view, which wasn't very good being that it was raining and overcast, Matt took up a seat on a bench in front of her. Doing his best to wipe the bench dry, it was a futile attempt, but he sat anyway.

Matt has always enjoyed alone time. Even as a young boy, he would often go for long walks, sometimes down to the bayou, sometimes down to the ballpark where he was sure to be able to people watch quietly. On this day in New York, Matt was taking in as much as he could since he didn't know when he'd be back. He always found the actions of people fascinating. Watching someone do the most mundane thing can sometimes be captivating. Earlier in day, he had observed a woman in the park; Matt estimated her to be about fifty-five years old. She sat on a bench, two down and across from Matt, also near the carousel. She had had a bag of what Matt thought to be bird seed at first but, after watching for a while, realized it was popcorn kernels.

As Matt watched the women as stealthily as he could, he wondered what her story was. Everyone has a story, you see. Some are filled with a lifetime of adventure and excitement while others were filled with days sitting on a park bench, feeding corn kernels to pigeons, though Matt knew that sometimes these two extremes often intersect. A person who seemingly lives a mundane life at present might very well have lived a life full of excitement and intrigue at one point. Often, while watching a person, Matt would fill in the blanks.

This woman, whom he named Sophie, was a widow, childless, and now alone. But at one point, she had a full life, full of people, activities, and love. Looking at the care in which she threw the kernels to the city-dwelling birds, Matt could tell she was a loving woman. She cared for these birds as much as she once cared for those who filled her life. *But they're gone*, Matt thought. *They are gone, and now Sophie has her pigeons.* Matt wondered if these birds knew just how lucky they were to have such a caring person as Sophie to spend time with them and feed them with such care. Doubtful, he thought.

Now sitting at the base of the great Lady, Matt continued to watch people passing by—people walking alone, couples walking together, families and even larger groups all doing their best to stay dry while taking in Lady Liberty. A family caught Matt's eye, maybe twenty feet away. Matt could barely make out what he assumed to be the father, explaining to the young boy, maybe nine, the son no doubt, Matt thought, while the woman, the mom, stood by, looking up into the rain at the tall statue. Matt could tell from the father's accent that they were probably from Africa, maybe West Africa, Senegal, maybe Liberia. Over his four years at Columbia, Matt had taken classes with and had met many students from around the world and many from African countries.

As Matt was watching the family, the father keeping his son's attention with facts being read from the guidebook, the man glanced over in Matt's direction and they made eye contact. Matt turned away quickly, somewhat embarrassed that he was caught red-handed eavesdropping on the private conversation. The man walked toward Matt rather directly.

"Excuse me," the man said to Matt. Matt immediately thought Liberia.

"Hi, how are you?" Matt replied.

"Oh, we are very well. Abu!" the man called to the young boy, standing by his mother.

"I'm Matt."

"Hello, I am Joseph. Joseph Hali." The young boy was now standing at his father's side. "This is Abu, my son." Waving the woman over, he said, "And this is Monji, my wife. We are visiting from Ghana." Immediately Matt was disappointed at his Liberia conclusion.

"Hi...hi, nice to meet you," Matt said as he extended his hand to Joseph. The men shook hands, and then Matt extended his hand to both Monji and Abu, in that order.

"I was wondering if you can help me. It seems as though there is a misprint in the guidebook." Pointing at the guidebook, Joseph showed Matt the error. "As you see here, it states that the Statue of Liberty was gifted to the United States from France on 1786," Joseph said while underlining the sentence with his finger as he showed Matt.

Seeing the misprint, Matt said, "Well, that's odd. I can't see how they didn't notice this."

"So it is wrong?" Joseph confirmed.

"Oh yes, that's clearly wrong. It was dedicated in 1886, so only a century off," Matt said, which drew a laugh from Joseph.

"I will have to bring it to the attention of the management," Joseph said.

"Yeah, that's a good idea," Matt said. "So how long are you visiting?"

"We are here for three weeks. I am a doctor with the WHO and I had the opportunity to bring my family. So we will leave on Wednesday to head to the capitol of Washington, DC. I have another conference to attend on Friday before heading back to Ghana."

"Oh, wow, that's really cool," Matt said. Looking at the young boy, Matt asked, "So are you having fun, Abu? Do you like the United States?"

Looking up at Matt a bit sheepishly, he nodded in the affirmative but then said, "I like McDonald's."

"Nice. Most people who visit enjoy McDonald's. I like Big Macs myself."

"I had chicken McNuggets," the boy responded.

"Ah, okay," Matt said, turning his attention back to Joseph. Glancing at his watch, Matt realized it was much later than he had thought and waited for a pause in between Joseph's detailed description of their visit to the United States.

In the politest way possible, Matt explained that he was running late and must be going. Shaking each of the family member's hand one more time, wishing them luck for the rest of the trip, Matt, seeing the ferry preparing to depart, started running full speed to the dock, looking back one last time and waving to the family while trying to avoid colliding with other visitors. Luckily, Matt made the ferry just in time and, checking his watch once more, calculated how much time he had until the party started. Just two hours to get back to Battery Park, uptown, shower, and change and then head back to midtown. *It's going to be close*, he thought.

Matt arrived at Samantha's apartment at 8:02 p.m. At this time of the year, the sunlight reflecting off all the steel and glass of the buildings can be quite beautiful, but this night, it was murky and wet, still raining as it had been on and off all day. Before Matt knocked on the door, he shook his umbrella off, removing as much of the water as possible. When Matt entered the apartment, he saw the decorations, balloons, and streamers strung about, one with the words *Good Luck, Matt* on them.

"Hey, buddy!" Steve said to Matt as he handed him a beer.

"What's up, Stevie boy?" Matt said, taking the beer and looking around at all the guest. Some he didn't recognize at all; he assumed they must be Benny's friends. Steve lit a cigarette and offered Matt one. Still not having been able to quit totally, Matt took one and used Steve's already-lit cigarette to light his. Looking around the apartment, he didn't see Samantha.

"Where's Sam? She's been acting weird all week," Matt asked Steve as he took a long swig of beer.

"You know, I haven't seen her in a while," he said as he scanned the room. "Maybe she's in her bedroom."

"All right, I'll find her. I'll catch up with you in a bit," Matt said as he walked through the apartment, saying hello to friends, stopping often for a few minutes at a time to chat. As Matt got closer to Sam's bedroom door, he was stopped by a well-lubricated Skip.

"Matty! Matty!" Skip yelled as Matt approached him, slightly slurring the *Y* at the end of each *Matty*, grabbing Matt and putting him in an awkward drunken hug.

"What's up, Skip?" Matt said while he continued to look around the room while breaking away from the drunken bear hug at the same time. Matt had known Skip for almost all the four years he'd been in New York. So seeing Skip in this condition was not a big surprise to Matt; the key was how you deal with him. He was a good guy, but he was not the guy you wanted to get stuck next to at a party, so Matt did his best not to be rude and told Skip he needed to use the bathroom and was able to break away.

Matt knocked on Samantha's bedroom door and walked in, closing the door behind him. He was surprised to see Sam sitting on her bed with her head hung low. Matt could tell she had been crying. Benny was sitting on one side of Sam with Petra on the other side, seemingly comforting her.

"What's going on?" Matt asked but was not getting a reply.

"Hey, Matt," Petra said, looking at Matt but not moving from Samantha's side.

"Hi, Matty," Benny said while he stroked Sam's hair.

Matt was confused and, for a second, thought that Samantha was simply upset that he would be leaving the following day, but he had a feeling it was something more. "Hey, baby," Matt said to Samantha as he walked toward her, kneeling down in front of her.

"Hi, baby," she said, but not yet looking up, seemingly still crying.

"Can we have a minute?" Matt asked his friends.

"Are you okay, Missy?" Benny asked Sam. She responded with a simple nod for yes.

"I'll see you in a bit," Petra said as she picked up her wine glass from the dresser, took a sip, and looked back one more time before she walked out of the room. Standing up, Benny hugged Matt and kissed him on the cheek. "I'm going to miss you, Matty boy," Benny said before walking toward the door. "I'll be right out here if you need me, Missy," Benny said to Samantha.

"Thanks, Benny," Samantha said, still not raising her head.

Benny closed the door behind him, and Matt sat down beside Samantha and placed one hand on her knee while he brushed her hair off her shoulder with the other. Giving her a kiss on the side of her head, Samantha reacted. She turned to Matt and wrapped her arms around him and gave him a hug, one that was so tight it was noticeably peculiar to Matt.

"What's wrong, baby?" Matt asked while still in embrace. Trying to pull away to make eye contact with Samantha, she didn't allow it and continued to hold Matt in her firm grip. "You've been acting weird all week," Matt said in a whisper.

Barely able to vocalize the words, she said in a tone close to, but not quite, a whisper as possible, "I was pregnant, Matt."

"What's that, baby?" Matt said, not able to understand what she had said.

"I was pregnant," Samantha said, only slightly louder than she had previously.

"You're pregnant?" Matt asked with surprise and excitement in his voice, this time using enough force to pull away from the hug to make eye contact.

Wrapping his arms around her again, he said, "Oh my god, baby. How long have you known? Why didn't you tell me sooner? Is this why you've been acting weird?"

Realizing Matt had misheard her, she broke away from his arms and stood up. "I was pregnant, Matt! I was…"

Matt, a bit confused and afraid of the reality of the situation, asked, "What do you mean?" looking over at Samantha, leaning against the doorframe of her closet door. "What do you mean *was?*" Matt asked again, this time with impatience in his voice.

"I was, Matt. I was!" Samantha snapped back at Matt. "I had an abortion! I had an abortion, Matt," she said, her eyes dotting up and back down again from the floor to Matt, making eye contact for as long as she can before she felt the need to look away. The tears started to rain down her face as she heard herself say the word *abortion*. Devastated at what he was hearing, Matt looked up to the ceiling, trying to comprehend what he had just heard. "Why?" he asked, now looking down at the floor. Looking at Samantha, with anger in his voice, he asked, "Why, Sam? Why would you do that?"

"Because, Matt," she snapped back at him, "we aren't ready! You said it yourself! You said we weren't ready!"

Sitting on the edge of the bed, looking down with his face in his hands, Matt was doing his best to rationalize what had just happened. Seemingly in a matter of minutes, everything changed. Not knowing exactly what to do, Matt stood up and stormed out of the bedroom, passing partygoers as many tried to stop him to wish him well on his new endeavor. Standing by the dresser for only a few seconds more, Samantha chased Matt out of the apartment. Out in the hallway, she looked over the stairway railing, seeing Matt rushing down the stairs.

"Matt! Matt! Wait!" she yelled to him as she rushed down the stairs after him. Coming out onto the street, she looked right and then left to see Matt walking away. Samantha ran as fast as she could, feeling pain from the procedure just a few days prior to catch up with Matt, grabbing him by the arms to stop him. "Wait!" she said. Matt was still trying to walk away, but Samantha had him by the wrist and jumped in front of him, forcing him to stop.

"Matt, wait!"

"Wait? Wait? Sam!" Matt said in quick succession, with anger in his voice.

"Matt, we talked about this. You told me."

"I told you what, Sam? I told you I wanted you to have an abortion?" Matt snapped back, clearly upset.

"No...you told me." Samantha stopped herself to rethink her choice of words. "Matt, baby...we aren't ready," Sam said as they both stood on the sidewalk in a steady mist of rain. "Matt...we weren't ready. We need to finish school. I know you, Matt. If I told you I was pregnant, it would have ruined all your plans...our plans! You need to finish school, and you can't do that while interning at the State Department and raising a baby." Samantha was standing in front of Matt as he did his best to avoid eye contact, as she held his wrist, not willing to let him go.

"I can't believe this. What did you do?" Matt asked, looking up into the rain and into the sky. But he wasn't talking to Samantha; he was asking God. "What did you do?" Lowering his head, he said, "I can't believe this."

"Matt," Samantha said, trying to catch his eyes. "I'm not ready. You're not ready. We are not ready, Matt," She implored.

"I have to get out of here," Matt said as he pulled his wrist away from Sam's grip and started running up the sidewalk.

"Matt! Matt!" Samantha yelled to him as she watched him make his way up the busy Saturday-night sidewalk, eventually losing sight of him among the crowd of people. Standing in the rain, Samantha began to cry; she put her hands to her face. Second-guessing her decision, she leaned up against the bus stop enclosure and cried, not concerned about the rain or the people watching—none of it matter. Eventually, she made her way back into the apartment building and slowly up the stairs.

When Matt arrived at Penn Station at 8:45 a.m., he had all that he could carry—a backpack full of books and personal items as well as his father's duffel bag fill with clothes, which was evident by the weight and the effort that Matt needed to carry it. His briefcase was stuffed way down in the duffel bag at the bottom, not wanting to look at it and give him a reason to think about Samantha. Penn Station, regardless of the time of day, was always a busy place. People coming in and people heading out, going in all different directions, and today, it was Matt's turn. He was leaving.

It had been a long night for Matt; he didn't get to bed until after 3:00 a.m. After he left Sam's apartment, he began walking and walking and kept walking. First up to the park and then by the Museum of Natural History and then past his own street. It wasn't until he hit 153th Street up in Harlem did he notice where he was—Trinity Cemetery. In his second year, he had to take a biology course, so he took ornithology. One of his classmates had told him that James J. Audubon was buried at Trinity, so one Sunday after church, he took a nice long walk. He hadn't been this far uptown since that day.

Matt's ticket was for the nine ten Silver Star, with stops in Philadelphia, Baltimore, and finally, Washington, DC. The Silver Star made this trip every day, day in and day out, back and forth, and after leaving Washington, DC, it continued on down to Savanna, Tampa, and then, finally, Miami.

Though he had passed Penn Station countless times over the past four years, he had only been inside a handful of times. Most of those times, he was headed to Boston to visit Jamal. Sitting on a hard, old wooden bench, Matt started to think about all the people who must have sat in this very spot throughout the years. Men and women both, many probably with children, families heading to someplace new, either on a vacation, maybe down to Florida or up to the Green Mountains of Vermont, and maybe some of them were running away from something, never to return to New York again. Looking up at the huge clock above the impressive arch, seeing it was three past nine, Matt looked down at his watch and it read one minute past nine; he synchronized it with the clock. Standing up, he put his backpack on and threw the heavy duffel bag over his shoulder, taking one last look around. Of course, he was taking in this last view of New York he'd probably see in sometime, but really, what he was really doing was looking for Samantha. She wasn't there.

As Matt walked toward the entrance of the platforms, he took a glance up at the departure board to reconfirm his platform—number 9. As he handed his ticket to the elderly ticket taker at the entrance but before he walked through the turnstile, he took one last look around for Sam. Nothing.

"Where you headed?" asked the elderly ticket taker.

"DC," Matt responded somberly.

"Safe trip," the man said as Matt walked toward platform number 9. He boarded the Silver Star and was on his way to Washington.

Chapter 12

WASHINGTON, DC

A long time had passed since Matt had lived in New York though he did travel there on occasion for work. And every time he did, as much as he tried to avoid doing so, he couldn't help but scan the faces in the train stations and on the trains, in the parks and the restaurant, or wherever else he was for Samantha. He never did see her on any of those trips; in fact, he hadn't seen or talked to her since that night outside her apartment. Though she never left his mind, she would always be an enduring tenant in his heart.

The summer of 1991, the summer Jamal spent in DC was a wonderful time for both Jamal and Matt. Though Jamal had a very hectic and demanding schedule throughout that summer, Jamal did a great job at lifting Matt's spirits. For two young men, working toward careers in law, being in Washington was a dream come true. And they made sure to thank God regularly in their daily prayers and also every Sunday. The boys would alternate churches weekly, going to a Baptist church, the First Baptist Church of Washington, DC, one week and then a Catholic church, St. Ann's, the following.

Matt's small but adequate apartment was on the corner of North Carolina and Seventh in the Lincoln Park neighborhood, just a few blocks behind the Supreme Court and the Capitol building. The apartment, on the second floor, was next door to a liquor store which, on some days, could be and was beneficial while other days not so much. Often, it was a convenient location for drug dealers to peddle their products as well as the occasional prostitutes looking for a john. Matt didn't mind so much as they never seemed to bother the residence in the neighborhood, and in fact, he had had a number of interesting and valued conversations with many of them on how they came to sell their products. Matt loved hearing people's personal stories. He couldn't help but wonder about who the people were, where they came from and how they got where they are, and most importantly, where they were going. Matt believed that the more you understand a person, the more you can understand or empathize with their particular situation, many of them cast aside by society, doing what they needed to, to get by. Well, Matt could relate all too well. He was a good listener.

That first summer went by far too fast. Jamal and Matt had tried their best to see as much as they could before Jamal had to head back to Boston in late August. Between Matt's internship at the State Department, which was a full-time commitment and Jamal's clerkship, their only real free day to spend together was Sunday. So after church, Matt and Jamal would go for lunch and then see the sights of the nation's capital. Sometimes they would sit on the mall or by the Lincoln Memorial, often talking about Jefferson Parish, the people they missed there, and of course, the food. But Washington, DC, was different from Jefferson Parish and even New York or Boston. There was an incredible vibe, a buzz in the city that was evident, and it attracted people from all over the country. And as young men, they didn't lose focus on what most young men enjoyed, young women, and Washington had plenty of them.

When Jamal arrived in DC, he knew Matt was hurting; he knew how much Matt loved Samantha, and he did his best to help him get through it. Jamal tried to pick his best friend's spirits up, and that often meant introducing Matt to young ladies that were also clerking at the court. There were a few nice girls, like Amanda St. Clair from Chicago. She was twenty-three and had just graduated from George Washington Law School in May. Tall, at least five foot eleven, maybe even six feet, she could just about look Matt in the eyes without having to get on her tiptoes. She was a dark-haired beauty with green eyes, olive skin, and a vocabulary that would rival any congressman holding office at that time. In fact, she had a habit of correcting Matt's southern so often they only went on four dates.

Then there was Stephine from Cape Cod, Massachusetts. Stephine was, well, she wasn't exactly the sharpest knife in the drawer. But after just a few conversations, Matt found out her father was a certain Massachusetts congressman's attorney and realized how she came to be a congressional intern. Now he wasn't exactly naive to how the world works. Hell, back home it was understood that when a new parish president was elected, he would most likely give his brother-in-law a job on the fire department or as a school custodian, so he wasn't surprised much. But Stephine just didn't trip his trigger though they did remain good friends, and a few years later, she married a freshman congressman from California. He lost his reelection campaign two years after the marriage, and with that, he also lost Stephine. Matt was always happy that he had dodged that bullet.

Jamal, as good as he was at finding new and interesting young ladies for Matt, didn't indulge himself; he had a girl waiting for him back in Boston—Jazmine. They had met in International Business Law, Professor Keen's class, and while it wasn't love at first sight, it was pretty damn close. Jazmine was the first in her family to attend college, like Jamal, from Athens, Georgia, and in addition to being the top in their class, she could cook as good as Jamal's momma. Now southern food from Georgia isn't exactly like the food in Jefferson Parish, though it's a lot closer than anything Jamal had had from the so-called southern restaurants in Boston or DC. So while Matt did his best to move on from Samantha and meet new women, Jamal abstained. In fact, though he never said it to Matt, he couldn't wait to get back to Boston to be with Jazmine.

At the end of that summer, Jamal did go back to Boston, and Matt was on his own; he often felt as alone as one can feel after that in DC. He found law school to be much different from his time at Columbia. In law school, especially in Washington DC, everyone was focused, so focused they often don't take time to interact. You see, most folks in DC aren't there for anything else other than career opportunity. No one moves to DC for the weather or the culture or even the amazing history; people move to DC to work in government or, in Matt's case, attend school and then go to work in government like many of his classmates, and that's what he did. After he graduated from Georgetown Law, he was offered a full-time position at the State Department. He had thought about applying for a position at Justice, but Matt wanted to be overseas. He wanted more adventure in his life, and he knew he wouldn't find it in some federal prosecutor's office in Des Moines, Iowa, or some other place like that, so State it was.

In the six years since graduating from law school, many things have changed in Matt's life as well as in those he loved. Jamal and Jazmine were married and living in New York City with one child—a daughter named Charlotte. The ceremony took place in the summer on 1996 back in Jefferson Parish. Matt, of course, was Jamal's best man and gave wonderful speech about friendship, Jamal's loyalty, and his love for Jazmine but couldn't help but include a story about walking in on Jamal pleasuring himself back in middle school. That part got the biggest laugh and most applause by far. It was a small ceremony with less than a hundred people, and the reception was held on the church picnic grounds. With plenty of shrimp and crawfish, greens and gumbo, the day couldn't have been better. Jamal landed a high-paying corporate gig with one of those big four-named law firms you see in New York City. Jazmine could have gone to work for one of those high-priced firms herself, but she chose to work as a public defender instead.

With the money Jamal was making at his firm, they made more than enough to live a very comfortable lifestyle while Jazmine could actually help people who needed it. While Jamal was under no illusions that he was basically making rich people richer with the cases he handled, he just hoped he'd work his way up that ladder and make some of his own. Jazmine, well, she was always thinking of other people, and it showed. She helped those in the community that couldn't help themselves, with plenty of pro bono work and in her mothering of Charlotte and how much she loved Jamal, well, that was clear. Jamal wasn't the only one who adored Jazmine either. Matt grew to love her as a sister as well.

Throughout those years, Matt would sometimes go up to New York City for a few days when he could to visit Jamal and his family. He would actually visit New York more often than he would go back to the parish, but that wasn't because he didn't love his family, but rather he just had more to say to Jamal. Back in the parish, conversations with William, Karen, and sometimes even Edith were fraught with awkward silences. That never happened with Jamal or Jaz. On occasion, he'd even get to meet up with Petra, who worked in the United Nations, though living in London she'd have to come over every now and again. When he could, he'd head back home, down to Jefferson Parish, to visit his folks, mostly for Christmas, but the stays were always shorter than he would plan. In the twelve years since Matt had moved away, first to New York and then Washington, his parent had never visited. This was not lost upon Matt, and though he tried not to let it bother him, it did.

Working at the State Department was often demanding and very time-consuming. Over the past nine years in DC, Matt had a few relationships, but none longer than a year. He was too focused on his career for a real relationship, and he moved up the ladder quickly—first as the assistant to the assistant lead attorney for overseas operations, then assistant and eventually he moved to supervising attorney to the office of foreign affairs. But of those rather short-term relationship, there was one girl he had feelings for, Baily. She was a nice girl; she worked for a lobbying firm and was very successful in her own right. Matt had started to fall for her and made the mistake of bringing up the future, something Baily wasn't ready to entertain. It wasn't long after that, one morning, on a day of no particular importance, Matt woke up to find a folded note on his nightstand from Baily; it said, *We are headed down different paths even though we occupy the same space. I can't do that anymore. Baily.* While his love life wasn't a success, the sacrifices have paid off and his career was progressing.

Mondays in Washington were always crazy, the busiest day of the week. The reason being that most government offices, federal and state, are closed on the weekends, so that means Mondays are a bit of a catch-up day. The events of the weekend needed to be addressed, and it usually wasn't until Wednesday that Matt was completely caught up. When he got to his office, his secretary, Claire, was already at her desk. She was a lovely older woman, well, older than Matt; he always assumed she was late forties, maybe fifty, but would never dare to ask. Now Matt was always an early riser and took pride in that but so was Claire, and over the past few years, Matt had tried to beat her in on a few occasions though the handful of times he showed up before eight, Claire was already at her desk. Matt never inquired why she was such an earlier riser; he just assumed she had her reasons.

"Good morning, Claire. How was your weekend?" Matt said as he filled up his Columbia University mug with bad government coffee from the dated coffee machine.

"Good morning, Matt. It was good. Kevin and I took the kids down to Hilton Head," Claire responded.

"Oh yeah? How was the weather?"

"Oh, it was great, a bit overcast yesterday, but still beach weather. The boys were on their boogie boards all day."

"Nice. I bet they had blast," Matt said as sipped his bad coffee and took the files Claire handed him as he walked into his office.

Sitting at his desk, Matt looked at the headline of the copy of the *Washington Post* he bought at the newsstand at the Virginia Avenue bus station. The headline was not dissimilar from most major papers that day, all filled with the headlines from the Democratic National Convention in Los Angeles.

Matt loved going to work in the Harry S. Truman building every day. History was never lost on Matt, and he knew the significance of the building and the people who worked there day in and day out, some spending a career, serving our country, not for money or accolades, but for love of country. Unlike his father or grandfather, Matt didn't serve in the military but felt what he was doing was in service of his country; working for the State Department made him feel patriotic, and he liked that.

But deep down, he always wondered if William would respect him more if he had forgone college and joined the military as Billy would have if he had lived. But that was just another answer to another question he'd simply have to live without.

Though Matt loved his work, he felt he was growing stagnant. He wasn't in any meaningful relationship; he didn't have any what he would consider close friends in DC, and his work was becoming, well, it wasn't as challenging as it once was, and Matt missed being challenged. He had fallen into the trap as many people do of getting comfortable and forgetting why he wanted this job in the first place. So about three months ago, he had put in a request for an overseas posting. Being that he spoke French and Arabic, he had requested any post that had opened up in countries where either were the primary language.

Through the intercom, Claire said, "Matt, the undersecretary wants you in his office at ten thirty."

"Did he say what it was pertaining too?" Matt asked inquisitively.

"He did not," Claire replied.

"Okay, Claire, thanks. What do I have scheduled before then?" Matt asked.

"Nothing that I see."

"Okay."

Sitting at his desk, doing some of the catching up Mondays always required, Matt's mind began to wander. It was back in Jefferson Parish with Em, Jamal, Grandma, and his parents. It didn't take long before it wandered back up to New York with Sam. Remembering all the good days, days spent in the park, the walks, the dinners out, and even the lazy nights lying in bed watching TV. But it was that last night together that was most memorable, unfortunately. Realizing his mind was going down a road he didn't want to take, he decided to go for a walk before his meeting.

One of the best things about working at the Harry S. Truman Building was its close proximity to the Lincoln Memorial. It was less than half a mile from his office, and it always, without fail, gave Matt the solitude he was looking for even when it was crowded with tourist. Like back in New York at the Museum of Natural History, Matt would often sit on the steps of the memorial and watch people. There were always plenty of war veterans milling about and hordes of tourist and endless assemblies of schoolchildren visiting Washington, DC; they were always inspiring to Matt. It reminded him of his trip to the

Johnson Space Center in Houston back when he was in the eighth grade. He missed being that age. How would his life have changed, for better or worse, had Billy lived? He missed his big brother more so now than he had in a long time.

After sitting in the shadows of the memorial of the great statesman for a period, Matt made his way back to his office. After a quick straightening of the tie, combing of the hair, and brushing of the teeth to rid his breath of the cheap government coffee, Matt said to Claire as he left the office, "Wish me luck."

Looking up from her computer, Claire said with a smile, "Good luck, Matt. Finger crossed."

Looking at his watch as he reached the undersecretary's office at ten twenty-five, Matt said to the secretary's assistant, "Hello! Matt Laurent to see Undersecretary Burns."

"Ah yes, Mr. Laurent. The secretary is running a few minutes late, so if you'd like to take a seat in the left chair in front of his desk, he shouldn't be much longer," she said.

"Okay, thank you," Matt said as he walked toward the secretary's office door. "The left chair?" Matt asked, looking back.

"That's right, the left chair," the woman replied without looking up from her work as though she had been asked this question many times before.

As Matt sat in the left chair in front of the desk, he started to second-guess himself. Could she have meant the undersecretary's left? But just as that thought was creeping through his mind, Undersecretary Burns was entering the office. Standing in the doorway and looking out toward his secretary, he said, "Okay, tell Representative Allen I'll see him in his office at one thirty and not two."

Matt rose to his feet as soon as he heard Secretary Burns, still hoping he was in the correct chair.

"Mr. Laurent, nice to see you. Take a seat."

"Thank you, sir."

When the secretary came into the room, that was when it dawned on Matt. Secretary Burns had lost his left eye years ago and wore an eye patch. So sitting in the left chair in front of his desk would allow him to see Matt better.

As the undersecretary sat down, he picked up a memo from his desk and started to read to himself, holding up his index finger to Matt, indicating for him to sit tight. Matt took the opportunity to glance around the room at all the photos on the wall, the most impressive being the three of the undersecretary with the current president, Clinton, and his two predecessors. Matt couldn't help but be impressed.

"Hey, Matt," Secretary Burns said as he laid the memo down on his desk and looked up at Matt. "You know, Matt, we are pretty impressed with your work. How long have you been at State, four years?"

"Six, sir."

"Ah yes, I have your file around here somewhere," he said as he moved a few manila folders around until he found the one labeled Matthew Laurent. Opening it up, he spent a minute or so reading while Matt sat silent, knowing full well that was all that was required at that moment.

"So why did you wait so long to apply for an overseas posting?" the secretary asked.

"I guess I always assumed there would be time…sir," Matt said after a moment of searching for a better answer than the one he gave.

"Well, never assume you'll have time, son. Take advantage of every day as if it is your last."

"Yes, sir. Good advice, sir, though I do feel this would be a good time for me to serve overseas in that I don't have any family obligations."

"Single, no children, correct?" asked the undersecretary.

"That's right, sir."

Looking up from Matt's file, the secretary said, "You studied under Professor Adkins, correct?"

A bit surprised by the question, Matt responded with a sense of pride in his voice, "Yes, sure, sure did. He was my mentor."

"Dr. Adkins and I were at Harvard together. He was a hell of a boxer. In fact, you got your interview as a personal favor to Dr. Adkins. But in hindsight and after reviewing your file and, admittedly, watching you from afar for the past six years, it was a favor that paid off." Sitting back in his chair while tapping the eraser end of a number 2 pencil on his desk, he said, "There's an opening in Riyadh. You'll have to leave in thirty days. Is that doable?" He expected the same answer he always got—yes.

"Yes, of course, sir. Not a problem," Matt responded.

"Good, good."

Trying to contain his excitement but not doing a very good job, Matt said, "Yes, sir. Thank you, sir!" Shifting around in his chair, making sure he was sitting at attention, he could only try to contain the smile that was doing its best to encroach on his face. "Sir, when will I get the details of my—"

Cutting Matt off in midsentence, he said, "Don't worry about that right now. You'll get all the details in a matter of days." Sitting forward and putting the pencil down, the undersecretary interlocked his fingers, like a person does when he prays, and looked directly at Matt and asked, "What I don't understand is, why not private practice? You clearly have the ability. You could make a lot of money at a lobbying firm. You have the education and credentials. Why in the world would you want to be stationed in Saudi Arabia?"

Matt again shuffled in his seat, his eyes turned up to the ceiling and then to the photo of the undersecretary and President Bill Clinton and then he responded, "Family tradition."

The secretary shot Matt a puzzled look and repeated Matt's response, "Family tradition? How so? From what I understand, you are the first in your family to attend college."

"Yes, sir, family tradition, sir. Yes, sir, I am the first in my family to attend college. But I am not the first in my family to serve our country," Matt said proudly.

"Military?" the undersecretary asked.

"Yes sir. Both my father and grandfather. My brother would have served if he had lived."

"So why didn't you join the military? Are you some sort of pacifist?" he asked with a hint of sarcasm.

Again, readjusting himself in his chair and taking a few seconds to formulate the response in the order in which he wanted to respond, Matt said, "No, sir, I'm not a pacifist...exactly."

"Then what are you?"

"An idealist, sir," Matt said with confidence.

Impressed with Matt, the undersecretary got up from his chair, moved over to his window, running his right hand over the golden tasseled American flag standing just to the right of the window frame. Looking out toward the Lincoln Memorial, he said, "Good luck, Laurent." Interpreting that as his cue, Matt stood from his chair and said, "Do you have any advice, sir?"

Turning away from the window and toward Matt sharply, the undersecretary responded in a quick and direct fashion, "Don't expect to find idealism in Riyadh."

"Yes, sir." Matt reached his hand out toward the undersecretary, his hand hanging in the space between him and the undersecretary for what felt like an eternity to Matt. Secretary Burns eventually took his hand. "Good luck, son."

Matt walked out of the office, still trying his best to contain his excitement; he clapped his right hand into his left, unable to contain himself anymore. The slap made such a loud smack that all the heads in the cubicles turned away from their work and toward Matt to identify the source. "Sorry. Sorry. Sorry," Matt said, turning his head at random folks.

It didn't take long for Matt to sell off or give away the belongings he would no longer need. Always a minimalist, he never acquired a mass amount of possessions in the first place and had very few sentimental feelings for inanimate objects. Unlike his momma or grandmomma who never throw anything away, Matt could always fit his most prized possession in a single bag. Heck, this time he was even giving most of his books away, only keeping his favorite five. The Salvation Army came and picked up his furniture a few days before he left. Matt figured it was better to give it away to people who needed it than make a few hundred bucks being that he wasn't hard up for money or anything. Instead of flying out of DC, he figured he'd head up to New York for a few days to spend some time with Jamal and his family before heading over to Saudi Arabia.

Chapter 13

MANHATTAN BOUND

att boarded the Silver Star, northbound from Union Station in Washington on September 9, 2000. Jamal would be waiting for Matt at Penn Station some four hours later. Matt was early as usual, so he was able to get a window seat. Matt always preferred a window seat over an aisle seat; aisle seats were just too dangerous to knees when traveling, especially for a man with some height.

Though his bags were full, mostly with clothes—four suits that he will need to have pressed once he arrives in Saudi Arabia, underwear, socks, two pair of shoes, dress shirts, and so on Matt brought his new cell phone as well as a file with all the information he would need upon arrival in Riyadh. Matt had had a cell phone for the last few years; the State Department had issued him one for his job and was often essential. This one was an overseas phone that would first connect Matt with the embassy operator who would then patch him through to any number he was calling. He thought the whole procedure to be a bit much, but the tech guy who brought it by Matt's office a few days earlier had said something about the calls being secure.

As he was flipping through the stack papers and what seemed like endless information—information on his apartment location and his required duties—he realized that being stationed overseas entitled him a pay differential of 12 percent plus an additional 5 percent because his station location was in what was deemed a potential danger zone, as well as travel expenses and moving allowance. Looking at all the benefits, Matt was wondering why he waited so long to request an overseas post. The train was starting to fill up with more passengers when an older woman sat in the seat next to Matt, the aisle seat.

"Hello," the elderly woman said. Matt guessed her age to be in her sixties but knew as soon as she said hello she was from Louisiana.

"Hello! How are you today?" Matt asked.

"Oh boy, I'm tired, young man." The woman turned to Matt and said, "Boy, aren't you handsome."

Immediately embarrassed, Matt could only assume he was blushing. "Well, thank you, ma'am. Are you from Louisiana, ma'am?"

"I sure am. Baton Rouge. As a matter of fact, this is the farthest north I've been in my sixty-eight years," she said, clearly looking overwhelmed.

"Jefferson Parish," Matt said with pride and in an effort of commonality.

Looking toward Matt, she said, "Why you don't say? I can hardly tell."

"Well, I've been up here for so long I'm probably losing my accent some. So where are you headed? If you don't mind me asking?"

"Don't be silly! Of course not. I'm heading to New Haven, Connecticut. Going to visit my grandson. He goes to Yale," the old woman said directly.

"No kidding? My friend Jamal went to Harvard in Boston. He lives in New York now. I went to Columbia."

"Well, isn't the world a small place?" she said as she reached in her knitted bag in an effort to remove something though she was having difficulty.

"Here, let me get that for you," Matt said.

"Well, thank you, young man," she said as she sat back in her seat and let Matt do the digging. "Can you give me my ball of yarn and my needles? If you don't mind."

"Not at all," Matt said as he moved aside a Bible to reveal the knitting tools. "So why did you get on here in Washington? My names Matt, by the way, Matthew Laurent," he said as he awkwardly offered his hand in the confined space.

"Gloria. Gloria Armstrong. Nice to meet you, Matthew," she said as she shook Matt's much larger hand. "We'll, since this was my first trip by train and since I ain't never been farther north than Jackson, Mississippi, I figured I'd make a few stops along the way. So I got off in Atlanta for a few days, then I stopped here in Washington for a few more, and I'll be in New Haven by the end of the day." Looking over at Matt and putting her weathered hand on Matt's knee, she said, "Thank Jesus. Amen." She folded her hands and looked up at the roof of the interior of the train and said it again, "Thank Jesus! Praise Jesus that I have the health to make such a long trip at such an advanced age."

"Well, ma'am, I have to say you look like you are in great shape. In fact, you look like you could make it all the way up to Canada with no effort," Matt said, looking over at the elderly woman, doing his best to induce a smile.

"Well, thank you, Matt, but I have to say, I won't be doing this again anytime soon, and I certainly won't be heading to Canada."

"I hate to ask, but how are you getting back to Baton Rouge?" Matt said, afraid of the answer.

"Oh, I'm taking a plane. When I got to Atlanta, I called Enos. That's my grandson. Well, I told him that if he didn't buy me a plane ticket back home, I would have to live with him in New Haven. Needless to say, he bought that ticket right fast."

Matt began to laugh at the nice woman's humor. "Well, that sounds great. That was very nice of your grandson."

"Well, he's a good boy. A real good boy. He lived with me for sixteen of his twenty years, and I doubt he wants that number to go up."

That gave Matt another chuckle. "Where are his parents?"

"Well, seems like so long ago, but his daddy went to Angola back in '81 and his momma was killed by a trick three years later. So he's been with me ever since. But he's a good boy, a good God-fearing boy. He's going to be a lawyer," the woman said as she slapped her hands together with pure jubilation and held them up to the train

134

ceiling. She said again, "Thank you, Jesus! Thank you Jesus for my boy! Amen! Amen!"

"He sounds like a great kid."

"Oh, he is," she said, looking around, making sure no one could hear her. "Far too many boys down there either end up dead or at Angola. But after I lost my boy to the devil and he started sticking up grocery stores and such, I knew it was only a matter of time before someone got hurt," she said with disappointment permeating through her voice. "He killed a man. He killed a man for forty-three dollars. God help him. That boy is right where he belongs." She shook her head from side to side, then placing her hand back on Matt's knee, she said, "And my boy Enos is right where he belongs. That boy has made me so proud. And that's why when he asked after three years of being up in New Haven if I'd go up and visit, I couldn't say no. I'm all he's got."

"Well, it sounds like he's right lucky to have you, ma'am."

Matt looked at his watch and then out the window for a minute, taking advantage in the pause in the conversation. "So what does Enos want to do when he graduates?" Matt asked, filling the void of silence.

"He wants to be a lawyer," she said, looking up at Matt from her knitting with a look that said, "I already told you he was going to be a lawyer."

Not wanted to dive deeper into the different types of law, as Matt was referring to, he went with, "Wow, that's great. I'm a lawyer. I went to Georgetown."

Thinking for a second or two, she said, "That's right here in Washington, isn't it?"

"Yes, ma'am. Yes, it is," Matt responded.

Looking away from Matt and around the train car, seemingly trying to recall something, she said, "Oh, you know what? I saw that. I took one of those bus tours around the city yesterday and I remember the man. You know the guy in front?"

"The guide?" Matt said, trying to help the woman remember.

"That's it, the tour guide. He pointed it out as we drove by though I wouldn't know it from any other of those big stone buildings in that city even if I was standing right outside it," she said with a chuckle. "These cities are just too big."

"Oh yeah. I can understand that for sure," Matt agreed.

Time passed by and Gloria kept knitting away. Matt had started reading his copy of Jack Kerouac's *On the Road*, one of the five books he felt was worthy of international travel. Matt appreciated that when he started reading, Gloria stopped talking as she had continued about everything under the sun before that. It's not that Matt minded hearing about Gloria's church choir or her recipe for gumbo, which she claimed was the best in all the South but felt no need to enter any of those silly gumbo contest because she didn't have anything to prove, it was just that Matt more so than most enjoyed quiet time.

As the Silver Star made its way North and deep into New Jersey, the Manhattan skyline began to appear. It was dusk by now and the setting sunlight was reflecting off the skyscrapers just as Matt had remembered. Looking out the window, he said, "Gloria."

"Yes, Matt?" she said, first without looking up but then getting her first glimpse of the big city. "Oh my lord. I have never," she said in amazement.

"Beautiful, isn't it?" Matt asked with a bit of pride since he still considered himself to be part New Yorker.

Thinking for a few seconds, wanting to convey her sentiments correctly, Gloria said, "Well, Matt, when I was a young girl, in grade school…" She was thinking to herself and looking up again, searching her memory. "I couldn't have been more than nine years old. Well, there was this man out in Monticello. That's where we lived back then, Monticello. Well, there was this man who served on the town council. And this man was a beautiful man. I mean, even at nine years old, I could tell a good-looking man when I saw one. He was one for sure." She put her hand on Matt's knee again. Matt, with his head turned toward Gloria, listened intently. "Well, this man, David Sale was his name. Mr. Sale a white man, a white handsome man who was also a member of the local chapter of the KKK, and in 1942, he was charged along with four other white men with the lynching of a nineteen-year-old black boy. They were all acquitted."

Looking over at Matt, she said, "So sometimes things can seem beautiful from a distance, but up close they are very ugly."

Before Matt got off the train, he gave Gloria his card to pass on to her grandson, Enos, and wished her well on the rest of her journey. He couldn't help but notice how much easier it was for him to talk to total strangers than many of the people closest to him. As he walked through the turnstile, he noticed Jamal's big smile right away.

"What's up, brother?" Jamal said as he embraced Matt.

"How's it going?" Matt replied as he started walking toward the exit.

"Woah, woah!" Jamal called after Matt. "Let's head down to the Battery."

"Yeah?" Matt asked, surprised, looking at his watch and seeing it was seven thirty. "I thought Jazmine was making dinner?"

Jamal grabbed Matt's bag and started carrying it for him as they walked toward the subway turnstiles. Jamal inserted a token and motioned for Matt to go through, then he followed.

"Yeah, well, change of plans," Jamal said as they walked down the steps to the platform for the 1 train. "Jazmine had to work late, so the sitter still has Charlotte, so I figured we'd go check out the Lady and then maybe grab some dinner ourselves. Sounds good?" Jamal asked though not meant it to be a question as he had already decided.

"Sure, let's do it," Matt said, happy to be back in the city he loved and with his best friend. He was feeling pretty good.

The subway down to the Battery didn't take all that long, usually about twenty minutes or so. But the train stopped at the Hudson Street station for what seemed longer than it actually was; the conductor made an announcement that they were waiting for a train to move in front of them before they could continue on. This wasn't all that uncommon, and they were back underway within a few minutes. For all the years he lived in New York, Matt always had a hard time understanding those conductors over the public-address systems, like most people, but somehow Jamal always understood them clearly. Today was no different; when the announcement was made, Matt turned to Jamal and said, "What did he say?"

They only spent about thirty minutes on Liberty Island, doing a single lap around the old girl and then grabbed the next ferry back. Jamal could have done without going, but he knew that it was one of Matt's favorite places in the city. They grabbed the train uptown and got off at Fiftieth Street and headed west to Tenth Avenue to Jake's Steak House, Jamal's favorite restaurant. It wasn't too busy at the time, so they were seated rather quickly.

Looking around at the fancy decor, Matt leaned in toward Jamal and asked, "Do you come here a lot?"

"Yeah, couple times a week," Jamal responded. Seeing a friend a few tables over, Jamal waved. "Hey, Dennis! How did you make out with the Rider Project?"

"We did well. Took us long enough, but it all turned out," the man said from two tables away.

"Nice, nice. Let me know when you're ready to move forward with that thing we talked about."

"I sure will."

"Who's that?" Matt asked, feeling a bit intimidated by his surroundings.

"He's an attorney. Works for Chase. Good guy. Helped us out with a project we were handling," Jamal said as he was reading the menu. Matt nodded in approval and then began to look at the menu.

"Jesus Christ, this place isn't cheap!" Matt said, louder than he had planned, drawing a look from the women at the next table.

"Don't worry about it. I got it," Jamal said while he continued to read his menu.

"Normally, people will tell you to get the fillet, but I'm telling you, the rib eye is amazing!" Jamal said to Matt.

"Dude, it's $48," Matt said in astonishment.

"Don't worry. Just try the rib eye."

"Yeah? Actually, that does sounds good," Matt said as he closed his menu and placed it on the table. Still looking around at the decor and, for a second, wondering why he hadn't gone into to corporate law, he asked, "You like places like this?"

"Why? You don't?" Jamal asked, slightly put off.

"Well, it's not that." Thinking to himself for a second, he said, "It's just... Is it really necessary?"

"Jesus, Matt."

"No, no. I didn't mean—" he said, afraid he offended Jamal.

"I know what you meant," Jamal interrupted. "Don't worry about it, Matt."

"It's just...it seems a bit much."

"It is a bit much, and that's why I like it. That's why I worked my ass off down in the parish and that's why I busted my ass at Harvard so I could afford a forty-eight-dollar steak if I wanted. And today, I want one," Jamal said with an unapologetic tone.

"Listen, you deserve a forty-eight-dollar steak and then some. I'm not saying—"

Jamal interrupted Matt again, "I know what you're saying, Matt, but just shut up and enjoy the damn steak! Okay?"

A grin came over Matt's face and he said, "Okay, I'll enjoy the damn steak. I think after I enjoy my damn steak, I'll enjoy a damn hot fudge sundae as well."

"Now you're talking, brother," Jamal said.

After they finished their dinner, they decided to walk back to Jamal's apartment up on East Sixty-Third street. The lights of the city were beautiful, and the bustle of the city was in full effect, and Matt was taking it all in again. After being in Washington, DC, for so long, just walking the streets of New York City again was a welcome change. He hadn't realized how much he had missed New York. Some people think that all big cities are alike, but that couldn't be further from the truth. Though Matt had only been to a handful of big cities, he always picked up on the unique subtleties of each. When it came to education, culture, and history Boston stood alone. Washington, DC, well, it can feel like the center of the universe sometimes with diplomats and government leaders coming and going on a daily basis; it's hard not to see it that way, and New Orleans is just one never-ending party. But New York...New York City is like its very own universe. Matt loved New York not only for its size but also for having so many unique neighborhoods. He loved the diversity of the city and the sanctuary of Central Park. And

Broadway. Well, Matt had learned to love Broadway, the museums, and even the opera. Thanks to Samantha. He was happy to be back, if only for a few days.

When Jamal and Matt arrived at the apartment on the tree-lined upscale neighborhood, Matt was impressed. When they walked into the brownstone building, Jazmine was waiting with Charlotte to greet Jamal and Matthew.

"Hi, baby," Jazmine said to Jamal before giving him a kiss on the cheek.

"Sorry we're so late. Where's my little girl?" Jamal said as he bent to his knees and opened his arms as his little girl, Charlotte, ran into his waiting arms. Only a tiny little thing, Matt thought the little girl packed more energy per pound than anyone he had ever known before. With her mother's high cheekbones and her hair full of white beads, she was a beautiful kid. Jazmine kissed Matt on his cheek after she kissed Jamal. "Hi, Matt. How are you?" she asked.

"Oh, I'm good," he said as he put his bag down on the hardwood floors.

"Are you excited?" she asked.

"Oh my god, yes. Excited and a bit nervous, I guess. Heck, I've never left the country, so yeah, I'm expecting some culture shock, but I'm looking forward to the experience."

Jamal grabbed Matt's bag and started walking up the stairs. "I'll put your bag in your room. It's the second door on the left."

"Thanks, buddy," Matt said as he bent down to say hello to Charlotte. "Hi, sweetie! Can Uncle Matt get a hug?" he asked of Charlotte. The little girl, a bit shy, used her mother's skirt as a defense mechanism. With a look of uncertainty on her face, she clearly didn't recognize Matt from his last visit over a year ago.

Bending down to Charlotte's level, Jazmine said, "You remember Uncle Matt, don't you, sweetie?"

Still hesitant, Matt relieved the pressure and said, "That's okay. I'll make sure to get my fair share of hugs over the next few days."

"Ha-ha, I'm sure you will. Come on, baby girl, time for bed-dy-bye," Jazmine said as she picked up the toddler and headed upstairs. Halfway up the stairs, she said to Matt, "Matt?"

"Yeah?" he responded as he was looking into the living room just off the foyer.

"Feel free to make yourself at home."

"Okay, thanks"

"It's real nice having you here. There's beer in the fridge. Oh, there's also wine in the rack on the island," she continued.

"Okay, Jazmine. Thanks," Matt replied as he walked down the very long hall, as most halls in brownstones are, and into the kitchen. Matt was a bit startled when the lights came on as he entered the kitchen, prompting a "Shit!" Looking around, he realized the lights must be on a motion sensor. As he looked through the different bottles of wine in the rack, Matt settled on a Cabernet Sauvignon. By no means was Matt a wine connoisseur, but he always enjoyed drinking it. He thought, one day, maybe in the future he'd get to spend some time in France, maybe Spain as well, wandering through the various vineyards, learning all the differences and subtleties of the grapes and the growing processes, but that wouldn't be possible for some time, so the best he could do tonight was drink. As Matt was searching through the drawers for a corkscrew, already into his third without any luck, Jamal walked into the kitchen.

"I still can't believe you're going to Saudi Arabia," he said as he walked directly to a drawer not yet searched by Matt, opened it, and removed the corkscrew. Taking the bottle from Matt, he started opening it as efficiently as a sommelier.

"Looks like you've done that before?" Matt said, clearly impressed, reaching up to the rack above the island and taking three glasses down.

"Just two. Jazz doesn't like red wine."

"Oh, we can have white. I don't care either way."

"No, it's okay. There's an open bottle in the fridge," Jamal responded as he popped the cork.

"Yeah, well, you know I've always wanted to go to the Middle East. Now I get to work there."

"How long?"

"A year minimum."

"Minimum?" Jamal asked with trepidation in his voice.

Taking a seat at one of the bar-type stools at the island, Matt slid his glass over to Jamal, indicating to him to fill 'er up, with Jamal waving the bottle above, using both his hands and arms in dramatic fashion to indicate the wine must breathe first.

"Breathe. The wine must breathe, my friend," Jamal said.

"Yeah, well, the Matt must drink," he said as he slid his glass even closer to Jamal. Getting the point that Matt's thirst outtrumped the wines needed to breath, Jamal filled Matt's glass and then his own.

"So, Matt, are you looking forward to Saudi Arabia?" Jazmine asked as she walked into the kitchen.

"Is she sleeping?" Jamal asked of Charlotte.

"Like a log. I have never seen a kid go out as fast as her. Her head hits the pillow and she's gone."

"That's dang good," Matt said.

"You ain't kidding," Jamal interjected.

"So? Looking forward to Saudi Arabia?" she asked again while she opened the refrigerator and removed a half-full bottle of white wine, Chardonnay.

Taking a sip of wine, Matt said, "Oh yeah." Taking a second sip, he reiterated, "Definitely."

"Let's go into the den." Jamal picked up the bottle of Cabernet Sauvignon. "Matt, grab the Chardonnay," he said, looking back as he walked out of the kitchen and down the hall.

Looking at Jazmine as he grabbed the bottle and started walking toward the door but waiting for Jazmine and allowing her to go first, Matt said in a low tone, "Den? You guys have a den?"

Looking back at Matt and giving him a bit of an eye roll, she said, "He wanted a den. It was a requirement. We looked at three other places without dens before we found this one. Whatever! He makes the money, not me. I'm just a government employee like you."

"I can relate with that," Matt responded.

The den was beautifully wood paneled with walnut, a fireplace, and plenty of books. It reminded Matt of Father John's office at St. Pat's back home. After an hour or so, Jazmine had gone up to bed while the boys finished off three bottles of wine, all red, while smoking cigars. The den was the only room Jazmine allowed smoking. As the hours went by, Jamal and Matt talked about the past with great fondness even though each would be perfectly justified in bitching and complaining about it.

"Do you remember that summer we spent day after day looking for Lafitte's treasure?"

Jamal asked, sipping his wine, "Are you kidding me? Of course."

Matt said, looking back toward Jamal and then back out the window into the cool autumn night once again, "I bet Lafitte didn't live this well."

Jamal took a long draw on his cigar, looked at the lit end, and then took another draw. "I don't know. He was a very successful pirate. But this ain't bad either. You like the cigar?" Jamal asked of the cigars they were smoking.

"Yeah, damn good," Matt said, puffing his cigar and watching the lit end change in brightness. "I have a friend in DC who used to get me some every once in a while."

"Oh yeah? Who's that?" Jamal asked. "You want a whisky?"

"Sure," Matt responded. "Friend of mine. She works at USAID and went down to Cuba a few months back for a humanitarian effort."

"Humanitarian, huh?" Jamal asked with great skepticism.

Looking back at Jamal again, Matt asked, "Yeah, why?"

"Well, USAID?" Thinking for a moment to make sure he worded the sentence correctly as lawyers tend to do, Jamal said, "I just don't believe their efforts or motivations are strictly humanitarian on Third World development. I mean, do you really think they aren't promoting American interest?"

Thinking for a few seconds, Matt responded, "Well, yeah, maybe, but—"

"But what, Matt?" Jamal said, cutting Matt off. "You're going to be in Saudi Arabia in a few days, working at the embassy, and you don't think they'll be intelligence agents stationed there posing as embassy employees?"

"CIA?" Matt asked.

"Hell yeah! Who knows, you might be CIA for all I know," Jamal said while raising his eyebrow.

"Ha-ha, yeah, no. I'm not CIA," Matt said.

"Well, would you tell me if you were?" Jamal asked just before sipping his wine.

"Nope, and—"

"And you'd have to kill me, right?" Jamal said, cutting Matt off.

"Exactly."

"I'm just saying. Be careful. The election is coming up. New administration. New agendas. Personally, I don't know why you do it. I told you, I could get you in at my firm anytime you want. Don't you get tired of working for government wages after all the hard work you've put in over the years?" Jamal asked as he stood up and moved behind the leather chair, leaning on the back of it. "I just think you deserve more."

"More? Like what? This?" Matt asked, gesturing around the room. "You know this isn't me. I don't want more. I don't need more, Jamal," Matt said, slightly offended at Jamal's suggestion.

Walking over to Matt and standing by him, both men looking out the window onto the night street, Jamal said, "I'm sorry, Matt. It just seems like…at times—and I don't mean this in a bad way. I say it because I care. It just seems as though you never recovered from Samantha."

"Samantha?"

"Yeah, Samantha. You haven't been in any significant relationship since Sam. What's that, eight years ago now?"

"Jesus, it's not like I don't date or get laid or anything."

"That's not what I am saying. What I'm saying is, you don't give anyone a chance. What happened to that one down in DC? The girl you told me about. What was her name? Britney? Bethany?"

"Baily."

"That's it, Baily. Wat happened with her? For nine months, every time we talked all you did was brag on her."

"She just wasn't the one," Matt said dismissively.

"What the hell does that mean?" Jamal said, starting to get frustrated.

"I brought up our future and she wasn't having it!" Matt snapped.

Starting to regret the conversation he had started, Jamal looked toward Matt and said, "I'm sorry, bro. I didn't know."

"I know you didn't know. You didn't know because I didn't tell you. I didn't tell anyone. It's not the kind of thing you go bragging about. She was a great girl. A smart girl. A pretty girl. Successful," Matt said with an undertone of disappointment in his voice. "You know how she ended it?" Matt asked his friend.

"No," Jamal said in a somber tone. "How?"

"A goddamn note. She said she wasn't ready for a long-term relationship or marriage. Just in not so many words. It was to reminiscent of what happened with Sam, and I didn't want to talk about it."

"I'm sorry—"

"Nothing to be sorry about," Matt said, cutting Jamal off mid-sentence, taking his last sip of wine. "I'm heading to bed." And he walked out of the den.

"Night," Jamal said with no expectation that Matt heard him.

Over the next few days, the two old friends, along with Jamal's family, would enjoy themselves immensely. They picnicked in the park and watched some ball games. Jamal and Matt had a boys' night out, but what was most enjoyable for all, especially for Matt, was the day they took Charlotte to her first Broadway show, *Marry Poppins*. The day Matt left was a hard day for all. Both Matt and Jamal did their best to hide their emotions as best they could though they knew how the other felt without having to say a word. Jazmine gave Matt a big hug and a kiss and wished him well, imploring him to stay safe. But what was the hardest thing for Matt to do was saying goodbye to Charlotte. Of all the hugs over the past few days that Matt received from Charlotte, this one was, by far, the longest and tightest and the hardest to let go of.

Chapter 14

SAUDI ARABIA

As Matt's plane touched down at the airport in Riyadh, he was feeling somewhat uneasy. On the approach, Matt was looking across the empty desert, miles and miles of nothingness, desolation as far as the eye could see, and he couldn't help but wonder why he or anyone would choose to be there.

After retrieving his bag, he walked out of the baggage claim area and into the main terminal. Almost immediately he heard his name being called.

"Laurent! Laurent!" a man called out, a black man in a fine dark-blue suit and red tie. "Hey, Laurent." Matt walked toward the man since no one else was calling out his name, and the chances of two Laurents arriving in Riyadh on the same day from the same plane where probably quite slim.

Reaching out his hand to Matt, the man said, "Hi, I'm Stevens. I'm from the embassy. I'm here to bring you to the compound."

"Hi, how you doing?" Matt replied while looking around, trying his best to absorb his surroundings as quickly as possible.

"Come on, let's walk," Stevens said. "It's never a good idea for us to stay in one spot too long."

"Really? That bad?" Matt asked, looking over at Stevens while trying to keep up.

"Well, it can be. Better safe than sorry, right?" Stevens said, looking over to Matt with a grin.

The men exited the main terminal, and Matt felt that hot blast of dry desert air hit his face. The difference from inside the airport was astounding. Stevens walked over to a desert-camoed Humvee with two Marines in full camo fatigues with weapons waiting for them. One of the Marines opened the rear door while the other took Matt's bag and his well-worn attaché case and put it in the back of the vehicle. Once everyone was securely in place, they sped off.

Loosening his tie a bit, Matt looked over to Stevens and said, "It's hot as hell here." Matt could hear a chuckle from the Marines in the front seat but ignored it.

"Haven't you ever been to Vegas?" Stevens asked, looking over at Matt for a second while he shuffled through some papers.

"No, never," Matt replied. "Don't gamble."

"Well, it's kind of like Vegas but without all the fun," said Stevens, which drew another chuckle from the front seat.

"Oh, okay. I'm from Louisiana."

"Oh hell, you guys get some heat down there. Humid, right?" Stevens said, looking at Matt one more time.

"It ain't this hot," Matt replied.

Stevens handed a file to Matt. "We have about thirty minutes until we get to the compound, so why don't you try and get through as much of that as you can. It will be helpful to get as up to speed as quickly as you can."

"Thanks," Matt said as he took the file from Stevens and then looked out his window at the vastness that surrounded him. As Matt started to go through the material, he realized it was all personal information and not related to his work. There was his compound identification pass, his apartment keys, a poorly printed map of the compound with a red circle around what he assumed was his apartment building, and three pages of dos and don'ts.

"What's it like?" Matt asked Stevens.

"Here?" Stevens replied.

"Yeah, what's it like?" Matt said again.

Thinking for a moment, Stevens replied as he looked over to Matt, "Necessary. You'll figure it out. In a few weeks, you won't even notice the heat and you'll get used to all the security procedures we have in place."

"How long you been here?" Matt asked.

"Nine months last Wednesday."

"How much longer you got?"

"Around 451 days," Stevens replied. Matt assumed Stevens's precision was an indication of his readiness to move on, so he felt no need to ask.

As they got closer to Riyadh, Matt started to notice more and more structures—some small homes, with both men and women working in gardens, men working on vehicles, and some just sitting around in groups. Matt was surprised at how many modern buildings there were as they entered Riyadh. The contrast of the empty desert and the business of the metropolitan area struck him as odd, but he assumed by this point that odd was going to become the new normal.

The Humvee pulled up to a compound checkpoint, manned by Marines in fatigues who have no shortage of weapons. After checking all the vehicle's occupants' identification, the three-cylindrical columns that once blocked the path lowered into the ground to allow passage. The commanding officer of the post walked out and said hello to Stevens. Matt assumed they were well acquainted. Leaning down a bit to make eye contact with Matt, the major said, "How are you doing, Mr. Laurent? Welcome to Saudi Arabia. Now if you just follow me, I'll bring you over to your new home." And he walked away.

"Thank you, Major," Matt said, louder than he had planned, leaning over Stevens in an effort to have the officer hear him. Sitting back comfortably, he said to Stevens, "Sorry."

One of the Marines who was sitting in the front of the Humvee was nice enough to carry Matt's bag into the building. Matt felt bad afterward that he didn't catch his name or have the opportunity to thank him before he left. Stevens showed Matt around his apartment which was nicely furnished and even had a balcony. The location of Matt's new home for the next year was nice being he was on the third floor and he had a nice view. From his balcony, he could see not only much of the compound but also into the civilian area as well. Matt was also surprised when Stevens open the refrigerator to show it was almost fully stocked with food, saying, "Don't get used to this. This is a one-time deal for new arrivals." Stevens then reached in the refrigerator and pulled out two bottled water, offering one to Matt, which he gladly accepted.

"I'm going to leave you alone now to get settled in. If you need anything or have any questions, just call. Hit 0 on the phone and it will connect you with the compound operator, and they can connect you with anyone here or back in the States for that matter." Reaching out his hand while standing in the doorway to Matt, Matt walked over to shake it.

"Thanks, Stevens."

Stevens started walking down the hallway toward the elevators, and Matt started to close the door when he opened it up quickly and yelled down to Stevens, "Do you have a first name?"

Stevens walked into the elevator out of Matt's sight and yelled back, "Mark."

Matt wasn't required to report for duty for forty-eight hours, so he used the time to relax and recover from the jetlag, something he had heard a lot about but had never experienced firsthand. He walked around the diplomatic compound, doing his best to get his bearings, and in doing so, met some nice fellow employees. A woman by the name of Marge, a secretary at the embassy and the wife of one of the diplomats, gave Matt a tour. Marge, somewhat older than Matt, was an attractive woman from Seattle and had been in Saudi Arabia going on two years. Matt wasn't aware that, often, the US government hired wives or husbands as nonessential embassy personnel in an effort to make the diplomats' lives and post assignments more bearable though Marge also told him that many of the nonessential posts were filled with Saudi civilians.

The next day, Matt walked over to his assigned building, Building S. It was barely 8:00 a.m. and the heat was already unbearable. In the lobby of Building S was a security checkpoint, manned by Marines who helped Matt find his office. When he walked in his office, he was surprised at the size and that it was bigger than he had expected though simply furnished. Sitting back in his chair, behind his desk, he reached into his attaché case and pulled out some supplies, pens, a pad, and a calculator. The phone rang, and when it did, Matt looked up at the clock on the wall which read eight thirty.

"Laurent here," Matt said into the phone.

"Mr. Laurent?"

"This is."

"This is Deputy Station Chief Douglas's secretary. Could you please find your way up to meet with Chief Douglas at 9:00 a.m.? He is located on the fourth floor, room 4A. Just ask when you get to the fourth floor."

"Yes, ma'am," Matt responded before hanging up the phone.

Matt made sure to leave early to give himself time to find the chief's office. He wanted to stop by the men's room to comb his hair and make sure he was presentable. When he first started at State, he made the mistake of showing up to a superior's office with his tie a bit too loose. It didn't go unnoticed, and he never made that mistake again.

As Matt approached the secretary's desk, she said, "You can go right in, Mr. Laurent. The deputy chief is waiting for you." Looking at his watch as he walked into the office, he saw it was eight fifty-eight.

"Hello, Mr. Laurent. Nice to meet you," the deputy station chief said, walking around his desk to meet Matt and shake his hand. "Have a seat."

"Thank you, sir."

"How was your flight coming in? Have a seat," he said again, pointing to the chairs in front of his desk.

"Fine, just fine," Matt replied as he sat down.

"Bullshit! That flight is terrible. Where did you connect through, Germany?"

"No, sir. London," Matt stammered.

"Either way, it's a long flight. Long layover. Cheapest way possible. But then again, it is taxpayer money, right?"

"Yes, sir."

"So you all settled in? Apartment okay? Any problems?" he asked though Matt doubted his sincerity of the questions and quickly realized that if he had had a problem, the station chief was not the man to tell.

"No, sir, no problems. The apartment is great, thank you."

"Well, listen, Laurent. I've seen your file, and it looks good, very impressive," he said, looking up at Matt. "I just want you to understand that overseas post can be difficult at first. The food, the culture, the customs all take time to understand, but we expect you to pick up on them quick."

"Yes, sir, of course," Matt responded as he adjusted himself to sit taller in his seat.

"What we do here is very important," the deputy station chief said as he leaned forward in his chair, folding his hands and placing them on his desk. "It's very important to the security of the United States and also to the mission of spreading our way of life around the world."

Sitting across from him, Matt could tell this was a serious man who took his job and responsibilities to heart. Douglas, in his early sixties, had been stationed all over the world at different points in his career. He had served eight years in the Army before losing a leg curtesy of an antipersonnel mine in a rice paddy in Vietnam. He was on his third tour of duty, when on patrol—*bam!* He woke up in a Saigon military hospital three days later. It was 1973, and after being medically discharged, he went to college and earned his degree in international studies and joined the State Department; that was over twenty years ago.

The deputy chief got up from his desk and, with a noticeable limp, walked over to the coffeepot and poured two cups of coffee. Watching him, Matt couldn't help but be impressed. He also wondered if he'd have such a long and distinguished career himself. Douglas put the hot cup of coffee in front of Matt and noticed Matt's trepidation.

"It's Ethiopian. Drink it. You'll never have better." Sitting back in his chair, Douglas took a sip carefully. "Listen, Laurent, I expect my people to take their jobs as seriously as I take mine."

"Yes, sir," Matt said as he took a sip of the coffee, surprised at just how good it was. And to this point, it has been his experience that the United States government was unable to acquire good drinkable coffee at any level.

"I want you to read our field manual and the ethics and code of conduct manual and know them inside an out, understand?"

"Absolutely, sir. Yes, sir."

"Good. I think you'll be just fine. Just learn from your colleagues and pick up as much as you can, and you'll be good," Douglas said as he stood up and walked around his desk to walk Matt to the door. Standing up, Matt shook the deputy chief's hand and walked to the door.

"Thank you, sir. I'll do my best, sir."

"Good, good. I'm going to have one of your colleagues stop by your office later and you can shadow him for a few days. You'll start getting regular assignments next week."

"Thank you, sir. Pleasure to meet you," Matt said before turning and heading toward the elevator.

When Matt arrived back at his office, there was a woman sitting in the small waiting area outside his office. In the waiting area outside his office, in addition to some chairs, there was a receptionist's desk, and Matt was told he would be assigned a secretary in time but was a little surprised it was so soon. As Matt got closer, the young woman, a Saudi native, stood and extended her hand.

"Hello, Mr. Laurent. I am Fatin Najjar, your new secretary," she said as she shook Matt's hand.

"Hi, how are you? Wow, I didn't think I'd see a secretary for a week or so."

"Oh, I don't know. I was assigned to Mrs. Morgan for the last six months, but I was reassigned and instructed to report to you late last week," Fatin said in a low tone.

"Okay," Matt said as he walked toward his door. "Come on in, have a seat." Matt pointed to the chairs in front of his desk. Sitting down at his desk, looking across his desk, Matt said, "I'm sorry if I look a little shocked. I wasn't expecting…"

"A Muslim?" Fatin said in a less timid voice.

"No, no," Matt said as he sat up taller in his chair.

"It's okay. I understand."

"What do you understand? I meant I was surprised I already had a secretary assigned to me," Matt said in a defensive manner.

"Well, I've been working at the US Embassy for just over two years and have been assigned to four different staff members, and all were a bit shocked when I showed up."

Readjusting himself yet again, Matt said, "Well, I guess I am a little surprised. I didn't realize until I got here that many employees were Saudi citizens."

With her legs crossed at the ankles, wearing an abaya as well as a somewhat stylish head scarf, she looked across at Matt, shuffling papers about his desk, clearly, to some extent, uncomfortable. Matt said, "I'm sorry. I don't want to give you the wrong impression, I'm just—"

"Not to worry, Mr. Laurent," Fatin interjected.

"No, no, my reaction was inappropriate, and I apologize," Matt said, interrupting Fatin.

With a smile creeping across her face, almost as if she enjoyed making him feel a bit uncomfortable and leaning forward slightly, she said, "Well, thank you. I accept your unnecessary apology."

"So, Fatin?" Matt asked, doing his best to get the pronunciation correct.

"Yes, Fatin, Fatin Najjar."

"That's a lovely name. Does it mean anything?"

"Yes, intelligent. It means 'intelligent.'"

"Oh, okay," Matt said, ruffling his brow a bit.

"You look a little surprised," Fatin replied.

"Well, I would have thought it had to do with your beauty," Matt said.

Thinking about her response very carefully for a second or two, Fatin said, "Thank you, Mr. Laurent, but I believe my former supervisors would say that the meaning of my name is indicative of my work." She said it with pride.

"I'm happy to hear that, and don't doubt your ability," Matt said in a consolatory manner. "What is your background, if you don't mind me asking, Mrs. Najjar?"

"Ms. Najjar."

"Ms. Najjar," Matt said in correction.

"Unfortunately, I was not able to attend college, but I did graduate first in my class in high school and then went on to secretarial school."

"Why didn't you go to college?" Matt asked, sitting forward in his chair, leaning on his desk.

"My father didn't feel it was in my best interest, seeing that eventually I would be married and would not need to work," Fatin said succinctly.

"Oh. Are you engaged?" Matt asked.

"No, no, not as of yet anyway."

"Do you like working here at the embassy?"

"Yes, yes, I do, very much so. It's different than my normal life outside of this compound."

"How so?"

"Well, can I speak frankly?" she asked.

"Of course," Matt reassured her.

"Because outside these walls, my value as a human being drops by half. Outside these walls, I am subservient. Inside these walls, I am, for the most part, treated with respect."

"That's disappointing. I'm sorry, Fatin," Matt said as he moved about his chair.

"Well, thank you, Mr. Laurent. It's just the way things are here. The way they've always been though working at the embassy does allow me to practice my English."

Walking over to the mini fridge built into the wall console on the other side of his office, Matt removed two bottles of cold water. Fatin had felt a lock of hair fall from her head scarf while talking with Matt and took the opportunity to slip it back under her scarf without Matt noticing. Matt wrapped each of the bottles in a napkin he got from the stack neatly piled on the counter and handed Fatin the bottle and returned to his seat.

"Obviously you've been here longer than I have, so if you don't mind, I'd like to draw from your knowledge and experience from time to time?" Matt suggested.

"That would be fine, Mr. Laurent."

"Good, good," Matt said as he opened his water and took a long swig.

Standing up from his chair, Fatin did the same and walked toward the door. Matt looked at his watch and saw it was nine forty, realizing he was scheduled to meet his direct supervisor at 10:00 a.m. As they walk toward the door, Matt behind Fatin, he couldn't help but notice Fatin's lovely shape, and as difficult as it was to discern in her abaya, Matt used his imagination.

"Thank you, Ms. Najjar. You can just get settled, and I'm sure things will pick up in the days and weeks to come." Stepping back into his office for a moment and then back out into the outer office, he said, "I hope you brought a good book."

Fatin, one step ahead of Matt, reached into her oversized bag and pulled out a copy of *One Hundred Years of Solitude* by Gabriel Garcia Marquez. Matt gave Fatin a smile and said, "I've been meaning to read that. Is it good?"

"Yes, it is," she said as she opened the book to the page with the bookmark, turning her attention from Matt to her book.

"You should try *To Kill a Mockingbird* by Harper Lee," Matt said, never missing an opportunity to share his favorite book with others.

"Is it good?" she asked as she wrote the name down on a yellow legal pad by the phone.

"Very," Matt said as he walked toward his door.

"Thank you, Mr. Laurent," Fatin said with a hint of a smile on her face.

Later that night, Matt was alone in his apartment, sitting on his balcony, smoking a cigar. Jamal's coworker was able to score a box of Cohiba, and he had given Matt a small supply to tide him over until he found a reliable supply in Saudi Arabia. Looking toward the night lights of Riyadh and wondering what the people were doing back in Jefferson Parish or even New York only enhanced Matt's feelings of isolation. Looking at his watch, seeing it was just past midnight, he quickly calculated the time difference between Saudi Arabia and Jefferson Parish, two places separated by thousands of miles and incalculable ideas. He had been dreading of calling home all day, but the time was right.

Poking out his cigar on in the side of a small ceramic cup filled with water since he didn't have an ashtray, he thought to himself, he had better pick one up soon. Picking up the phone, he said, "Hello? Can you please connect me to 504-555-8183? Thank you."

The phone rang a few times before he heard Father John's voice say, "Hello?"

"Father John!" Matt said with excitement in his voice, clearly happy to hear a familiar voice.

"Matthew?" Father John questioned.

"Yes! It's Matt."

"How are you, Matthew? Is everything okay?" the father asked.

"Yes, yes, Father, everything is good. You know, still getting settled in, but yeah, I'm good. How are you, Father? How are my folks?" Matt asked as he walked around his apartment randomly.

"They're all okay. As good as you'd expect, I suppose."

"Yeah, I know what you mean."

"When did you talk to them last?" Father John asked.

"Ummmm, it's been about a week."

"Matthew?" Father John said with surprise in his voice. "You haven't called them since you got to Saudi Arabia?"

"Well, I called the day before I left Washington, but I've just been so busy I…"

"Matthew, call your folks. Let them know you are okay."

"I will, Father, but you know—"

"I understand, Matt. Believe me, I do, but you need to call them," the father said, interrupting Matt before he could finish his sentence.

"I miss our talks, Father," Matt said, looking back at the night lights of the city.

"I as well, Matthew. Call your parents, Matt. We'll talk soon." Matt heard the line go dead.

Matt checked his watch once again and decided to take a shower before calling his parents. It had been a long day, and Matt still wasn't used to the heat which he found odd being he grew up in it. Though he hadn't spent any long periods back in the Parish for a dozen years, he just assumed he lost his tolerance for the heat.

After his shower, he changed into his pajamas, the old-fashioned kind with the buttons down the front. They were cotton and lightweight and suited the desert climate. Growing up, Matt's family never had air-conditioning, and even now he was reluctant to use it, but when he did, it was used sparingly. So he went into his bedroom and turned it on; he figured no need to cool the whole apartment down since he'd be sleeping shortly. He felt bad that he needed to prepare mentally to call home. He could never understand—truly understand—why talking with the people who should know him best was so difficult. Over the years, he had spent countless hours trying to figure it out, trying to understand, but never really knowing why. He liked to pretend that it didn't bother him, but it did. He called the operator once again.

"Hello?" Karen said in her distinctive Louisiana drawl.

"Hey, Momma, how are you?" Matt said. And even though Matt had always felt his and his family's relationship was challenging at best, he was delighted to hear his mother's voice.

"Hi, baby!" Karen said with excitement. "It's Matt!" she yelled to the others in the house. "How are you doing? Are you okay?"

"Yep, yep, I'm okay. Everything is okay here. How is everything back home?"

"Oh my goodness, it's so nice to hear your voice, Matty."

"I miss you too, Momma. How's Dad? How's Grandma?" Matt asked as he sat down, lifting his legs and putting them up on the sofa, feeling a little guilty that he often found it difficult to talk to his parents though, on this night, it wasn't difficult at all.

"Well, you know your daddy. He's your daddy, but he's okay. He's out front working on that old Ford with Johnny."

"Grandma?" Matt asked.

"Well, she ain't doing so well. She's forgetting a lot lately. She was making soup the other day, and after she put it in the bowl, she forgot to turn the fire off."

"The burner?" Matt asked.

"Yeah, the burner. Well, it eventually melted the handle and smoke filled the house and Mrs. Grisly next door saw the smoke coming out the window and she called the fire department and, well, we decided she's better off moving in with us here."

"Oh well, Jesus, Momma. That could have ended badly."

"You ain't kidding," she agreed.

"Is she there now?" Matt asked, hoping to talk to his grandmother.

"Well, she's down for nap. You want me to wake her?"

"No! No, Momma, that's okay. I'll talk to her next time," Matt said, making sure his mother understood.

"I love you, Matty. Amen! I love you!"

"I know, Momma. I love you too."

"But I'm not sure you know exactly how much I love you, Matty. I know your daddy and I aren't exactly—"

Matt cutting her off said, "I know, Momma. It's okay."

"The older I get, the more I realize it's not okay, Matt. I just wish—"

Cutting her off again, Matt said, "Me too, Momma. I got to get to bed, Mom. I'll call you next week. I love ya."

"I know, Matty. I love you too."

"Bye, Momma. Make sure to tell everyone I said hi and I love them," Matt said.

"Oh, I will, Matthew. I love you, honey."

"Love you too, Momma," Matt said as he hung up the phone.

Chapter 15

As the days passed, they slowly turned into weeks and then a month, and Matt was starting to feel comfortable in yet another home. His routine was becoming as normal as it would have anywhere else in the world though Saudi Arabia was unique. No escaping that, Matt thought. But for the most part, things were going well, and Matt had even made a few friends.

Robert Whitman, or Bob, as he was known around the office, Warmed up to Matt rather quickly. Bob was from Pine Bluff, Arkansas, but went to LSU and even played on the 1986 SEC conference championship team. As a second-string defensive back, he didn't get many snaps on defense, but because of his speed, he played on special teams as well. Another friend Matt made was Allen Kim, a first-generation Korean American from Portland, Oregon. What Matt liked so much about Allen was his sense of humor. Allen would always crack a joke when things would get to tense though he could really only do this among his peers. The one time Allen made a joke in a department meeting with his superiors, well, it didn't go over well, and he never made that mistake again.

As Matt, Allen, and Bob walked into the embassy cafeteria, Matt saw Fatin sitting alone, eating her lunch, and reading *To Kill a Mockingbird*. Over the past month, Matt had noticed Fatin had a regular routine and saw that she always sat alone.

"Hey, Matt," Allen said as they walked toward the food options.

"Yeah?" Matt replied as he kept looking over at Fatin. Matt did his best to hide the fact that he was attracted to Fatin and not just for her obvious beauty. He was impressed by her; he was intrigued with what he had learned from small talk with her over the last month and was anxious to learn even more.

"What do you call someone who doesn't get into Harvard Law?" Allen asked.

Looking over at Fatin, Matt asked, "What's that, Allen?"

"A Georgetown Law student," Allen said, which drew a laugh from Bob.

Looking over at Bob and shooting him a look, Matt asked, "Where did you go to school?" lowering his brow.

"AU Law," Bob said.

"Exactly," Matt said, feeling a bit of a retribution.

As Matt selected his food—a steak and cheese sandwich and fries, a piece of chocolate cake, and water—he kept looking back at Fatin, still sitting alone. While the three men were selecting their food, Bob said under his breath, "I don't trust these sand niggers," referring to the Saudi man serving the hot food. Matt was completely taken aback by Bob and pretended like he didn't hear it though he couldn't forget it.

As he was standing at the register, waiting to pay for his food, he looked toward Fatin again and saw her looking at him but quickly looking away. Allen had waited for Bob and Matt after paying the cashier, and when they were both in earshot, Allen said, "Where we are sitting?"

Looking over at Fatin one more time, making sure she was still sitting alone, Matt said, "I'll catch up with you guys later" and walked off toward Fatin's table.

"Where is he going?" Bob asked Allen as they both watched him walk away.

As Matt got closer to Fatin's table, he realized he didn't know what he was going to say, and he could suddenly feel his mouth becoming dry with a lump forming in his throat. With his tray in his hand and now standing at her table, he was relieved when she looked up at him and said, "Mr. Laurent. Do you need me for something?"

In a quick response, Matt said in succession, "No, no." As subtly as possible, Matt licked his lips to extricate the dryness that might hinder a coherent sentence.

"No…I just thought I'd join you for lunch," Matt said in such a way that would give Fatin the opportunity to say no if she chose.

A bit hesitant, Fatin looked around the cafeteria and said rather sheepishly, "No, I don't mind. That's okay. Please sit." She moved her tray slightly to make room for Matt's. "You do know this isn't really condoned?" she asked him while scanning the cafeteria to see what kind of attention they might elicit.

"What's that? Eating?" Matt said, trying to make light of the situation while not taking his eyes off hers.

"You know…, the fraternization between staff and subordinates," she said, a bit surprised that he wasn't aware.

"Well, this is just lunch," Matt said as he took a bite of his sandwich. With a mouthful of steak and cheese, he chewed and covered his mouth as he said, "We both have to eat, don't we?"

After a few second's pause, Fatin said, "Yes, yes we do" as she took a bite of her salad.

"Mr. Laurent—"

"Matt," he said, interrupting her.

"Excuse me?"

"Matt. You can call me Matt."

"I'm not sure—"

He interrupting her once again. "I mean when we are alone. You can call me Matt when we are alone. And since we are alone…" With his back toward the rest of the cafeteria and Fatin looking out over the room, Fatin said, covering her mouth slightly, "There are a lot of people looking at us." Looking back over his shoulder, Fatin lowered her head in embarrassment. Taking a bite of his sandwich, he said, "Not that many."

"Seriously, Matt?" she said, a bit exacerbated.

"Well, not all of them anyway. You look like a long-tailed cat in a room full of rocking chairs."

"I'm sorry?" she said, not understanding the southern reference.

Clearly not as concerned with what others might think as Fatin was, Matt assured her that he read through the State Department Code of Ethics manual, and he found no clause that would prohibit them from eating lunch together. While this was reassuring in the immediate, Fatin started to wonder.

"Mr. Laurent."

"Matt," he corrected her again while covering his mouth full of food.

"Matt...Can I call you Matthew instead?" She asked hesitantly after calling him Matt.

Matt nodded his head. "Yeah, sure."

"Matthew, I just don't think it's a good idea."

"You don't think lunch is a good idea?" he said, trying to lighten the mood and attempting to get Fatin to relax. Getting a bit of a chuckle and a relaxing smirk, Fatin said before taking the last bite of her salad, "No, I think lunch is a great idea. In fact, I find it to be a necessity and try to do it daily." Wiping her mouth with a napkin and closing her book, Fatin stood and said, "Thank you for your company, Matthew, but there is work to be done" and walked away from the table and out of the cafeteria.

Still sitting toward the wall and facing away from the rest of the people in the cafeteria, Matt tried his best to determine the number of eyes burrowing into the back of his head, but to no avail. He sat alone, facing the wall and enjoyed the rest of his lunch, all the while a small grin would encroach on his mouth in between bites, as pleased with himself as the cat who ate the canary.

After lunch, Matt had a few meetings, rather innocuous in content, and then went back to his office. As he walked down the hall and with the outer office in sight, he could see Fatin was on the phone and seemed to avoid making eye contact, so he just walked by and into his office. Sitting at his desk for a few moments, contemplating his next move, he saw the little light on the phone go out. He immediately called Fatin over the intercom.

"Fatin, can you come in here for a moment?"

"Yes, Mr. Laurent," she replied over the handset.

Fatin picked up her yellow legal pad and pen, and with the other hand, she fixed her abaya and made sure no hair had fallen out from her head scarf. She took a deep breath and walked into his office, standing in front of his desk, waiting as Matt, with his head down, was writing something and had yet to acknowledge her. Without looking up, Matt said, "I'll be with you in a moment." He motioned to her to take a seat, and she did. He picked up the phone and dialed an extension; he got voice mail.

"Harry, Laurent here. I was wondering if we could get together sometime tomorrow to talk about that thing we discussed earlier. Well, just get back to me when you can. Thanks."

Sitting patiently with her right foot crossed over her left, back erect, and ready to take notes, Fatin was under no illusions. She is fully aware of what Matt was doing. Her first reaction was to be offended that he would think he can fool her with his childish antics, but her second reaction, which came also immediately after the first, was to be flattered. As she sat there looking down at her pad and then up again at Matt, just having finished his voice mail ploy, she admitted to herself that Matt was an attractive man. As Matt hung up the phone, Fatin said, "Mr. Laurent, can we talk a second?"

"Talk? Talk about what?" he replied while moving papers around his desk in an attempt to further his ruse.

"Mr. Laurent—"

"Matt," he corrected her.

"Okay, Matthew. Matthew, I think I know what you're doing and I—"

"Oh yeah. What am I doing?" he asked, leaning forward, finally giving her his full attention.

Leaning forward herself, Fatin said, "This can't happen."

Reassessing himself and contemplating his words carefully, Matt said, "Is there anything wrong with wanting to get to know you better?" He sat back in his chair, pleased with himself.

Slightly hesitant herself in her response, she sat back in her chair a bit and, for the first moment, felt an ease she hadn't felt before with Matt. "No. No, I guess not. What do you want to know?"

"How old are you?" Matt asked quickly.

Leaning forward in her chair and placing her hands on his desk and calling his bluff, she said, "You know. Matthew, I'm sure you have access to my file and probably know full well how old I am."

Knowing he was caught, a slight grin came across his face and he said, "Yeah, yeah, I do."

"So how old am I?" Fatin asked Matthew.

"You're twenty-five. You live with your mother, father, and younger sister. Your older brother works in construction and has two wives and four children."

"Very good. What else?"

"You were a straight A student and never married."

"Yet," Fatin interjected.

"Sorry?" Matt asked.

"I haven't married *yet*," she corrected him. "But from what I understand, neither have you."

Somewhat unsure of her inference, Matt asked, "You haven't gotten engaged, have you?"

"No, not yet," she said, starting to enjoy the playful banter.

"No, no, I haven't either," said Matthew. "And how would you know that anyway?" Now very intrigued.

"While I might not have access to your file, I am not without my own resources. So why is that?"

"Why is what?" Matthew asked.

Why haven't you gotten married yet?"

"Oh, that," Matthew said, playing coy. "Well, there was a girl once."

"What happened?"

"Didn't work out," Matt said after a short pause.

Sensing that wasn't a subject Matt cared to talk about, Fatin quickly asked a follow-up question though in a different direction. "How old are you? As you know, I don't have access to your file."

"I'm thirty-one."

"What else?" she asked.

"I'm from Jefferson Parish in Louisiana. My parents still live down in Louisiana. That's where I'm from." Pausing for a second, he said, "I had an older brother...but he's dead."

"Oh, I'm sorry."

"It's okay. It was a long time ago." Looking up at the ceiling and thinking a moment, he said, "It's been twenty years. Jesus," not realizing he said out the last part loud.

"I'm sorry, Matt," Fatin said, leaning in and not realizing she had called him Matt and not Matthew.

Looking back at Fatin, Matt collected himself and said, "It's okay. It really is. I just don't think about it much."

"Maybe you should. Maybe you should remember him more often," she said.

"Maybe you're right," Matt said, nodding in agreement.

A few seconds of silence passed though not awkward silence, just emptiness. In fact, it was somewhat odd at how comfortable they were both feeling. Fatin said, "So what do you want, Matthew? I've noticed the way you've looked at me over the past few weeks, and I'd be lying if I said I wasn't flattered." Taking a deep breath and a few seconds to build up the courage to admit out loud, she uttered, "I'd be lying if I said I didn't find you attractive as well." A feeling of shame came over her almost instantly, causing her to unconsciously lower her head. She hated that feeling more so than any other emotion. She hated that she couldn't openly express how she felt without some adjoining emotion that made her feel guilty over the first.

"I don't know what I want. I mean, I know I want to get to know you better but—"

"And you know that that is not possible, Matthew."

"Anything is possible."

"There's too much difference. Difference between us, where we come from. Our religion. Our families. Everything," she said as she stood up from her chair in a huff and walked toward the door. Matt got up quickly and watched her walk out of the room. For the rest of the day, Matt would not leave the office and would intentionally wait until Fatin had left for the day before he went home.

Chapter 16

A few days had passed, and to say things were a bit awkward between Matt and Fatin would be an understatement. Matt did his best not to ask Fatin for anything he could avoid, and Fatin did a good job at looking busy when Matt walked by even when she wasn't. Sitting in his office thinking, Matt hit the intercom button on the phone. "Ms. Najjar? Would you come in here for a moment?"

"Yes, sir," Fatin's voice came through the speaker.

This time, as Fatin walked through the door, Matt wasn't trying to look busy at all; in fact, he was waiting for her. "Yes, Mr. Laurent?" Fatin said.

Matt was surprised and thought to himself, *Back to Mr. Laurent apparently?*

"I need you to attend a meeting at my apartment tomorrow night at 7:00 p.m. We need a notetaker," he said in a matter-of-fact manner.

She was thinking to herself for a second before she said anything. "But, Mr. Laurent…Matt?" She felt this was another ploy.

"Don't worry. It's just a working dinner meeting, and we need someone to take notes and minutes." Feeling a little uneasy and fidgeting a bit, Fatin stammered, "Well…I guess I can…"

Cutting her off, he said, "Okay, be there at 7:00 p.m. sharp. I'll make sure to leave you the address before I go home tonight, and I'll make sure the guards will be expecting you. Thank you." He finished and proceeded to pick up the phone and dial with Fatin still a bit taken aback, standing there motionless. Matt said, "That'll be all, Ms. Najjar," dismissing her.

Slightly dumbstruck, Fatin stood there for a few more second which triggered Matt to say into the phone, "Hold on, Allen." Looking at Fatin, he said again, "That'll be all." And she walked out of the room.

The next night, Matt was in his apartment, finishing getting ready. He was tying his tie while looking into the floor-length mirror mounted to the backside of his bedroom door. As he slid the knot up tight to his collar, the small photograph of him and Samantha sitting on a blanket in Central Park that was taken on a day of no distinct significance other than they were together and were in love caught his eye. It was in an antique putter frame sitting on the nightstand, the same location Matt would place it, regardless of city, whenever he wasn't in any sort of relationship. Matt walked over and sat on the edge of the bed, picking up the frame and looking at the photo. He could remember with great detail the events of that nondescript day. It was a cool autumn day, evident from the sweater Samantha was wearing in the photo; they ate meatball subs with provolone from Tony's Pizza on Sixty-Third. Matt and Sam had so many of those ordinary days, days where nothing significant happened, but it was the accumulation of those ordinary days that made what they had so special. Matt always thought that people put far too much significance and unintentional pressure on themselves and their relationships on days with high expectations. Anniversaries and birthdays, days like that were overrated in Matt's opinion. The days that matter most were the random days—autumn day in the park, a lazy Sunday curled up on the sofa, each reading a book or walking through one of New York's many museums, listening to Samantha explain the artwork while never totally understanding but never once losing focus on what she was saying. Matt heard a knock on the door. Opening the drawer of the nightstand, Matt placed the framed photo back in the nightstand, not sure if or when it would appear again.

As Matt walked toward the door, he stopped momentarily to glace in the hallway mirror, checking his teeth as he was eating chips and spinach dip a bit earlier. With his teeth free of any greenery, Matt took a deep breath and opened the door.

"Hello. Come on in, Fatin," Matt said, letting Fatin walk past, allowing him to close the door behind her.

A bit surprised she didn't see any other people in Matt's apartment, she asked, "Are your guest not here yet?"

"No, not yet. Will you join me on the balcony?" Matt asked while leading the way.

"You have a lovely apartment, Matthew," she said as she looked out over the lights of Riyadh, the warmth of the desert heat still lingering.

Thinking to herself for a moment, Fatin said, "Listen, Matthew. I know no one else is coming."

Not surprised that Fatin had saw through his ruse, Matt looked over at her, but only for a quick moment, and the back over the lights of the city before saying, "And you still came?"

Turning toward Matt and using her hands to turn him slightly toward her, she said, "I like you, Matt. I really do. But—"

"But what?" Matt asked, now looking right at her.

"But you know how complicated this would be," she said, looking down at Matt's feet, avoiding eye contact. Using his index finger to lift her chin and compelling her to look into his eyes, he said, "I don't care" before he started kissing her. She didn't resist or hesitate to kiss him back, and while the first few seconds of the kiss would be considered by most standards as soft and sweet, it soon became teemed with passion.

The couple moved back into the apartment as the desert night started to cool as it often does. Sitting down on the sofa, they continued to kiss, sometimes softly and other times more intensely. Only in between kisses did they talk about both the good and the bad of this unsanctioned relationship. Fatin was sitting with one leg folded under the other, and the tie that Matt had spent so much time getting just right was now off and thrown on the chair. Fatin halted the kiss and said, "Do you know what a mess this is going to create?" As she leaned in for a few more pecks in between his answer, she reached up and removed her head scarf, exposing her jet-black hair for the first time to Matt.

Never fully stopping kissing her, Matt said, "You're beautiful." Giving her another kiss before saying, "Yeah, I know. We'll just have to keep it a secret." All the while, Matt, being as respectful as one can be in such a situation, caressed Fatin's shoulders and arms, eventually deciding to risk moving his right hand down to her waistline. She didn't object.

As the pair softly exchanged kisses on the lips and then the cheeks, Fatin made her way toward Matt's ear, making sure to leave a path of ever so tiny kisses on the way. Reaching her destination, she whispered, "Where is the bedroom?"

The two walked down the hall, hand in hand to the bedroom.

After that first night, others would follow, both always aware of the consequences of their romance. A few weeks had passed from that first night together and the couple had been able to maintain their secret. Both realizing the significance of this relationship, it wasn't a subject they needed to remind the other about. Over the past couple of weeks, Fatin would make up excuses to tell her family in order to sneak off with Matt. Most of the time they would have dinner in Matt's apartment or watch a movie. Fatin loved American films but didn't have a satellite at home, so getting to see many movies she had heard about but never seen was enjoyable for her. And then there was the lovemaking. Being that Matt was Fatin's first, she was, as most are during their first time, a bit clumsy and awkward and, of course, nervous, but that didn't last long. In just that short period of time, Matt was amazed at what a lover she had become.

Often, the office was the most difficult for them, even more difficult than the nights they made love and Fatin had to say good night, leaving Matt's warm bed and his secure embrace. The office was like a covert operation, each always having to be aware not to let a glance linger too long or to let a first name slip in front of other employees as they have become so accustomed to using when alone. The fact is, the stress of keeping the love affair hidden with no clear outcome was beginning to overwhelm both Matt and Fatin.

Every Monday morning at ten o'clock sharp, Matt's department held its weekly staff meeting. Deputy Station Chief Douglas would facilitate each individual department meeting, all of them taking place on Mondays throughout the day. Matt was no fan of staff meetings and was thrilled when they were over. He didn't like speaking in large groups and was always just better at dealing with people on a one-on-one basis.

It was already late November, just a week past Thanksgiving. The State Department made sure each of the embassy employees received a turkey for Thanksgiving as to try to maintain the traditions the American employees were accustomed. On the nights she was able to sneak over, it was always just more convenient for Matt to cook ahead of time than to wait for Fatin as she had frequently offered to cook. Matt didn't want to waste time cooking together when they could be doing more enjoyable things together. Matt used the turkey he received to make Fatin a full Thanksgiving dinner, and she was surprised at the variety of food that Matt was able to prepare. The turkey and stuffing, the mashed potatoes and gravy, and of course, the sweet potato pie. He neglected to tell Fatin that he had called home to get all his grandma's recipes beforehand; he just figured she didn't need such details.

As Matt and the other employees made their way into the conference room for their weekly meeting, Allen asked Matt, "What happened to your Saints? Man, they blew it."

Taking their seats around the oval table, Matt responded, "Yeah, I know I saw. It was terrible."

"Okay, okay, everybody take your seats," Chief Douglas said as he walked in the room, last as always. He was the kind of man who liked to start meetings on time and didn't care for no dillydally as he called it. Sitting at the head of the table, he put on his glasses, but only halfway up his nose; that way, he could look over them when needed being as he only needed them for reading. Looking at the file in front of him, he said, "Who handled the Miller case?" He peered over the top of the frames of his glasses waiting for a response. "Kim?" he asked.

"No, sir. That was Matt," Allen replied, giving Matt a kick under the table simultaneously. Matt's mind was wandering, and he hadn't heard the question.

"Yes, sir. That was me, sir. I handled Miller," Matt said, adjusting himself in his seat and making eye contact with the chief.

Leaning over to the man on the side of him, Bob whispered, "Seems a little preoccupied."

Hearing Bob, Matt ignored him but stammered slightly, trying to recall the case, "Ummm...yeah, the Saudis dropped the disorderly conduct charges, and they, the whole family, returned to the States on Friday."

The chief gave Matt a stare over his glasses a bit longer than Matt or anyone in the room ever enjoyed; it was anything but a look of satisfaction. The meeting continued for another thirty minutes and then adjourned. But throughout the meeting, Matt's mind seemed to wander, something that rarely ever happened to Matt in meetings. In fact, Matt, in his short time at the embassy, was widely regarded as the most talented lawyer though, on this day, his mind was somewhere else. As everyone was making their way out of the room Bob, under his breath, said to no one in particular, "That's why they keep us away from the natives."

Matt heard Bob and choose to ignore it, Allen giving Matt a pat on the shoulder as they walked toward the door, as a fellow teammate might do after the coach tore you a new one.

"Laurent, hold up a minute," the deputy station chief said as he signed a document for his secretary. "Make sure that goes through today," the chief said to her as she walked away.

"Yes, sir," the young lady replied as she walked out the door, leaving only Matt and the chief in the room. Still standing, the chief said to Matt, "Take a seat."

"What's going on, Matt?" the chief asked, looking directly at Matt from a standing position.

"I'm sorry, sir. I just lost focus," Matt replied.

"That's not what I mean."

"I'm sorry, sir. What do you mean?" Matt asked, a bit puzzled at where the chief was going, but more aware than he let on.

"I think you know what I mean."

"Sir?" Matt asked.

"The rumors, are they true?"

Knowing full well there was no need to lie anymore, Matt said simply and shamefully, "Yes." The shame, as most shame does to most people, triggered that effect as it does in anyone with pride to drop his head, but not shamefully in that he was regretful of his and Fatin's relationship, but shameful in that he felt like he had let the chief down. The way a child feels when he lets a parent down by not doing his chores or for getting bad grades.

The chief walked over toward Matt and sat down in the chair next to him. Running his finger through his thinning hair and finishing off with a double-handed scratch of the bald part of his scalp, he asked, "What is the nature of the relationship?"

Still looking down, Matt raised his head to make eye contact with the chief before he said, "Love."

"Fuck, Matt. You know this goes against every goddamn regulation we have? Shit!" he said as he sat back in the reclining office chair, gathering his thoughts for a moment. "You know, I understand these things happen, but you need to understand they are not like us."

"Chief?" Matt said as his head turned quickly to look at the chief, a bit surprised to hear that from him of all people.

"Now just wait a minute. I can't blame a man for falling in love, but it should have never got this far. I mean, I'm sure she is a wonderful girl, but do you have any idea what kind of problem this can create?"

"Yes, sir," Matt replied as he looked back down at the desk, his anger at the chief's remark quickly shifting back to shame.

"No, Matt. I'm not sure you do because if you did, I wouldn't be in this position right now." Standing up and walking around to the window and looking out onto the embassy courtyard, he said, "You know I'm a Southern boy too?" Not getting a response from Matt, the chief snapped, "Matt!"

"Yes...yes, sir, I do." The chief's raised voice seemingly snapped Matt out of whatever state he was in. Thinking to himself for just a second, he said, "Georgia? Right?"

"Macon, Georgia. Beautiful part of the country," he said with pride.

"Yes, sir."

Looking over at Matt, he said, "When I was in high school, I had an affair, a relationship, whatever you want to call it. With a girl, a black girl."

A bit surprised at what he just heard, not so much because he thought the chief was a racist on anything, though the chief never did seem to overly sympathetic to people of color. Matt never thought of him as a racist, but rather just from a different generation where lots of people thought a different way about race.

"We kept it a secret for months. Shit, we had to. It's Macon, Georgia, for Chrissake. It was 1965. Well, word got out. Not really sure how, but you know? Small town and all." The chief paused and took his seat at the head of the table, seemingly waiting for Matt to respond. A few seconds had passed, and he did.

"What happened?" he asked.

"They beat her bloody. She was in the hospital for a week. A month later, I left for boot camp and never went back. Doubt they'd want me back. My daddy disowned me, never talked to that son of a bitch again." The chief paused for a few seconds, his thoughts taking him back to that painful time. "He died a few years ago," he said of his father, looking over at Matt again.

Matt realized then that the chief wasn't so much mad at the relationship as he was concerned for Matt and his future, but only second to Fatin. "What happened to her?" Matt asked.

Looking down at the table, the chief said, "I don't know." Raising his head and looking over to Matt, he said, "I just want you to understand what you're getting yourself into. I know you are an educated man and you're going to make your own decision, but keep in mind it isn't going to be easy, especially for her." Pausing again, the chief continued, "But then again, what is?" He stood up from his chair and turned toward the whiteboard behind him, writing. "I'm going to forget we had this conversation and play dumb for a bit though it's not in my nature. I'll give you some time to figure out what you want to do." Looking back over his shoulder at Matt, now standing, he said, "But I think you know as well as I do you aren't going to be able to stay at State and maintain this relationship." Turning back toward the board, he continued writing, and he said, "Do what makes you happy, Matt."

Matt gathered up his things and placed them into his attaché case, the gold leaf thread having been worn clean for some time now. Matt walked toward the door. Looking back at the chief, Matt asked, "What was her name?"

"Eugenia. Gene," he said without turning around.

Chapter 17

O ver his time stationed at the embassy, Matt had become friendly with many of the Marines stationed there. He often felt for them being that many had wives and children back home, but unlike diplomatic personnel, they weren't allowed to get their wives' nonessential jobs. Jamal and Karen would sometimes send Matt care packages with all sorts of things. Jamal sent over a full box of Cohibas and a bottle of Jamison and Karen had sent over new socks and underwear as well as two bottles of Matt's favorite hot sauce, a brand only found in Louisiana. Two of the Marines were on guard duty that Matt had become friendly with over the time he had been stationed in Saudi Arabia. He had made a deal with them, and it only cost him two hundred Saudi riyal, the equivalent of fifty dollars and two of Jamal's Cohibas for each Marine to turn a blind eye and allow Matt to borrow one of the embassy's four-wheel drive vehicles. Being it was Saturday night and most of the bigwigs were back in Washington for a congressional oversight hearing on Monday, the risk of getting caught was limited, so Matt figured if he was ever gonna get away with it, now was the time.

He and Fatin had driven about an hour's distance outside Riyadh into the desert to lessen the chance of getting spotted by anyone. The stress of sneaking around had started taking a toll on both Matt and Fatin. The temperature was almost mild, being it was well into December. People who haven't spent any time in the desert think it's always hot when, in fact, it can get quite cold, especially in the evening hours. It was a beautiful night in the desert, the sun beginning to drop off in the distance, dry of course, but a breeze was sweeping across the sand that was creating what could only be described as desert whitecaps. They had found a nice spot on the blindside of some sand dunes, out of sight of any vehicle that might pass by. Both lying down on a blanket, the sand still warm from the sun beating down on it all day, it radiated up through the couple. The sun was encroaching on the horizon, stretching the shadows longer and longer with each passing minute.

"Why are you so quiet tonight?"

"I don't know. Just thinking, I guess," Matt replied.

Rolling over on to her side to be able to see Matt's face, Fatin said, "Thinking about what, my love?"

"Us," he replied.

"What about us?" Fatin asked with concern in her voice.

"I just don't know."

Sensing the seriousness of the direction the conversation is taking, Fatin sat up to look into Matt's eyes though he wasn't making much an effort to look into her eyes just yet. "What are you talking about?" she asked with determination in her voice, leaving no doubt that she expected an answer.

"The deputy chief knows about us," Matt said as he looked over to Fatin. He sat up and with a look of concern on his face he said, "I have to resign."

Without hesitation, Fatin said, "No! You can't."

"I have to, Fatin. I have no choice. The only other option is for us to end it, and I'm just not going to do that."

Looking off into the endless desert, taken aback by this revelation, Fatin said forcefully, "I can't let you do that. I'll quit." Her head snapped around to make eye contact with Matt. "What are you going to do if you resign? What are you going to do here in Saudi Arabia if you don't work at the embassy?" she asked in a somewhat frantic manner.

Looking out into the desert, the darkness increasing as the sun seem to hold on for only a few more moments, and then looking back toward Fatin to make eye contact with her, he said, "There are oil companies, or I could teach."

"Matthew, you never once talked about working in business or teaching," Fatin replied. "You love the law. You told me all you ever wanted to do from when you were a child was to become a lawyer."

Picking up a handful of fine desert sand and watching it slowly flow through the spaces between his fingers, he looked to Fatin and said, "Well, how would you feel about coming to the United States with me?"

Fatin sat in silence for more than a few seconds, again looking off into the distance which didn't give Matt a feeling of reassurance. He brushed the sand residue from his hands and reached over and took her by the hand and said, "Fatin," drawing her attention. She looked over to him and he said, "I love you. I want to spend the rest of my life with you."

"I love you too, Matt. But—"

"But nothing," Matt interrupted, not allowing Fatin the opportunity to deny him.

Leaning over and kissing Matt with a series of intermittent kisses, Fatin said, "But where will we live in the United States?" Grabbing Fatin by the shoulders and pushing her back slightly to create space to get a better look at her face, which was now occupied by a large smile, Matt leaned back in and started kissing Fatin.

"Are you sure this is what you want, Matt? Do you really want to leave the State Department?" Fatin managed to ask as Matt continued to kiss her.

"No, I don't really want to leave State, but given the choice, I choose you."

"But why?" she asked.

"Why? Why? Because I love you! Because you are as rare as a desert butterfly. Because I can get another job, but I'm not about to walk away from love, from you."

"Where will we live?" she asked with obvious excitement in her voice.

"Jefferson Parish," Matt said, looking at his watch and realizing the hour. "We should get going."

Matt started picking up the blanket and shook the sand off, and Fatin grabbed the other end; working together, they folded the blanket, and Matt placed it on the back seat of the vehicle. It was unusually quiet between the couple as they started their drive back into Riyadh before Fatin asked, "Why Jefferson Parish?"

Not taking his eyes off the road, Matt said, "Well, I'd want my family to meet the woman I hope to marry one day," glancing over at Fatin to catch any response, facial or other, before looking back down the empty desert road.

"I'm just a little surprised. I thought you'd want to go back to New York," she said, looking over at him.

"I thought about that, but I just think I..." He stopped himself midsentence and looked over at Fatin again. "We need to head back to Jefferson Parish. It's just what I think I need to do right now." But what Matt didn't say to Fatin as they drove down the empty road was he connected New York City with Samantha. He didn't think it would be fair to Fatin if everywhere they went and everything they did was measured consciously or subconsciously against his past experiences. The last thing he wanted for what he thought of as his future wife and mother of his children was to live in anyone's shadow.

By the time they got back in Riyadh, it was already dark and, therefore, safe to drop Fatin off close to her family home. When she walked inside, her mother, Asisa, and little sister, Azzah, were in the kitchen, preparing food for the next day. Kebabs, both chicken and lamb, sambusa filled with spiced potato and lentils, and other traditional Saudi dishes filled the table for the next days' meals. Fatin noticed her favorite sweet cake, Basbousa, at the other end of the table. Made with coconut and rose water, it always made Fatin think about her childhood every time her mother made it.

Fatin's family were definitely more progressive than most Saudi families, which was often a source of embarrassment for her father, Aiman. Asisa was far more assertive than most Saudi women, and her example has had a profound influence on her daughters. As much as Aiman would complain and tell Asisa how her disobedience made him look bad, his love for his wife and his daughters would always overshadow any feeling of self-consciousness. And while Asisa was proud of each of her daughters' confidence, she was also well aware of the limitations their culture afforded them.

"Hello, Momma. Hello, Azzah," Fatin said as she leaned back against the kitchen counter.

"Do you remember Hamza?" Azzah asked Fatin, looking up while continuing to thread lamb onto steel skewers.

Thinking to herself for a second and crunching her face up slightly in an effort to concentrate, Fatin said, "Nasser's son?"

"Yes, Daddy thinks he'll make a good husband for me one day," Azzah said with an abundance of sarcasm not meant to be overlooked.

"Yuck!" Fatin said, making an unpleasant face.

"Right? I know," Azzah said.

"How old is he?" Fatin asked her mother.

"I think he's twenty-four," Asisa said. "He's not that bad." She looked up at Fatin.

"Momma, he's gross!" Azzah chimed in.

"He is in medical school," Asisa said to bolster her argument.

Standing up from the table and walking toward the door, Azzah looked back and said, "I want to go to university myself and support myself." She walked down the hall to the bathroom.

Sitting down in Azzah's seat and taking over her skewering duties, Fatin asked, "Where is Father?"

"He is with your uncle." Pausing for a moment, Asisa said, "Are you asking because you have a secret to share?" Looking over at Fatin, hoping to catch a glimpse of what was on her mind and in her eyes. But Fatin gave no clues with her eyes or her expression; in fact, she didn't respond.

"What's his name?" Asisa asked her daughter.

Still looking down at her work, Fatin simply said, "Matthew."

"And when I do go to university, I want to go to Cambridge in England," Azzah said as she walked back into to kitchen and over to the refrigerator, removing some juice and pouring it into a glass she retrieved from the dish strainer. "That's where Stephen Hawking went." She took a drink that emptied half the glass. Looking at both Fatin and then her mother, Azzah said, "What's wrong?"

"Nothing's wrong," Fatin said quickly, not allowing any time for her mother to answer the question.

"Azzah?"

"Yes, Mother?" Azzah replied before finishing off her juice, tapping on the bottom of the glass with her other hand as a child does, making sure to get every last drop.

"Do you remember that white lace tablecloth Teete gave me before she passed on?"

"I think so," she said though she didn't remember.

"I want you to go into the linen trunk in my room and find it. I believe it's at the bottom."

Not terribly pleased that she had to miss out on whatever conversation she anticipated would take place when she left the room, she walked toward the hall door, dragging her feet the whole way. As she was halfway down the hall, Asisa said in a raised voice, "Make sure you refold everything correctly before putting it back." Looking over at Fatin, she placed her hand on top of Fatin's hand, impeding her from doing her work.

"Fatin?" Asisa said, prodding her daughter to look up from the table.

As Fatin looked up from the table and over at her mother, at a pace that concerned Asisa, she asked, "Do you love him?"

After a short pause, not because she wasn't sure if she loved Matt or not, but simply because she knew the ramifications of their love, she replied, "I do. Very much, Mother." With certainty in her voice and her eyes so full of moisture, a tear cascaded down her cheek. Asisa, like any mother, reacted, catching the tear before running off her cheek. "Then why do you cry, my love?"

"We are going to move to the United States," Fatin said, fearing a reaction of disappointment from her mother. Fatin and her mother have always had a close relationship, more so than Fatin and her father or even Asisa and Azzah. Fatin never felt inhibited to talk with her mother as many of her friends had with their mothers growing up. Their relationship was unique that way, and that's what each of them cherished about it.

"I don't think it's in here!" Azzah yelled from the bedroom.

"It's in there! Keep looking!" Asisa yelled back.

"How long have you known?" Fatin asked her mother as she started to skewer the lamb and vegetables again.

"Oh, well, over a month. At least."

Surprised by the response, Fatin asked, "Why didn't you say anything?"

"There was no need. I was pretty sure you were in love." Looking at Fatin, she said, "It's easy to see when someone is in love—in your look. Love is not easily masked."

"Does Father know?" Fatin asked with a bit of hesitation in her voice, afraid of the answer.

"No. Now your father, well, he's a man. A man doesn't always see love the way we do." Looking away from her mother and back at the lamb, Asisa said to her, "There are things your father chooses not to see as I'm sure many fathers choose not to see in their daughters."

"I found it!" Azzah yelled from the bedroom once again. "I know, refold everything."

"I love you!" Asisa yelled back to her youngest daughter.

Looking over at Fatin and seeing that she was still carrying a heavy weight, Asisa asked, "What is wrong, my love?"

"I feel shame. I worry how disappointed Daddy will be in me, how it will look."

Asisa wiped her hands with a towel and stood up from the table, and walking behind Fatin, placing her hands on either side of her face from behind, making sure to only use the palms, tilting it back slightly in order to kiss her daughter on her forehead, she said, "Don't you worry about your father. I'll take care of your father." Asisa walked over to the sink and began washing her hands.

Looking back over her shoulder at her mother and feeling better than she did before their conversation, Fatin said, "I love you, Mother."

Still washing her hands, Asisa asked, "When will you go to the United States?" Asisa turned toward Fatin while she dried her hands.

"Matt said he already made arrangements to get my green card expedited, so less than a month."

The women heard the front door open and close, which prompted a look between them and for Asisa's finger to move up to her lips. "Shhhhh. Keep your secret, and I'll take care of everything, sweetheart."

Aiman walked into the kitchen, a large man with an extended belly, tall, but definitely more round than tall, but tall nonetheless. "Hello, my ladies," he said in a jovial voice.

"Hello, Father!" Azzah yelled from the bedroom, still doing her best to fold all the blankets and sheets she had removed in order to find the lace tablecloth her grandmother had given her mother and hoped she would receive one day.

"We are well, Father. How was your day?" Fatin asked, clearly in a much better mood.

"Wonderful, wonderful wonder," he said as he started to snack on the vegetables designated for the next day's meal.

"Hey!" Asisa said. "Stop that! That's for the guest tomorrow."

Rubbing his big belly, he said, "Okay, okay, okay." Aiman had the habit of repeating things in threes. Everything in threes.

"Where is my baby, baby, baby?" Aiman asked in his booming voice to no one in particular as he walked down the hall.

"I'm in here, Father," Azzah said.

Sitting back down in her chair, Asisa said to Fatin in just above a whisper, "You just do what you need to do. Your happiness is my happiness, so go and be happy, my love."

Standing up from her chair and kneeling in front of her mother, she wrapped her arms around Asisa and said into her ear, "I love you, Mommy."

Chapter 18

K aren had just finished collecting the laundry from the clothesline and was making her way to the back door of the screened-in porch. She could hear the phone ringing through the screen door and knew she had better hurry because last she looked, William was fast asleep on his recliner in front of the TV. As she walked into the kitchen, she picked up the phone mounted on the wall closest to the back door and was pleasantly surprised to hear Matt's voice on the other end.

"Hey, Momma!" She heard come through the phone.

"Hi, baby. How are you, baby?" Before he could answer, she said, "Your daddy's fast asleep in his chair." She poked her head into the living room just enough to confirm her suspicion; she was right.

"I'm good, Momma. How are you?" Matt asked.

"Oh, you know, happy as a clam."

"Hey, Momma?" Matt said, waiting for a response.

Taking a seat at the kitchen table, Karen began to separate the clothes, colors from white, so she could fold them, the phone wedged between her shoulder and ear, a skill it seems all mothers acquire at one point or another. "Yeah, baby?" she responded, not missing a beat with her folding.

"I met someone," Matt said.

"Oh, well, that's wonderful, Matt. Does she work at the embassy?" Karen asked.

"Yeah, yeah, she does work at the embassy."

"I'm sure she's beautiful. Is she from the South?" Karen asked as she stuck her finger through a hole in one of William's socks before throwing it into the trash barrel just a few feet away.

"No, no, she's not from the South, Momma. She's from Saudi Arabia. Her name is Fatin," Matt said as he almost held his breath waiting for his mother's response but thought better of it. After a few seconds of silence that seemed much longer, Matt said, "Momma?"

"Yeah, well, that's nice, Matty," Karen said.

"We're moving back home, Momma. Back to Jefferson Parish," Matt said, again with bated breath, waiting for a response.

"Do you think that's a good idea, Matthew?" Karen asked as she got up from the kitchen table and walked over to the door separating the kitchen from the living room. Looking in at William, sleeping in his chair. Three beer cans on the TV tray next to his recliner, no doubt empty, she started to ask, "Do you think—" She walked back into the kitchen but was cut off by Matt before she could finish her question.

"I love her, Momma." He let the emptiness of the silence float in the air for a few moments, separated by thousands of miles. He said again, "I love her, Momma."

Walking over to the back door, leaning on the doorframe and looking out into the backyard, hearing Matt say he was in love brought a smile to his mother's face. Though always worried about her youngest and only living son, she had learned through the years that Matt was a strong personality, a boy and now a man who, for the most part, with few exceptions, made well-thought-out decisions. Curling the phone cord around her finger, the natural worry a mother takes on when having a child, regardless if that child is an infant or a full-grown man, kicked in. It didn't bother Karen that Matt had fallen in love with a Saudi girl; what worried Karen was how it would bother others in the community and possibly even those in her own home. Though she knew when Matt made up his mind, there was no changing it. She said, "Well, if you love her, Matty, I'm sure I will too."

"Thanks, Momma. It means a lot," he said.

"Well, you're my boy, and I love you, Matty," Karen said in a tone of assurance that clearly wasn't present just a few moments prior.

"I'll give you a call as a soon as I get my plans figured out."

"Okay, baby," Karen said, holding the phone to her ear for a few moments more until she heard the line was dead. She hung up the phone and continued folding her laundry, thinking, finishing with a single sock, the second in the pair to the one with the hole; she walked it over to the trash can and placed it in with the other. It wasn't that Karen didn't want her baby back home or that she had a problem that he had fallen in love with a Saudi girl; it was that small part of the old South that still existed in Jefferson Parish that concerned her.

* * *

Three weeks had passed, and everything was a falling into place. Matt opened his eyes, still lying in bed, the call to prayer waking him up as it had every morning since arriving. He thought to himself that he will miss it when they leave Saudi Arabia.

Matt had given his notice of resignation, and they were planning on leaving in just a week's time. Fatin's immigration status and green card was approved in an expedited manner, thanks to Deputy Chief Douglas. Douglas was undoubtedly going to miss Matt though he would never tell him so. He showed his appreciation for Matt by pulling some strings and allowing Matt to move into the next chapter of his life unfettered.

It was Monday morning again. As like every Monday morning since Matt arrived in Saudi Arabia, Matt and his colleagues had their department meeting. Chief Douglas, not one for fanfare or anything like that, made a simple announcement at the end of the meeting that Matt would be moving on from State and heading back to the United States. Though everyone had already known for the past few weeks, a slight murmur still occupied the room for a second or two.

"Matt, would you like to say anything being this is your last department meeting?" Deputy Chief Douglas asked Matt.

A bit surprised and not at all prepared, Matt said, "Ummmm, yeah." He looked around the conference table at his colleagues. "I just want to thank all of you for making my time here an enjoyable one. It was an honor to work with each of you."

"Well, I'd be lying if I said I wasn't a little jealous that you'll be eating gumbo and apple pie in just a week or so. And while I know our cafeteria staff does a great job and tries their best, they can't make a goddamn apple pie worth a shit!" Douglas said which drew a laugh from everyone in the room.

"I'm not kidding. I've been here for two years and ain't had a decent piece of pie yet. So, Matt, enjoy that pie, son," he said, looking over to Matt.

"Thank you, sir," Matt replied.

"Okay, people, dismissed. Make your country proud," the chief said as he walked out of the room before anyone else.

Matt gathered his paperwork and stuffed them into his attaché case, and as he did, his coworkers wished him well and took turns shaking his hand and patting him on the back. As Matt exited the room, he overheard Bob say to the closest colleague to him, "Fucking guy is putting his dick before country, if you ask me."

As Matt walked down the hall behind Bob, he debated for a second or two and decided that since this opportunity wouldn't come again, he'd take it. So he said loud enough for Bob to hear him, "You know, Bob, I've been pretty patient over the last bunch of months with your ignorance and lack of empathy or compassion for what we do here. Personally, I don't know how you can stand yourself." Matt walked past Bob and continued down the hall.

Bob, embarrassed by the retort and momentarily at a loss for words, said, "Well, at least my wife isn't a sand nigger."

In one fluid motion, or at least that's the way Matt would describe it every time he told the story for years to come, Matt swung around, fist clenched, and connected square on Bob's jaw. Bob fell onto his ass and reached for his jaw, looking up at Matt looking down at him, Allen and a few others staring in shock, some wishing they had done what Matt just did. Taking a step closer to Bob, still sitting on the floor, not even attempting to get up, Matt said, "You know, Bob, you're the problem in this world. People like you who think you're better than other people." Shaking his head, Matt said again, "I just feel sorry for you." And walked away.

A week later, Matt and Fatin would arrive in Jefferson Parish.

Chapter 19

January 17, 2001, Jefferson Parish, Louisiana

Matt and Fatin arrived at the Laurent family home by taxi at about three in the afternoon. Even though it was January, and it can get quite cold in Louisiana in January, this day was unreasonably warm. As the taxi made its way out of the city limits of New Orleans and closer to Jefferson Parish, Matt rolled the window down. It had been sometime since he'd been back home, since he had smelled the murky air blowing off the bayou, since he had heard the frogs, cicadas, and crickets fill the humid air with what Matt considered the symphony of the swamp, and he didn't want the window to impede his senses and deprive him of these simple pleasures that he just now realized how much he actually missed.

When they pulled up in front of Matt's boyhood home, he saw not much had changed. Making a quick scan of the front yard which was often filled with William's mechanical projects, Matt noticed an older model Ford pickup truck he had never seen before. Matt thought it looked like a '62, maybe a '63. And then he saw his momma, Karen, who was sitting on the porch with a pitcher of lemonade on the table beside her chair, a glass half full in her hand, beads of condensation running down onto her hand. When Karen saw the taxi pull up in front of the house, she rose to her feet.

Putting her glass down on the table, never taking her eyes off the taxi, not wanting to miss who stepped out, she finally set her eyes on her baby boy. Her hands clutch her chest and then both up to her mouth, she made her way down the rickety stairs, still in a state of disrepair; she took firm grip of the railing to assure her steadiness.

"Matthew!" she said as she made her way toward the taxi. Karen wasn't a big woman; in fact, she was rather petite though, over the last few years, she has felt the negative effects of age, as most people do. Her movement could never be confused with running; though she was moving as fast as she could, the gout in her foot didn't allow for running. A more accurate description would be a quick walk.

"Matthew! Matthew!" she said the closer she got to the taxi.

Fatin had gotten out on the driver's side, and by the time she had walked around the car, Karen and Matt were clinched in an embrace he feared she would never let go. Then for one inexplicable moment, he feared she would.

"Hi, Momma," Matt said as he pulled away just enough to kiss her on the cheek.

Karen pulled away for a moment to get a better look at him and then hugged him once more, saying, "Well, it looks like you've been eating just fine" before finally letting go and stepping back.

"Yeah, Momma, I've been eating just fine." Taking a few steps over toward Fatin, Matt took her by the hand and said, "Momma, I want you to meet Fatin." Karen took the two steps needed to get into handshake range before Fatin raised and offered her hand to Karen. "So nice to meet you, Mrs." Fatin started to say before being cut off and, needless to say, being a bit surprised by the embrace Karen imposed on her. After a second or two of awkwardness, Fatin's frigid reaction relented, and she eagerly reciprocated the warm embrace.

Karen broke the embrace, only to step back a moment, looked both Matt and Fatin up and down, reached over, and pulled them both back into an awkward three-way hug.

"Dear Jesus, I missed you so much. Amen!" Karen said as she broke her hold on the couple but continued to hold on to Matt's hand.

Realizing he'd need both hands to get the bags, he said, "Momma, I have to get the luggage."

"Oh yes, of course," she said before letting go of her baby boy's hand.

With his duffel bag slung over his shoulder, his attaché case in one hand, and pulling Fatin's oversized suitcase with the other, Matt struggled across the overgrown lawn. When they got in the house, Karen immediately started apologizing for the condition of the house even though it is well-kept—as kept as it could be anyway. The years of neglect by William weren't totally concealable.

"Oh, my Lord," Karen said as the three of them crowded the kitchen. "Matty, why don't you take your bags into the other room."

"You have a lovely home, Mrs. Laurent," Fatin said as she looked around the kitchen.

"Well, that's nonsense. You call me Momma, you hear? Take a seat, honey," Karen said, pushing the one unmatched kitchen chair away from the table.

"Oh, thank you, Mrs. Laurent," Fatin said as she sat down, conscious to ease the weight of her body down slowly on the questionable chair.

"Momma!" Karen said as she reached into the fridge for a fresh pitcher of sweet tea.

"Momma," Fatin corrected herself.

Karen placed the pitcher of sweet tea on the table and reached into the cupboard for three glasses. She held each of them up to the light one at a time, looking for watermarks or spots of some kind though none were found; in fact, none was ever found. It was a habit she had since childhood. Two of the glasses Karen placed on the table matched while the other did not. The unique and unmatched glass was the remnant and sole survivor from a set well over twenty-five years old. The three others had all been broken through the years though the only one Karen could remember breaking was the one that caused her to need to get eleven stitches to close the wound. She always assumed William had broken the others while drunk and then hid the evidence.

"Where's Pop, Momma? Work?" Matthew asked loudly from the other room.

"Oh yeah, he's working. Hopefully, he brings home dinner because I haven't had a chance to get to the market this week," she said as she poured sweet tea into each of the glasses. She reaching across the table and took Fatin's hand into hers. "My goodness, you are lovely, my dear."

Fatin's timid nature kicked in, triggering her eyes to lower to the table before working their way back up to Karen's. "Thank you, Mrs. Laur—" Catching herself before finishing, she corrected herself, "Momma. Thank you, Momma."

"Don't mind me asking, honey, but aren't you supposed to wear something on your head?" Karen asked as she pointed toward Fatin's head, swirling her finger about.

"It's called a hijab, Momma," Matt said as he entered the kitchen.

Looking over to Matt and then back at Fatin, Karen said, "A hijab?" muttering the pronunciation.

"Hijab," Fatin said slowly, making sure to hit each syllable clearly.

Looking over to Matt again, Karen gave it another try. "Hibab?" she said with slightly more confidence.

"Yeah, Momma, that's just fine," Matt said in surrender.

"Hibab," Karen said once again. Pleased with herself, a smile came across her face.

"Well, Matt wanted me to wear it." Looking up from her seat at Matt, love overflowing from her eyes, she said, "But I decided not to wear it here in America."

Sitting down next to Fatin and before taking a sip of his sweet tea, Matt said, "Yeah, well, I don't want you to change for me. I don't want you to change for anyone." After his sip of tea, he said, "You are who you are, and that's why I love you."

Smiling at her son, Karen looked over to Fatin and said, "That's right, baby. You are who you are though it would be a shame if you covered up that beautiful long hair. And besides, Jesus wants us to be who we are, sweetie."

Matt couldn't help but to give Fatin a look of "told you so" before saying, "Are you tired, honey? You want to lie down for a bit?"

"Oh my goodness, that's right," Karen said. "You kids had a long flight and you must be exhausted." Looking over at Fatin, she asked, "Would you like to lie down a bit for a nap?"

Matt, looking over at Fatin, said, "I could go for a nap."

"Yeah, sure. I am a bit tired."

Karen said, "That's a good idea. You kids go lie down a bit, and when you get up, we'll have supper. Your daddy'll probably be home by then too." Karen hugged each of them, and then she kissed each on their cheek before they head into Matt's old bedroom.

A few hours had passed, and Matt emerged from his bedroom, wiping the sleep from his eyes, each strand of his hair seemingly going off in its own direction. He yawned and stretched, extending his hands high over his head, his fingers nearly touching the ceiling. Taking a seat at the kitchen table and pouring himself another glass of sweet tea, he picked up the copy of the *Times-Picayune*, reading each of the headlines before turning the page.

Karen walked into the kitchen through the screen door to the porch, carrying two grocery paper bags, one in each arm. Looking up from the *Picayune*, Matt asked, "You need any help, Momma?" Looking over her shoulder and giving Matt that look people give, as if to say, "Are you kidding me?" While she continued to take the groceries out of the bags and placing them onto the counter, she said, "No, no, you just relax, baby. You know I've been doing this for more time than I care to remember." Placing a package of chocolate chip cookies on the table, she said, "Have a cookie. Supper won't be done for a while."

Looking down at the paper, Matt said with a tone of disbelief, "Darrel Lee Martin is parish president?"

"Oh yes, three terms now."

"Holy shit, Jesus! How the hell did that happen?" Matt asked rhetorically, remembering Darrel from back in the old days. Darrel was a few years older than Matt's brother, Billy, but he was known to be quite a prick around Jefferson Parish and an overt racist.

"Matthew! Don't be talking like that in this house!" Karen admonished Matt quickly for his blasphemy.

"Sorry, Momma. I just can't believe the people of Jefferson Parish elected that fool."

"Well, that fool has done quite well for himself over the last ten years or so. After his daddy died, he inherited quite a bit of money." Rinsing off the vegetables in the sink, she turned back toward Matt. "Money buys an awful lot of respect around here." Turning her attention back to her vegetables, she said, "I'm sure it buys respect most places."

Matt had heard Fatin get up from her nap a few minutes ago, but she didn't come out of the bedroom right away. When she walked into the kitchen, he could tell she must have been fixing herself up nice before coming out. Karen, hearing Fatin walk into the room, turned and asked, "Did you have a nice sleep, honey?"

Walking over to the back of Matt's chair, standing behind him, wrapping her arms around him, and leaning over, she snuggled onto him. "I did, thank you," Fatin responded.

"Oh, you don't got to thank me, honey."

Walking over to Karen, Fatin asked, "Can I help with anything?"

"Well, sure. Can you chop onions?"

"Onions are my specialty," Fatin said, picking up two of the onions sitting in the colander in the sink.

Karen handed Fatin a chef's knife and said, "Why don't you take a seat there at the table?"

Sitting down in one of the two sturdier-looking chairs, Fatin asked Karen hesitantly, "Momma, do you have a cutting board?" She was still not fully confident in calling Karen momma.

"Oh yes. I'm sorry, honey. Let me get you one," she said as she reached over the counter to retrieve one and placed it in front of Fatin. Not able to resist expressing her happiness, she kissed Fatin on top of her head, which caught Fatin by surprise though she didn't mind at all. In fact, she looked over at Matt with a big smile, the kind of smile one has when they know they are welcome.

Sitting at the table, still reading through the *Picayune*, something Matt hadn't done for well over a decade, this simple and inconsequential activity would be one of many more to come that would help Matt reacclimate to life in the parish. The reacquainting of past routines, as well as friends and family, would be an inevitability that Matt would accept at times and loath others. But when he heard the unmistakable sound of his father's heavy boots walk up the neglected stairs, creaking each time William took another step up, Matthew wasn't just accepting; he was happy.

When William opened the screen door and walked into the kitchen, his sturdy frame blocked out the setting sunlight that was shining in only moments before. He was a middle-aged man now, well into his fifties, and while he will be a large man until the day God takes him, time nor the alcohol have benefited William. Casting him in silhouette, his lunch pail in one hand and a large bag of shrimp in the other slung over his shoulder, for an instant devoid of any facial features, the figure was immediately recognizable to Matt. Fatin, on the other hand, squinted her eyes in an effort to regulate the light and get a better look at William. Her initial thought of the nondescript figure in the doorway was one of intimidation.

"Hey, Pop," Matthew said as he rose to his feet.

"Hey, boy, long time no see," William said as he walked over to Karen and placed the bag of shrimp and lunch pail on the counter. Moving at a slower pace and slightly hunched over from the last time Matt had seen his father, William asked, "When did you get in?"

Glancing at his watch momentarily, Matt said, "About three, I guess." Fatin rose to her feet, waiting for Matt to introduce her, but before he could, William walked down the hall and into the bathroom, closing the door behind him. Fatin slunk silently back into her chair and continued to cut onions.

A few minutes had passed and the only noise from the kitchen was that of food preparation before William walked back into the kitchen. "How you doing, son?" William asked as he placed one hand on Matt's shoulder and extending the other for Matt to shake. Though the hand on Matt's shoulder was to prevent him from standing up, he maneuvered around it and got to his feet and hugged his father. Matt's hug was that of a son who hadn't seen his father in a few years and was clearly happy to see his old man. William, well, William wasn't much of a hugger; in fact, he wasn't an affectionate man at all. Matt had once tried to remember each of the times his father had told him he loved him growing up; he could remember seven.

Walking over to Fatin's side of the table, Matt said, "Daddy, this is Fatin." At which point, she rose again to her feet and extended her hand. "Hello, Mr. Laurent, it's so nice to meet you."

"Nonsense," Karen said as she continued to peel and devein the fresh shrimp in the sink. "You call him William or Billy or even Daddy, but don't you call him Mr. Laurent. You leave that Mr. Laurent nonsense at the door. You hear me, young lady?" she said to Fatin, turning her head around enough to see Fatin and get confirmation of her edict.

"Yes, Momma," Fatin said as she looked back toward William. "It's nice to meet you, William. Matt has told me so much about you."

Extending his hand from where he stood, the two shook hands. "How do you say your name again? Fatten?" he asked as he walked over to the fridge and removed two beers, placing one down in front of Matt.

"Fatin," Matt corrected his father.

Looking back at Fatin, William tried again, "Fatin."

"That's right," she said before a smile came across her face.

"Hey, Pop, why don't you show me that new '62 Ford."

"It's '63," William corrected his son as he walked toward the door.

Kissing Fatin atop her head before he followed his father out the door, Matt said, "I'll be back in a few minutes, honey."

Fatin gave Matt a silent nod of acknowledgment before asking Karen, "Do you need any help with the shrimp, Momma?"

Chapter 20

Matt and Fatin had only been back for a few days when Matt realized that not much has changed in the parish since he last called it home. Of all the things Matt had wanted to do upon getting back to Jefferson Parish, seeing Father John was on top of the list. While Matt lived away and called regularly to keep in touch, the majority of the conversations were with Karen and Father John. The conversations he had with his dad while away were succinct to say the least. They typically consisted of "How you are doing?" "Staying out of trouble?" and such. For better or worse, the parish was the parish, but most of all, upon returning to the parish, Matt was anxious to introduce Fatin to Father John.

Of all the places in the parish that Matt missed most over the years, St. Patrick's was certainly one of them. When the couple walked into the church, Fatin's eyes were drawn upward into cavernous space. While entering the church felt like coming home to Matt, Fatin was awestruck at the elaborate interior, seeing she had never been in a Catholic church before or any church for that matter. She was also anxious about meeting Father John. Even though she and Matt had only been together for less than a year, she knew how much the father meant to Matt. She was even surprised at times at the reverence Matt would exhibit when talking about Father John and, even more so, that she never noticed this admiration when he talked about his father. As the couple got closer to the altar, a much shorter man, much balder than the last time Matt had seen him, a man in a robe much different than she had envisioned, emerged. But there was one thing that she could see immediately, and that was his love for Matthew.

"Matthew!" the father exclaimed louder than he would tolerate any of his parishioners doing in the holy place.

"Hello, Father," Matt said before embracing Father John. After their long-awaited reunion, the father turned to Fatin, standing there, looking at them with joy in his eyes and said, "As-Salaam-Alaikum" to Matt and Fatin's surprise.

"Wa Alaykum S-Salam," Fatin responded in delight.

"And when did you learn Arabic, Father?" Matt asked as the three walked back around the altar toward the father's office. Leaning in toward the couple, the father said, "That's all I know," which drew a chuckle from Matt and Fatin.

"Come on in. Sit down," the father invited the couple as he walked behind his large oak desk.

Sitting in Father John's office brought all kinds of fond memories rushing back to Matt. When Matt turned twelve years old, he became an altar boy just as his brother, Billy, had when he was twelve. Technically it didn't pay anything, but Father John would give Matt and whichever other altar boy or girl worked that Mass five bucks each. Doesn't seem like much, but five bucks could buy a heck of lot of candy or pay for a couple of movies at the showcase cinema back then.

Sitting in the two plush leather chairs in front of Father John's desk, Fatin and Matt held hands, occupying the space between. Fatin looked around the dark wood-paneled office, a fireplace on the far wall with photographs displayed across the mantel.

"Father, your office is beautiful."

Looking around his familiar environment, impossible to conceal his pride, he said, "Well, thank you, my dear. Sometimes I forget just how blessed I am, so thank you for that reminder. And if I may say so, you are lovely," which brought the hint of a smile to Fatin's face and induced blushing.

"Thank you, Father," she responded.

Taking his attention off Fatin and turning it to Matthew, the father said, "So, my son, it's so nice to have you back in the parish." Looking back over at Fatin, he said, "Do you know that I never worried about what this young man would achieve? Oh, back in the '80s, things were difficult in Jefferson Parish. Still can be for some. But Matthew had a focus that most children his age didn't." He looked over at Matt. "We had some tough times."

Nodding his head in agreement, Matt said, "Sure did."

"But you've done great, my boy. I am so proud of you. Actually, when you told me you were heading back home, I started to think how I can use you."

Matt and Fatin looked at each other with a look of curiosity. Matt said, "Sure, Father, how can I help?"

Standing up and walking over to his fireplace, the father looked over the top of his glasses at his many pictures; he picked up two framed photos and brought them over to Matt and Fatin, standing off to the side of his desk. "You know, it's important to have role models." Pointing up to the crucifix on the wall behind his desk, the father said, "There's my role model." He handed one of the photos to Matt. "This man was an inspiration to me as well."

Matt, holding the photo and showing it Fatin, said, "Oh wow, Father, very cool." Pointing to the photograph, Matt said to Fatin, "That's when Pope John Paul came to New Orleans."

"When was that?" she asked.

"Oh my goodness, a long time ago, dear," the father said as he sat back down in his well-worn high-back leather chair.

"I remember that," Matt said, looking up from the photo and at Father John.

Turing his attention to the other photograph, Matt said, "Oh my god, I've never seen this picture, Father."

Showing it to Fatin, she asked, "Is that you?"

"Yes."

Taking the picture from Matt to get a better look at the old, somewhat grainy photograph, she said, "Aww, Matthew, you were so adorable."

"He was a good boy," unsolicited, the father responded.

Placing both photographs down on the father's desk with care, Matt asked the father, "So how can I help?"

Leaning forward in his chair, folding his hands, interlocking his fingers as though he was praying, the father said, "I would love if you could come in and talk to the kids in our youth program about things. You know? Setting goals and how best to achieve them. As you can imagine, their home lives are difficult." He paused and sat back in his chair. "Complicated situations."

"Of course, Father. Whatever I can do."

"Thank you, son. We can discuss it more later, but you said you wanted to talk to me about something?"

Looking over at Fatin, which caused her to look back at him, Matt squeezed Fatin's hand slightly, a clear indication of his nervousness. Releasing her hand and shifting in his seat somewhat, placing his hands on the father's desk, Matt said, "We want to get married."

Sitting back in his chair with a look of satisfaction on his face, Father John said, "Now how did I know you were going to say that?"

Looking over at Fatin, and she back at him, both with a look of surprise, Matt said, "I don't know, Father. How did you know?"

"Oh, Matthew, come on now. Before you went to Saudi Arabia, our ten-minute phone calls were filled with the cases you were trying or the work you were doing at the State Department, but the calls I received from Saudi Arabia were much different."

"How so, Father?" Fatin chimed in as she leaned in.

"He was in love." Looking over at Fatin, the Father said, "That was obvious." He looked back over to Matt. "The ten-minute phone calls were nine minutes about this wonderful woman you met. So I'm not as surprised as you thought I might be."

Taking Fatin's hand back in his own and looking over at her before he said with trepidation in his voice, "Well, we have something else we want to tell you."

A look of concern came across his face, furrowing his brow slightly, the father said, "Okay. What is it?"

Looking back over at Fatin, Matt said, "We're pregnant," which induced a smile between the young couple.

While the father had deduced the fact of the couple's plans for marriage, he was clearly taken aback by this revelation. Standing up from his chair, Father John picked up his watering can and started to water his ferns hanging in the windows on either side of his desk. A minute or so of silence filled the room, prompting Matt to speak up as the father continued to water his plants.

Matt said, "Father?"

Father John carefully placed the water can down in its designated location on a side table under the windowsill, on an old folded over paper towel stained from the bottom of the can and said while looking at the couple, "Matthew, Fatin, while this is clearly not the ideal situation in the eyes of the Catholic church, I wouldn't be exercising the compassion that these circumstances require if I turned you away. So if you are asking me to preside over this marriage and the baptism of this child, I will do so on two conditions."

"Sure, Father," Matt said as he looked over at Fatin for approval.

Sitting forward in his chair, leaning against his desk to ensure he had both Matt and Fatin's attention, Father John said, "I would rather you wait until the baby is born before the two of you to get married."

"That's fine!" Fatin said excitedly as she looked over at Matt and then back at Father John.

"And?" Matt asked.

"The child must be brought up in the Catholic faith."

Matt, somewhat surprised, looked over at Fatin for a response and was a bit taken aback at her quick response of "That's fine too."

"Are you sure, honey?" Matt asked.

With her hand holding Matt's and looking deep into his eyes, she turned back to Father John and said, "I'm sure. I couldn't ask for a better man to be the father of my child, and as long as he has God in his life, I will be happy."

Pleased at everything he heard from Fatin, the father shook his head in agreement and said, "Great." Looking over at the clock on the wall and realizing the time, he said, "Oh boy, I'm late." He stood up from his chair. "I'm sorry, but I'm running late." He took his glasses off and looked at them before putting them back on his face.

"These glasses are just useless. We'll talk soon, Matthew. We have a lot to discuss." Shaking Fatin's hand, he said, "So wonderful to meet you, my dear. I'll see you on Sunday, Matthew?" And he walked out of his office, leaving the couple.

"Sure thing, Father," Matt said loudly, making sure he was heard.

Chapter 21

SUMMER, 2001

Matt and Fatin had moved out of the Laurent family home a few months back and into a little cottage owned by a Mr. Tyler. Matt didn't know Mr. Tyler beforehand, but he was a parishioner at the church, and he gave Matt and Fatin a very fine deal on the rental cost. They figured they would rent the Tyler cottage for a year or two while they saved enough money for a down payment on their own place. The house had been empty for a few years at this point since Mr. Tyler's momma had passed away while sitting in her recliner, TV still playing when he found her some three days later. It was less than a mile from the Laurent family home, and Matt was familiar with the place. Growing up, all the kids in the neighborhood, including Matt, thought the place was haunted. Old Mrs. Tyler, as the kids called her, was very rarely seen, so when she was, people often thought she was some kind of ghost or something. While those stories spooked Matt when he was a kid, for the deal he got he wasn't going to let them scare him away. The place needed some freshening up, so Matt agreed to repaint the cottage and do some other little odd repairs around the place to get it looking spiffy again.

Fatin, well into her second trimester, was growing faster than any weed that she would remove from the vegetable garden she planted out back behind the cottage. The backyard of the cottage had sun all day, from sunup to sundown being it was on the south side. She had never grown a garden before, so Karen had come over a few months earlier to help lay down the top soil and plant some seeds and, most importantly, help her with the fence to try to keep the pocket gophers out. Though they always found a way into the garden at the Laurent home, Karen would try all sorts of methods to keep them out, and she had a year's long feud with every pocket gopher in Jefferson Parish. It didn't take long for Fatin to adopt Karen's view of the pocket gopher and often caught herself cursing the little bastards, only to ask Allah for forgiveness immediately following. Just a few weeks ago, Karen had stopped by to visit and check on Fatin and her garden, and when she saw the gopher holes bordering the garden, she let loose a profanity-laced tirade, which shocked Fatin at first, but moments later, she broke out laughing hysterically. Fatin and Karen got along well, better than either had imagined they would, to that point not only did Fatin enjoy calling Karen momma, she was also starting to look at her as a second mother.

Matt had taken a job at a small law firm in New Orleans, offered to him by an old friend, David Sanders. Matt and David had been schoolmates up until the tenth grade until David's daddy had gotten himself a job over in St. Tammany Parish on the other side of Lake Pontchatrain. The firm only consisted of David, Matt, and David's secretary, Betty Jo, who happened to be his second cousin on his momma's side. Most of the work that came in were probate cases, but occasionally there were some personal injury cases or divorce as well. Matt didn't have any experience with this area of the law, but David knew Matt was a quick learner from back in school. He always remembered that Matt was either first or second to finish when they'd take test back in school. Now that ain't saying a whole lot if you fail the test, but since Matt was able to get into Georgetown Law and David only got into the Louisiana Academy of Law, well, that was confirmation enough for David that Matt would be able to pick up quick. And he was right.

Though there was always more than enough work for one lawyer, there was sometimes not enough for two. David was working on some new marketing ideas that he hoped would bring in more business that would grow the firm. He rented out a few billboards out on

Route 61, and he was scheduled to make one of those commercials you see lawyers do on TV nowadays. But for now, during the slow periods, Matt would take advantage of the extra time and location of the office in New Orleans to walk down to the Southern Charm Nursing Home and visit with his grandmomma, Edith.

Matt would walk over to the Southern Charm Nursing Home from his office on Camp Street usually a couple times a week. It was a short walk, just a few blocks down to Sixth Street, then north a few blocks, and there it was, directly across from the Lafayette Cemetery Number One. He often wondered if the owners of the nursing home picked its location for its proximity to the cemetery. But then he would think to himself that that would be incredibly insensitive although convenient, and Matt hated to think the worst of people, so he'd let it wash on over him and think better of it.

This particular day was an extremely hot and humid August day, even more so than usual for Louisiana for this time of year. David was meeting with the production company for the commercial he was going to shoot, Betty Jo had left for a doctor's appointment at 11:00 a.m., Matt had finished up his work for the day, so he locked up shop and walked up to the nursing home. He always enjoyed spending time with Edith, especially since her health was failing recently and wasn't sure how much time she had left, so on this uncomfortably hot day, he made his way up to the nursing home, but truth be told, he had his sights set on a nice cold beer later in the afternoon.

The people that worked at the nursing home were always very pleasant and extended Matt a fine greeting when he walked through the door. The receptionist, Rita, a rather large black woman of probably sixty who always seemed to be eating when Matt arrived, was one of his favorites. "How you doing, Matty?" or "How goes the battle, Counselor?" she'd ask, often covering her mouth politely, being she was chewing on something. Matt would often walk a block out of his way to stop at Pernille's Bakery to pick up some beignets for Rita and Edith, but not on this day; it was just too damn hot.

"Hey, Rita," Matt said as he walked through the door and past the reception station.

Fanning herself with a copy of *US Weekly*, she said, "Hey, Matt. You feel like a turkey out there in that oven?" ending with a chuckle that made her entire upper body jiggle.

Looking back at Rita as he kept walking toward Edith's room, he said, "Are you kidding me? I don't need heat to feel like a turkey. It just comes natural."

Still fanning herself, Rita let out a boisterous laugh and said out of Matt's earshot before taking a bite of an already half-eaten donut, "That boy's a good hoot."

As Matt walked into Edith's room, she was sitting in her chair in the corner of the room, looking out the window and over the Lafayette Cemetery. "Hey, Grandma," he said, happy to see the fragile woman.

Turning back toward the door, she said with joy in her voice, "Oh my goodness."

Edith was now an old woman, well into her seventies, and it showed not only in her physical demeanor, but also her memory. Matt always knew this day would come but, like anyone else, was surprised at how quickly it snuck up on him. When Matt had gone off to college in New York and then Washington and eventually overseas, he made a concerted effort to only get back to Jefferson Parish when he couldn't avoid it. While he never meant no harm and thought it was the best way of dealing with differences and seemed like a good idea at the time, there was no doubt he was regretting that lost time now. When he had left all those years ago, Edith was strong-willed in body and mind, and it wasn't easy for him to see her this vulnerable.

Edith had been diagnosed with dementia and Alzheimer's a few years back; the diabetes had been around for much longer than that. William and Karen had started to notice subtle signs a year or so before her diagnosis but avoided that battle they knew it would take to get Edith to go into a home though, eventually, they needed to take action, which went over like fox in the henhouse, but in time, the old girl relented. As much as she hated the idea, she wasn't a stupid woman and saw the writing on the wall and, at the last minute, decided to surrender the fight and go along with the program.

Sitting on the edge of the bed, Matt untied his tie and put it in his sport coat pocket. Reaching over, taking Edith's hands into his, he said, "How are you doing, Grandma?" He gave her a kiss on her forehead, just below her hairline. Looking weak and frail, her false teeth currently serving no purpose, they were sitting in a cup of water on the nightstand by the bed.

"Oh, I'm doing okay," she said before her focus wondered from Matt and back out the window.

Turning back from the window and toward Matt, the old woman smiled at her grandson, the kind of smile that conveyed peacefulness, but Matt was afraid to ask why she was smiling. Matt avoided looking at his grandmother for long periods, instead focusing on her for a bit and then finding something useful to do, like refold her clothes or check on her hygiene products; it gave him an incredible feeling of sadness, so he looked away a lot. That day, the sequence went like this: out the window and back to her, down at the floor and back to her, at his watch and back to her. When he looked up from his watch and back at his grandma, she said, "You know, Matthew, your grandfather would be so proud of you."

A bit surprised at the statement, it widened Matt's eyes and perked his ears, the way a dog's ears perk up when he hears the electric can opener open a can of dog food or he hears a gopher in the front yard. Looking deep into his grandmother's elderly gaze, it was almost like she was looking through him and not at him. He asked, "You think so, Grandma?"

"You have his eyes. I saw that the day you were born, when you were in your momma's arms. Your brother, Billy, God rest his soul, had your daddy's eyes, but you"—looking into her grandson's eyes the same way she had for the first time that night he came into this world—"you have his eyes," she said with a smile that conveyed the kind of love that only a grandmother knows.

Matt decided to stay with Edith for lunch—tuna sandwiches, a garden salad, and some runny peach cobbler. It wasn't something Matt did on a regular basis; he certainly didn't do it for the food, but rather the company of his dear grandma. Seeing the ageing process right before his eyes wasn't easy for Matt. He liked to remember

Edith in her younger days when she wasn't reliant on anyone, when she didn't take shit from anyone—and she didn't have to. Now they tell her when it's time for a bath, when it's time to eat. Hell, they even have to change her diaper. *Now, well, it's just the cycle of life*, he thought to himself, *as shitty as it is.*

As Edith and Matt finished up their lunch in the dining room, a nice elderly man by the name of Nathanial P. Turner approached. He was much older than Edith by ten, maybe fifteen, years or so, Matt thought to himself, a black man with a full head of white hair and a small pencil mustache. Matt had seen him before on his visits with Edith but never actually met the man.

"Hello, Edith, did you enjoy your cobbler?" Nathanial asked, standing beside the table.

"Please take a seat," Matt said to the aged man as he quickly stood to his feet.

"No, no, no, that's all right there, young man. I just came over to ask Edith if she would like to join me for bingo." Putting his hand on Matt's shoulder as he sat back into his chair, he said, "So this must be that talented young grandson of yours?"

"Sure is," Edith said proudly.

Extending his hand upward slightly, Matt said, "How are you, sir? Nice to meet you."

"Oh, I'm doing just fine. The Lord has blessed me with an extremely long life. Good health for the most part," he said as he gave his left bicep a squeeze, which gave Matt a little chuckle. "But he also made sure to take all my kin long ago."

Reaching over the table, Edith touched Matt's hand to draw his attention. "Now how old would you say Mr. Turner is, Matthew?" This was a question Mr. Turner didn't mind being asked. In fact, whenever he heard that sentence, *how old do you think Mr. Turner is?*—and he heard it a lot—he got this prideful look that would wash across his face while he waited for the response.

A bit perplexed and not wanting to overestimate his age and insult the man, Matt decided to guess a bit low. "Seventy-nine?" he said, looking up at Nat. That was what most people in the home called him, Nat.

The seventy-nine guess gave Nat a big laugh, and he reached down and put his hand on Matt's shoulder once again and said with pride, "I am 101 years old, young man."

Matt's jaw dropped, and he quickly looked over at Edith who, with a constant nod, confirmed the old man's claim and then back up to Nat. Quickly standing up, Matt said, "Please, Mr. Turner, take my seat."

"Nonsense," he replied. "I'm off to bingo anyway." Looking over at Edith, Nat asked again, "So what do you say, Edith? You up for some bingo?"

Edith looked over at Matt, and he could tell she was looking for a nudge. "Go on, Grandma, have some fun. You always were lucky at bingo."

"Yes, yes, that's true," she said. "I'll tell you what, Nathanial. You head over into the activity room and save me a seat, and I'll be there just as soon as I say goodbye to my grandson."

Standing up from his chair, Matt extended his hand once again to Mr. Turner. "So nice to meet you, Mr. Turner," Matt said.

Shaking his hand, Mr. Turner said, "Nonsense! You call me Nat just like everyone else round here." Nat liked the word *nonsense* and used it whenever he could fit it into a sentence though sometimes he'd fit it in like a square peg into a round hole.

"Yes, sir," Matt replied, not able to drop the formal overture that all government employees become accustomed to.

Sitting back in the hard plastic chair while watching Mr. Turner shuffle off toward the bingo game, Matt couldn't believe what great shape he was in. He was sharp as a tack and he certainly didn't move like a man of 101, but then again, Matt thought, most people 101 are dead so there ain't much to compare it to. Taking Edith by the hand, Matt looked down at his watch and said, "Well, Grandma, I really should get going."

Taking a moment to gather her thoughts, Edith, using both her hands to hold Matthew's hands, pulled them closer to her. Though she loved when Matt would come to visit, she couldn't help but wonder each time she saw him if it would be her last. She knew her health wasn't what it once was and, frankly, will never be again. She doubted she'd have the longevity that good ole Nat has, and she was pretty sure she wouldn't want it anyway.

Looking at Matt, but almost past him, like she was gazing into a long-ago past, she said, "That watch was the first gift I ever bought your grandfather." This caused Matt to look down at it. "He was headed off to boot camp, and he had never owned a watch before." She looked up at the ceiling a bit and back down at Matt. "You know I met your grandfather when we were both working at the Higgins boat factory?"

Listening to his grandma intently, he said, "No, I didn't know that, Grandma."

"It was May 12. We went on our first date on May 12, 1943. He could barely read, but he was a good man. I was pregnant with your momma when he left for boot camp." Looking up at the drop ceiling panels in the dining room, she said, "Never did see her." Then she shook her grandson's hands slightly to make sure she had his attention, which she did. "I see him in you. You have his eyes and you have his kindness, and I'm sure he'd be happy you have his watch."

Matt walked his grandmother over to the activity hall and peeked in. Mr. Turner, true to his word, had a seat saved for Edith, and when he saw her and Matt at the door, he waved her over, patting the chair, indicating it was reserved for her. Matt gave Edith a hug, careful not to squeeze too tight; he kissed her on the side of her head and said, "I love you, Grandma."

"I love you too, Matthew," she said as she carefully walked to Nat and the seat he saved for her.

As Matt was walking down the hall and toward the exit, he was nodding at and saying goodbye to folks, both employees and residents, that he had met while visiting Edith since she arrived at Southern Charm. Matt was always good with names and faces and placing them together even if he had only met a person once. Lots of time, people are either good with faces or names, but less frequently both. He thought to himself that he'd like to sit down with Mr. Turner sometime soon and just listen to some old-time stories of times past, the way things used to be, the good and the bad. But unfortunately, that would never happen. Nat died just three days after Matt had the pleasure of meeting him.

While Matt always enjoyed spending time with Edith, he was really anxious to get a sip of that first beer. When Matt walked in the door of the old Redd's Tavern, his eyes took a few seconds to adjust from the bright Louisiana sunlight to the rather dark and smoky barroom. There was Leo, as always, though instead of working the bar and taking care of customers, he was perched on one of the tall barstools at the end of the bar. His knee hadn't gotten better with time; in fact, he just had it replaced two years ago, and when asked about it, he'd go into what seemed to be a never-ending silique about the whole procedure. Matt found that out the hard way. He made that mistake when he first got back to Jefferson Parish and has since avoided all discussions about knees, elbows, sleeping habits, or general health with Leo ever since.

Once Matt's eyes adjusted to the light in the bar, he gave Leo a wave and walked toward the other end—the empty end. Matt didn't often drink alone, but he just wasn't in the mood for any long difficult kind of conversations today.

"Hey, Evelyn, can I get a beer?" Matt said as he slid the barstool under his backside.

Without answering him, Evelyn reached down into the beer cooled on the back side of the bar, took out a cold one, and popped the top. Evelyn was Leo's niece and had been working at the bar for the last five years or so. She wasn't a bad-looking woman, just a few years younger than Matt; she had three kids with two different men. In her relatively young life, Evelyn has lived some hard years. Her first child's daddy was killed in a shoot-out with police back in '95 after he walked out of the First Saving's Federal Bank, not realizing one of the tellers had tripped the silent alarm. Well, when he walked out the door, he must have had a dozen guns pointed at him, and it only took him to start raising his gun hand before he was cut down. The daddy of baby number two and three was doing a five to seven stretch in Angola for the same crime, armed robbery, though his sights were set a bit lower. He wasn't expecting to be shot in the back as he ran out of Flippy's Liquors over on Clayton Avenue, but ole Flippy had been robbed three times that past month and wasn't going to let it happen again. He was just lucky Flippy only had a .22 and not a .44 or a .357 or he'd be as dead as Stonewall Jackson.

Taking that first swig of beer on a hot day was something Matt knew he'd never grow tired off; in fact, his affinity for little things like that seemed to only increase as he got older. A cold beer on a hot day, the sound of the cicadas on a hot summer night, and of course, silence. But being the Southern gentleman he was, Matt asked, "So how's it going, Evelyn?" He immediately regretted the question though she hadn't even responded yet.

"Oh, you know, Matt, living large," she said sarcastically as she lit a cigarette. Matt didn't notice the brand, but he saw they were 100s simply by the sheer length of it. The glow of the match cast a light on Evelyn's face in the softly lit bar when struck that allowed Matt to see the advanced age in this young woman's face. Crow's-feet and lines around her mouth seemed to arrive a decade early for Evelyn, the cost of living hard. She always hung around with bad boys as Matt remembered, but she was a fine-looking girl back in high school. As he took another swig of his beer, he decided not to ask any more questions of Evelyn.

"Come on, fuckhead! Break already!" Matt heard from the open doorway that led to a side room which housed two pool tables that had seen much better days. He thought he recognized the voice and considered asking Evelyn who it was, but he thought better of it and just continued to drink his beer.

The crash of the white ball slamming into all the others echoed through the bar. Seemingly not happy with the results, Matt heard a different voice say, "Well, Jesus Christ! How the fuck you expect me to get a good break when this damn felt is all worn-out?"

Leo stood up from his stool, folded up his paper, and said, "I have to do a few errands, Ev. I'll be back later on, about eight." As he walked toward the door, he gave Matt a nod and was gone.

"You know, Perry, you always were a bitch. Bitchin' and complainin', bitchin' and complainin'." Matt heard a third man's voice laughing at the insult.

"Don't you owe us shots, Tommy?" And that's when Matt's assumption was confirmed.

"Yeah, yeah, hold your fucking horses," Tommy said as he walked through the doorway leading into the bar. Wearing a stained and stretched out white tank top, ripped jeans with blotches of roofing tar all over them, a cigarette hung from his mouth as he walked toward the bar, pulling singles out from his wallet, still attached to those worn jeans by a chain.

Sipping his beer, Matt glanced over, knowing exactly who it was, noticing numerous bad tattoos, no doubt jailhouse tattoos, covering each of his arms and the one cross just below and off to the left of his left eye. "Hey, Ev, get me three shots of Wild Turkey." Downing the last of his beer, he slammed the empty bottle down on the old bar top, startling Evelyn and causing her to jump.

"Jesus! Tommy!" she yelled.

"Get me a beer too," he said as he threw the one-dollar bills on the bar until he had what he thought was enough.

"You know, Tommy, you ain't got no manners," Evelyn said as she placed three shot glasses in front of him, pouring the Wild Turkey in each.

Taking one of the shot glasses, he pounded down his drink, pointing to the now-empty glass, saying, "Another."

Evelyn popped open a bottle of beer and poured him another shot. Picking up the one-dollar bills, she walked toward the register counting them, looking back and saying, "What? No tip?"

"I don't believe in tipping," Tommy said before taking a swig of his beer.

"Yeah, whatever," Evelyn said, loud enough for Tommy to hear. "Cheap son of a bitch," she continued, but only loud enough for her to hear.

Tommy, standing at the bar, was staring at Evelyn's behind in her tight jeans when, from the next room, someone yelled, "Yo, it's your shot." Ignoring the call, Tommy watched Evelyn walk down to the other side of the bar, which drew Matt right into his eyeline. Almost spitting up his mouthful of beer, he said, "Holy fuck! Look what we got here." He turned his body to face Matt sitting only three barstools away. "I heard you were back in town."

"What the fuck, Tommy? Where's my shot?" Perry said when he walked in through the open doorway and into the bar area. Perry made a beeline to his shot and drank it. Standing next to Tommy he said, "Come on, asshole, it's your shot."

Elbowing Perry in the side and not just a nudge, he said, "Don't you see what we got here? It's college boy Matt Laurent."

Matt took a sip of his beer, still looking straight ahead. He said, "Hey, Tommy."

"Holy shit! Look at that. Hey, Albert, come here!" Perry yelled to the other room.

Taking a few steps closer to Matt, Tommy stumbled just a bit on one of the legs of a stool. Matt could smell the alcohol coming from Tommy's breath and permeating out of his pores.

"You know I heard you was back in town." Leaning against the bar to hold himself steady, he leaned in closer to Matt, uncomfortably close, but Matt didn't move an inch.

"I heard you was back in town, and I heard you were married to some Arab nigger bitch," Tommy said with the confidence that only alcohol and two friends can give a man.

Albert walked into the bar with his cue in hand. Looking over and seeing Matt, he said, "No fuck!"

Matt stood up from his stool and pulled out his wallet. "How much, Evelyn?" he asked.

"Three bucks," she said.

Matt placed a five-dollar bill down on the bar and took his last swig of beer, finishing off the bottle. Turning toward Tommy, he said, "I see you're still going with the swastika," referring to Tommy's necklace hanging around his neck, lying flat on what looked like the top three letters of a KKK tattoo on his chest. The bottom half was obscured by his ratty old tank top. "Well, you heard wrong, Tommy," referring to Tommy's derogatory comment.

"Thanks, Evelyn," Matt said as he turned to walk toward the door.

"No, no, no. He did marry a nigger," Albert jumped in. "I saw them at the Piggly-Wiggly not three weeks ago. Matter of fact, she's pregnant."

Slamming his hand down on the bar, Tommy said, "No fuck! Laurent's gonna have a nigger kid."

Matt stopped before walking out the door; he didn't bother turning his whole body, just his head, enough to catch Tommy's eyes. "Watch it, Tommy."

Taking a step closer to Matt, Tommy said, "Now come on, Laurent. You know, I'm just fuckin' with y'all," looking back at Albert and Perry with a big grin on his face and then back to Matt. "But I ain't surprised."

"You aren't surprised about what, Tommy?" Matt said, quickly second-guessing even engaging with Tommy.

"I ain't surprised that you married a coon. Hell, you was best pals with that nigger back in school." Looking back again toward the other two, he said, "What the fuck was that ole sambo's name?"

Quickly chiming in, Perry said, "Jamal."

Snapping his finger as one sometimes does when recalling something, Tommy said, "That's it! Fucking Jamal. How's old Jamal doing anyway?"

"Better than you, Tommy, better than you," Matt said in a dismissive manner before turning his head as he walked out the door.

After Matt walked out of the bar, Tommy sat down in one of the chairs at the table closest to the door, and almost instinctively like the geese at the rear of a flock flying South for the winter, Perry and Albert followed him though Perry turned his chair around and leaned over the back. "Evelyn, get us some beers!" Tommy shouted, which was uncalled for since she was only six feet away. The boys sat in silence for a few moments, which was rare as they waited for Evelyn to bring over the beers.

"Anything else, king shit?" she asked as she walked through the poolroom and into the storage room in the back. By the time Tommy thought of something he thought was clever, she was out of earshot but said it nonetheless, "Whore." It didn't have the effect he had intended.

"Man, I hate that motherfucker. Always have," Tommy said as he took a big swing of beer.

"He's a fuckin' pussy," Perry added to the conversation empathically. "I mean, any self-respecting southerner, a white man, who would knock up some Arab who don't belong in the South?"

"You ain't shittin'," Alberts said.

Tommy sat quietly, sipping on his beer, lighting a Marlboro Light cigarette, seemingly stewing in his anger. Perry and Albert both knew through years of retribution, through tongue-lashings and, on some occasions, a knock to the head, to sit back and wait for Tommy. There was no question who the alpha male of this pack was.

Taking a long drag on his cigarette, the ashes now long and gray and seemingly defying gravity, finally fell to the floor. It caught Tommy's eye, but he paid it no mind and took a swig of beer. Leaning over to his right, trying to get a better look into the back room, he said, "Where is that bitch?" He finished off his beer with the last large swig. "I need a shot."

"You know what the problem is?" Tommy asked rhetorically, pointing toward the door Matt had just walked out of not ten minutes ago. "These nigger-loving white southerners. Everything was fine back in the '30s and '40s and then that fuckin' Dr. King showed up and fucked shit up. Equal rights, voting rights, desegregation, fuck! Back then, if a nigger acted up, you just lynch 'em."

"Fuckin' right," Perry said with a tone of nostalgia in his voice.

"Hell, if you ask me, they should take away a nigger's right to vote. They all dumb motherfuckers anyway."

"Damn right," Albert said, making sure to keep his input to a minimum, not because he didn't agree but because of possible retribution on Tommy's part for interrupting him.

"You know what?" Tommy asked as he saw Evelyn walk back into the room from the back, but not looking for a response. "I'd take away a woman's right to vote too."

"Big fuckin' surprise," Evelyn said in response as she walked behind the bar.

"Go get us some beers and some shots," Tommy said to Albert in a milder tone. Albert didn't say a word and just got up. Tommy lit another cigarette and stood up and walked over to the bar. "You know I'm just fuckin' with y'all, right?" he said to Evelyn as she popped the top of three beers. She looked back at him in disgust and started to pour the Wild Turkey. Tommy picked up his shot and, in one swift motion, gulped it down, leaving it to Albert to bring Perry over his beer and shot. Taking a drink of his beer, he said, "Hey, Ev, I'm just fuckin' with y'all. Everybody knows women are one step above a nigger." This caused all three of them to laugh. Never surprised by Tommy's misogyny or his racism, Evelyn had learned long ago to brush it off.

"I'm just sayin'," Tommy said as he looked at the guys. "Men are supposed to work, and women belong in the kitchen cookin' or in the bedroom making babies."

"Damn straight!" Perry said before taking a sip of beer.

"Speaking of, you said you saw Laurent's woman?" Tommy said, looking over at Albert sitting at the bar.

"Yeah, I did. At the Piggly-Wiggly. Looked like she had a bunch of Arab food in her buggy." Albert was looking for a laugh but got no response. "She ain't bad lookin'," he said before realizing what he said, which drew a look from both Tommy and Perry. Quickly, he amended his statement with, "I mean for a nigger is all."

"Give me another shot, Ev," Tommy said as he stared off into the emptiness of the room. He took a long swig of beer before saying, "I'm gonna get that motherfucker."

Placing a new shot glass down on the bar and as she was pouring the Whiskey, Evelyn said, "Why don't you just leave them alone? They ain't bothering nobody."

Looking down the length of the bar, first right and then left, Tommy reached into his pocket and pulled out an eight ball of coke. Holding it up, like someone teasing a cat with a piece of string, and knowing full well Evelyn had always liked to party though she had been doing her best to stay clean, even marijuana, which she's been able to do for the past five weeks, he asked, "Want a little toot, Evey?" swinging the little plastic bag full of coke back and forth as if to tantalize her. Evelyn kept drying yesterday's beer mugs, looking down at the mug and then up at the baggie more than a few times Tommy knew she couldn't say no. She took down a small Jack Daniels's mirror off the wall from behind bar and walked toward the front door to lock it and turn over the Open sign to Closed.

"Just one," she said, which Tommy and the boys knew was meaningless.

Chapter 22

HOLY NAME CEMETERY

Edith passed away quietly in her sleep on a Tuesday evening. It was a day that could have been confused with countless others. The sole difference of this day for Matt and his family was this one was without Edith. Rita told Matt and his mother, Karen, that Edith was in good spirts the night before she died, went to sleep, and simply didn't wake up. She had eaten one of her favorite meals for dinner, chicken fried steak with mashed potatoes and white gravy, and she played bingo with Mrs. Monte, one of Edith's schoolmates from years ago, and even Kenny, one of the night shift orderlies.

It made Matt feel somewhat better to hear that his grandmother had a good day before she passed. Though he couldn't help but feel, even though in a nursing home and surrounded by friends, both old and new, somewhat selfish that she was gone and regretful for all those times he could have visited from New York and Washington but didn't.

The service at St. Patrick's was simple, no fuss. Edith hated funerals with lots of fuss. Matt, Fatin, Karen, and William occupied the front pew; behind them were a few old friends, including Johnny and Doris and, as always, at any funeral at St. Pat's, the neighborhood widows, dressed in black, as they had been since the day that each of their husbands had passed. Also in attendance was Louise, Jamal's mother.

After the service at the church, the procession made its way over to Holy Name Cemetery, not more than five city blocks from the church. Down in Jefferson Parish as in most parishes in south Louisiana, the dead are placed in crypts, above ground. Luckily, the Davis Funeral Parlor supplied some pallbearers to help Matt, William, and Johnny carry Edith's casket. There was a dozen or so chairs set up in front of the crypt though only half would be needed. It was a sunny day, and being early September, the sweltering summer heat had started to break and was very comfortable. Matt always thought the ideal weather for a funeral day should be a bit chilly and overcast to reflect the somber occasion, but he was happy that it wasn't today.

Father John was standing in front of the crypt and behind the casket as he gave his benediction. As Matt was sitting there, holding Fatin's hand to his left and Karen's hand to his right, listening to the father, he realized this was the first funeral he had been to since Billy died. He was sad that Edith would miss the birth of his child, her great-grandchild by only a month, but he was also grateful that she would once again meet up with his grandpa in heaven. Just then, Matt felt a hand on his shoulder. Looking up, he saw it was Jamal.

Waiting for Father John to finish, Jamal, Jazmine, and little Charlotte stood behind Louise. Jamal bent over and kissed his mother on the cheek, her hand reaching over her shoulder, holding his. She motioned to Charlotte to come on around to sit on Grandma's lap, and she did. As Father John finished, as all Catholic Masses do, "Now go in peace," Matt got to his feet and gave Jamal a hug. No longer restrained by the silence that is required at any funeral, Louise stood and said, "My baby! My baby! My baby boy!" giving Jamal a hug and covering his face with kisses until he put a stop to it by saying, "Momma, Momma, please. We're in public."

"Oh, I know, but I don't care. The Lord knows how much I love my baby." Looking down at Charlotte, she said, "And my beautiful grandbaby!"

"Hey, buddy. Glad you could make it," Matt said to Jamal.

"Sorry we're late. There was a thunderstorm coming up in the East Coast and delayed everything out of New York," Jamal said. He gave Karen a hug and his condolences and shook William's hand.

"Hello. So you're Fatin?" he said. "Well, look at you, you're about ready to pop." Fatin extended her hand, and Jamal was having nothing of that and gave her a hug, minding her extended belly. Though hugging a man you just met in public isn't allowed in the Muslim religion, Fatin was growing rather fond of the open gestures of affection that she had found were simply part of the culture in the Deep South.

"Fatin, this is my wife, Jazmine, and our little one, Charlotte," Jamal said.

Shaking Jazmine's hand, she bent down as best she could and said, "Hi, Charlotte. Aren't you so pretty!" This drew a big smile from the little girl's face.

Reaching out and touching Fatin's belly, Charlotte said, "Is that a baby?"

Surprised at the young girl's inquisitiveness and understanding of reproduction, Fatin said while rubbing her belly, "Yes, it is, honey."

"Mommy has a baby in her belly too," the little girl said, unsolicited.

Matt surprised by the news looked to Jamal for confirmation. "Really?"

"Sure is, buddy. We just found out though we were going to wait and tell you at dinner tonight." Looking down and placing his hand on Charlotte's head, the young girl looked up at her daddy as if he were the only thing on earth that truly mattered.

Putting her hand on her belly, Jazmine said, "Just seven weeks."

"What do you say we go grab a beer before we head back to your place?" Jamal asked Matt. Looking at Jazmine for approval, he said, "You don't mind, do you, honey?"

"No, no, go on and have your beer, but not too many. Fatin and I will talk and get to know each other and talk about the joy of motherhood," she said in a jokingly sarcastic tone as she pointed to Charlotte chasing a butterfly, doing its best to avoid captivity and the clumsiness of an excited child.

Giving his wife a kiss teeming with gratitude, Jamal said, "Thanks, baby."

As the family walked down the gravel road, flanked by crypt after crypt, some dating back to the 1700s, Matt made his way over to his mother. Taking her hand, he walked with her to William's truck.

"Honey, take the car with Jazmine and Charlotte and I'll go with Jamal," Matt said.

"You know you're supposed to buy me one soon," Fatin said as Matt handed her the keys.

"I know, I know. I'm going to see Phil Deeds over on Route 61 on Monday." Looking over at Jamal and Jazmine, Matt said, "She's all excited about driving. She just got her driver's license last month and now she wants to drive everywhere."

"You just got your license?" Jazmine asked with trepidation in her voice.

Jamal said, "Hey, Momma, you go with Fatin and Jazmine and the baby and we'll see you in a little bit."

"Okay, baby. Don't take too long now," Louise said.

With a big smile on her face, Fatin said, "Don't worry, I'm a good driver."

Kissing his mother on the cheek, Matt said, "We'll be over the house in a bit, Momma. I'm just going to go have a few beers with Jamal."

"That's okay, honey. You boys take your time. I'm not going anywhere," she replied.

Before getting into the passenger's side of the car, Matt looked back at his father and said, "Hey, Pop, you wanna come?" knowing full well he'd probably refuse.

"No, I'm gonna take your mother home," William said without looking toward Matt before he hopped into the driver's seat of his truck. Looking over at Father John, Matt called over, "Father? A few beers?"

"No, thank you, boys. Another time. I have some work to do back to the rectory."

When Matt and Jamal arrived at the Redd's Tavern, the parking lot had a fair number of cars in it, but then again, being Saturday and with such pleasant weather, it shouldn't have been a surprise. As they walked through the door and into the bar, the smell of stale beer and cigarettes permeated the room. The choices of tables were limited to two, being the place was full of regulars, a fact that didn't go unnoticed by Matt or Jamal, or by the regulars for that matter.

While Matt and Jamal were both from the parish, they've both been gone so long; on top of that, they've both done well for themselves, and sometimes that can rub some of the locals the wrong way, and it wasn't lost in some of the dirty looks they got. It was funny that they either got fine hellos from old friends or dirty looks from old friends; either way, there didn't seem to be any in between. There were two bartenders working being it was Saturday, not including Leo, perched up like an old barn owl on the same ole stool. Matt waved over to Evelyn to get her attention, and when he did, he said, "Two beers, Evelyn, please."

Jamal was very much like Matt was when it came to Jefferson Parish; they both loved their hometown, but ever since they were young boys, they dreamed of getting out, achieving things, seeing things, doing big things, and they both had to a certain extent. So Matt wasn't surprised when Jamal said after taking his first sip of beer, "Why the hell did you come back here, Matt?"

Sipping his beer and taking a moment to think of a reasonable response that will satisfy his friend, he said, "The weather." And they busted out laughing before taking another sip of his beer.

"Seriously, why? I told you I could get you in at the firm. We have plenty of work, and the money is great," Jamal said.

"I know." Looking around the bar, realizing that Jamal was probably right, and he doesn't fit in like he used to, he said, "I don't know. I just thought I could settle some things."

"What things? Your father?" Jamal asked, leaning forward in his chair and resting his weight on the table, anticipating where Matt was going.

"Yeah, I guess."

"Matt, it is what it is, man. If he ain't changed by now," he said as he leaned back in his chair to a more relaxed position.

Rubbing his forehead and working his hand down to his chin, Matt said, "I know. I just thought maybe I could get some answers before he drinks himself to death or drops dead of a heart attack." Sitting back and biting his bottom lip, Matt looked up at the ceiling at nothing in particular, just gazing up. "You know, I'd like to say he was different before Billy died, and it was Billy's death that changed him. But the fact of the matter is, I don't remember if he was different. I mean, it feels like he changed." He looked down to Jamal. "It's weird. I don't know if my memories of before Billy's death are real or manufactured in my mind."

Realizing his beer was almost empty, Jamal waved over at the other bartender. "What's her name?" he asked Matt.

Matt, looking over at her, said, "I have no idea. Never seen her before."

"Miss? Miss?" Jamal called to her until she looked up from whatever she was reading laid out on the bar, holding up his bottle and giving it a bit of a wave, the universal sign for an empty beer. The young lady—in actuality looking like she was closer to a girl, eighteen, maybe nineteen—brought over two beers to the boys, placed them on the small table between them, and started to walk away totally uninterested in the thank-you Jamal extended.

"Have you read *Mockingbird* lately? Atticus?" Jamal asked Matt.

Looking up from the floor, Matt responded, "Few months back."

Looking at his friend and knowing him so well, Jamal said, "Man, you are so Atticus," shaking his head slightly side to side. "You want and, even worse, think everything should be right, that everything should be just, but that's not reality, Matt. And it wasn't for Atticus and it certainly wasn't for Tom Robinson. Life isn't fair, brother." After a few moments of silence between them, Jamal continued, "Matty, I love you like a brother, but you can't keep waiting for answers that might not come. You're going to be a father, you're going to get married. There is your answer. Right there! You know everything you shouldn't be, and you are everything you should be. You're a good man, Matthew Laurent. You are Atticus Finch."

Looking around the room before finally fixing his eyes on his friend's, Matt asked, "And where did you get all this wisdom?"

Without hesitation Jamal said, "Harvard! And if you would have got in, you'd have it too," making both the boys chuckle.

The bar door opened, and the sunlight streamed across Matt and Jamal's table, the sunlight illuminating the clouds of smoke and dust in the air, causing both men to squint their eyes and look toward the irritation. Matt wasn't exactly thrilled when he heard and recognized the voice coming from the silhouette figure walking through the door; it was Tommy with Perry and Albert in toe.

"Jesus Chris, you fucking retard. I told you to see that fuckin' Mexican over on Stafford Road. He's got the best shit. These niggers down here got shit," Tommy said as he walked in the barroom and toward the bar.

"Listen, asshole, the Mexican wasn't there," Albert responded.

"Well, where the fuck was he?"

"Maybe he went back to Mexico. Ha-ha," Perry chimed in.

"Yeah, maybe, back where he belongs," Tommy said as he leaned up on the bar. "Hey, Ruby, aren't you looking fine as all hell today?" Tommy said to the younger bartender as he looked her up and down. "When you gonna come home with me and show me tight little body?"

As she reached into the cooler, pulling three beers from it, she looked at Tommy and said, "In your fucking dreams."

"Cunt," Tommy said under his breath as he took a sip of his beer, turning away, leaning his back up against the bar. Finally noticing Matt and Jamal, Tommy said, "What the fuck! Hey, Perry, look at these two." Turning around, both Perry and Albert saw Matt and Jamal sitting at the table. The boys were almost hoping their three old classmates wouldn't notice them as unrealistic as it seemed.

Jamal said before taking a swig of beer, "Hey, Tommy, Perry, Albert, how y'all doin'?"

"What the fuck are you doing down here? You weren't wanted here twenty fucking years ago! Why the hell you come back?" Tommy asked.

Matt and Jamal both understood that a confrontation with these three fools who have nothing to lose could be detrimental to both of them. Realizing the option to ignore Tommy and his friends no longer existed, Matt motioned to Jamal to finish his beer so they can head out.

"Oh, oh! Ain't you heard? His grandmomma died," Albert said with excitement. Pointing at Matt, he said, "His fucking grandmomma died. I saw it in the paper."

Slamming his hand on the bar and busting out in a mock laugh, doing his very best to taunt Matt, Tommy said, "Is that right, Laurent? Did your grandmomma drop dead?" Matt was always good at keeping his composure, but Tommy was getting to him. His face becoming flush, the carotid artery on the right side of his neck visibly expanded, Tommy could see the fruits of his labor. "You know, I saw that Arab girlfriend of yours the other day. She ain't bad for a sand nigger," Tommy said as he turned toward Albert and Perry; the three started laughing.

At that moment, Matt leaped out of his chair and decked Tommy—a right hook that sat Tommy on his ass and just about shocked everyone in the bar. Matt stood over Tommy, and neither Perry nor Albert even considered stepping in. Looking up from the barroom floor, and with his hand on his left cheek, Tommy said, "You still hit like a pussy, Laurent."

"Come on, Matt," Jamal said as he stood, just wishing it was him who had the pleasure of knocking Tommy on his ass.

Tommy, still looking up, said, "You know, Laurent, why don't you take your nigger girl and your half-nigger kid and get the fuck out of this town? Ain't no one want you here anyway."

"Tommy, shut the fuck up," Evelyn said from behind the bar, out of Tommy's sight.

"Ain't no one talking to you, Evey," Tommy yelled back in her direction.

"Matt, let's go," Jamal said, fearing Matt would do something he couldn't undo.

The door opened, and again, the sunrays burst into the bar like before and blinded the boys again. The dust and smoke still lingering in the air and in the doorway was a very large man. As the door closed behind him, the change in light revealed that it was Sheriff Kennedy. Wearing his Stetson hat, he looked almost seven feet tall and his broad shoulders consumed the doorway. A black man and sheriff for almost twenty years now, Sheriff Kennedy was a fair man, but a man who didn't tolerate shit. He knew long ago there was a certain segment of the population who didn't much care for him, which was fine by him because he felt the same way about them. But those who hated Sheriff Kennedy did so not so much because of his badge but rather his skin tone.

"Hey, boys," the sheriff said, looking at the three men he knew all too well and had plenty of experience with. "What the hell you doin' down there, Tommy?" he asked as he adjusted his Stetson.

"I dropped a quarter, why? What'd you think I'm doin'?" he asked with disdain in his voice. Even after all these years, Sherriff Kennedy's been sheriff, it pissed Tommy off to no end that he, a white man, had to answer to a black man. Tommy got to his feet and turned, looking back toward the sheriff before taking a sip of his beer. Albert, not wanting any part of Sheriff Kennedy, made a beeline to the men's room.

"Hey, Jamal," Sheriff Kennedy said as he shook his hand. "Haven't seen you in a bit. Hi, Matt. Damn shame about your grandma. Edith was a good woman. Did a lot of good over at St. Pat's. Real sorry for your loss, son."

Matt extended his hand to the sheriff's and shook it. The sheriff's hand totally encompassing Matt's hand, which wasn't small either; the man was just that big.

"You boys take off. I'm gonna stick around here a bit and make sure nobody makes Tommy drop any more quarters."

Tommy didn't appreciate the comment, and he swigged the last of his beer, slammed the bottle down, and said to Evelyn, "Another!"

Jamal placed a twenty-dollar bill on the bar, and as they walked past the sheriff, they each gave him a nod of acknowledgment and thanks. Once outside in the car, Jamal looked over at Matt and said, "You know, it ain't ever gonna change down here." Matt heard Jamal very clearly but chose not to respond; he simply continued to look forward as Jamal drove off.

Chapter 23

A week or so had gone by since Edith's funeral and Matt and Fatin had had some serious discussions regarding their future. Those billboards ole David rented didn't pan out like he had hoped and that commercial, well, folks around town found it to be more comical than anything. Because he had to shell out so much cash and because work had been slow at the law firm, Matt wasn't due into work until 11:00 a.m. And since he didn't have to be in to work for a while and since Fatin had the biggest belly Matt ever did see a pregnant woman have, he was making Fatin and himself some eggs with shrimp and grits; it was the least he could do. Fatin had really acquired the taste for shrimp and grits and loved when Matt offered to make them. She was sitting on the living room floor, knitting a baby blanket, and it was coming along. Karen had taught Fatin how to knit a few months back and she's been slowly adding to it though not as quickly as she had hoped when she started.

Matt was the ideal partner for Fatin, and she knew it. She was always so appreciative of his natural caring nature. She was just about three weeks from her due date, and being as big as she was, it wasn't so easy to get around. Even going back a few months when things started to get difficult, like tying her shoes or making the bed or doing laundry, Matt stepped right in and took care of all those chores.

"That smells so good, sweetie. Is it almost—" Fatin yelled to Matt from the living room floor, looking over at the doorway. But before she could finish the sentence, Matt was walking in with two fried eggs, toast, shrimp and grits, and a glass of orange juice on a tray.

"Where you want this, baby?" Matt asked Fatin.

Looking over to the couch and coffee table, she said, "Over there." She dropped her knitting needles and the almost, but not quite, finished baby blanket.

Matt placed her breakfast down and then stood over her. "I suppose you'd like some help getting up?" he asked.

Raising both her hands in the most helpless way with the cutest smile she could muster, she said, "Please."

Matt bent over and wrapped his arms around her and lifted her to her feet and gave her a little swat to the butt, looking over at the TV. "What ya watchin'?"

"The *Today Show*. I like Al Roker. He's cute," Fatin said as she first tried to lower herself slowly, but the full weight of her pregnant body took over, and she plopped down like a bunch of bricks.

"Al Roker?" Matt asked as his eyebrow crinkled and his head lowered, not 100 percent sure he heard her right.

"Yeah, Al Roker," Fatin said as she scooped up a heaping spoonful of grits with a large shrimp topping it off. With a mouthful, she said, "He's cute. He's sweet."

Looking over at the TV, seeing Matt Lauer interviewing a man, Matt asked, "Who's this guy?"

"That's Matt Lauer, silly," Fatin said as she dipped her toast into the runny egg yolk and then took a bite.

"No, not him," Matt said as he rolled his eyes. "The other guy."

With a mouthful of toast and egg, Fatin said almost incoherently, "I don't know."

Turning away from the TV and looking down at a very pregnant Fatin enjoying her breakfast and probably doing so too fast, Matt was washed over with a feeling of contentment. "I'm gonna go read the paper, baby."

Without looking up, her eyes fixed on Matt Lauer and this other man, she said, "Okay, honey."

Fatin took to American life like a sparrow takes flight. She was truly happy. And that's not to say she wasn't happy back in Saudi Arabia, but life, customs, and expectations were just different. She liked driving, something she could never do in Saudi Arabia. She liked how helpful Matt was. And not just since she was as big as a small cottage, but even before. He was thoughtful. He'd run baths for her, he'd bring her flowers for no reason, he'd cook dinner without Fatin even asking. She was truly in love with Matt and he with her. Though she really hadn't made any friends, she was happy at how close she and Karen had become over the months.

As Matt sat down at the kitchen table and started to read the *Picayune*, he flipped to the sports section first. He always kept up on the local high school sports as well as LSU football, and when he was done with that, he went back to the front page.

"He wrote a book about Howard Hughes!" Fatin yelled from the other room. Matt could tell she had food in her mouth when she said it and it sounded like *Oward Ughes*.

"What's that, baby?" Matt asked without lifting his head from the paper.

"The guy on TV. The guy Matt Lauer is interviewing."

"Oh, okay," Matt said trying his best to not sound dismissive though he could care less.

"I wish we weren't waiting until after Christmas to move to New York. I'm gonna miss your momma so much," Fatin said from the living room.

Flipping back to the front page to read what Matt thought of as not nearly as important as sports, he said, "Yeah, I know, baby. But it's for the best."

"I know it is, but still," Fatin said as she took her last bite of shrimp and grits from the bowl she had resting her on belly. "Did you talk to Father John?"

"I did."

"And? Was he upset?"

"Not at all. He totally understands. In fact, he said when we do set a date next spring that he would fly up to New York and preform the service if we'd like," Matt said as he got up to pour himself another cup of coffee.

"Oh, that's nice of him. Why didn't you tell me?"

"I just forgot, baby," Matt said as he looked out the window. There was a cat in the front yard that Matt saw from time to time. He was mostly black with a few white patches on his back. He was crouched down, stalking a swamp sparrow. He seemed to have it in his sights, moving closer and closer with the sparrow seemingly unaware. At the last moment, the cat made its move and sprung at the small bird. Today wasn't the cat's day; it was the sparrow's. He flew off, leaving the disappointed cat firmly on the ground as he took flight.

"Do you think they'll still have the Christmas lights up when we get up there?" Fatin asked.

"I don't know, baby."

"I hope they do. I'd really like to see them. And that big tree. Where is that big tree again?"

"Rockefeller Center, baby."

"Oh yeah, Rockefeller Center," Fatin repeated slowly in a low tone only meant for her to hear, paying careful attention to each syllable, doing her best to say it without her accent. She repeated it a few more times to herself, "Rock-e-fel-ler Cen-ter, Rock-e-fel-ler Cen-ter."

"Are you all done, honey?" Matt asked as he sat back down and continued to read a story about new housing development that was being built less than a mile from the cottage. Sipping on his coffee, he realized it tasted burned, not so surprised being he had made it at 6:00 a.m. and then decided to go lie back down and ended up falling back asleep until eight.

Matt took another sip and decided to make another pot, but before he did, he walked over to the doorway to the living room and said, "You full?"

Looking over, rubbing her very pregnant belly with a big smile, Fatin said, "Very."

Still looking at Matt, she said, "Do you remember what next Tuesday is?"

Looking a bit confused but realizing he should know this, he said not confidently at all, "Yeah, of course."

"Matt?" Fatin said, disappointed that he forgot.

Realizing he was caught, he submitted, "Okay, sorry. What's Tuesday?"

"My appointment with Dr. Wells," she said in a tone that let him know he should have remembered.

"Oh, Jesus! Yea, I'm sorry I forgot."

"And?" Fatin asked, lowering her head as if to look over the top of a pair of glasses she clearly didn't have on. Matt stood, biting his lip, looking at the ceiling. After a few seconds, he heard a sigh come from Fatin. He looked back down at her and said, "Anniversary." This aroused one of the biggest smiles he'd ever seen on Fatin's face. September 18 would be one year since he and Fatin had met. He walked back into the kitchen and poured the burned coffee down the drain.

Finally realizing the man Matt Lauer was interviewing had written a book about Howard Hughes, Fatin said, "Who is Howard Hughes?"

"Was," Matt replied quickly.

"What?"

Realizing what Matt meant, she said "Was. Who was Howard Hughes?"

"A very rich man, but he's dead. Been dead for a long time now," Matt said as he scooped the coffee grounds out of the tin can and into the filter. But he realized he lost count and couldn't remember if he had put in four or five scoops during the Howard Hughes discussion and had to start over.

"He sounds interesting."

"That's one way to put it," Matt said under his breath.

"I might have to buy this book," Fatin said as she sat back down on the floor, doing her best to lower herself as carefully as possible. She was determined to finish the blanket before the baby came, and with the pace she was on, she might just make it.

Matt started to scoop the coffee again—one scoop, then two—when Fatin said, "Matt, there's something happening in New York."

Doing his best to ignore her for the moment—three, four. "Matt!" Fatin said loudly in a tone that got Matt's attention.

"Something is happening in New York!" This time, she was yelling, making sure he heard her.

Dropping the fifth scoop of coffee back into the tin and moving to the doorway somewhat hurried, he said, "What's going on, baby?"

Pointing to the TV, she said, "Look!"

Looking at the TV, Matt saw the World Trade Center with smoke billowing from a large gaping hole in the side. "Oh my god!" Matt said as his eyes widened and his mouth was agape. He moved over toward Fatin. "Let's pray baby," he said.

Chapter 24

THE LAURENT HOME, SEPTEMBER 14

S eptember in southern Louisiana isn't a particularly wet month historically, but for some God-awful reason, it's been raining like cats and dogs for the past two days. Normally, William wouldn't let a bit of rain keep him from his work, but the weather forecast called for swells of four to six feet, and that just isn't the kind of seas to be shrimpin' on. It was just past 11:00 a.m., and while William was sitting at the kitchen table reading the *Picayune*, Karen was preparing lunch—turtle soup. William loved turtle soup so much he never had to ask Karen to make it; she just knew instinctively when he needed his fill.

The art of making turtle soup is one Karen learned from her momma as her momma learned before her. Lots of places down in the bayou sell turtles already dressed and ready for the pot, but Karen would have none of that; she does her own gutting and removed the head and all the other parts you don't want in your soup. It's a bit of a lengthy process, and she'd been at it since 9:00 a.m., but she feels it's worth doin'. Every once and a while, Karen would take a peek back at William reading his paper in silence, as usual, and attempted some small talk, which typically didn't go very far. William is and always has been very big on one-word answers: yes, no, okay, and such. But on this day, Karen was determined to get past his typical defenses and broach the subject that's been on her mind.

Looking back over her shoulder as she removed the cheesecloth from around the turtle carcass, she began picking the meat away and said, "You know, she ain't like those other people, the ones that did that." But got no response. As she continued to pull the hot meat from the turtle, having to blow on her fingers every so often to cool them down, not getting a response from William, not even one of his grunts of acknowledgment, she said again, "She ain't like them, William." This time, pausing her work and turning totally around, resting on the cabinet behind her, she expected a response.

William instinctively knew he needed to respond and lowered the paper. "I know," he said before raising the paper back up, shielding his face.

"Oh no, William Laurent, you ain't getting off that easy," Karen said before sliding the chair closest to him out, sitting down, and pulling the paper down from in front of William's face rather gently.

"Billy," she said, which she very rarely called him to get his attention, compelling him too look up at her from his paper now lying flat on the table. In the Laurent house, some things kind of work in reverse. Normally, William is William, but when Karen called William Billy, he knew she was serious.

"I said I know she ain't like those son of a bitch cowards!" he said at a level that was surprising to Karen as William didn't often raise his voice.

Looking around the kitchen at nothing in particular, showing his dismay that he even has to have this conversation, William asked as he stood up and walked over to the coffeepot, pouring himself a cup, "What do you want from me?"

"She's a good girl, Billy. And more importantly, she makes Matt happy."

"I can see that," he said, looking up from his cup and over at Karen. "You'd have to be a blind fool not to see that." As he sat back down, he folded his paper over, which, to Karen, was a good sign that he was at least willing to listen.

"What do I want from you, you asked?"

"Yes, what do you want?" he responded.

"I want you to show some love, damnit!" Karen said, matching William's tone from just a few moments ago. "I want you to imagine what that poor girl is going through right now. I want you to imagine being in a strange place where no one wants you there, but you ain't got no choice."

Taking a sip of his hot coffee, looking off into the living room, just the distance from where he sat at the moment and the peace and quiet he wanted, he realized it wouldn't be that easy. "Don't you think I know what it's like to be somewhere I don't wanna be?" he exclaimed. Slamming his hand to the table, he said, "Do you think I wanted to be in that jungle? Don't ya think I know we weren't wanted there? So don't give me some lecture about being a stranger in a strange place!"

Realizing what William was saying, maybe for the first time in a long time, Karen said, "I want you to stop thinking like most of these damn fools around here and be your own man." This got William's attention, but not in a good way; his stare back at Karen was piercing and full of momentary anger. She reached over, taking his hand off the coffee mug, and then taking the other one, she shook them gently and said, "William, I know where we both come from and where we are, and I know what you've been through hell and back. All that time you were over there, I was over here, and day after day, I worried if you'd ever make it back. Me with a baby, not knowing if he'd grow up without a father like me or, even worse, a childhood like yours. How do you think that made me feel?" Pausing for a moment to select her words wisely, she continued, "I've been through much of the same hell as you have." She paused for a moment. "It's made you into the man you are today and the woman I am. Now I know I love the man who sits across from me now because the struggles we've gone through together. I love that man," she emphasized. "But I need you to love this girl. Matt needs you to love this girl!"

Looking back from the living room and directly at Karen, the beginning of a small but evident crooked smile started to come across William's face. "You know, Momma, that's why I love you. You don't take bullshit from anybody, not even me."

"I need you to open up. Give her a chance. See in her what Matty sees. You know that boy ain't stupid. He's got one hell of a head on his shoulders. He wouldn't be fallin' for some woman who wasn't good at heart. And I know she is William. I can feel it. I can see it."

Taking another sip of his coffee and placing the mug back on the table, he said, "Okay, Mrs. Laurent, you got me. I'll try."

"You'll try?"

"I'll try damn hard. How 'bout that?" he said as he reached over and touched her shoulder softly.

Felling like she has made some inroads, she leaned in and kissed William on the forehead, got up, and began picking the turtle meat again. "Oh wow, it's cooled off quite a bit."

William picked up his paper and began to read again when, from behind the paper, he said, "You know, I just don't know any better. This is all I know."

This prompted Karen to turn around with a sympathetic look, and she said "I know. I know."

Karen had loved William for a very long time, well over thirty years now, and she knew what she was getting when she said, "I do." But Karen was brought up in a home and around people that were much more tolerant of others than William's upbringing, and she knew it; she always knew it. She knew people aren't born bigoted; they are taught bigotry. And while she always knew William, while she never considered him a racist or a bigot, he was brought up to feel differently about certain folks—black folks mostly. And more recently about folks from the Middle East. And while William was brought up around black folks his whole life, worked with them, attended the same church with them, he'd never socialize with them, which unfortunately was all too common with most of his generation down South. But she was always happy he never passed his beliefs on to Matt, not even when he became best friends with a black boy named Jamal or fell in love with a young bi-racial girl named Emily.

In fact, when Jamal started coming around all those years ago was when she first noticed William letting his guard down some, though never completely. Well, now that he's gonna have himself a biracial grandbaby, Karen figured there's no time like the present. And with all of William's flaws, and she could always rattle off a few at a moment's notice, she also always knew him as a man of his word. So if he said he was gonna try, she believed him.

Chapter 25

September 18

A full week had passed since the attacks on 9/11, and while the overwhelming feeling in the country was one of just wanting to curl up in bed, everyone knew we must persist, we must carry on, we must live. So that's what people did, including Matt. If not for the attacks a week earlier, this Tuesday could have been confused with dozens other Tuesdays past. Matt was sitting at his desk, finishing up his draft for opening statements in a case later that day. When he looked up, he noticed David standing in the open doorway, leaning against the doorframe. It made Matt wonder just how long was David had been watching him.

"Hey, David."

"Are those the opening statements for the Tristate case?" David asked, gesturing with a finger.

Looking down at the papers in front of him, Matt responded, "Yeah, yeah, it is. I think it's strong, but once we get into the medical evidence, we get a little soft." He looked back up at David.

"Can I come in?" David asked.

"Of course, sit down," Matt said as he pointed to the lone but old and somewhat rickety wooden straight-backed chair in front of his desk. Matt had thought about buying a new one after a new client had walked in his office who was rather large. Throughout the whole meeting, Matt kept praying in between sentences that the chair wouldn't collapse, and thank God it didn't. But with the lack of work in the office, he just hadn't had the extra money to buy a new chair.

Avoiding eye contact, David sat in the unstable chair and noticed the unsecure feeling immediately. "Jesus Christ, this chair is terrible," he said as he wiggled it, gently holding on to the seat with both hands.

Finally looking up at Matt and making the eye contact that Matt could tell he was avoiding, he asked, "What's wrong, David?"

With little hesitation, David said, "I gotta let you go."

With a look of surprise and disbelief, Matt asked, "Why?"

"Matt," David said as he fidgeted with the cuticle of his fingernails, looking down and then up at Matt again, almost as if he had been searching for the strength to get through this. "Matt, after what happened last week, I just can't keep you on."

Matt's body seemed to be slinking into his plush brown patent leather chair ever so slowly, as if he were a balloon from a child's birthday party that inevitably lost its strength to stay afloat and sank to the floor. Matt brought both hands up to his face, covering it and moving them up slightly and then down.

"Matt, you know I hate to do this but—"

"But what!" Matt asked in tone that conveyed disappointment, anger, and definitely fear.

"Matt," David said as he leaned forward and rested his forearm on the desk and looked back at the open door to make sure no one was within earshot. "Matt, you know I hate this, but in the past week, we've had three clients drop us because of you, well, actually, Fatin." With that, the hardest part over, David sat back in the unstable chair as comfortably as he could.

"Three?"

"Yes, three."

"And they said it was because of Fatin?" Matt asked as he was doing his best not to look at David.

"Yeah, well, they didn't say her by her name. Called her something else actually." After what seemed like a minute of silence but was only about four or five seconds, David continued, "Matt, I really hate to do this, but you know we're struggling, and I just can't afford to lose the business."

"What did they say about Fatin?" Matt asked, this time looking David dead in the eyes, almost looking through him.

"Matt."

"What did they say, David!" Matt asked, making sure to hit every word as hard as verbally possible without raising his voice.

"They called her a terrorist, Matt. They called her a dirty Muslim. They said she wasn't like us. They said they wouldn't do business with me as long as you were associated with the firm."

Shaking his head and leaning forward, resting his elbows on the desk, Matt couldn't feel more defeated at this moment. How would he tell Fatin? How would he support Fatin and their baby until they move to New York? It was then he looked down at his desk calendar and saw written in his own hand, "One-year anniversary, 6:00 p.m., Chet's Shrimp Shack."

"Matt, you know I love you…and Fatin, but I have to do what's best for me and mine."

With his head down, biting his lower lip as he often did when he was perplexed with a situation, Matt said, "I know, Dave." Looking back up, no longer biting his lip and with clear eyes, he said, "Do you want me to leave now?"

"No! No, of course not. I know one of the attorneys from the insurance company assigned to the Tristate case, and he told me they might be willing to settle. This was last week, but I think I can convince him if we drop our demand by 10 percent. If that happens, I'll advance you your commission immediately instead of the sixty-day finalizing period. Is that okay with you?"

Nodding his head yes, Matt accepted the situation and started to think of a way out of this mess. David rose to his feet; the men shook hands, and he walked toward the door. Before walking out, he turned and asked, "By the way, boy or girl?"

"We'll find out today. She has an appointment at four thirty. We were just going to wait and be surprised, but eight-plus months has gotten the better of Fatin." David patted the dark wooden doorframe a couple times and said, "I'll see you at the christening." And he walked out the door.

Sitting at his desk and finishing up some paperwork, Matt looked down at his watch and, for a few moments, didn't see the time even though he was staring right at the watch. As he was looking at the watch, all he could see was the old black-and-white photo that sat on the mantel of his parents' house of Edith and his granddad on their wedding day. And he kept remembering the look in his grandma's eyes when she said, "*Your granddad would be so proud of you.*" This brought a small but meaningful smile to his face. Once his eyes regained focus and he saw the time, he noticed that the lunch hour rolled around quicker than he had realized. He put on his sport coat and picked up his worn attaché case and went to lunch.

Matt decided to walk on down to Pot Belly's on Dauphine Street over by Washington Square for lunch. They had a great pulled pork sandwich there that people traveled from all over to get. Matt's been sittin' at the lunch counter on more than one occasion and had met people from all over the South—Georgia, Florida, and even a couple from Massachusetts one time. But as he walked, he decided to call Jamal and tell him the bad news.

After a few rings, Matt heard through the receiving end of his cell phone, "Jamal Jenkins, attorney-at-law."

"Hey, I need a good attorney. You know where I can find one?" Matt said as he navigated the walking traffic down Dauphine Street. It's always heaviest at lunchtime in New Orleans because they call New Orleans a walking city though Matt had never been to a city that wasn't considered a walking city, so he wasn't exactly sure what the alternative was.

With his unmistakable laugh, Jamal said, "What's up, brother? I miss the hell out of you."

"Yeah, we'll see if you say that once we move up there. You might get sick of me right quick." The funny thing about southerners is, when they move out of the South for any stretch of time, they tend to lose their southern accent a bit, and I would imagine vice versa. That is, until you get two Southern boys back together. It doesn't matter how long they'd been out of the South; that southern drawl comes right back—even stronger sometimes.

"Come on, man. You know I love ya," Jamal said.

"What's that?" Matt asked as he held his other hand up against his ear to reduce the street noise as the connection wasn't too good.

"I said I love ya, bro."

"Oh yeah. Love you too. But that ain't why I'm callin'," Matt said as a man, looking backward as he was walking, almost walked right over Matt.

"So what's up?" Jamal asked.

"Any chance you can get me in sooner than Christmas?"

"What happened? What's going on? Fatin okay?" Jamal asked with concern in his voice.

"Oh yeah. Fatin is great. Couldn't be better." Just then, Matt stopped at the window front of Kleinman's Jewelers. A ring with a diamond in the middle and two smaller diamonds on either side had caught his eye. It was displayed on one of those hand mannequins. Not the whole body, mind you, just the hand with extended fingers. And this diamond ring on the wedding finger. Matt stood as close to the window as he could, doing his best not to impede the people walking by, and said, "Fatin is great, but I'm just having second thoughts about waiting so long."

A bit surprised by Matt's request, but not in the habit of letting his best friend down, he said, "Let me see what I can do. Can I call you later tonight? About seven or eight?"

"Can I call you in the morning? It's our one-year anniversary, and we're going out to dinner and then headed home afterward," Matt said, still not looking away from the diamond.

"Yeah, yeah, that's cool. I wouldn't want a call on my anniversary either. You tell Fatin I said hello and happy anniversary and I'll see her soon."

"Of course, bro, and thanks," Matt said. Matt hung up the phone, bit his lower lip as he did the math in his head, thinking about what he'd clear from the Tristate case, and walked into Kleinman's.

Chapter 26

Since arriving in the States, Fatin had done well to adapt to customs that she wasn't used to back at home in Saudi Arabia. Driving, for one, which is illegal for women to do in her home country, was very enjoyable to Fatin. And now with her own car, a small SUV, she had the freedom to come and go as she pleased, something that is all too rare back in Saudi Arabia. The fact that Matt often cooked and enjoyed cooking—no doubt from all those years living as a bachelor was also a plus—back home only the women cooked. But picking out a greeting card was a custom she hadn't mastered nor warmed up to. She had only had a handful of occasions to tackle this task, but each time she found the process overwhelming. Standing in front of the baby section of the greeting cards in Murphy's Drugstore, Fatin took an overview of the section. It looked like there must have been hundreds of choices, maybe a thousand, so she dove right in and started reading.

Since she or Matt didn't know the sex of the baby and wouldn't until her appointment later in the day, she thought it would be cute to buy two cards, one of each, "It's a boy" and "It's a girl." She had thought about swinging into Murphy's after her appointment, but she knew she had to meet Matt for dinner, and she'd be pressed for time. Anyway, she could always keep the second card for the next baby.

As Fatin read and read and read, she finally found an "It's a girl" she liked. It had a drawing on the front, painted in watercolors of a beautiful little girl wrapped in a pink blanket with the caption "God's Little Angel" above her. As she continued to look for the second card, she glanced over the card display which was only about four feet high. She could see the people on the other side of the card display, and down just a bit she could see that two women kept looking over at her and were clearly talking about her. This wasn't totally uncommon for Fatin to experience, but this time, it seemed the women took no effort in concealing their conversation. Fatin kept reading though a little faster and with a sense of urgency, and she finally found her second card, "It's a boy." With a smile on her face, she walked toward the register, cards in hand, and as she past the section of display across from the two women, she heard one use the word *terrorist*. Though she didn't hear anything else or any other part of the conversation, she concluded it couldn't have been complimentary but simply ignored it.

As she reached the register, there was a young lady, a girl of maybe seventeen or eighteen; her hair was three different shades of green, and she had a ring in her nose. Fatin gave her a smile, and the girl responded with a simple and polite hello. The girl pressed a few keys on the register, and the total of $4.98 appeared in the digital display. Fatin began looking in her purse for a five-dollar bill. She knew she had one because Matt had given her $100 in cash not a week ago—four twenties, one ten, and two fives. She knew she used the ten-dollar bill and one of the fives two days ago at the Piggly-Wiggly when she picked up milk and eggs and a *Vogue* magazine, along with a few other things, so it had to be in there.

"Why don't you go back to where you came from?" a woman said at a level that would be considered inappropriate even outdoors. Fatin was startled by the older woman who was standing just a few feet away. She hadn't even noticed her; she was so focused on finding the five-dollar bill. Fatin didn't say a word, ignoring her, and continued to look for the elusive five-dollar bill though at a more frantic pace.

"Why don't you go back to where you came from?" the woman asked again, even louder this time, which got the attention of every customer in Murphy's. Fatin looked up, finally pulling the five from her purse and looking around the store, seeing all the faces looking back at her, but each one of them silent. Handing the cash to the green-haired girl, Fatin avoided eye contact with the women, hoping the problem would go away, but to no avail.

Taking a step even closer, the woman yelled," No one wants you here!" Fatin glanced over at the woman and was surprised and in disbelief at the anger she saw in her eyes.

"My son was killed over there fighting you people in 1991!" The register girl slammed a roll of pennies on the corner of the counter, which startled Fatin again, though the girl did it inadvertently.

"Those were not my people," Fatin said as meekly as possible, avoiding eye contact with the angry woman. Her hands shaking, waiting for her change, she shoved the two cards into her purse and started for the door. As Fatin walked to the door, and even after she got outside, she could still hear the woman ranting.

"Now they did it again! We don't want you here! Go back to where you came from! They don't even believe in Jesus!" the older woman continued to yell. "They don't believe in Jesus!"

Fatin rushed toward her vehicle as fast as any pregnant woman could while not running. Not waiting to find her keys, her right hand was buried deep in her purse, again, thrashing around like a gator with its prey in its mouth as she hurried toward the car, the whole way cursing the purse and, in that short distance, making up her mind to buy a new one, a more convenient one, one with less pockets.

With her hand shaking, it took a few attempts for the key to find its hole, looking back over her shoulder, making sure the old woman was not in pursuit; she wasn't. Fatin started the vehicle and was ready to break down and cry but thought better of it, put the car in gear, drove out of Murphy's parking lot and down Slade Street a few blocks, pulled over in front of a vacant lot, and broke down.

After a few minutes, the tears subsided and Fatin finally caught her breath; she put the car in Drive and made her way to Dr. Wells's office. It was only a few miles away from Murphy's Drugstore, but for some reason, to Fatin, it seemed much farther today. As she pulled into Dr. Wells's office parking lot, she sat for a few minutes and relaxed. She started thinking about Matt and the baby and being in New York, and her mind went to a better place than just a few minutes before. Her excitement of finding out the sex of the baby would be evident to anyone in the proximity, and she looked forward to seeing Dr. Wells. He was a good man who treated everyone the same—rich or poor, black or white, Christian or Muslim—a quality that Fatin was realizing was far too rare.

Looking down at the clock on the dashboard, Fatin saw it was four thirty. *Right on time*, she thought to herself. But before she headed in, she thought she'd give Matt a call at the office. "I'm going to have wait in the waiting room, a good ten or fifteen minutes anyway," she said out loud, justifying her impending tardiness. She wiped away any remnants of tear residue and cleared her throat before she hit Send on her phone.

"Matthew Laurent, attorney-at-law," Matt said when he answered the phone.

"Hi, honey, how is your day going?"

"Hi, baby." Looking down at his watch and seeing the time, he said, "Shouldn't you be at your appointment?"

"I'm here. I'm sitting in the parking lot. I'll head in in a minute. So how's your day going?" she asked again.

"Oh, it's going okay," he said as he moved some paper about his desk, stacking a bunch of nine or ten firmly on the desk so they are all aligned while holding the phone between his shoulder and ear.

"What's that?"

"Oh, it's nothing. The Tristate people settled. We did pretty good."

"That's great, honey. Do you think David will give you a bit of time off after the baby comes? A week or so maybe?" she asked.

"Yeah, I think so," he said, not wanting to tell her the truth just yet.

Putting the papers neatly off to the side, Matt opened the center drawer on his desk and removed the ring box, placed it on the desk, and opened it, continuing the conversation while looking down at the diamond. "So are you excited to find out the sex?"

"Yes!" Fatin exclaimed. "As long as you are?" She was second-guessing their decision.

"Of course, I am," Matt said. And he was. Though he wasn't sure how he was going to tell Fatin about being fired from the firm, he knew that it wasn't something he wanted to talk about on the phone and would be better done face-to-face later at the restaurant. Matt had also stopped at the CVS during lunch and bought an anniversary card though he had yet to write anything in it.

Rubbing her belly with one hand and holding the phone with the other, Fatin could tell she was starting to get emotional again. She could feel the tears developing in her eyes, and her voice suddenly began to break. She said, "I love you, Matthew."

Leaning back in his chair a bit, Matt responded, "Well, I love you too, baby." After a short pause and no response from Fatin, Matt asked, "Are you okay, baby?" Quickly, Fatin responded as not to let on she'd been crying or to give a hint that she had a terrible encounter at Murphy's; she simply said in her most convincing tone, "Never better." Though she heard her voice crack slightly, she could only hope Matt didn't.

"You know you are my papillon du desert," Matthew said in the most loving voice one could ever imagine or hope to be on the receiving end.

When Fatin heard him, even though she didn't know what "papillon du desert" meant, the tone of Matt's voice conveyed love. "What does that mean?" she asked.

"Desert butterfly."

Matt could immediately hear Fatin start to cry and said, "Oh, baby, don't cry."

Sitting in her car, a single tear running down each cheek, she was not sad; on the contrary, these were tears of joy. Fatin was the happiest she'd ever been and couldn't wait to start her family in New York. Looking down at the clock again, she saw it was now four thirty-six and said to Matt, "I better head in, babe."

"Okay, honey." After a few second pause, Matt said, "You are going to be an amazing mother, papillon du desert."

"I love you, Matt. I'll see you at the restaurant at six."

When Fatin entered the office, there were no other women in the waiting room, which was a relief. She approached the reception-ist's counter, and Ashley, Dr. Wells's receptionist, slid the glass win-dow open and said, "I'm sorry, Ms. Najjar, but Dr. Wells is over at the hospital." Looking up at the clock behind her, she said, "He's running a little late."

"Oh, okay," Fatin said. "Is everything all right?"

"Yes, everything is fine. Mrs. Eckhoff went into labor at about noon. She just gave birth to a baby boy."

Fatin, placing her purse down in an empty chair, used both hands to balance her weight and lower herself slowly into the chair next to the first. "Oh, that's wonderful!" she said. "That's a short labor."

"Yes, that's ideal," Ashley said from her receptionist's area though Fatin could only see the top of her head. "He was…let me see." She looked down at a file. "He was eight pounds, six ounces."

"Oh boy," Fatin said under her breath in response to the size of the child, secretly hoping her baby isn't that big. The office phone rang, and Fatin could hear Ashley's one-sided conversation. "Yes, she's here, Doctor." After a short pause, she said, "Okay, Doctor. Hmmmm, mmmmm. Okay, I'll tell her." And then she hung up the phone. "Ms. Najjar?"

"Yes?" Fatin responded without getting up, being it was always such an ordeal once she was comfortably sitting and only did it when absolutely necessary. Realizing the same thing and just a few seconds later, Ashley stood to talk to Fatin.

"Dr. Wells is on his way." Looking at the clock again, she said, "He should be here in about twenty minutes."

"Oh, great." With that news, Fatin felt it reasonable to start the process of getting to her feet. Ashley met her at the door that led to the examination room and walked her down to exam room 3.

"Okay, if you want to put the johnny on, the doctor will be here shortly."

"Thank you, Ashley."

Fatin changed into the johnny which she found to be as difficult or even more so than sitting or standing with her big belly. There
were a few magazines in a rack mounted on the wall; Fatin grabbed
People and wiggled her way onto the examination table. She began
to read an article about Andy McDowell, who Fatin had never heard
of but thought looked lovely in the full-page photo in the magazine.
She woke up to Dr. Wells voice saying, "Hello, Ms. Fatin. How are
you?"

Forty-five minutes later, Fatin walked out of the office and
toward her car. She was beaming. It would be impossible for anyone
to not notice if they were around, but there was no one around.
Looking down at the clock in the car, Fatin saw it was now five fifty
and she was going to be late to meet Matt. She opened the manila
envelope and removed the sonogram photo and began to tear up.
She slid the photo back in the envelope careful, making sure not to
damage it whatsoever; the thought of denying Matt the same exact
pleasure she experienced would be devastating. She then reached into
her purse and removed both cards and a pen. She reread both the
cards and then placed one back in her purse and began to write in
the other.

"Congratulations, Daddy!" With a little heart, she signed,
"Love, Mommy, a.k.a papillon du desert."

As Fatin started driving down the road on her way to meet Matt
at the restaurant, she noticed the colors of the sky. For a second,
she thought it looked like a brightly colored painting with different
shades of reds and oranges. The colors peeking through the clouds
looked like God had stroked his brush across the sky numerous times
to create this beautiful canvas of art. Her cell phone rang.

"Hello?" she said in a jovial voice, noticeably different from
before her appointment.

"Hi, baby. I just pulled into the restaurant," Matt said.

Looking down at the clock again, seeing it was five fifty-nine,
she said, "I'm running late. Mrs. Eckhoff had her baby, so Dr. Wells
was late."

"Oh, okay. No big deal. What did she have?"

"Boy, eight pounds, six ounces."

"Wow, big boy," he responded. "Well, don't rush or anything. I'll save the table."

"Okay. I'm probably fifteen minutes away."

"So? What are we having?" Matt asked.

"Seriously?" she said. "You can wait fifteen minutes until I get there."

"Okay, I'm just playin' anyway. I love you, papillon du desert. I'll see you soon."

"Okay, Daddy. See you soon. Love you," she said before hitting the End button on her phone.

The sun was going down fast, and the colors of the sky kept changing. There were more purples in the sky now than just a few minutes before, and Fatin thought, what a wonderful color it would make for the nursery when they get to New York.

Driving down the empty country road, she realized her headlights weren't on and reached over and flipped the switch. As she looked up, the reflection of lights in the rearview mirror caught her eye. The vehicle was quickly approaching, which caused Fatin to look down at the speedometer to ensure she was driving within the speed limit, and she was. The vehicle was getting closer and closer and didn't seem to be slowing down. Fatin gripped the wheel a little tighter. Now right on her rear bumper, the horn started wailing over and over again, but not like a normal horn; it was unique. Fatin, gripping the wheel even tighter than before, looked down the road and into the mirror, down the road and into the mirror again.

The truck swerved into the oncoming lane in an attempt to pass her but clipped her rear bumper, compelling Fatin to grip the wheel even tighter as she began to spin out of control.

"Matthew!" she screamed.

Matt, sitting alone at a table for two, overlooking the bayou, reached into his pocket for at least the third time to confirm he remembered the ring; he did. Looking down at his watch, he saw it was now six fifty-five and began to dial Fatin's cell number; he hit Send and looked up to see Sheriff Kennedy standing at his table.

"Hey, Sheriff."

Chapter 27

MID-OCTOBER

O ver a month had passed since the funerals for Fatin and baby Zoe had taken place, and Matt was no closer to feeling any better today than any of the past thirty-plus days. He was grief-stricken and heartbroken. Spending hours upon hours lying in bed, alone, staring at the ceiling in the dark of night. The conversations he had with God were all one-sided and offered him no comfort. For the first time since the abortion, Matt was angry at God. He hated that he was questioning his faith, but it was clear that he was, and it was undeniable by any measure.

One of the most difficult things Matt had to do after the accident was to call Fatin's parents and break the bad news. His guilt was almost unbearable, and he took 100 percent of the blame though they didn't cast it upon him and said, "It was God's will" and only asked that she be buried in the Muslim tradition. When Matt heard that, he was taken aback at their grace, and he only wished he had a tenth of the faith in God that the Najjar's possessed. While they saw it as God's will, Matt saw it as unfair in every sense of the word. He saw it as the loss of his family. He saw it as what someone might feel if paralyzed from the neck down, with the ability to only think and contemplate what he had lost but powerless to change the outcome. Only one hundred times worse. And then there was the anger.

As a Muslim woman living in the United States and in a relationship with a Catholic, Fatin still prayed her Muslim prayers five times a day. Though she also attended mass with Matt and often Karen and William on Sunday, she still considered herself a Muslim. In her short time in Jefferson Parish, Fatin began to embrace the Catholic faith and often struggled with it, once even asking Matt if it was okay to love Allah and Jesus at the same time, for which he responded after a few seconds of thought, "I can't see why not." That might have been the single thing Matt loved most about Fatin— her openness and her acceptance of differences while condemning hatred and her childlike way of looking at the world, always seeing the best in people, often when others around didn't. Matt was always impressed and even envious of Fatin that he had never heard her use the word *hate*, not even in jest.

Father John was able to find a local Imam to perform the funeral for Fatin while he preform the services for little Zoe. While lying Fatin to rest was the hardest thing he ever had to do up until that point, the following day would prove to be even harder. Anyone who's ever attended the funeral services for a child can understand— the tiny casket, the idea of a whole lifetime of opportunity, experiences, adventures, and most of all, love gone. Matt was inconsolable, though both Karen and Jamal did their best. But what can you say to a man who just lost the love of his life and an unborn child? Answer: nothing.

On the day of Zoe's funeral everyone gathered at the Laurent home after the services. Karen and Doris had been up late the night before preparing all sorts of food, inevitably making far too much. When everyone was eating, and all occupied with conversation, Matt snuck off into his parents' room. He went into William's nightstand drawer and removed a key. He walked to the other side of the room and unlocked the lower door of William's gun cabinet and removed a snub-nosed .357, nickel plated.

He stuck that gun down deep in his waistband, locked the door back up, returned the key, and went to the bathroom. There, he slid the release forward and pushed out the cylinder chamber to find six rounds—fully loaded. He stuck it in the back waistband of his pants and rejoined everyone else. He didn't once think William would miss the gun being he hadn't been shooting in probably ten years though he was a bit concerned that when people hugged him; they might feel it in his waistband though no one did.

Matt had gone home that day and put that gun into his nightstand. He took off his grandfather's watch and placed it in the nightstand as well, as though time had stopped for him. The gun fully loaded, it sat in the drawer. Each day after that, Matt would think about that gun and terrible thoughts would flood his mind. Jamal's family had gone back to New York, but Jamal stayed behind to try to help Matt as any good brother would do. On some days, his presences did help, others not so much. But after he left, Matt seemed to get worse, falling into a deep depression that no one could bring him out of. Karen, as hard as she tried, was also heartbroken and often prayed with Father John for Fatin and Zoe, but most of all, for her suffering son.

The days passed, one after another to the point that Matt had lost track of the date and even the days of the week. He was spending most of the day, sometimes twenty hours, in bed, only getting up to use the bathroom and sometimes not even to eat. Each time he woke up, he thought of Fatin and then Zoe and then, almost without question, the gun. Each day, every day he'd either open the drawer just a bit too see the gun or take it out, wrap his hand around the grip, and hold it to the floor, begging God for strength, wanting to join Fatin and Zoe. But each day he was compelled to return the gun to the relative safety of the drawer.

He could feel he had lost weight, maybe five or even ten pounds, he thought, but didn't care enough to step on the scale in the bathroom. Before Jamal left, he begged Matt to come back to New York with him but rarely got a response, and when he did, Matt would say, "Not yet." Since he had left, Jamal had called every day though often Matt neglected to answer any phone calls, prompting Jamal to leave a message on the answering machine. They were all pretty similar, "Hey, brother. Just calling to check on you, see how you're doing. You know we all love you, and we're always here for you, and anytime you're ready to come up, we have a place for you. Okay, bro, call me back when you want to talk." But Matt hadn't called back once. In fact, he hadn't called anyone back, so the only time he talked with people was on days he was willing to answer the phone or when they'd stop by.

Of the four or so hours a day Matt was out of bed, often they were in the middle of the night. He'd go down to the kitchen in the middle of the night, never turning on a light, make a sandwich in the dark, utilizing whatever moonlight there was or even sometimes just the light of the refrigerator. Sometimes he'd sit at the table or other times in front of the TV, often turning it on and leaving it on whatever channel it was on the last time he shut it off. He'd watch men and women dehydrate food, clean carpets with some new and unprecedented technology, or even watch an old man hang upside down by his ankles on some contraption he invented that was supposed to help back problems. It didn't matter. None of it matter to Matt anymore.

Over at the Laurent home, there was an overwhelming feeling of helplessness. As much as Karen wanted to be there for her baby boy, she knew he needed some time on his own to sort through his feelings though she did stop by every other day, sometimes sitting beside Matt's bed in silence while he slept, holding his hand or stroking his hair, just as she did when he was a child and he was sick. She'd make him some food and do her best to watch him eat as much as he could though she had a suspicion that the days in between her visits, he was neglecting to eat very much. On her last visit, she told Matt as she stroked his hair, his back to his mother, that the official report of the accident was done, and she left it on the kitchen table. He didn't respond in any meaningful way. This day had ended like many others before it with Karen saying, "Okay, baby. Momma's gotta head home. I love you. We all love you. I'll call you tomorrow and see you in a few days." Then she would kiss him on his head, replace the glass of water on his nightstand with a fresh glass, and quietly make her way downstairs and out the door, often in tears.

The sun had long since gone down, Matt had barely moved, staring out the window from his side. He had watched as the sky turned from a vibrant blue to shades of red and yellow to purple and, finally, black speckled with stars. The backdrop of the sky was almost irrelevant as he looked out the window because all he saw was Fatin and Zoe. What felt like mere moments but in actuality was hours later, though Matt totally unaware being there was no way to measure the time passed, his watch still safely tucked away in the dresser. He was feeling rather weak, so he decided to go downstairs and eat some of the shrimp gumbo Karen had left him. He also knew there would be no way to avoid looking at the police report.

When he got downstairs, he found a note on the table on top of a manila envelope, folded twice, into thirds, written on the outside was "MY BABY, LOVE MOMMA!" Just like that, in all capitals followed by an exclamation point. Matt sat down and opened the envelope, but realizing he couldn't read it in the dark, he went and turned on the light. It took his eyes a few moments to adjust to the light, but when they did, he started reading:

Dearest son,

Oh, Matthew! Matthew, Matthew, where do I begin? From the moment I looked in your eyes on the day you were born, I could tell you would do great things one day. While I loved your brother, Billy, just as much as I do you, you were always different, but in a good way. Billy had so much of his father in him, and while I'd like to say you took more after me, you really didn't. Even from a young age, you were so unique, already with a sense of self, like you knew where you were going. I've always admired that about you.

Now I know all children seem to think that their mother was also born on the day of their birth, but that ain't so. Before I met your daddy and we got married and had Billy and you, I had a life, and it is was fun. I had friends, and I was even in love. When I was fifteen years old, I met a boy. His name was Oscar Bramble. He was a fine boy, and we had a wonderful summer together, and I love him. Oscar worked with his daddy cutting down trees and clearing brush and such during that summer. Just a week before school started, Oscar was killed by a falling branch. As you might be wondering why I never told you this story, well, all women have secrets, and some are not the kind to share with her children. But today I decided to make an exception, hoping that my pain of the past will lessen yours of today.

My heart was broken, and like you, I didn't understand why it happened. I cried and cried, and your grandma couldn't get me out of bed for weeks, much like you in the past many days. I know how much you love Fatin. I want you to know that I did as well. She was a wonder girl, and I couldn't wait to hold my grandbaby in my arms. But you are alive, Matthew. You can't wither away and die. You have far too much to do yet before you leave this world.

I know I don't tell you as much as I should, and I know your daddy don't either, but I—we— couldn't be prouder of you than we already are. And it breaks my heart to see you in such pain. But I beg you, please, Matthew, get out of your bed and live.

Love,
Your momma

After Matt read the letter, he carefully folded it twice on the existing folds and set it off on the other side of the table. His mouth was parched, so he went to the fridge and poured himself a glass of orange juice. Sitting back down at the table, Matt's eyes wandered around the room, and he noticed little things that had been there since he and Fatin had put them there but paid them no mind before this night: three small paintings of mallard ducks hung to the wall, each offset and one lower than the next, the crucifix above the front door (no doubt given to Fatin by Edith or Momma to hang there), and a set of salt and pepper shakers on the counter in the shape of roasters. His eyes, after touring the room slowly, would eventually land on the manila envelope on the table.

Matt flipped over the envelope, bent the two metal fasteners back, and removed a single sheet of paper. On top of the page was the official Jefferson Parish Sheriff's Department letterhead. Matt began to read the short report:

> On September 18, 2001, at approximately 6:00 p.m., the automobile driven by Ms. Fatin Najjar, twenty-six years old, was in a single car accident on State Road. Brake marks on the road indicate she lost control of her vehicle and ran off the road and into the bayou. Initially only partially submerged, she did not die on impact. Muddy footprints on the window indicate that Ms. Najjar survived the initial accident.
>
> After an examination of Ms. Najjar's cell phone, it is clear she made several attempts to call Matthew Laurent, but due to the water damage to the phone, those calls were unsuccessful. The vehicle slid deeper into the muck of the bayou and continued to fill with water. The results of the autopsy confirm that Ms. Najjar's cause of death was drowning.
>
> Pending any new evidence, this case is closed.

Chapter 28

For the past month, for Matt, time had somewhat stood still. He was lost in his memories of Fatin and the thoughts of the future they were planning on building together in New York with Zoe. A new job, a new city, and of course, Fatin and Zoe. But when Matt woke up on this morning, he felt just a little light. The heaviness that had weighed him down for the last month was lessened. He didn't know if it was divine intervention or his mother's letter or a combination of the two that led to lightening. He swung his legs around and sat for a moment before opening the nightstand drawer; sitting next to the fully loaded gun was his watch. He picked it up and looked at the face. It was 10:10 a.m. He closed the drawer and put his watch on, the first time since he had taken it off after the funerals.

After taking a shower and cooking breakfast, something he hadn't done since the deaths, Matt hopped in the car and started to drive. He wasn't headed anywhere in particular; he just felt like driving a bit. He lowered the windows of the vehicle and took in some deep breaths; the air was fresh, and the indelible smell of the bayou was on the wind. After driving around the parish for about an hour, he looked at his watch and saw it was two ten; he realized he wasn't far from the tavern and decided to stop in for a few beers. He had also decided to call Jamal later that night and tell him he'd be heading up as soon as possible.

It was Friday afternoon, and that was evident from the amount of people in the tavern. Matt looked around and saw some folks he knew and said hello and gave the applicable acknowledgments as he made his way to the bar and mounted one of the high stools. Evelyn was behind the bar, and Ruby, the new girl was waiting on customers and clearing tables.

"Hey, Leo," Matt said as he looked down to the end of the bar, which prompted Leo to look up.

"Hey, Matt," he said as he took off his glasses and before a bit of an awkward pause, the kind of pause when you see someone who just experienced the loss of someone and you don't know exactly what to say.

"How are you doing?"

But Matt understood and responded, "Better. I'm doing better."

"That's good, Matty," he responded as he put his glasses back on and returned his focus to the racing form laid out on the bar in front of him.

"Hey, Evelyn, can I get a beer when you get a chance?" Matt said.

"Sure, Matt, just give me a second," she said as she cleared a couple of empty mugs and wiped down the bar. She grabbed a cold beer from the cooler, popped the top, and placed it down in front of Matt. In the most careful way she could, she asked, "How you doing, baby? I'm so sorry."

"Well, I'm doing better, I guess. First day out of the house since the funerals actually," he said.

Evelyn reached over with both hands and clasped Matt's; her eyes were welling up with tears when she said, "I'm so sorry, Matt." Looking back at Evelyn, Matt was appreciative of Evelyn's condolences and shook his head up and down ever so slightly and hung his head a bit; he could feel the tears coming as well. The lighter feeling he had experienced that morning was suddenly becoming heavy again. He realized the sooner he gets to New York, the better.

Matt sat and drunk his beer and then another and was finishing his third, and throughout his time at the tavern, he noticed Evelyn kept glancing over at him, which he found to be a bit odd. The next time she was in earshot of Matt, he called her over. "Hey, Evey," he said as he used his hand to call her over. She saw and gave a nod of acknowledgment. As she made her way over to Matt, he could see she had a look of distress on her face. When she got over to Matt, he said, "What's wrong?"

As she stood in front of Matt, the bar between them, she was hesitant. She looked to her right and over to her left, scanning to see if anyone was within hearing distance; there wasn't. Still unnerved, she called Matt down a few more barstools, creating even more space between them and Leo at the far end of the bar.

Matt leaned both arms on the bar, doing his best to reduce the space between them. Evelyn, almost instinctively, did the same. Looking at her, he said, "What is it, Evelyn?" Her eyes down, avoiding contact, Matt said again, "Evelyn, what is it?"

She looked up at Matt, and she had a look of pain on her face, but it was accompanied by guilt in her eyes. "I know something," she said, which increased Matt's attention and spiked his interest.

"What do you mean?" he said as his brow furrowed.

"Last Saturday night I was working, as usual. Leo hired another bartender the Tuesday before, Kevin Brit. You know him?"

"No."

"I thought you knew him. He was in your grade, I think. Anyway, he got pulled over on Thursday. He had a half ounce of coke, so he's still in lock up. Needless to say, he didn't make it into work on Saturday night, and we were slammed. So I was running around here like a chicken without a head," she said as she lit a cigarette and took a deep drag and then another.

"And? So what happened?" Matt asked, all his attention directed to Evelyn.

"Well, you know I party from time to time," she said, feeling embarrassed having to say it out loud. It was one thing to talk about it with a close friend or even someone in her circle, but she admired Matt. Those kinds of things are usually kept within certain circles, a circle Matt wasn't a part of. But she admired him for being able to follow his dreams and even to get out of the parish, and she didn't like the idea of him thinking poorly of her.

"So anyway, I don't do it often," she said, doing her best to minimize her guilt and fearing being judged. "But I used to buy my stuff off Kevin." She took another long drag on her cigarette, clearly uncomfortable, fidgeting around, looking out the window, and avoiding eye contact with Matt.

"Okay, so?" Matt asked. "No big deal. You do a little coke, lots of people do." He felt she was doing her best to skirt the main part of the story. Picking up the pack of Marlboros 100s, he said, "Can I have one of these?"

Evelyn nodded and said, "I didn't know you smoke."

Matt used Evey's lighter to light his cigarette, and he took a drag. As he exhaled the smoke, he was reminded how much he missed smoking. "Yeah, I smoke from time to time." He took another drag, then blew on the red burning end. "I used to smoke more, but I cut back over the years. So Saturday night?"

"Oh yeah," she said as if she truly forgot what they were talking about.

"Well, it was about midnight on Saturday and we were slammed and down a bartender. So I wanted some to pick me up. You know, just a little to get me through the night," she said as she took the final drag of her cigarette, poking it out in an ashtray with the picture of a pelican in the bottom.

"Well, Tommy came in with the other two. He hooked me up. He gets his stuff from some black dude." She thought a second. "Maybe a Mexican. A fifty, but he gave it to me for forty. Then they started doing shots, Turkey. Then he started buying me shots. By 2:00 a.m., I was pretty fucked up, and I was also out of coke. So he said he had more at their place and he'd hook me up if I went back there with them." She lit another cigarette.

Matt took the last swig of his beer and said, "Can I get another?"

Reaching down into the cooler, she reached around her back and pulled out her bottle opener from her back pocket and popped the top. Matt took a sip of his beer and said, "Go on."

"Well, anyway, we got back to their house, you know, that old broken-down house they rent? Anyway, we did a shitload of coke."

Taking a drag on her cigarette, she said, "Your name came up." This got Matt's attention as his focus was starting to wane slightly.

"My name?" he asked.

"Yeah."

"What about? May I?" he said as he picked up Evelyn's pack of smokes.

"Yeah, sure. He was going on about how you think you're better than he is, and you always have. He was calling you a punk."

"Yeah, so what else is new?"

"Yeah right," she said with a chuckle in her voice. "I was just sitting there on the shitty old couch, and Tommy started taking about all the people he fucked up in his life. You know, war stories, typical shit. And I was only half paying attention when your name came up again…and Fatin's." This got Matt's attention more so than anything she had said up to that point.

"What did he say?"

Evelyn poured herself a glass of water and took a sip. "They were there."

Leaning forward, he said "Where?"

"There, the night Fatin died."

"What?" Matt asked in disbelief.

Evelyn took another sip of water. "They saw her drive by. They were at Tuffy's garage. You know, down there on State Road. Well, they saw her drive by and they wanted to scare her. So they came up from behind her, and I guess they were just trying to scare her by riding her ass, you know?" she said as she took a drag of her cigarette before poking it out on the pelican. Matt's eyes drifted away from Evelyn's and down to the bar top. Evelyn continued, "I guess they were honking the horn and riding her ass, but when Tommy went to pass her, he clipped her bumper. They kept driving."

Sitting in silence for a few seconds after she finished, Matt said, "You have to tell the sheriff."

"Matt, I can't. I can't, Matt," she said with a combination of fear and anxiety in her voice.

"Why not? They killed her!" Matt said as he clinched his fist and as loud as he could without anyone else hearing.

"Matt, I can't. If I tell the sheriff and if it ever went to trial, I'd lose my kids." She exhaled a large cloud of smoke from yet another cigarette. "I got to live here, Matt. This is my goddamn home," she said as she looked around the bar. "Unfortunately, I can't move away like you can, Matt. I'm stuck here."

Matt sat for a moment thinking, first as a man who lost the love of his life and his unborn child, but moments later, the lawyer in him started thinking legally. He thought, it was her word against theirs. Evelyn wouldn't exactly make a great witness with all her baggage. Add the fact that she was high and drunk at the time they told her. He knew it was useless. He'd have to find something else, some physical evidence that tied them to the crime.

Evelyn looked at Matt and said, "I'm so sorry, Matt, but I can't say any more than I have." She emptied the ashtray out and began to wash it in the sink behind the bar.

Matt took the half-full bottle of beer and guzzled it down in one motion. He placed it on the bar and walked toward the door. "Matt!" Evelyn called out. It prompted Matt to stop and turn. "I'm sorry." Matt turned and walked out the door.

Matt drove away in a huff, peeling out as he left the parking lot of the tavern; the depression he had been feeling for the last month quickly turned to anger. The more he thought about the details of the situation, the more he knew he or his family would never get justice. Even if they were found guilty, the best he could hope for would be vehicular manslaughter, and that would be if everything went well. It's more likely they'd get involuntary vehicular manslaughter if anything.

As he was driving, he thought about Fatin's SUV. *Could there be any evidence on the car?* he thought to himself. He pulled into Circle K and turned around and headed over to the impound yard. When he arrived, it was already three thirty, and the gate was locked, the attendant was gone, most likely for the weekend. Matt knew his curiosity wouldn't wait until Monday and began to walk along the outer perimeter of the fence. Looking around to make sure no one was around and which direction the surveillance cameras were pointing, he found a good location to hop the fence.

Once inside the yard, Matt walked down a row of smashed-up vehicles and then up another when he noticed the front end of the SUV. He made his way over and took another look around to make sure he wasn't in view of any cameras; he began to go over the car. He looked through the broken window of the driver's side, and the first thing he noticed were the muddy footprint on the passenger's window. He took a moment as he could feel himself sinking—sinking into a nonexistent hole. He felt empty and hollow. Alone. He envisioned Fatin, trapped in the vehicle, sinking into the muck of the bayou, trying to call him on her damaged phone while kicking the window. He took a few deep breaths and began to investigate the exterior of the car.

Most of the damage was to the driver's side of the vehicle, the roof on the driver's side buckled somewhat, the front and rear windows smashed out, but much of the vehicle looked rather untouched. Images of Fatin started flashing through his mind. Like a slide show playing over and over, still pictures and short video clips of what Matt imagined Fatin went through kept playing over and over—how she must have been calling out for Matt, trying to call him with no success, all the while the water rising.

He walked around to the rear of the vehicle and right where Evelyn had described he noticed an unmistakable indentation in the bumper. No other damage in the area, just the indentation in the bumper. It was sinking in that Evelyn was telling the truth. Matt's mind quickly shifted to Tommy and Perry and Albert. He stood there for a moment, trying his best to control his rage, to think clearly as a levelheaded man, as man of the law should. But it wasn't easy. He thought, even levelheaded men other than him must feel rage. Other men of the law must, in certain circumstances, want revenge. And then he remembered the fully loaded gun, the snub-nosed .357 in his nightstand drawer. He got back in his car and drove off.

Matt was kneeling in the third pew of St. Pat's, saying a prayer in what would be considered a whisper. There was no mass until the next morning, so he was alone in the cavernous space; he thought he was anyway.

"Mind if I join you?" Father John asked, standing in the aisle at the end of the pew.

"No," Matt said as he slid himself back onto the pew. "Sure."

"Haven't seen you in a while," Father John said to Matt. Matt, sitting wearing his coat, his head hung low, simply nodded his head up and down, accompanied by a softly spoken, "Yep."

"You know, I know how hard this past month has been for you." Father slid closer to Matt and put his hand on Matt knee. "When you give your life to the Lord, you are blessed to see and participate in so many wonderful blessings. Baptisms, first communions. Weddings have always been my favorite. Weddings are just a delight. For everyone," he said as he turned to face Matt. "Even me. To preside over two people, committing themselves to each other in front of family and friends and, most importantly, God. Well, it just makes my job worth waking up for every day." Matt turned to Father John. Tears have filled his eyes but have yet to fall.

"What makes me want to stay in bed, what makes my job difficult is the grief, the loss. Helping people work through their grief is the most difficult job I have. And I must admit, Matt, I don't always know what to say. I have scripture and doctrine to fall back on, but that, well, sometimes it's not always as effective as we'd like it to be. I know how much you loved Fatin, and it was clear, profound the first day I met her that she loved you very much. But sometimes we just can't understand why the Lord would take such a young life...two young lives. But we must have faith in him. You must have faith in him. We have to. If we don't, if we don't concede he has a plan, then what is it all for? Then we truly have nothing."

After a long pause, for which Father John was most patient, Matt said, "Father...the Lord didn't take her. She...they were taken from me and was sent to the Lord."

Looking curiously at Matt, the father said, "What are you saying, Matthew?"

"I'm saying, she was run off the road. It wasn't a one car accident like it said in the police report. She was killed, Father."

Father John had been as much a part of Matt's life as his own father had been, even more so at times, taking the time to play catch with him when Matt was a young boy or help him with his home-work because Father John knew William was on some barstool some-where and was in no condition to father young Matt. He was puz-zled by what Matthew was saying, or not saying. But the father had learned long ago, with in his first few years in the church, that some-times parishioners hold back, and often, they hold back for a reason. Looking over at Matt staring straight ahead at the twelve-foot cruci-fix hanging on the wall behind the altar, with his arms outstretched, nails through his hands and feet, the father said, "Vengeance is not yours, Matthew. It is God's and God's alone," which seemed to draw Matt out of his fixated gaze.

"I have to go, Father," Matt said as he stood up and started down the aisle. As he walked away, the only thing Father John could do for him was to pray.

Chapter 29

As Matt walked out of the church, he was angry; he was sad as well, and he felt lost. But the anger was most prevalent, the most obvious of emotions, and he embraced it and just started walking. No destination in mind, he just kept walking. He just wanted to keep moving. He thought if he stood still for too long, all the pain of his past would catch up to him and it'd be even more overwhelming, so he walked. But as he walked down some random street in the parish, a street he recognized and knew he had been down probably dozens of times in his life, even though he couldn't remember the name of the street, a question washed over him: what does his future hold?

His pace started to slow down, his gate closed, and soon he was standing still. The thoughts of the future, what possible future he'd have started to reverberate in his mind. *How can I go on without them? How could I ever justify a day, an hour, a minute of happiness down here when they are up there? How could I live with myself?* he thought, seemingly as if he were meant to be on this street, the street for which he cannot remember the name, at this particular moment of the day his focus was broken.

"Mister? Mister?" he heard, which caused him to look to his right. It was a little boy, maybe ten years old. Matthew looked at the child and didn't say a word. "Can you give me my ball?" Not sure what the child meant, Matt looked at him with a confused look. The boy pointed in front of Matt's feet. A small pink rubber ball was resting still. Matt looked over and, behind the boy, saw six or maybe seven other children, boys and girls, playing stickball.

"Sure," Matt said as he bent down, picked up the ball, and handed it to the young boy.

"Thanks, Mister," he said before throwing it back to the group and yelling, "It's my at bat!"

Matt walked over to a bench and sat down. He watched the children play ball, run, catch, slide, and do everything children do when playing a game of stickball. Memories of his brother, Billy, came rushing back. He wondered what it would be like if Billy was still around. He wondered if his relationship would be as strong today as it was on the day he was killed in that accident. He was mad at Billy for leaving him. This was the first time Matt had ever been mad at Billy, alive or dead. He could only wonder what the comfort of an older brother would be like right now at his most difficult time. He wanted to know. Matt started to pray.

When he got back to his car, he sat for a moment and remembered his brother—his brother Jamal. He looked at his watch and saw it was four fifteen, but meant it was five fifteen back in New York. Matt hated to call Jamal during work hours. Always fearing Jamal would be in some big meeting with millions of dollars at stake, he hesitated to call but did anyway.

The phone barely made it through one complete ring when he heard, "Jamal Jenkins?"

"You busy?"

"Atticus! No, I was just finishing up a few things before I take off for the weekend. We're taking Charlotte down to Atlanta this weekend to visit Jazmine's parents. Driving down as soon as I get home and pick up the girls. How are you doing?"

"They killed her. Killed them," Matt said, correcting himself.

"What do you mean? Who killed them?" Jamal asked as he stopped moving papers around his desk to give Matt all his attention.

"Tommy and the other two."

"How do you know?"

"I know. I just know. They ran her off the road. They ran her off the road to get at me."

The lawyer in Jamal kicked in immediately like it did with Matt. "Matt, you have to take this to the sheriff. You have too—"

Matt cut Jamal off midsentence. "I have too what? There's no hard evidence. Nothing that would hold up in court."

Perplexed and unsure of his next words, something very foreign to Jamal, he said, "What are you going to do?"

As Matt started up his car and put it in Drive, he said in a tenor that sounded worrisome to Jamal, "I don't know. I'll talk to you later, bro." And he hung up the phone and drove away.

After driving around for the better part of an hour, thinking about his future, Matt made his way home. He wasn't expecting to see his mother's car parked in the driveway though she wasn't in it; she was sitting on the swing on the porch. As he walked up the steps of the porch, he knew this wasn't a coincidence. "Hi, Momma," he said as he took a seat next to her. She didn't respond. "Jamal call you?" he asked but got no response.

As they both sat there on the swing, the autumn sun starting to set, Karen was wearing a heavy coat, the type a person up North would wear on a cold New England day. Her circulation had been getting worse over the years, and the cold was sometimes unbearable. Matt, with just a sport coat, didn't realize if it was hot or cold or something in between.

"Let's go inside. I'll make coffee," Karen said.

Matthew sat in silence while Karen scooped the coffee into the filter, poured the water in the machine, and then sat down in the chair closest to her son. She took his hand in hers and said, "I know your father isn't exactly the father you read about in books or see on TV or the movies. He ain't like that Mike Brady on the Brady Bunch or the one from Happy Days or, for God's sake, Atticus Finch." Matt, caught off guard by his mother, looked up at her from the floor with an odd look. "I know who Atticus Finch is. I read books too, you know. Not as many as you but…" she said as she got up and walked over to the cupboard, removed two mugs, and sat back down.

Taking Matt's hands back in hers, see continued, "Your father has lived a very pained life. What we never told you, you or Billy, was that he was orphaned as a little boy."

With a crook eye and a ruffle of his brow, Matt said, "What are you talking about? When?"

Karen noticed the coffee stopped dripping, and she got up and got the pot. "He was six." As she poured the coffee, first in Matt's cup and then in hers, she returned the pot to its cradle. "He was bounced around from foster home to foster home."

"Wait. What about Grandma and Grandpa?" Matt asked, still confused by the whole conversation.

"We just told you boys that they were killed in a car accident when you were young because it seemed easier. It's what he wanted. He didn't want you boys to know."

"But why?"

"He was always ashamed. Though he never said it, I knew. You know, Matt, inside that silent man is a hurt little boy. I know he looks tough on the outside—and God knows he can be, along with pigheaded—but he's never gotten over that."

"So they just abandoned him? Just like that?"

"Yeah."

Matt looked around the room at nothing in particular, but seeing everything just the same, he said, "Oh my god."

"You see, Matty, he didn't know how to be a father. He barely knew how to be a husband. But I always knew one thing. I always knew how much he loved you boys. It's just no one ever taught him how to show it."

They both sat in silence for a few moments, drinking their coffee. "I knew when you came home with Fatin and you told us she was pregnant, I knew deep in my heart you were going to be a great father, Matt. But they're gone, Matthew. They are in the arms of the Lord. Right now, as we speak. But you have to live. You are a young man, and you will fall in love again, Matt. And I know you will still be a great father one day."

"Momma, they killed them."

"I know, baby." Karen said, "But—"

"But nothin', Momma!" Matt yelled as he pounded his fist onto the table, causing coffee to spill all over. Karen rushed over to grab some paper towels and began to soak up the coffee. "Matthew, please, please just go to New York. Go to New York and start over. Go to New York and—"

"And what, Momma? Forget? I can't forget, Momma! For the rest of my life, this will always be a part of me." Sitting back down, Karen's shoulders slunk some in defeat. She wasn't sure of anything she could say could stop him from whatever he was thinking. Seeing the disappointment and pain his mother was in, Matt finished wiping up the coffee, threw the towels in the garbage bin, and sat back down. He reached over to his mother and stroked her arm.

"You know, Momma, I'm glad you told me that about Daddy." This caused Karen to become a bit more erect and looked at her son. "There were times when I was a kid where I hated him for not being the father I guess I always wanted. I feel guilty now."

"Don't feel guilty, Matthew. You didn't know. He just didn't want to be pitied." Karen moved her chair closer into the table, getting as close to Matt as possible and said, "Why don't you come to Biloxi tomorrow?"

"What's in Biloxi?"

"Doris and I are going to Biloxi, Gulfport for the night, to the casino."

"Oh, I don't know, Momma," Matt said, cringing at the idea.

"Come on, Matthew. It will do you good to get away."

"Momma, I can't. I just can't."

"Well, you should. Sitting in this house all day isn't good for your mind. All you have is time to think. You need to get out, be around people, and live."

"I'm just not ready, Momma. I'm just not."

"You play bingo with me and Doris."

"Jesus Christ, Momma," Matt said, which drew a laugh from Karen and, in turn, made Matt laugh a bit.

"Well, I'm going to head on home then. Your daddy's got to be wondering where I am and, more importantly, where his supper is." Karen stood and put on her thick winter coat. She looked out the window and said, "This cold is going to be the death of me." She turned and hugged Matt and said softly, "I love you, baby. Please don't do anything that will break my heart." She reached up and kissed Matt on his cheek and walked out the door.

Matt sat back down at the table and took a sip of his coffee. His mind was calm for a few moments but then started racing. He was finding it difficult to think clearly, so he crossed his arms and laid his head down right there at the table. When he woke up, it was pitch-black. Dark outside and dark inside. He looked down at his watch but couldn't see the hands. He put the coffee mugs in the sink and turned to go upstairs. As he did, he looked on top of the fridge and saw a bottle of scotch. It was a gift from William for some occasion though Matt couldn't recall which. He took the bottle, went to the cupboard, grabbed a glass, and headed upstairs.

When he got upstairs, he cracked the seal and pour himself what might be considered a double in any bar, maybe even a triple. He sat on the edge of the bed and sipped the scotch. Scotch wasn't something Matt particularly cared for or drank often; he just thought it was appropriate for the occasion and would get him drunk quicker, the state he wanted to be more than any other right now. For a second as he sipped his scotch, sitting on the edge of the bed he thought to himself that maybe he now understood why his father drank so much—to numb the pain.

After Fatin had died—was killed—he considered taking her photos down on advice from some folks at the funeral, but he wouldn't hear of it. In fact, after the funeral, he put a few more up in the corners of his mirror in the bedroom and bathroom. He wanted to see her face as often as possible. His greatest fear was forgetting what she looked like.

It didn't take but a few glasses of that scotch, which he suddenly started to gain a taste for before he started crying. He took out a photo album that Fatin had put together one day while Matt was at work. She was always doing something productive, like planting a garden, making a photo album, or knitting a baby blanket. Matt started flipping through the pictures and reliving every day through each photograph, and he started to cry and couldn't stop, nor did he want too. He wanted to feel the pain; because it was that pain that was the only thing making him feel human at the moment. He was on an emotional roller coaster, and it didn't seem like it was slowing down. His thoughts were jumping all around—from Fatin to his father, to Jamal and Billy when they were boys, back to Fatin and Edith and his momma, and back to Fatin again. He could feel the effects of the scotch starting to kick in and lay back on the bed, causing the album to fall on the floor, and Matt just cried in his pillow for a bit.

Matt, throughout his life, had spent much of his time alone, much of his time in thought and tonight was no different. He was torn. He wanted revenge, to make those bastards pay for their actions. He wanted justice. The kind of justice that the courts could never deliver, let alone the courts with no hard evidence. He wanted to be with Fatin and the baby, then he thought of the gun, loaded in his nightstand. And then he thought to himself, *Fatin would never condone what he was thinking of doing.* And then he thought of Jamal and Jazmine and little Charlotte in New York and wiped away the tears and sat up.

He opened the top drawer of his dresser and took out a pair of black socks and underwear. Matt went over to the closet and removed his duffel bag; he moved the hangers enough to get a better look at each suit, picking one, then a second and third. He threw them on the bed and continued in the closet, moving hangers as he dismissed suit after suit until he got deep in the closet and saw something he hadn't seen in a long while—a one-piece pair of mechanics overalls that William had given him when he got back to the parish to use to paint the cottage. They were covered in paint, red and yellow and also blue. Matt looked down and noticed his attaché case wedged between the bed and nightstand. He picked it up and saw the stitching had worn through on the bottom. He rubbed the leather and stuck his finger clear through to the inside as one does when they discover an unexpected hole.

Standing there for a minute or two, staring at the overalls, paint—dried paint, old paint—splatted about. He took the overalls out of the closet and laid them down on the bed. He walked around the bed and over to the nightstand and removed the nickel-plated revolver and tossed it on the overalls. He went over to the bottle and poured himself another triple, and he gulped it down.

273

Chapter 30

LAURENT HOME

I t was a cool and clear morning on this October day; a chill filled the southern air, dew had gathered on each and every individual blade of grass, and from a distance a lovely sheen was evident, just like a freshly varnished piece of furniture. William's head was under the hood of a '71 Chevy pickup in the front yard when Matt pulled up. William had removed the air cleaner, and he was now working on removing the carburetor. He heard Matt's car pull up, but that didn't interrupt his work.

"Hey, Pop," Matt said as he approached his father with his head still under the hood.

"Hey, Matt," William said in a strained voice as he struggled to loosen a bolt. With one more thrust, the bolt's grip finally relented, and it was removed.

"Is that Mr. Underwood's truck?"

"Yeah," William said as he finally exposed himself, stepping back from under the hood, carburetor in hand. He rubbed his finger in the fuel bowl vent and then blew into it.

"What are you doin'?"

And then he wiped the gunk on his overalls. William loved wearing overalls and would wear them to church if Karen would allow it.

"Ah, this damn carburetor keeps stickin'. I tried some cleaner, but it didn't work to well." William wasn't a mechanic by trade, but he's been pulling apart motors and putting them back together since he was a kid. The first motor he ever worked on as a kid was Mrs. Willis lawnmower. She was little old lady, a widow with no children who used to pay the first kid in the neighborhood she'd see in the morning to mow her lawn. It didn't take William long to realize she didn't care who cut her lawn just as long as it was done early in the morning. All the other kids in the neighborhood would charge a full dollar to cut someone's lawn, but William would only charge seventy-five cents per lawn. He always did all right cutting lawns as a kid though, often, it was taken away from him as quick as he made it by his drunken forester parents.

William used his foot to kick the lid of his toolbox closed and sat on top of it while he fiddled with the carburetor. Matt looked around the front yard, which was scattered with all sort of random things most would consider useless, but not William; everything had a purpose. He saw an empty five-gallon paint bucket, turned it over, and sat down. He wasn't more than five or six feet from his dad when William peeked up and saw Matt holding his temple. "Rough night?" he asked his son.

"Yeah, a bit. I cracked the seal on the scotch you gave me awhile back."

"Your momma go by last night?" William asked Matt without losing focus on the carburetor. "Son of a bitch," he uttered under his breath as he continued to work on the faulty device.

"Yep," Matt replied as he picked at the dewy grass, plucking a random blade from the ground and using two fingers to remove the droplets and holding it up, closing one eye, and using it to block the sun which was still low on the horizon being it was only just past ten. "She up?" he asked.

"Oh yeah, for a while now. She's packing her bag for her trip to Biloxi. She told me she asked you to go?"

"Yeah, she did."

"And?" William asked as he finally looked up.

He pursed his lips and looked away. "Nah." Looking back over at his father, he said, "What am I gonna do with a couple of church ladies at a casino?" This drew a chuckle out of William, a feat not easily accomplished.

"Yeah, that's what I said when she asked me. Besides, LSU is on tonight at eight." After a pause that seemed longer to both Matt and William than it really was, William said, "But...maybe you should go." He once again looked up from his work and at his son.

"Me? Why you say that?" Matt asked his father.

William put the carburetor down on a piece of cardboard he had laid out and stood up, walked over to a bunch of cans closer to the truck, picked one up, and poured some of the contents onto a rag he pulled from his pocket. He began using the damp rag to clean off the black muck from around his fingernails as he sat back down.

"Well," he said as he looked up though he continued to clean his dirty fingers, "I don't have your education. And I don't read a whole lot of books. But I know trouble when I see it. And, son, you look troubled. More so than I've seen in a long time."

Tossing the blade of grass down and using his foot to gently disturb the grain of the grass, Matt said, "Well, I guess you'd be right in sayin' so."

Rubbing his hands together and realizing his nails were as clean as they were going to get, William dropped the rag beside the toolbox he was sitting on and looked up at his son and said, "Matthew, you're the only boy I have left, and I don't want to lose you too. I hear things. I hear things around town. And believe me, I'm pissed." William looked off down the road, doing his best to conceal any emotion from his son. Matt knew better than to acknowledge his father's emotions, and he simply looked away, doing his best not to make William uncomfortable. Matt always knew his daddy loved him, deep down. He just had his own way of showing it, which meant if Matt wanted acknowledgment of William's love, well, he had to pay attention. Because those acknowledgments came in the simple wink of an eye when Matt was fourteen and showed his parents a report card with straight As. It was in a simple look of pride he'd see on his father's face when Matt would look out at his parents from the altar during mass at St. Patrick's when he was an altar boy. But outright displays of affection from William, well, they were nonexistent.

"Go with your momma, boy," William said. But Matt didn't respond. He sat in silence and wiped the tears away that began to fall from his cheeks.

He cleared his throat and said, "You putting that thing back in?"

William got to his feet and said, "Why don't you help me putting this carburetor back in?"

Surprised at the offer, Matt said, "Okay." This was how William showed his love and affection for his only son, not with words but with subtlety.

William took his time explaining to Matt how a carburetor worked as he reinstalled it in the old truck. Matt, like anything else, had a curiosity about all things and didn't stop asking William questions throughout the process, but William didn't mind at all. "Why does this go here?" and "Why does that do that?" Matt asked his father. It was during this time and others like it that Matt was reassured of his father's love though each were very memorable to Matt because there were only a handful. It only took a half an hour to reinstall, but it was one of the lengthier conversations either could remember having in sometime. Once William tightened the last bolt, he said to Matt, "Go around to the cab and turn her over."

Matt walked around and got in the cab. He yelled out, "Do you want me to pump the gas?"

To which William replied, "Yeah, just two pumps and then turn it over." Matt did as his father told him—pumped the gas twice and turned the key. The truck started right up. She was a little rough at first, but William made a few adjustments, and it settled down and started to idle just fine. Matt walked around the front of the truck while William fidgeted with a few other things under the hood before putting the air cleaner back on and closing the hood.

"Hey, Pop, you got an extra pair of gloves?" Matt asked.

He pointed at the closed toolbox and said, "In the bottom. Why you need gloves?" William asked, knowing it wasn't typical for Matt to get his hands dirty if he didn't need to. "I got a dead squirrel in the attic. He used to run around and keep us up at night. I put traps up there awhile back and forgot about him. Well, I got 'm."

Matt reached into the bottom of the old rusted box and removed the gloves. "Thanks," he said.

"I got an extra pair anyway," William replied.

Using his thumb like a hitchhiker, he gestured toward his car and said "I should get going, Pop." William walked toward Matt, slow and almost meandering, seemingly taking a few moments to think of what he wanted to say. "Son," he said only a foot or so away from Matt. "Son, I'm asking ya one more time, go with your momma."

Matt looked into his father's eyes and saw something he had never before. He took the opportunity to wrap his arms around William, which surprised him at first, but he really didn't mind. Matt held tight for a second or two before feeling his father's arms embrace him. For a moment, Matt felt like a little boy again, and tears rolled gently down his face. "I love you, Pop," Matt said only loud enough for William to hear. If someone had been two or three feet away, they would have heard nothin'.

"I love you too, son," William replied without hesitation.

Matt walked over to his car and got in; he started it up as his father looked on. William said, "Sounds like it could use a tune-up. Maybe we could do it next weekend."

Turning back at his dad, Matt said, "Sure thing, Pop." A small grin came across William's face. "Why do you still work on other people's cars anyway?"

William replied, "That's what I do. I fix things." William gave Matt a wink of the eye, turned, and walked back toward the '71 Ford. Matt nodded, put the car in reverse, backed out of the gravel driveway, and drove on down the road.

After Matt left his parents, he stopped off at a few places around the parish to pick up a few things. He got back to the cottage at around noon—the sun high in the sky, the dew long burned off—and went inside. He started to unpack his packages when the phone rang; it was Jamal.

"Hey, bro," Matt said when he answered.

"How you feelin'?" Jamal asked without the requisite pleasantries.

Sitting down at the kitchen table, Matt continued to remove items from the bags and laid them out on the table as he continued talking with Jamal. "Where are you?" Matt asked.

"Remember, I told you I was taking Jazmine and the kid to visit her relatives this weekend?"

"Oh yeah," Matt remembered.

Jamal could tell Matt wasn't fully engaged in the conversation and asked again, "Are you okay?"

"Yeah, of course," Matt said, intentionally more enthusiastic to reassure Jamal, but not really knowing what to say next to his friend. "Oh, my momma wants me to go to Biloxi with her and Doris to the casino," he said, just to keep the conversation going.

"Really?"

"Yeah, can you believe that?"

"I think you should go," Jamal said.

"What? You crazy?" Matt asked Jamal as he took a roll of duct tape from one of the bags and started picking at the end. After a few seconds, he was able to lift the end, and he pulled off about two inches and folded it back onto itself and laid the roll back down on the table.

"Matt, I got to be honest, I'm worried about you." Jamal waited for more than a few seconds for a response, but never got one. "Matt?" he said into the phone.

"Yeah?" Mat replied.

"I'm worried," Jamal said with concern in his voice.

"Yeah, well, don't," Matt said back in a bit of a huff.

"You ain't planning on doing something stupid, are ya? Something you're gonna regret?"

"Regret!" Matt exclaimed. "Regret!" As he stood up from the chair, he grabbed a coffee mug from the counter and threw it against the wall. Jamal heard the shattering cup but stayed silent. "Jamal, I can't imagine having another regret for the rest of my life. What could I possibly do that would be regretful, Jamal? What could I possibly do that wouldn't be just? I haven't had a single goddamn thought that wasn't justified, that wasn't owed to me." Jamal continued to stay silent, giving Matt all the room he needed to say his piece.

"What those motherfuckers stole from me…" Jamal could hear Matt's voice break and took advantage of the opportunity.

"Matty, I know. I know what they did. But whatever you do ain't never gonna bring them back," Jamal tried to reason with Matt. Hearing Matt as broken as he was, was hard for Jamal. Jamal knew, and always knew, that the one person he could always count on if he ever really needed anything—anything—Matt was that person. It killed him to hear his best friend, his brother so broken.

Matt sat back down in the chair, but not like he or anyone else would normally sit down in a chair; this would be as close to collapsing into it as there ever had been. His energy had evaporated. His tank was empty. He felt hollow. A few more seconds of silence passed before Jamal said, "Matt, brother. Go with your momma. Get away. Please."

"I'm gonna go lie down for a bit." And he ended the call. Rubbing his forehead with his index finger and thumb and then up to his hairline, he looked over at the small table next to the door. A photo of Fatin and himself sat in a simple rectangular frame. His eyes welled with tears again. He thought to himself that the pain just wouldn't go away. He wondered, *How long can a man deal with such pain before he gives up?* And he finally realized why some men take matters into their own hands. *Death would be a relief,* he thought.

He stood up and walked over to the sink, turned on the cold water, and began splashing himself with handfuls, one then another and another. He turned off the faucet and made his way upstairs. Sitting on the edge of the bed, he reached down and loosened the laces of his shoes. His face cupped by the palms of his hands, he reached over and picked up the gun off the overalls. With the gun his right hand, he pushed the cylinder release and checked the cylinder. Six rounds.

Later that night, just past 1:00 a.m., Tommy, Perry and Albert walked out of the Redd's Tavern. They passed a couple headed into the bar and Tommy said, "Hey, baby, fuck that asshole and come home with us. We'll show you a good time." The couple heard but didn't respond and kept walking into the bar.

As the three got into Tommy's truck, he backed up and tore out of the parking lot. "Does that nigger know we're comin' by?" Tommy asked Perry.

"Yeah, well, I talked to him about thirty minutes 'go. So yeah, I guess," he said. Tommy looked over at Perry in the passenger's seat with an angry look, a look of disdain. The kind of look he usually reserved for those he despised or people that crossed him. But tonight he was in a particular bad mood though unjustifiable.

"I'll call him again," Perry said.

When they pulled up in front of their house, they exited the truck with more enthusiasm than which they got in; the difference, they had more cocaine. Drunk and high, but not as high as they were when they were in the bar and not as high as they would be shortly, all three men failed to notice the vehicle across the street though that's not particularly odd being on the whole street there wasn't one streetlight working. The only light on the street came from the full moon, which created a dark shadow under the southern maple tree, the kind of shadow someone with revenge on their mind could appreciate. The car and its lone occupant sat in that shadow of that southern maple for an hour before the door opened and a boot came out and touched the pavement.

Well past two in the morning, the neighborhood silent, the figure emerged from the shadow and made its way across the street and to the front door. With a lone and violent kick, the front door swung inward. "What the fuck!" someone inside screamed.

Six blast echoed in the small run-down house, each blast accompanied by a single flash of light. If someone had been outside the house or even up the street a bit, they would have heard six somewhat muffled shots, separated in pairs and each with its own muzzle flash that temporarily illuminated the dark house. But there wasn't anyone outside the house. And there wasn't anyone up the street a bit. Not long after the last blast, the figure emerged from the empty space that, moments ago, was occupied by the door. The figure walked across the street and back into the dark shadow of the southern maple got into the car and off—just like that.

Chapter 31

MONDAY MORNING

T he sun had just started to make its way into the cottage, and Matt was still fast asleep in his bed when a knock at the door came. Three quick knocks, all in rapid succession. With an interval of only a few seconds, three more and then three more. Matt had started to wake up but was in that state of sleep when you can't tell if what you're hearing is real or a dream. On the fourth set of rapid knocks, Matt realized they were real.

He wiped the sleep from his eyes, threw a pair of pajama bottoms on, and hurried downstairs. The fifth set of knocks started as he approached the door, saying, "Yeah, yeah, I'm comin'." When he opened the door, Sheriff Kennedy and two of his deputies were standing in the doorway. "Hey, Sheriff, what's going on?" Matt said a bit surprised by the visit, but unconcerned.

Sheriff Kennedy took one step into the doorway, and Matt stepped back and said, "Come on in." The sheriff was going to anyway but appreciated the invitation. "What's going on, Sheriff?" Matt asked again.

Scanning the kitchen, the sheriff said, "Matt, do you mind coming down to the station with us? We have a few questions." Matt was in the middle of a yawn accompanied by a big stretch of his arms over his head when the sheriff asked the question. Not alarmed by their presence, Matt said, "Sure. What's this all about? Did you talk to Evelyn?" Matt asked as he started up the stairs, the sheriff not far behind.

"We have a few questions is all."

"Yeah, sure. Do you mind if I hop in the shower for a minute?" Turning back, Matt asked as he reached the top of the staircase.

"Ummm, yeah, actually I do mind. In fact, don't wash your hands either. Just throw some clothes on," the sheriff said as he followed Matt upstairs and into his room.

A little taken aback, Matt asked again as he started to put on a pair of jeans that were crumpled up on the floor, "What's this all about, Sheriff?"

The sheriff, in the room with Matt, said, "Don't worry, we'll discuss that when we get down to the station." Matt still wasn't fully awake, but he was starting to get concerned.

It was barely past 9:00 a.m. on Monday morning and Matt found himself sitting in a small interrogation room in the police station; he hadn't slept much the night before and had his head resting on the table. The sheriff walked in and closed the door behind him. The sound of a lock could be heard from the outside. "Sheriff, what's going on?"

"Did they swab your hands?"

"Yeah, they did. I'm just not sure why."

"Is that right?"

"Yes, yes, that's right. Now will you tell me what the hell's going on here?" Matt exclaimed.

"Tommy Martel, Perry Walsh, and Albert La Rue were all murdered late Saturday night. Sunday actually. The medical examiner estimates the time of death between midnight and 4:00 a.m."

Matt suddenly got erect in his chair. Still not fully awake moments ago, he was now. "What happened?" he asked.

"Matt, do you own a gun? Or do you have a gun in your house?" the sheriff asked, looking directly at Matt for any hints or subtle intimation of a guilty man as he sat down in the unoccupied chair on the other side of the table. Matt's shoulders shrunk, and he replied, "Yeah, I do. It's in the nightstand drawer in my bedroom."

"Well, we're already in the process of getting a search warrant for your house, but it would make this go a lot quicker if you gave us permission to search."

Matt, realizing it would be futile to deny the sheriff access to his house, gave a simple nod. The sheriff, in turn, looked up at the small window in the door and gave a nod of his own to one of his deputies who was watching through. Looking down at his wrist, Matt realized he had left the house without putting his watch on. He looked up at the clock on the wall and saw it was now ten thirty. The sheriff, who didn't smoke, took out a pack of cigarettes and matches and placed them on the table next to the ashtray. He stood up and said, "I'll be back in a bit, Matt. We'll need a statement." And he walked out the door.

Picking up the pack of cigarettes, he removed one and lit it. On the first drag, he realized the cigarettes were old, but he didn't mind. He smoked two more before he rested his head back down on the desk, waiting for the sheriff to come back. The sound of the door unlocking woke Matt up from his shallow sleep. The sheriff walked back in, the door closing behind him and locking once again; he had a recorder in his hand. He sat down and said, "I need a statement."

More than an hour, but not quite two, had passed when the sheriff was interrupted by a soft knock at the door. He pressed the Stop button on the recorder and said, "I'll be right back, Matt" and walked out the door. When he closed and locked the door behind him, two detectives were standing there, one of them holding a VHS tape labeled Palace Casino Biloxi.

"Well?" the sheriff asked the second detective with anticipation in his voice.

"Wrong caliber," he replied. "It's a .357."

"And what was used?" the sheriff asked.

"A .38."

"No shit?" the sheriff responded. "And?" he said as he looked at the other detective.

The detective inserted the tape into a VCR that was set up on a movable stand with a TV monitor. The tape started to play. On the tape was Matt, Karen, and Doris walking through the Palace Casino in Biloxi with a time and date stamp from Saturday night.

"No shit!" the sheriff said to no one in particular. "Anything else?" the sheriff asked the two detectives.

"Yeah," The first detective said as he took out his ringed notebook from his inside coat pocket. He flipped a few pages and started reading, "I talked with a pit boss who remembered Matt playing blackjack. Apparently, he gave Matt three complimentary buffet tickets." He paused for a moment and said, "He had to show his license to get some players card or something. He's faxing over a copy of the card now."

"And the ladies?" the sheriff asked, referring to Karen and Doris who were each in their own interrogation room.

"They confirm everything he said."

The sheriff took off his Stetson hat and rubbed his bare scalp for a few seconds. He looked back at the interrogation room door and walked back in. When he got in, he asked Matt, "Do you have your wallet?"

Reaching into his back pocket, Matt removed his wallet and placed it on the table.

"Do you have a players card from the casino?"

Matt remembered he did and quickly looked through his wallet, pulling it out and handing it to the sheriff. Deputy Larsen walked into the interrogation room and handed the sheriff the fax copy of Matt's players card.

"Let 'em go," the sheriff said.

Chapter 32

In the week that followed, Matt had cleared out the cottage and brought all the things he wouldn't need in New York over to his parents' house. As Matt made his last trip from the car to the house, William was standing on the front porch. He opened the door, and Matt placed the box down on the kitchen table. He stepped back out onto the porch with his father and said, "I guess this is it."

William, leaning on the porch rail, said, "Yep, guess so."

Matt took a step closer to William, just close enough to put his hand on his shoulder, which made William turn slightly toward Matt. "I'm gonna miss you, Pop," Matt said.

William stood upright and turned to his son and said, "All those years you were gone, I forgot how nice it was having you around."

Matt extended his hand and William took it but then, with his other, pulled Matt into an embrace for which Matt fully submitted. Father and son embraced on the front porch for as long as Matt could ever remembered. When the men each stepped away, they walked toward the Matt's car.

"You know, Matt," William said, "I was thinking of taking your mother up to New York for Christmas."

Matt looked over at his father with an air of surprise, but not wanting to show it, and said, "That's great, Pop. I think she'd love that."

"Yeah, me too. I'm also gonna cut back on the drinking."

"Really?" Matt said with a sound of approval in his voice, not able to hide his delight.

"Yeah, yeah." William said. "I suppose I've drunk my fill."

The two men reached the car, and Matt turned to his dad and didn't wait for him to initiate an embrace. As he and William were hugging, Karen came out on the porch and down the steps. "Don't you think you're going anywhere without saying goodbye to me, young man?" she yelled as she walked toward them.

"I wasn't, Momma. I wasn't," Matt replied.

"William, you get back in the house and get my washing machine working again."

"I better get back inside. If I don't, I'm gonna have me some dirty britches for work tomorrow," William said as he walked away from Matt and swatting Karen on the backside as they passed each other. She let out a "Yelp!" and turned back at William with a smile.

When she reached Matt, she took her little boy in her arms. Regardless of how old he is or how big he got or what he accomplished in his life, he would always be her little boy. Stepping back and looking up as she always had to do she said, "Matthew, I just can't tell you how much I love you." A tear started to roll down her cheek, and she wiped it away. "All I ever wanted for you was to be happy."

"I know, Momma," Matt said.

"Are you?" Karen asked. "Are you happy?"

Matt looked up to the sky and thought for a second or two and looked back down to his mother and said, "I'll get there, Momma."

A smile came over Karen's face, and she pulled her son back in for one more hug. Matt kissed his mother on the head and said, "I love you, Momma." She reached up and touched his face and started to walk away.

"Drive safe," she said without looking back.

"Hey, Momma!" Matt called to Karen, which made her stop and turn. She didn't say anything.

"Take care of him. He's trying," Matt said.

"I know he is, Matthew. I know he is," she said as she turned and kept walking, up the stairs and into the house. Matt watched her the whole way.

* * *

Matt stopped in Washington and spent the night. It was late when he arrived in DC, so he checked into the Holiday Inn on E Street and then decided to go for a walk. He wandered around the city for longer than he realized, just thinking—thinking about Fatin, thinking about the baby, and thinking about how he must move on. As much as it pained him to concede, he realized he'd have to let go of the past if he was going to have any future. He stood awhile and looked up at the Lincoln Memorial, sitting stately in his chair and decided that he'd start over in the morning. He walked back to his hotel, went to his room, got undressed, took out and placed a photo of Fatin on the nightstand, and cried, eventually falling asleep.

When Matt woke up the next morning, just past 7:00 a.m., he felt alive. He felt a weight that he'd be carrying for some time no longer there. He swung his feet over the edge of the bed and looked down at the photo of Fatin and said out loud, "I love you my, papillon du desert. I'll see you again." He took the photo out of the frame, folded it up, and put it in the trash can.

Six hours later, Matt was crossing the Washington Bridge and heading down Riverside Drive. He had made plans to meet Jamal down at Battery Park. Matt sat for a while, reading his old beat-up copy of *To Kill a Mockingbird* on a park bench when he heard Jamal's unmistakable southern drawl from behind, "My brother!" Matt stood, and the two old friends embraced.

"Come on, let's go see Liberty," Jamal said, referring to Lady Liberty.

Matt stuffed his book into his beat-up attaché case, now with duct tape, the only thing keeping the contents from falling to the ground, and they walked toward the ferry. Jamal was dressed as fine as any man you'd see in Manhattan. He had on an Armani suit with Bruno Magli shoes, and his briefcase was alligator skin. His position at the firm had made him a lot of money and had given him the power to get Matt a job.

When the men reached Liberty Island, they found a bench and sat in the shadow of Lady Liberty. It was almost November, and it was getting quite cold out. Matt reached into his pocket and removed a pair of gloves and put them on. Jamal looked at them and asked, "Where the hell did you get those things?"

"My pop," Matt replied.

"They've seen better days," Jamal said.

Holding them up slightly and then placing them back down on his lap, Matt said, "I guess, but they do the job." He paused for a moment and looked over at Jamal. "Speaking of job." Jamal knew exactly what Matt was going to say before he said it. "You're not taking the job?" he asked, looking over at his friend, his breath visible in the cold air.

"No. No, I'm not," Matt replied. He couldn't help but feel like he was letting Jamal down. But Jamal knew him too well. Matt never dreamed of having Armani suits or a three-hundred-dollar pair of shoes, and Jamal knew that. While they came from the same place, and all they had in common, their motivations were totally different.

"What are you going to do?"

"I'm going to apply to the public defender's office," Matt said, looking over at Jamal.

Jamal was looking at his closest friend, and he wasn't surprised; he wasn't surprised one bit. In fact, he was almost relieved that Matt turned down the job. The thought of Matt in an Italian suit just didn't seem right.

"Listen, I have to head back. I have a meeting." He handed Matt a set of keys and said, "Just come by when you want. We have the spare room all set up for you. Jazmine will be there with Charlotte." Jamal opened his expensive briefcase and pulled out a large manilla envelope and handed it to Matt. Jamal stood up and started to walk back to the ferry launch.

"What's this?" Matt asked.

"Just a little something." He turned and kept walking. He turned back yet again and yelled, "From one brother to another."

Matt stuffed the envelope into his attaché case and walked around the island for a bit longer. He saw and heard people of all ethnicities speaking a multitude of language, and that made him happy. It should have felt weird that he felt more at home in this environment than he did back down in Jefferson Parish, but he didn't. He was home.

He looked at his watch and saw it was getting late, so he made his way over to the launch and boarded the ferry. It started back to Manhattan Island. The trip would take thirty minutes or so being that the ferry makes a stop at Ellis Island. So Matt went to the stern, removed the envelope from his case, opened it, removed a single-page letter, and started reading.

> *Dear Matt,*
>
> *For all these years, I have jokingly called you Atticus. And like Atticus, sometimes you'd have to set me straight, like he would do with Scout. I joked about it because I never meet anyone else who personified goodness the way that you do. I envied this quality of yours since the day we met.*
>
> *On that day we met, all those years ago, you could have walked away and pretended you didn't see anything or, even worse, joined in with those fools beating on me. But you didn't. You took a stand, you stood up for what is right, not popular but right. Just like Atticus would have done. There's a line in* Mockingbird *in which Atticus says while talking to Scout, "I wanted you to see what real courage is, instead of getting the idea that courage is a man with a gun in his hand. It's when you know you're licked before you begin, but you begin anyway, and you see it through no matter what."*

I'm no Atticus, Matt. I knew you were too good
a man to do what needed to be done. It took courage
not to do anything, more courage than I have.

Sincerely,
Your brother

Matt looked up from the letter to see Liberty in the foreground and Staten Island way off in the distance. He reached into the large envelope and removed a small manilla envelope, the kind jewelers use, and removed it. It kind of jingled a bit. Folding the two-metal clasp forward and flipping the top of the small envelope open, he turned it upside down and the contents dropped into his other hand. It was Tommy's swastika necklace.

Matt gripped it firmly in his left hand for a moment before opening it and looking at it sitting in his palm. He clinched his eyes closed as tight as he could for a second or two and took a deep breath and then exhaled; a sound escaped, accompanying his breath at the same time. It wasn't a sound of joy or happiness or pain or hurt, but simply relief. He took that thing in his right hand and tossed into the harbor, where it would sink to the bottom and, in time, be covered in muck where it belonged.

When Matt was folding up the letter, he noticed a postscript at the bottom.

PS: Take a walk by 651 Sullivan Street in SoHo.
There is always time to start over.

He looked down at his watch and set the time for six fifty-one, leaving the crown disengaged so it wouldn't run. He took that letter and ripped it up into as many tiny pieces as he could, looked around to make sure he was alone, and then tossed in New York Harbor. Matt walked the twenty minutes from the ferry launch to Sullivan Street in SoHo, there in the middle of the art capital of New York, some might say the world. He glanced down at his watch, seeing the six fifty-one, and then looked up at the number on the building, 651

Sullivan Street. Looking through the floor to the ceiling windows, he saw Samantha, just as beautiful as he had remembered. She was showing her work to a young couple in her very own gallery. Matt stood and watched her for a minute or so, gazing through the window and admiring the excitement he could see in her eyes talking about her work. He took out a pack of cigarettes from his inside coat pocket, removed one of the cigarettes and raising it up to his mouth. Never taking his eyes of Samantha, he lit the cigarette. He took a long drag and then another…his eyes finally broke away from Samantha and down to the cigarette. He thought to himself; *I guess today is a good a day as any to quit.* He dropped the cigarette to the ground and crushed it out and walked toward the door and into the gallery.

Maybe there is always time to start over, he thought to himself.

ABOUT THE AUTHOR

Born and raised in Massachusetts, Michael Hull is the son of an electrician and a computer networker. As a young man, Michael worked in the electrical trade for some years before returning to college to earn his BA in political science from the University of Massachusetts, Amherst. Over the last thirty years, Michael has traveled extensively around the world in an effort to experience and learn firsthand about as many cultures as possible.